DUPLICITY

VICKI HINZE

St. Martin's Paperbacks

DUPLICITY

Copyright © 1999 by Vicki Hinze.

All rights reserved. No part of this book may be used or reproduced in any manner whatsoever without written permission except in the case of brief quotations embodied in critical articles or reviews. For information address St. Martin's Press, 175 Fifth Avenue, New York, N.Y. 10010.

ISBN: 0-312-96894-9

Printed in the United States of America

St. Martin's Paperbacks edition / April 1999

10 9 8 7 6 5 4 3 2 1

EXTRAORDINARY ACCLAIM FOR VICKI HINZE'S *SHADES OF GRAY*

"SHADES OF GRAY is such a wonderful book: it successfully combines thrilling suspense with equally compelling romantic elements."

—*The Milwaukee Journal-Sentinel*

"SHADES is very fast-paced, filled with the kind of intrigue and plot twists that make for a great action movie . . . a great read if you're a fan of Clancy-type novels and movies. I enjoy books that combine intrigue with romance and found SHADES to be a perfect combination of the two."

—*The Middlesex News* (MA)

"A great storyline that easily could sell as a romance or an action thriller. Hinze is clearly one of the leaders of military romances that emphasize action, suspense, and romance. A winner for fans of romantic suspense."

—*Affaire de Coeur*

"Page-turning intrigue with action-packed drama will keep you immersed in this piercing drama . . . fascinating."

—*Rendezvous*

"The complications here go beyond the usual hurdles and make the romance more touching for being hard-won. And if the main action—Laura and Jake must combat terrorists amassing anthrax in the Florida Everglades—seems far-fetched, just read *The New York Times*."

—*Publishers Weekly*

more . . .

"A first-class military romance loaded with non-stop action, plenty of intrigue, and a great romance. The crisp storyline is driven forward at a frenzy pace by a brilliantly developed set of secondary characters."

—*BookBrowser Review*

"An edge-of-your-seat thrill ride."

—Barnes and Noble.com

"Suspense is paramount, the stakes high, the bad guys truly bad, and the main characters inseparable from their work for the American military. Hinze writes with convincing authenticity about the complex military world of exacting rules, rigid discipline, constant preparedness, and covert missions, a world in which men and women, and their families, make tremendous sacrifices to protect their country. In Jake and Laura, Hinze creates two people of exceptional honor and self-control whose struggle to resist the pull of love goes down in glorious defeat."

—Amazon.com Reviews

"Twists and turns abound. A crazy ex-wife, a terrorist group, and the rigid discipline of the military all come together to make this book a real page-turner."

—WCRG on America Online reviewer board

St. Martin's Paperbacks titles
by Vicki Hinze

SHADES OF GRAY
DUPLICITY

To my mother, Edna Sampson
The loveliest angel of all. . . .

Author's Note

As a nation, we expect a lot from our men and women in uniform. Often we have no idea of their trials or sacrifices, or of what serving us costs them professionally or personally. I write these military-theme novels to offer readers an opportunity to become aware, to understand, and to appreciate those who dedicate, and sometimes sacrifice, their lives for us.

When writing, it is an author's responsibility to weigh the value of depicting characters and events in their natural forms against the potential impact of those depictions. Having been a military wife for over twenty years, I consider the impact of what I write on current military members of paramount importance. For that reason, as in my first military-theme novel, *Shades of Gray*, I have implemented artistic license in *Duplicity*. Laurel Air Force Base and the chemical retrosarin exist only within these pages (though sarin is in fact real—and a deadly threat). Some of the disciplines and procedures in this novel have been altered. Our soldiers operate in a world with over fifty thousand chemical weapons, many of which once belonged to the now-collapsed Soviet Union and its economically stressed countries: conditions which demand consideration and caution. I ask your indulgence and assure you that the differentiations have been made not in ignorance, but out of respect and concern for the soldiers who perform sensitive missions, and for their families. I hope you'll agree that their gifts to us warrant our concern and protection, and compensate for the deviations.

Blessings,
Vicki Hinze

Chapter 1

This couldn't be happening to her. Not now.

Again, Colonel Jackson's edict reverberated in her ears. *Keener, I've assigned you to defend Captain Adam Burke.*

Captain Tracy Keener, a Staff Judge Advocate relatively new to Laurel Air Force Base, Mississippi, swallowed a knot of dread from her throat. "Is that a direct order, sir?"

"If necessary, yes, it is, Captain."

She tensed her muscles to keep her boss from seeing how appalling she found the notion. Only a sadist would be elated at hearing they'd been assigned to defend Adam Burke. What attorney in her right mind could be anything but appalled at being ordered to defend him? If the rumors proved true, he'd *deserted* his men. *Abandoned* them to die.

Refusal burned in her throat, turned her tongue bitter. This had to be a bad dream—a nightmare. It couldn't be real.

But from the look on Jackson's face, it was real, and there was no escaping it.

"This won't be an easy case to defend." He passed a file across the desk to her. "On paper, Burke's assigned to Personnel, but he actually works for Colonel Hackett."

"Burke is in Intel?" Could the news get any worse?

Jackson nodded. "And because he is, the prosecutor is

going all the way on this one. So far, the charges are conduct unbecoming, disobeying direct orders, cowardice, and treason."

Choking back a groan, she fixed her gaze on an eagle paperweight atop a neat stack of files at the corner of his desk. Sunlight slanted in through the blinds at his coveted office window. Washed in its stripes of light and shadows, the bird looked arrogant. Sinister.

"It gets worse." Jackson grimaced. "Four counts of murder are coming down the pike."

"Murder?" She really should have seen this assignment coming. Burke's was the last case *any* Staff JAG officer would want to take on. It was a guaranteed career-breaker. A ball-buster—which is why, as low man on Laurel's Judge Advocate General's office totem pole, she'd gotten stuck with the unholy honor. "Wasn't this an accident during a local war-readiness exercise?"

"The incident occurred during a local readiness exercise, but it was no accident—at least, not in the way you mean." Jackson rubbed at the bridge of his nose. "The troops were split into two teams, Alpha and Omega. Omega played the enemy. Burke headed Alpha team with orders to infiltrate Area Thirteen—Omega's 'enemy' territory—to jam their communications, and gather intel."

"Sounds typical, so far."

"It was," Jackson said. "But the woods are dense in Area Thirteen. Burke got lost and led his men onto an active firing range."

"He got *lost*?" An Intel officer who can't tell directions? That didn't fit.

"According to Hackett, it happens all the time out there. The terrain disorients." Jackson leaned forward. "The worst is that Burke realized he'd screwed up and bugged out."

A shiver crept up Tracy's back. "He admitted that he deliberately abandoned his men?"

"He's admitted nothing. In fact, he's not talking. But

he was the only Alpha team survivor. Four skilled operatives died.''

"So why murder charges?''

"Burke threatened two of his team less than a week before the exercise. Investigators are about to conclude he carried through on the threat, and the other two men were sacrificed.''

Could anyone be that cold? "Why did Burke threaten the men?''

"That's classified.''

How could she defend him against murder charges when the basis for them was classified? Killing and sacrificing men—during an exercise, for God's sake. And she had to defend him? *Now?*

She had to get out of this assignment. That, or kiss off her career.

Desperately seeking a chink in Colonel Jackson's armor, she studied him. He was a big, imposing man with an intelligent face, pushing fifty and graying gracefully at the temples. In the months she'd been at Laurel, he had earned her respect. More than once during case discussions at the morning staff meetings, compassion had burned in his eyes, and that compassion had come through in his recommendations. According to Tracy's overqualified assistant, Janet Cray, the only thing that sent Jackson through the ceiling was clutter, and that melded into an odd combination of human characteristics, to Tracy's way of thinking. How could he show a murderer compassion but lack so much as the scent of it for any staff member who tolerated a staple on the carpet near his or her desk?

Yet Tracy had worked for worse. Gutless wonders who'd rather fold than fight were a dime a dozen in the military. Fortunately, so were the dedicated, the proud, the sincere. Soldiers who took their oaths to serve and protect into their hearts, and did their best to live by them.

Jackson fell into the ranks of the latter. Yet no compassion shone in his eyes now, nor any latitude. There was no chink; his armor unfortunately appeared intact, but he did look . . . guilty.

Smoothing her uniform's dark blue skirt, Tracy set out to find out why. "You do realize that in taking on this case now I'd be begging for career disaster, right?"

The veiled empathy flickering in Jackson's eyes snuffed out. He darted his gaze to his office door, as if assuring himself of privacy, and then nodded. "Frankly, yes, I realize the risks."

His tone removed any doubt about his damage-assessment expectations. Enormous risks. Enormous.

Should she feel relieved that he had acknowledged the risks, or despondent that he had realized them and had put her in the direct line of fire anyway?

Before she could decide, he rocked back in his chair. The springs groaned and his stern expression turned grave, dragging down the creases running alongside his mouth, nose to chin. "I'm not going to sugar-coat this situation, Captain," he said. "The Burke case has tempers running hot and hard up the chain of command and the local media is nearly out of control. Between the two of them, they're nailing our asses to the proverbial wall."

Hope flared in Tracy. If he could see that, then surely he would see reason and assign someone else to the case. "I'm up for major, sir," Tracy interjected. "My promotion board meets in about a month."

"I know." A frown creasing his lined forehead, Jackson doodled with a black pen on the edge of his blotter; a frequent habit, judging by the density of his previous scrawls. "And I know that you're up for Career Status selection."

Bloody hell. Tracy hadn't yet even considered Career Status selection. This was her fifth year in the Air Force. Her first and—by new policy adopted three weeks ago— her last shot at selection. If not selected, she'd promptly be issued an invitation to practice law elsewhere, outside of the military.

This was not a pleasing prospect to an officer bent on making the military a career.

Decidedly uneasy, the colonel fidgeted with his gold watch. It winked at her from under his shirt cuff. "I understand the personal risks to you, and the potential sacrifices you may be called upon to make, but there's more at stake here than your career. The Air Force Corrections System is on trial, Captain, and all eyes are watching to see if it's up to the test."

He let the weight of that comment settle in, then went on. "Burke is a sorry bastard who deserves to die for his crimes—and I have no doubt that he will die. Yet he is entitled to a defense and—"

"I agree, Colonel," she interceded, doing her best to keep her voice calm. "Burke does deserve a defense. But can't an attorney who already has Career Status defend him? If I lose this case—and we both know I will lose this case—then that's a huge strike against me with the boards. Competition is stiff and losses bury you. I'll be passed over for promotion and for Career Status selection. If that happens, my military career abruptly ends."

"I'm aware of these, er, undesirable conditions, Captain." Jackson lowered his gaze to his desk blotter. "But I'm afraid a reassignment is impossible."

The regret in his tone set her teeth on edge. This was another slick political maneuver; she sensed it down to her toenails. Some jerk with more clout, rank, or backing from his superior officers didn't want his butt stuck in a sling, so they were planting her backside in it first. The unfairness of it set a muscle in her cheek to ticking. "May I ask why not?"

"I'd prefer that you didn't."

She just bet he did prefer it. A stern edge crept into her voice. "I mean no disrespect, sir, but if I'm going to risk sacrificing my career then I think I'm entitled to know why it can't be avoided."

Unaccustomed to being challenged, even respectfully, Jackson clearly took exception. Red slashes swept across his rawboned cheeks and his tone chilled, nearly frosting the air between them. "Officially, you've developed a reputation as a strong litigator."

Tension crackled in the air and an uneasy feeling that she had indeed been slated for sacrifice crept up Tracy's backbone and filled her mouth with a bitter taste. "And unofficially?"

Jackson pursed his lips and held his silence for a long beat. "General Nestler specifically requested that you be assigned to defend Burke, and Higher Headquarters agreed."

A by-name request? From Nestler? Oh, hell. Oh, bloody hell. No one refused Nestler anything. Within two days at Laurel, while assisting Ted, a fellow attorney, on a contract case, Tracy had learned that. Now she'd learned Nestler's clout ran straight up the chain of command.

She was screwed. Screwed. Pure and simple. "I wasn't aware General Nestler even knew my name."

Jackson's resigned look faded and the corner of his wide mouth twitched. "Don't be fooled by the actions of some generals, Captain. General Nestler knows everything that goes on with his staff, on the base, and in the community—within *and* outside of the military."

No conflict there with what Tracy had heard and observed. At last month's First Friday gathering at the Officers' Club, Janet privately had referred to Nestler as Laurel's god. *Sees all, knows all.* Since then, others had used that same analogy, and Tracy innately knew she wasn't going to like his rationale for choosing her to defend Burke. "So why me?"

"Why *not* you?" Jackson issued a challenge of his own.

She could think of a dozen personal reasons, but not a single professional one.

Jackson stood up and turned his back to her, then stared out the window at the red brick building next door. Two airmen were washing its windows.

A long minute passed in taut silence, then he stiffened his shoulders, braced a hand in his pants pocket, and faced her. "Frankly, Captain, the general feels your professional acumen, poise, and appearance will be an asset in dealing with the media."

"What?" That response she hadn't expected. She forced her gaping jaw shut.

"I'm sorry, Tracy," Jackson said, for the first time calling her by her given name. "But it's vital we keep this incident as low-key as possible. That's why we're trying the case locally."

He plopped down in his chair. Air hissed out from the leather cushion, and he leaned forward, lacing his thin hands atop the blotter. "The truth is, the local media is chewing us up and spitting us out on this case. We don't want CNN crawling on our backsides and blowing this out of proportion. The last thing the military needs is another fiasco of the magnitude of Tailhook."

How could she disagree? That scandal had caused a lot of people sleepless nights, agony, embarrassment. Careers and lives had been ruined. And innocents had suffered the shame as much as the guilty.

"We need every possible advantage. We're fighting budget cuts at every turn, base closures that could include Laurel—we escaped the latest short list by the skin of our teeth—and the end of the fiscal year is breathing down our throats. This case has every military member's reputation on the line." Frustration knitted Jackson's brow, making him appear every day of his fifty years. "You're bright and attractive—that surely comes as no surprise to you. You're a media asset, and as unfair as you might deem it, we've chosen to exploit our assets."

He let his gaze veer to a bronze statue of Lady Justice on the credenza below the window, and then to the flag beside it. His voice softened. "Hell, Tracy. We have to exploit our assets. We're an all-volunteer force. A nation of people depend on us to protect them."

"I'm aware of that, sir." Who in the military could be unaware of that?

"Then you understand the challenge. Burke has complicated our mission. He's tarnished the image of the entire military, and it's up to us to salvage all we can, any way we can."

She was a means to an end. *It could destroy your career and your life, but, hey, it's nothing personal, Tracy.*

Her stomach churned acid. She stared at the eagle paperweight, at the dark shadows between the glints of light reflecting off it. As much as she hated admitting it, Jackson and Nestler's rationale made sense. As a senior officer in the same situation, she'd use whatever assets she found available to defuse the situation. Could she fault them for doing what in their position she would do herself?

Not honestly. Still, she couldn't stop visualizing her shot at promotion and selection sprouting wings, or imagining her forced exit from the Air Force. Burke was guilty. Everyone knew it. And while she might be media-attractive, she wouldn't get him off. She didn't want to get him off. But even F. Lee Bailey couldn't get Burke off, or come out of this case unscathed.

Yet the man was entitled to the best possible defense. Would any other JAG officer make a genuine attempt to give it to him, knowing personal disaster was damn near inevitable?

Probably not. And Tracy couldn't condemn them for it. Given the sliver of a chance, she too would have avoided this case as if it carried plague. But she couldn't avoid it, and that made only one attitude tenable. She had to handle the case and give Burke her best. Not so much for him, but because it was right. When this was over, she had to be able to look in the mirror and feel comfortable with what she'd done and the way she'd handled the case, and herself.

"We should have word on the murder charges later today," Jackson said.

Tracy nodded. Since she'd lost her husband and daughter five years ago, she often had imagined herself as an eighty-year-old woman, wearing the same gold locket she wore under her uniform now, looking in the mirror and asking herself where she'd screwed up, what she'd done or left undone that she wished she hadn't. In grief counseling, she'd learned that the death of a loved one changes a survivor's perspective, sharpens it, forcing the survivor to focus on what matters most. And she had long since determined that the one thing she would *not* face that eighty-year-old with was more regret. She had to do the right thing.

Resigned, she lifted her gaze to Colonel Jackson and accepted responsibility. "I understand, sir. I'll get started on it."

Jackson blinked, then blinked again, clearly expecting her to body-slam him with a sharp-tongued comment.

When it occurred to him none would be forthcoming, he gave her a curt nod. "Fine, Captain." He lifted a pen and turned his attention to an open file on his desk. "Dismissed."

Tracy unfolded her legs, hoping her knees had enough substance left in them to get her the hell out of his office before she crumpled. *Dismissed.* And how. From his office and, she feared, from her chosen way of life.

The office grapevine was operating at peak efficiency.

Walking directly from Colonel Jackson's office down the gray-carpeted hallway to her own office, Tracy realized that word of her defending Burke was already out. Sitting in their offices, her coworkers craned their necks and slanted her pitying looks, proving they knew she'd been tagged. The jovial moods of the attorneys behind her confirmed it. Their laughter rang out a pitch too high to be anything but relief that they had escaped the assignment.

All of her training—every damn course the Air Force offered and she was eligible to take: JAG School, Pro-

curement Fraud, Program Managers Attorneys Course,
Safety Officer's School, and the Government Contract
Law Symposium, a small coup for the junior-grade officer she had been at the time—and a hard-won reputation
as a crack litigator—and it could all flush down the tubes
because she was bright *and* media-attractive. That combination had gotten her stuck with defending Adam Burke
at an extremely critical point in her career.

Once, she might have vented her outrage to a co-
worker. But after Matthew's death, Tracy had learned not
to become emotional. So although she felt the others
gawking at her back, she walked wordlessly to her assistant's office, intending to go straight through into her own
and privately rage at the walls.

Janet stopped her. Her chin braced on the heel of her
hand, she shot Tracy a look of pure empathy. "How
about we skate out a little early, go stuff ourselves at El
Chico's, and bitch about how life sometimes sucks?"

Drowning her sorrows at Grandsen, Mississippi's sole
Mexican restaurant—the only one worth its salt between
Jackson and Hattiesburg—sounded like a great place for
a good pout, but Tracy rejected it. "Sorry, fiscal year-
end budget report is due in today."

"I see." Janet sighed. "I promised myself I was going
to keep my mouth shut and just let you dump out all your
righteous indignation. But I can't." Tapping the mug's
handle, she put a warning in her tone. "Don't do it,
Tracy. Burke's case will break you."

If she didn't find a strong legal hook, it definitely
would break her. "Thanks for the vote of confidence."
Tracy stared at her grapevine-attuned assistant. In her
mid-thirties, Janet was about three years Tracy's senior.
The lines under her eyes and around her mouth proved
Janet's were high-mileage years, not that Tracy's had
been easy, and physically, they had little in common. Janet was petite, sleek, and trim; Tracy tall, and damned to
curves. While Janet had gleaming black hair and the ex-
otic features of an Asian, Tracy fought with a wild mass

of summer-streaked blond hair and, thanks to Scottish paternal ancestors, skin that tanned to the color of a pale rose. Her nose was slightly crooked, her deep blue eyes a little too far apart, and yet tossed together, the package wasn't half bad. Janet's was more perfect—especially her nose. Pert and straight, flawless even now, with her nostrils flaring.

"File thirteen the sarcasm, okay? This doesn't have a damn thing to do with confidence. We both know you're good at what you do, but Burke's case carries all the signs of becoming Intel-intensive and that's no place for an Intel novice to cut her teeth. For God's sake, Tracy. Colonel Hackett, Burke's own boss, is pushing as hard as the rest of the honchos for four counts of murder and the death penalty."

"The death penalty?" That, Colonel Jackson hadn't mentioned. Tracy frowned, upset but also grateful that Janet's former Intel service still netted her the lowdown from on high.

"Intel Rule Number Six. Compromised cover equals death. Figuratively, or literally." Janet shoved her gold bracelet up on her arm. "Refuse the case. Just say no."

Tracy grunted. "I don't even rate an office window yet. I can't 'just say no.' "

"Claim you can't be objective." Janet licked at her lips, warming to her topic. "God knows, you're as opinionated as a heart attack on everything—especially Burke's offenses."

"That'll certainly impress my superiors," Tracy retorted, wishing she could say she had an open mind about Burke. But why lie? Janet had made another valid point, too. Tracy wasn't up to defending this case. She met life straightforward and head-on. You play fair, you deal honestly. If you deserve lumps, then you take them. But in an Intel-intensive case such as Burke's, being straightforward and head-on could jeopardize missions and endanger lives.

Tracy fingered Burke's file. "I'm not surprised they're

pushing for the death penalty." How could she be surprised? Even the compassionate Colonel Jackson thought Burke deserved to die. "But even if I were, I couldn't skate out on this case."

"Now isn't the time to be noble." Janet let out a sigh that ruffled her spiky bangs. "I'm not knocking nobility. I wish we had a little more of it floating around. But don't be stupid, Tracy. This is going to cost you big."

"Probably," Tracy admitted. But she had to do it.

How she'd do it, she had no idea. Not yet. Her sense of justice and trust in the system was at war with her disdain. Burke's crimes were inexcusable. Heinous. Even a saint would be challenged to defend him with conviction. Yet without conviction, she didn't stand a chance.

Somewhere, somehow, she had to latch on to something good. Something upon which she could build conviction—and her case.

"Tracy, think, okay? Is your nobility worth your life?"

"My life?" Tracy grunted, and shoved a wild tangle of hair back from her face. "This is a case. My career and professional future. But it's hardly my life." Her garden. That was her life. And her memories.

Janet rolled her eyes back in her head. "We *are* talking about your life. Literally," Janet insisted. "Burke is Intel." She tapped at her temple. "Lots of supersensitive stuff locked inside his head. And lots of creeps out there who'll use anyone—even his attorney—to get it."

Her life. Literally.

Tracy absorbed the gravity in silence. She'd known the risks when she'd joined the Air Force. True, she hadn't expected to actually be called upon to take them, but that wasn't the military's fault. The recruiter had been honest. She'd been in denial—and eager to leave New Orleans, her ex-brother-in-law Paul's domain. Yet Janet jerking Tracy out of denial changed nothing. She still had to do what she had to do. "I have no choice."

"Everyone has a choice," Janet argued. "I'm living proof."

Frowning, Tracy poured herself a cup of coffee from the pot on the corner cabinet. Janet had left active duty and taken the civil service job as Tracy's assistant—though she was overqualified for it—because she'd gotten tired of working Intel. She wanted a more normal life. One free of danger and intrigue. Because she had radically changed her life-style, she firmly believed anyone could choose anything at will. "Hear *and* listen, okay? I have no choice."

Realization dawned and gleamed in Janet's eyes. Bracing her forearms against the edge of the desk, she sucked in a sharp breath and stiffened. "Oh, hell. You got tagged to defend him. Word was, you volunteered, but you didn't. You got damn tagged to defend the jerk." Janet grimaced. "Who did it? Jackson? Higher Headquarters? Who?"

"The baseline is I *am* going to defend Adam Burke. To do it well, I need Intel expertise and insight, and I don't have it. I need your help."

"Oh, no." Janet sputtered a sip of coffee. "No way."

"You just said my life is at stake. The man's incarcerated and bail is out of the question, so I don't see how I could be in danger, but you obviously do. Doesn't that prove I need you?"

"It proves you should ask for different counsel to be assigned. Make the bastards give the case to someone with the credentials necessary to survive it."

"The bastards have given the case to me," Tracy said, deliberately flattening her tone to let Janet know this point of discussion was closed. "Help me, Janet. Please."

"You're asking me to sign your death warrant. I won't do it—and I can't believe you'd ask me to, knowing how I feel about this, and about Burke. Five minutes alone with him, and I'd fry his sorry ass myself."

A lot of people, particularly ones in uniform, shared her feelings. "I'm going to defend him with or without your help. My best chance of survival is if you assist."

"Forget trying to put me on a guilt trip. I have no

conscience. I'm Intel-trained, remember? Only rules and the drills survived my active-duty days.'' Janet twisted a scowl from her lips and narrowed her eyes, staring at her long nails. ''I've warned you, and that's it for me. You go on from here and get yourself killed, and your blood is on your own hands, not on mine.''

''Do you want me to beg?'' Tracy lifted a hand, palm upward. ''Okay, I will. I'm beg—''

''No!'' Janet let out an exasperated groan. ''I worked with Burke in Intel. I know how he operates. He's a shrewd son of a bitch, and I'm steering clear of anything to do with him. The fallout is going to be explosive, Tracy, and I'm not eager to find my skinny ass buried in the rubble.''

''But I need a background check on him,'' Tracy persisted. ''One that digs deeper than his manufactured personnel file.'' Shoring up her courage, she voiced her real need; one that for a truckload of reasons she feared being fulfilled. ''I need his Intel file.''

''Are you crazy?'' Janet screeched.

''I'm desperate. To build a case I can live with building, I've got to find something good about this jerk. I need to know how his mind works. Who he is inside.''

''He's a goddamn coward. A ruthless, treasonous coward who got four good men killed. Operatives who were my friends.''

They had been Intel, and at heart, Janet was still Intel. No one ever walked away, forgot the rules and drills, or the camaraderie. They put their lives on the line together, depended on each other to survive, and nothing broke those kinds of bonds. Not duty, family, or even death.

''I'm sorry your friends are dead, Janet. Maybe Burke did get them killed. Maybe he is a coward and in his years of service to this country he hasn't done one damn thing good or right, or made even one small sacrifice for someone else. But maybe he has. And if so, I need to know it.''

Janet glared at her desktop, her voice tight and grating. "Intel records aren't accessible."

"Ordinarily, they aren't. But I know you. If you want his records, you can get them."

"*Usually*, I can get access. But I'm not going to do it. Not on this one." Scowling, she focused on Tracy's locket. "The man is guilty as hell. How can you expect me to help him?"

No progress whatsoever. Those Intel bonds were tugging hard. Tracy reached across the desk and touched Janet's hand. "Quit huffing and listen to me. If I fail to handle this case right, we all lose. Me, you, your friends, the legal system, and ultimately our country. Don't you see? The only way we can win is to do the best job possible for him."

"Don't you see that it won't matter what you do?" Janet stabbed her pen into its holder. "His fate has already been decided. The man's crashed and burned, Tracy. He's going to fry."

Tracy's stomach soured, then filled with resolve. "Maybe. But he's not going to fry before I give him a defense that doesn't get me fried with him."

Janet stilled, dragged a frustrated hand through her hair. "Oh, damn. Your promotion."

Tracy nodded, her stomach turning. "And I'm up for Career Status selection."

Staring at the mural of a window on the far wall, Janet finally riveted her gaze back to Tracy. "Okay, you can quit rubbing your locket," Janet said. "I'll *try* to run the background check on Burke—for you, not him." She clenched her cup in a white-knuckle grip. "I wouldn't spit on his grave."

"Thanks." Grateful, Tracy let go of her locket, supposing she did rub it when in a crunch. It was her last gift from Matthew, one that held a cherished photograph.

"That's a pretty romantic habit for a sworn nonromantic," Janet commented. "Rubbing the locket to remember him whenever trouble strikes."

It was anything but romantic. "I wear it to remember losing him, Janet. And so I never forget how much loving someone can cost."

"Good grief." Janet slid her a sour look. "Talk about jaded."

"It's not jaded." Tracy let the pain of losing Matthew and their daughter, Abby, shine in her eyes. "It's realistic."

"No," Janet contradicted. Speculating had her irises flickering golden brown. "It's safe."

"God, I hope so." Tracy sipped at her coffee, praying hard that proved true. She had survived all the losses she could stand for one lifetime.

"I'll do what I can on the file—but no promises." Janet flattened her lips to a thin coral line. "After what he's done, there's not a soul in the world eager to help Adam Burke."

The truth in that remark had Tracy frowning and heading toward her office.

"Damn, I forgot," Janet called out after her. "Randall phoned. You should tell him about the assignment before he hears it somewhere else, Tracy."

Janet too often fantasized that Tracy's relationship with Dr. Randall Moxley was a heated affair: a ridiculous notion. Randall, a pathologist at the base hospital, was charming and a bit of a rogue, and he did love to playfully hit on Tracy. But if she were to hit back, the man would probably faint. He'd definitely run, which is exactly what allowed them to be friends. "I'll call him when I get home."

The dreaded call came through from Colonel Jackson's office just before the end of the duty day at 1620—4:20 P.M. Burke had officially been charged with four counts of murder.

The alleged threats remained classified information, and adding that bad news onto the heap had Tracy depressed to the gills. She drove to her suburban home in the Gables subdivision, pulled into the driveway, and stared at the three-bedroom, two-bath cookie-cutter house she called home. The windows were dark, the house empty, and she wondered how long she would live here after she lost Burke's case, failed to get Career Status, and they kicked her out of the military.

Janet thought the house felt cold, and Tracy agreed. It did. But that hadn't been an accident. It was a deliberate warning: *Don't get too comfortable. You're a guest here for a time, and you won't be invited to stay.*

Realizing that warning extended to herself, Tracy har-rumphed and tapped the garage-door opener on her visor. Maybe she had become jaded. Damn morbid, too.

The garage door slid up, and she drove inside. It was at times like this that she missed the perk of having a husband to talk to about her troubles. Before Matthew's death, that's how she'd always found her legal hooks. She missed feeling close to a man, too, but she'd resolved to move mountains to avoid losing someone who mattered too much again. And there were other times, such as when Janet was nursing her weekly broken heart, that Tracy felt grateful for the reprieve.

Catching the scent of vanilla potpourri, she locked the kitchen door behind her, then changed into a pair of soft jersey slacks and a baggy T-shirt. Feeling the locket against her skin, she recalled Janet's reaction to it. She clearly considered Tracy an emotional cripple. But Janet couldn't understand. She hadn't lived through loss. Tracy wasn't a cripple, she was a survivor. And for a survivor, she was content. Satisfied. Happy.

Liar.

Bristling at her conscience's tug, she opened her bed-room door. Okay, she was a *nearly* content, satisfied, and happy survivor. At least she had been, until the Burke case was dropped in her lap.

Slipping on the Winnie-the-Pooh slippers she always wore when she needed an attitude, she admitted that sometimes she did feel *slightly* crippled. But only *slightly,* and considering her past, that wasn't bad.

She walked down the short hallway to the kitchen, snagged the phone, then dialed Randall. Waiting for him to answer, she stared down at the twin Pooh heads on her slippers' toes and again heard her dad's voice: *When the world's kicking your ass, hon, kick back. Just make sure you're wearing steel-toe shoes.*

Randall answered, sounding as if he had a mouth full of toothpaste. "What?"

"Don't you sound chipper?" Glancing through the huge windows to her garden, a sense of calm settled over her. It was her refuge. Her candle in the window. "Most people say hello before biting your head off." Tapping the faucet, she filled the teakettle.

"Mmm, let me guess." His sigh crackled through the line. "She's had a bad day."

"She's had the ultimate bad day." Tracy set the kettle on the stove to heat and then told him she'd be defending Adam Burke.

Ten minutes later, after Randall had given her every reason conceivable to God and man why she shouldn't take Burke's case, Tracy began wishing she hadn't called him. "Would a little sympathy and commiserating be asking for too much?" The teakettle whistled. She filled a mug plastered with Mickey Mouse's smiling face full of hot water. "You're supposed to be my friend."

"You do something crazy and you expect sympathy?" Randall paused, cleared his throat, and tamped down his temper. "Look, I understand that you feel obligated to defend the man, but Christ, Tracy, you'll be committing career suicide. Claim a conflict of interest. Tell them your personal feelings negate your ability to defend Burke."

"The promotion board would love that." Her spoon clinked against the edge of the mug, and she grunted. "Their pencils would leave screech marks on my file, adding 'unprofessional' to 'too young and idealistic' in my bio."

"Hell, then lie. Say anything. Say you're in love with the man."

Revulsion coursed through her in shudders. How could *any* woman be in love with Adam Burke? "I won't lie. And I won't say I'm in love with a traitor and murderer. The boards would swear I was either crazy or stupid. Maybe both—and I'd agree with them."

"Do you grasp the severity of this? Your promotion and status selection are on the line."

"My whole career as a Staff JAG is on the line, Randall." Bobbing the tea bag by its string, she grumbled and glanced out the window at her roses. Beautiful—and still in full bloom, though the blazing heat had most gardens sun-scorched and burned. "Giving the board more ammunition against me won't help cinch my promotion."

"Well, you've got to do something to get out of defending this case." His frustration hissed static through the phone line. "My hospital board will go nuts."

About to take a sip, Tracy frowned into her cup. "Excuse me?"

"My board. It'll take a dim view of me being close friends with Burke's attorney, and the members will be very verbal about it. You know how they are about controversy, and you've got to admit, Burke's damned controversial."

Bloody hell. Didn't she have enough to worry about already? But Randall was right. His hospital board was extremely conservative and protective of its image. The members would take a dim view of their friendship. It was the nature of Burke's crimes that would turn everyone against her for defending him. It didn't matter that she'd been assigned; people felt too passionate about treason, murder, and sacrificed men. She stood in Burke's defense, and that would stick in everyone's craw. Emotion always buries logic. A fact, that.

Mentally seeing Randall standing front and center before the board members, his blond head bent, his lean shoulders stooped, she barely managed to stave off a sigh.

Regardless of what he said to them, the members *would* give Randall hell. "I have no choice." She let him hear her regret. "I didn't volunteer, I was assigned."

"So dream up an excuse and get out of it. My board would be fine with your refusal."

His board? Bristling, she stilled, the tea bag dangling in midair over the sink. What about *her* promotion and selection? *Her* career? All this case could—and probably would—cost *her*?

Irked that her challenges didn't weigh at all in Randall's considerations, Tracy slung the tea bag into the sink. It thunked against the stainless-steel bottom, and steam poured out of it. Any second, she expected an equal amount to pour out of her ears. "Careful, friend," she said in clipped tones. "You're sounding like your convictions only run as deep as you find convenient."

"Image matters." His voice turned cold and distant. "You know my personal goals."

Lord, did she. She snatched up a dishcloth, then mopped at a tea splash near the faucet. He drove her crazy with his strategy updates, but his attitude on this rated downright unfriendly.

She tossed the cloth onto the counter and cast her slippers a suspicious look. But Pooh wasn't responsible for this attitude. Truth was the culprit. Randall Moxley was a fair-weather friend. And knowing it, Tracy couldn't get off the phone quickly enough. "I think we'd better agree to disagree on this and let it go."

"Fine." He slammed down the phone.

Clenching her teeth, she put the phone down, and resumed searching for her legal hook.

Feeling as she did about Adam Burke, how could she defend him with conviction?

She had until tomorrow morning to figure it out. That's when she was due at the facility, commonly referred to as the brig, to meet Adam Burke.

Just the thought of having to look the coward in the face had her stomach revolting and her head throbbing.

She'd bet her bars he would play the innocent victim. He'd blame someone else—anyone else—for everything.

It was a safe bet. The guilty assigned blame elsewhere with monotonous regularity. And considering Burke's crimes were positively the worst that could be committed by man, God knew she should expect nothing better from him.

Disgust turned her tea bitter. She dumped the contents from her cup, then went out to her moonlit garden, needing to cleanse herself of her distaste for both men.

Dropping to a wicker chair beneath the huge magnolia, she lifted her chin and inhaled its blossoms' sweet scent. Randall—if he appeared genuinely repentant for being an ass about this—she might forgive, but Adam Burke?

Never.

Chapter 2

As jails went, the Laurel Correctional Facility wasn't bad.

Built this century, it was a lot newer than Leavenworth; tan brick with white trim and equipped with basic cable TV, central heat, and air-conditioning, though every prisoner Tracy had visited there had pointed out within the first ten minutes that the system was insufficient to cool the building. The grounds were nicely landscaped with a seven-acre garden that prisoners could, or could not, work in. All able-bodied prisoners worked. But the choice on gardening was theirs. Most chose it, considering sweltering outside in the heat preferable to sweltering inside in a six-foot cell.

From the prisoners' reports, the guards weren't abusive, they just wrote up infractions and breaches of military courtesy, which over the course of time had become definitively defined. But the group of prisoners known as Heavies were abusive, especially to child molesters, rapists, and military prisoners guilty of treason—like Adam Burke. From all accounts, the Heavies were cautious about their attacks, which was sensible on their part, considering that if a guard wrote up something on a prisoner, the prisoner was guilty. Disciplinary consequences were blatantly listed in the rule book, and it was common knowledge that military sentences were about three times as harsh as civilian ones. Tracy supposed there was logic in not opening to dispute every call the corrections officers made.

Too many write-ups, or too severe an infraction, and a prisoner earned himself a stay in the hole—the prisoners' pseudonym for solitary confinement. There, the rules were harder to live with. The prisoner was allowed out of his six-by-ten-foot cell only an hour each day, and he had to stay awake from 0330 until 2130—three-thirty in the morning until nine-thirty at night. He couldn't sit on his cot, only on the chair inside his cell. And he could read only the *Laurel Correctional Facility Rule Book* or the Bible.

Tracy signed in and then followed her armed escort down the two-story row of cells. The bays housing the men reminded her of those in basic training—except for the bars. Cramped space and the prisoners' penchant for making weapons from the most unlikely objects kept furnishings sparse—a cot, a chair, a toilet, and a footlocker—but the place was spotless: unmarked white walls and gray tile floors that gleamed and smelled of fresh wax. Yet the air felt stale and recycled; old and used, like many of the prisoners' expressions. Dressed alike in issue gray jumpsuits, officers were segregated from enlisted prisoners, as is custom military-wide, though none wore any rank. Those sentenced for longer than five years would eventually be transferred to Leavenworth. With a stint at "the castle" hanging over their heads, she didn't suppose they had much incentive to feel enthusiastic.

She walked swiftly through the center of the cell block. Early on at Laurel, she'd learned not to linger between the entrance and the attorney/client conference room, or to so much as glance at any of the men. Once a female attorney did that in Cell Block D, she was verbally tormented more every time she walked through the steel doors.

The attorney/client conference room was down near the far end of the long corridor. She often wondered if it had been placed there deliberately to diminish the number of visits attorneys made to clients. It didn't take much imagination to walk in and feel oppressed.

The feeling hit her every time she came here, as soon as the heavy steel doors slammed shut behind her and locked. But before today, she had never suffered such strong claustrophobic symptoms. Hot, clammy, and sweat-sheened, she felt dizzy and her throat threatened to squeeze closed. Why did the oxygen in the air feel like lead in her lungs?

A shade shy of panic, she issued herself a stern lecture. *Calm down, Tracy. You know why this visit is the worst yet. You know why . . .*

She did know. This visit, she had come to meet with Captain Adam Burke, a traitor and coward who had killed four of Janet's Intel friends. And from all reports, Burke was about as excited at the prospect of meeting her as she was at the prospect of defending him.

God help them both. And please—*please!*—let her find a legal hook.

She stepped into the postage stamp generously referred to as a conference room. It was empty of everything except bare white walls, a marred wooden card-size table that had seen better days, and three scratched and dented metal folding chairs that attested to some of the less-than-pleasant conversations which had taken place here. But the ceiling fan's paddles, thumping overhead, made the Lysol-scented room semicool.

Tracy slid her chair over so that when Burke arrived and sat down he wouldn't be between her and the door. No sense in taking unnecessary risks with a man who had little to lose. She checked her watch. Ten o'clock on the nose. Burke should arrive any—

A guard around thirty, sporting sergeant's stripes, a blond crew cut, and arms the size of steamship rounds preceded Burke into the room, blocking her view of her client. When he stepped aside and Tracy got her first look at Adam Burke, it took everything she had in her not to gasp.

His legs were shackled. His arms handcuffed. And his face was as raw as a pound of lean hamburger in the grocer's meat case. He'd been beaten—severely, judging by the swelling and bruising on his face, forearms, and hands. His neck bore choke marks, and his knuckles were scraped and cut, evidence that he'd tried to give as good as he'd gotten. From the gap-necked opening in his prison grays, she glimpsed a thatch of black hair and a purple bruise that muddied his left shoulder. Some ass had spray-painted a four-inch-wide yellow stripe up his back, neck, and over his hair to the crown of his head. That same ass, or another one, had branded a huge black *C* on his wide forehead with what appeared to be a permanent ink marker.

Outrage immobilized her. Her heart thumped erratically. Her blood began a slow, hard boil, fueling its wild beat, and putting a furious tremor in her hand. Damn it, she should have expected this. He'd been charged, formally branded as a coward and traitor. She should have anticipated that the Heavies—or the guards—would beat Adam Burke to within an inch of his life.

And she might have expected it, if she hadn't been so damn preoccupied worrying about how this case would affect her life instead of thinking about how it would affect his. Damn her for blowing that. This kind of vengeance, Lady Justice didn't need.

Tracy turned an explain-this-now glare on the guard.

The sergeant shuffled his feet, rested a hand on the butt of his holstered gun, and nodded toward the still-silent Burke. "We, um, found him like this first thing this morning."

"First thing?" Tracy pointedly looked at her watch. "It's ten A.M., Sergeant. Has the doctor seen him yet?"

The guard avoided her eyes and skimmed a beefy hand over his stubbly nape, rustling his hair. "Um, no, ma'am. The doc's been pretty busy."

Probably sewing up the men that had left Burke nursing raw knuckles. "I see," she said from between her teeth. "Would you tell the unit commander I'd like a word with him, please?"

The guard's eyes stretched wide. "He's a bit busy this morning, too, ma'am."

"Fine." Tracy slid the guard a chilling look and a saccharine smile. "I wouldn't want to interrupt. I'll just route my message to him through Higher Headquarters, with a copy to General Nestler." Mentioning Laurel's god should get some action. "What was your name, Sergeant?"

"Maxwell, ma'am," he said sharply, knowing as well as she that she could read his name badge from where she sat.

His Adam's apple bobbed hard, twice, and he looked as if he would love to handcuff her to the water tower on the far side of the base to keep her out of his way. "But I'm sure you won't need to bother the general. Things are calming down. Let me check to see if the commander is free yet."

"Thank you." She motioned to Burke, silently swearing that if she hadn't seen photos of him in his Personnel file, she never would have known him. *Why in the name of God didn't I anticipate and prevent this?* She swiveled her focus back to the sergeant. "Could you please remove the shackles and cuffs?"

"No, ma'am," Maxwell stammered, looking torn. "I mean, yes, ma'am, I could, but I'm not permitted to do it. Burke is Intel, ma'am. High risk. Maximum security."

Before she could say another word, the sergeant backed out of the room and closed the door. Staring at it, Tracy drew in and then expelled three deep breaths, steeling herself to talk with Burke. "Please sit down, Capt—" She halted abruptly, refusing to address him by a title he no longer deserved. A title she shared, and took pride in. "Please sit down."

Swaying slightly, he shuffled to a chair, his chains clanking against the tile. When he moved his left arm, she saw a smattering of blood on his shirt, though she didn't see an open cut. With the number they had done on his face, the blood could have come from there, though getting it past his broad shoulders and full chest to soil his shirt beneath his ribs took a stretch of the imagination. But maybe in the heat of battle . . .

Burke shifted on his seat. From his ginger movements, the man had to be sore from head to toe. "Are you in pain?"

No answer. He just continued to stare at her through those swollen slits of icy gray eyes. They didn't even vaguely resemble the soft dove-gray she had noted in his photo.

"My name is Tracy Keener," she said, not at all put off by his silence. He was taller than she had expected. At least six two. "I've been assigned to defend you."

No comment.

Maybe dangling a carrot of courtesy would get him to alter his attitude and open communications. "Do you have any questions you'd like to ask me?"

She paused, but Burke didn't utter a sound, so she again changed tactics. Glancing at a checklist, she had to resist an urge to rub her locket. The facility certainly hadn't wasted any time in seeing to the paperwork on this case. Personnel had been notified of Burke's change in duty status, and they had acknowledged receipt of a copy of the confinement order. "Most of the forms required have already been filed."

She looked up. "You have no dependents." That could present a challenge or two. Nothing major, but inconvenient. "What about your household goods? Your car?" She didn't bother to wait for a response she knew she wouldn't be getting. "Do you have someone you can give a power of attorney to take care of them?"

Not so much as a head shake. Now why didn't that surprise her?

Raking her lower lip with her teeth, she hid a grimace. "The government won't ship your household goods or store them," she warned him, trying to elicit a response.

"And they've already stopped your entitlements and processed a grade reduction."

That bit of news had his eyes glittering, but it didn't have his tongue moving. A mean streak surfaced in her, but she squelched it, and explained. "As you haven't yet been adjudged, the grade reduction won't be effective until fourteen days after your court-martial."

Scanning the listing, she noted his date of separation was listed as "Indefinite." That was expected, and convenient. Otherwise it too would have, if necessary, been extended to a date beyond his court-martial proceedings. The government couldn't muck up jurisdiction by having a military member legally separate from the Air Force in the middle of his court-martial.

"These matters of your personal property have to be dealt with." Tracy laced her hands atop the checklist. "It's a safe bet that your sentence will be longer than five years. You do understand that the prosecutor is going for the death penalty, correct?"

Burke watched her draw every breath, but said nothing.

Okay, whatever. She damn well couldn't help him if he wouldn't so much as speak to her. "Leavenworth is definitely a part of your future. So think about those powers of attorney. Otherwise, your household goods will be lost with the house, and the mortgage company will dispose of them. Your car will be impounded and sold at auction. You won't get the money from any of this, and if your home is financed with a VA loan, it won't be reinstated so you can use it again later." *Later? He'll never need another home loan. He'll never again see the light of day free from prison walls.*

Nothing she said gleaned a reaction from him, much less a response. She opted to press on. "I'd like to hear your rendition of the events leading up to your arrest."

Again, no answer.

Urged to fill the uncomfortable silence, Tracy forced herself to be still and just wait. Sooner or later the man *had* to say something.

Five minutes passed. Then three more. Her nerves were stretched razor-wire tight, and she glared at him. "Did the beating affect your hearing?"

"Burke, Adam B.," he said through puffy lips. "Captain, U.S. Air Force. Serial number five-two-one, three-eight, two-seven-five-nine."

Name, rank, and serial number. *Fantastic.* She withheld a groan and leaned an elbow on the table between them. Wobbly, it rocked. "In case no one has told you, you're not a prisoner of war, Burke. But you are in an enormous amount of trouble. Would you kindly cut the antics and elaborate on the event that led to your arrest—and tell me who beat you? Was it the Heavies, or the guards?" She hated the thought, but—Burke was a coward and traitor so it could have been either group. Her money was on the Heavies.

"Burke, Adam B. Captain, U.S. Air Force. Serial number five-two-one, three-eight, two-seven-five-nine."

Tracy grimaced, her patience shot. "Look, it's obvious you don't want me here. Well, I don't want to be here, either. The truth is, I was drafted to defend you. I have no choice, and you have no choice. Live with it.

"We both know you're guilty. But maybe we can convince the jury you made a bad judgment call or you had faulty navigational equipment. We'll find an honest angle and work for a sentence reduction to life in prison—*if* you'll help me by answering my damn questions."

"You're a real piece of work, counselor. You know only the charges, my name, rank, and serial number, and you have me serving life." He motioned toward the door with his cuffed hands. "Get the hell out of here. I need an attorney, not a piece of fluff posing as one."

Her lips tightened to a thin line. "I am an attorney, Burke. A damn good one."

"I need a damn good one who does her homework. You don't." He scowled, stood up, spun his chair around, and then straddled it, straining his shackles until the chains snapped tight. "Hell, I know more about you than you've bothered to learn about me."

"I sincerely doubt it." She tilted her crooked nose upward.

He hooked his arms over the back of his chair, his grim expression dark and dangerous. "You're the widow of Matthew Keener, one of two heirs to the Keener Chemical fortune. You worked your way through law school and married the youngest heir, Matthew, in your junior year. In your senior year, you and Matthew were in a car accident. His blood alcohol level was 2.5, well above the legal limit. You were five months pregnant at the time. Matthew was killed and you were seriously injured. You delivered a daughter, Abby. Four months premature was just too much, and she died within minutes of being born."

That hurt. He knew it, and was taking pleasure in it. The smart-ass probably thought she'd asked for it, coming in here with preconceived notions about his guilt.

"The senior heir to the family fortune, your domineering brother-in-law, Paul, handled the funerals, which you couldn't attend because you were still hospitalized. Correct so far, counselor?"

She sent him a cold glare and a warning. "That's enough, Burke."

"But hardly the whole story." He plowed on, tapping his fingers against the back of the folding chair. The metal pinged against his blunt nails. "After losing Matthew and Abby—and probably to stop Paul's interference in your life—you joined the Air Force, intending to make it a career. You're now up for promotion to major—Board meets in about a month, right?—and you're up for Career Status selection. By the way, that's a bit harder to get these days than it once was. You get one shot at it." He slid her an icy smile. "Knowing your distaste for research, I thought you might be interested in that piece of information."

She held her silence, and her glare.

Adam cocked his head. "What I don't know for fact—and I seriously doubt you've considered—is, if everyone but God thinks I'm guilty, then why would Command insist on assigning such a high-profile, volatile case to a junior Staff JAG like you?"

Adam paused a beat, and the question swelled in her mind. By all rights and logic, senior officers *should* be prosecuting and defending him to protect the military, as best they could, against bad publicity. That they had assigned a media-attractive woman might help them with the press, but it wouldn't do them a damn bit of good in official circles.

Another oddity was his being held over for trial here, in Mississippi. Why had Command held him at this base rather than taking the more typical route and transferring him to Higher Headquarters for trial? It was the convening group's call, true, but considering the nature of the case, and the timing—fiscal year-end was staring into the whites of their eyes—that decision didn't make sense to her.

"I didn't ask," she said. "But I suspect I was assigned your case because I'm pretty new to the office and I don't yet have a full caseload." She dropped her lids to half-mast. "Or maybe Command figured that with its mountain of evidence against you, any lawyer could get a conviction."

Burke grunted. "Looks and claws, and she's decided to bare them. Problem is, counselor, your answers are as fluff as the rest of you."

"Define 'fluff.' "

"No substance," he explained, his eyes keen and assessing. "Or are you being deliberately evasive to conceal the truth?"

"What's your supposition?" She slid Adam a hooded glare. "Why do you think I was assigned?"

He sent her a steely look that could curdle blood. "I suspect you came into the office with a full caseload—Staff JAGs are always overworked. And I also suspect

you were assigned to my case because the honchos too
know your distaste for research. They *want* me convicted,
and with you representing me, they feel certain I *will* be
convicted.''

Tracy flinched, angry because she hadn't considered
that possibility, hadn't wondered why a junior Staff JAG
had been assigned to this high-profile case. Angry because she hadn't done her homework and learned all there
was to know about Adam B. Burke and his case *before*
coming to see him today. And she was most angry because Burke could be right. She could have been assigned
to assure his conviction. God and Command, and likely
Higher Headquarters, had known from the onset that she
considered Burke guilty.

That bit of honesty turned her tone acidic. "Look,
Burke. You don't have to like me, and I certainly don't
like you.'' She hated him for bringing up her past. For
invading her privacy, and dredging up old hurts that
brought her fresh pain. For committing the god-awful
crimes he'd committed, and screwing up all their lives.
"But I am your lawyer. I'm all you've got, and you'd
best get used to it.''

"*Captain* Burke,'' he said through clenched teeth.
"I've worked my ass off for seven years to earn my rank.
I've put my life in jeopardy more times than you've put
on a uniform, and though everyone in the world thinks
otherwise, I've done nothing—*nothing*—to dishonor it.
All I've gotten since this nightmare started is humiliation
and degradation. I deserve better. You either prove me
guilty, or you acknowledge my rank, Captain.''

"When I'm convinced you've honored it, I will. But
not a moment before then.'' She stood up, gathered her
briefcase and her purse, then dug down into the leather
compartment holding her wallet. She fished out a quarter
and tossed it onto the table. "When you decide to act
civil and tell me something I can use to save your ass,
call me.''

"You? Save my ass?" He grunted, proving he couldn't fathom that possible. "Right."

Furious, she turned and walked out of the room.

Adam glared at her back. "Fluff."

Tracy seethed all the way back through Cell Block D. Defending the man threatened to destroy her career, to endanger her life, and he had the unmitigated gall to call her *fluff*?

He certainly had. He considered her a lightweight, totally incompetent. That infuriated her. Hell, everything about him infuriated her.

But even through her fury, she had to admit Burke was nothing like she had expected. From the photos Janet had pulled, Tracy had known he was gorgeous. Tall, broad-shouldered, lean-hipped. Strong chin, firm jaw, and a long, straight nose. Though little evidence of his good looks had been apparent under the bruises and swelling, those would heal. His physical appearance would definitely be an advantage in a jury trial. What she hadn't expected was his attitude. He'd broken the mold. Not once had he acted like a typical defendant. He hadn't justified his actions, blamed someone else, or rationalized.

That stumped her.

After a brief chat with the unit commander, a charming man miraculously no longer too busy to see her, she headed out to the shadeless parking lot, to her Caprice.

Breath-stealing heat poured out of the car. Tracy climbed in, started the engine, and cranked the air-conditioner up on High, still trying to puzzle out why Burke had broken the mold. His acting unlike the typical defendant brought her no comfort. In a sense, it made him even more dangerous. In only a few moments, Adam Burke had had her questioning his guilt, Command, Higher Headquarters, and herself.

She dumped her purse and briefcase on the passenger seat, then stared at the rearview mirror, into her own distrustful blue eyes. *Why would Command assign a junior Staff JAG to defend such a high-profile, volatile case?*

Chapter 3

Adam hated being wrong.

He had been wrong, of course, and he had admitted it. But this time admitting it grated deeper, and that made him hate it even more. He despised having to give that sanctimonious, biased incompetent credit for anything, but facts were facts, and Tracy Keener had been right. She was all he had.

He had refused to believe that was possible. Had been certain that *someone* would take his side. But not one person from Intel, one neighbor or friend or family member, had come to see him, much less offered to help him. His family avoiding him didn't surprise him. If they had come, that would have been a shock. He'd been an outsider since the day he was born, and he was damn grateful for it. And his friends numbered few. In his line of work, they had to; well-meaning friends could cause complications, and they would resent his secretive nature. But his Intel family . . . He couldn't believe they'd slashed and severed without hearing his side of this. Yet they had. And that cut him deep.

Stiff and sore from the beating, he paced his cramped cell, staring at the iron bars denying him freedom. How had this happened to him? How had he, a dedicated member of the United States Air Force, a man who had built his life on ideals that demanded duty, honor, loyalty— and more personal sacrifices than he cared to recall—

ended up behind bars as a criminal? He'd risked his life his entire career to prevent crimes against the United States and, by God, he had the scars to prove it. Yet no one—*not one single person*—believed him innocent. Hell, no one even gave him the benefit of doubt.

Stiff and sore and now tense, he forced himself to do some stretching exercises to loosen up, even though it was mid-afternoon and the heat inside the cell was at its smoldering peak. Bracing a foot flat against the wall, he leaned into it. Pain, sharp and swift, shot through his ribs. His head swam, and a wave of nausea rushed up his throat. Doubling over, he grabbed his side. No matter what that quack of a doctor had said, his damn ribs had to be broken.

When the pain dulled, Adam blew out a sharp breath and straightened up. If he had sustained such a beating on the street, he would have been put on leave and ordered to stay home to recuperate. If on a mission, well, treatment would have depended on whether or not he had already accomplished his tasks. If so, he'd hibernate until he was strong again. If not, he'd keep pushing until he had finished the job. That was the drill. *Duty first.*

But he wasn't on the outside or on a mission. He was locked up, accused of crimes he couldn't even imagine committing. And that angered him into breaching military courtesy and moving to the cot. What the hell else could they do to him?

He rocked back, letting his head drop down to the plastic-covered pillow. It crackled, irritating him more. He'd slept in worse places out in the field. In the blistering hot desert, after hiking miles through a hellish sandstorm to bring needed intel back to the unit. In a mosquito-infested swamp, armed to the teeth and awaiting orders to infiltrate enemy territory. In a mountain crevice during a blizzard, huddling there after gathering intel needed for a preemptive strike. But when he got out of here, he swore he would *never* again sleep on a pillow encased in plastic.

Would he get out of here?

Fear that he wouldn't surged through him, and his muscles clenched. Sweat beaded at his temples, trickled down his face, and again he heard Keener's voice. *You do understand that the prosecutor is going for the death penalty, correct?*

Didn't the incompetent realize he already had been convicted? That whether or not the honchos succeeded in getting him legally convicted and sentenced to death, they'd already stolen his life? He had been stripped bare. Left with nothing. Even if he proved his innocence, his Intel operative days were over. With all the publicity and exposure—he was worthless to Intel now.

Worthless.

He stared blankly at the ceiling, feeling isolated and empty. He had lived and breathed his life as an operative. Since his divorce from Lisa four years ago, he hadn't had a personal life, only his work. Even if he did get out of this, what was left for him?

Duty first.

The first Intel rule drilled into his head during basic training kicked in, commanding him with the authority of a direct order to keep a tight focus on the big picture. More important than what he'd have left, was what the country would have left. How would this incident impact it?

That, Adam didn't know. Until he did, he couldn't rest. His oath, his honor, forbade it.

He chewed his lower lip, thoughtful. Who had done this to him? Why had they done it? The war-readiness exercise had taken extensive planning. No one invested in extensive planning except to commit a deliberate act. And an act of this magnitude—one that sacrificed lives— established irrefutably that it had been committed for a specific purpose. A purpose, Adam sensed deep in his gut, that would cost his country plenty unless it was revealed.

He dropped a frustrated fist to his cot. He damn well

should let the nation pay those costs. But even after what had been done to him, he couldn't do it. Besides the bastards who falsely accused him, innocent people would pay the price. People he had sworn to serve and protect.

Folding an arm above his head, Adam fingered the shiny quarter he'd held like a talisman since Keener had tossed it at him. She was something else. Incompetent, but interesting. Beautiful, of course, or she wouldn't have been chosen as his defense counsel, yet not conventionally beautiful. More pretty with a haunted air about her that made her seem tragically mystical. That combination, he grudgingly admitted, was even more irresistible than classic beauty—and more dangerous. Men instinctively reacted to her beauty, and women sensed the tragedy behind her haunted air and responded protectively to it. Having an in with both sexes gave Keener a hell of an edge.

Adam let his hand slice down his prison grays, thigh to knee. Okay, so she had endured her fair share of problems. Maybe a few more than her fair share. And he had been hard on her. She'd deserved it, but she hadn't had to take everything he had dished out like a pro. Yet she had. She'd left the meeting furious with Adam, but she'd still stopped by the unit commander's office and, with a respectable amount of righteous indignation, she'd insisted Adam be isolated to avoid future beatings. She had also demanded a full-scale investigation of the beating to determine who had inflicted it—the Heavies, or the guards. That had taken guts.

Not that she realized it—or, believing him guilty, she wouldn't have done it—but her arranging his move to the hole had been a lucky break for him. It afforded him the privacy and latitude he needed to gather vital intel. Unfortunately, even with the move, there were still things he needed to do that he couldn't do from any jail cell.

I'm all you've got, and you'd best get used to it.

True. He flipped the quarter, caught it, then rubbed its ribbed edge with the pad of his thumb. But that didn't mean he should trust her with what he knew about the incident.

Should he take the risk?

That was the million-dollar question. The answer wouldn't come easily. The stakes were damn high. He'd pay with his life.

Adam gave his pillow a punch. Keener was also friends with Dr. Randall Moxley. That was worth remembering, considering suspicions regarding Moxley had been unofficially reported to Intel and to the OSI. He could be disseminating sensitive information on confidential programs to outsiders. The Office of Special Investigations had been given a heads-up on the doctor, but they had no authority to make an arrest, as a formal report had not been filed.

Adam understood the reason for that. It wasn't a matter of guilt or innocence, but a matter of evidence. Once a report was filed, with or without hard evidence, the OSI had to launch an investigation and follow the "guilty until proven innocent" military policy. Arrests would be made based on suspicion. Careers and lives could be ruined. So military and civil service employees had become wary of the formal reporting process, and they generally chose to meet informally with OSI agents to discuss "hypothetical situations." Of course, the OSI tracked everyone involved in those hypothetical situations, and they shared their findings with Intel.

Such was the case with Tracy Keener. The suspicions against Moxley had unofficially been extended to the incompetent captain because of their friendship. Guilt by association. And Adam wondered. Could either of them be using their positions to filter sensitive information on programs that would render new technology obsolete prior to it even being developed?

After what had happened to him, Adam knew anything was possible. Anything at all. And he'd be foolish to forget Keener had been counsel on research-and-development-project contracts before her ex-brother-in-law, Paul, through Keener Chemical, had started bidding on them. Paul's bids had made her acting as R & D counsel a direct conflict of interest, necessitating her transfer from her specialty, contract law, to criminal law. She had to resent that.

The steel door to the solitary confinement block opened.

Adam rolled out of bed. Springing to the balls of his feet, he focused his full attention on who was approaching. The Heavies had jumped him in the dead of night. He'd been sound asleep. That wouldn't happen again. Now, he had sharpened his two pencils and, whenever he slept, he tied his foot to the cell door with his shoestring. If the door opened, Adam would know it *before* someone blindsided him.

By all rights, the beatings shouldn't happen again. He was isolated in the remote northeast corner of the brig, separated from the others. But the guards had keys, and someone had given the prisoners access to them before or they wouldn't have gotten to Adam the first time. If it happened once, it could happen again. And if it did, this time, he would be ready.

His pant leg clung to his calf. Static electricity. He shook it loose and palmed his quarter. He had to find out who was behind this nightmare, and why they had dragged him into it.

Accept it, Burke. To find out the truth you need help. You need Keener.

He rubbed at his lower lip, angry at having been put in this position and hoping to hell her outrage at his being beaten was genuine. Surely a reaction that stark had to be honest. But either way, the bottom line read the same. He had to prove himself and protect the innocent. He had to risk trusting her. He had no one else.

Sergeant Maxwell appeared outside Adam's cell, carrying shackles and cuffs. He unlocked the cell door and then pulled it open. Its hinges whined and groaned.

''Let's go, Burke. You've got fifteen minutes' exercise time.''

Adam was supposed to have an hour. Evidently, three quarters of his time had been rescinded because of the fight. Of course it had been blamed on him. ''I want to call my lawyer.''

If Maxwell was surprised to hear Adam's voice for the first time, he didn't show it. ''Whatever.'' Working efficiently and effectively, he fitted the shackles onto Adam's legs, the cuffs onto his arms, locked them, and then backed off. ''It's your time and your dime.''

Adam didn't bother reminding the moron phone calls cost a quarter.

As they walked through the corridor, Adam covertly looked around. Six cells, all prepared and ready for prisoners, but currently empty. Odd, as the facility was supposedly overcrowded. Yet, from the lack of noise, he had suspected himself alone in the cell block. During his move there, his eyes had been too swollen to visually verify it. He would have had to turn his head to see into the cells, and looking would have been taken as a sign of weakness by the Heavies, a show of fear. The last thing a man who wanted to survive his facility stint showed the Heavies was fear.

At the end of the hall, they turned right, into the activity room, which closely resembled the attorney/client conference room. Both were sparsely furnished, hot, and empty of other prisoners. Circling a wide table, Adam walked over to the wall phone.

Maxwell plopped down on a chair near the window, letting out a respectable grunt. Close, if the need arose, but out of earshot.

Since Keener's visit with the unit commander, Adam had been treated with civility, if not with respect. He was grateful for that, though he hated owing her or anyone anything as much as he hated being wrong and her being right.

He palmed the receiver, dropped the quarter into the

pay phone's slot, and then dialed, resenting his lack of
options and praying that calling her wasn't a lethal mistake.

A woman answered. "Captain Keener."

Where was Janet Cray? He rolled his gaze to the wall,
betting his fluff attorney didn't care for answering the
phone herself. Wait. Keener was a junior Staff JAG.
She'd share a secretary, and answer herself when necessary.

"Hello?" She solicited a response, her tone soft and
throaty. "This is Captain Keener."

Adam swallowed hard, wishing her voice didn't sound
like music to his ears. Wishing it grated. He didn't bother
with courtesies, or with identifying himself. She'd know
it was him. During her visit, the woman had absorbed
everything about him like a sponge.

*Don't do this, Burke. She's incompetent. In with Mox-
ley. You're being stupid. The woman will get you killed.*

Adam cleared his throat and shut his eyes, blocking
out his thoughts. In a cold sweat, his hand clammy
against the phone receiver, he pretended the tremor rattling through him had nothing to do with the thought that
he was making a monumental mistake, pretended the
knots in his gut were remnants of the beating, knowing
damn well they were rooted in fear.

I'm all you've got . . .

Staring at a No Smoking sign above the phone on the
wall, he took the plunge. "Why does a junior captain get
assigned to lead a team of four even more junior-grade
operatives to jam communications in a war-readiness exercise when neither the team leader nor any member of
the team is communications-trained and, at the time, there
are no readiness exercises being conducted in the field?"

Chapter 4

Burke.

Stunned to hear his voice, Tracy jerked. The phone bumped against her chin, and she rubbed at it, trying to grasp the question he tossed out to her.

Cold fingers of shock bolted up her spine. *All* of the men on his team had been junior operatives? *None* of them had been communications-trained? Why *had* they been assigned? And why had Burke been assigned to lead them?

The dial tone buzzed in her ear a solid minute before Tracy could slow her racing mind enough to hang up the phone. He had surprised her, first by calling—she'd considered the odds of that slim to none—and then by throwing out his intriguing question and hanging up without another word.

She'd have to be an idiot not to recognize the call for what it was: a direct challenge to prove her worth. In the past, she had walked away from similar challenges—though if they were still alive, her parents and Matthew would find the notion impossible to believe. Yet she had no intention of walking away from this one.

Cradling the receiver, she gave the Simpson file one last look, closed it, and then retrieved her purse from her lower right desk drawer. The retired Major Simpson would just have to wait to test the strength of the regulations that demanded he forfeit part of his civil service salary because he was already receiving a military retirement pension. His was a valid common complaint of discrimination against regular commissioned officers who retired from active duty and then went back to work for the Department of Defense as civil servants. It had been challenged in the past without success and, Tracy feared, it would be again in the future. She'd give it her best, but the battle would have to be put on hold a while longer. Adam Burke didn't get into talkative moods often—in fact, this was the first one since his arrest—and Tracy didn't want him to clam up again before she learned anything from him.

She buried her hostility at what Adam Burke had done—her only hope of finding her legal hook and building a respectable defense—and left a note for Janet, who had gone to lunch with this week's heartthrob.

Out in the parking lot, Tracy cursed the scalding heat pouring out of the Caprice and climbed in. Even with tissues stuffed under her hands, holding on to the steering wheel proved to be an exercise in discipline.

Half an hour from the time she received Burke's call, she sat cloistered in the Lysol-scented, attorney/client conference room, suffering symptoms of claustrophobia and looking at a less swollen, if still shackled, Adam Burke.

He sat ramrod straight on the metal chair, his expression tense, his distrustful gaze hard and unbending. "Everything I say to you is confidential, correct?"

She nodded, determined that this time he would be the one talking—and that she would *not* leave here doubting everything on God's green earth because of what he said—especially herself.

"You will repeat it to no one?" he persisted. "Not under any circumstances?"

The hairs on her neck lifted. This wasn't going to be some Sunday-school disclosure. His caution proved it, and her instincts hummed it. "Not without your express permission, no."

He dropped his deep voice to an unmistakable warning. "I've learned the hard way not to trust others, Keener, and if I had any choice, I sure as hell wouldn't risk trusting you. Not knowing you consider me guilty."

She could challenge him to find someone who didn't consider him guilty, and she would have, but there was a bite of accusation in his tone. He resented knowing she believed him guilty, and afraid any reply to what he had just said would shut down communications, she tilted her chin and chose a less confrontational tack. "In the five years I've been practicing law, I have never—not once—breached attorney/client confidentiality."

"I'm glad to hear it." His gray eyes glittered. "Don't disappoint me by starting now."

She tossed a hank of unruly hair back over her shoulder and propped her elbow on the table, striking what she hoped would pass for a lazy pose. "Is that a threat?" It felt like a threat, and it had her uneasy. She resented that, though on some level, she understood it.

He didn't answer.

She gave him a sigh she meant for him to hear, then sat back and folded her arms akimbo. "Look, you've obviously made the choice to trust me—at least, insofar as you must—so why don't you just tell me what happened to cause your arrest?"

Adam couldn't sit down. Just the idea of trusting Keener had every nerve in his body knotted. Looking at the rank on her slim shoulders, knowing his own was about to be stripped from him, only jerked those knots tighter. "Are there any loopholes we haven't covered that would allow you to disclose what I'm about to tell you?"

She tilted back her head to meet his gaze, doing her best to bury her impatience. "Give doubt a rest, Burke. Just tell me the truth. I won't reveal anything you say to anyone without your permission. You have my word."

Give doubt a rest? Easy for her to say. Unconvinced, he knit his brows. "What's your word worth?"

"To me?" She looked up at him from under her lashes. "Everything."

Adam did his damnedest to stare straight into her soul. Hell, yes, he was being cautious. This was his life he was putting on the line, and he meant for her to realize it.

She didn't flinch or look away.

"Okay," he said, her steadiness giving him the reassurance he wanted. "Okay."

Settling back on her chair, she crossed her long legs at her ankles. He couldn't not react; she was beautiful, and that tragic mystical air hovered around her like a cool mist on a hot night. Trying to ignore it, just as he'd tried ignoring her subtle perfume and everything else attractive about her, he forced his mind back to the incident.

"Orders came down from Command for me to participate in a war-readiness exercise out in Area Thirteen. It was short notice—one day—but that isn't uncommon when O'Dell—Colonel Hackett's assistant, Major Gus O'Dell—spearheads missions."

Hating that bastard O'Dell for having involved him, Adam's stomach flipped over and he swallowed down a fist of bitterness from his throat. "I was assigned to lead Alpha team—me and four junior operatives—in the exercise. Our mission was to cross enemy lines, jam Omega's communications with their factions, and gather intel."

Adam's thoughts drifted to the day of the exercise and, low in his gut, anxiety coiled tight. "We hopped into a truck and headed out to the field. At Thirteen's drop-off point, O'Dell pulled me aside. There had been a change in orders, he said. He issued me chemical protective gear, a personal chemical alarm, and then ordered me to lead my men to Area Fourteen."

Keener's eyes registered shock and confusion. "But—but that's a bombing range."

"Yes, it is," Adam confirmed, his tone deadpan flat. "My reaction to the order was about the same as yours. I couldn't figure out why the hell my team was being ordered to infiltrate a bombing range during an active war-readiness exercise, or why I needed chem-gear and they didn't.''

''What did you decide?''

Tension lumped his muscles, and Adam rubbed at his neck. ''Military information is disseminated on a 'need to know' basis. Everyone in uniform is aware of it. I figured I had no need to know.''

He walked toward the window and looked out. A cardinal sat on an oak limb, just outside the window. Beyond it, prisoners worked in the garden, weeding. ''Intel operatives routinely face unorthodox situations, counselor. It seemed logical to be trained in how to protect yourself in a controlled readiness exercise rather than to be put in that position in the field and to have to figure it out then.''

''Sounds like valid judgment to me,'' she said. ''So far.''

A concession, but Adam had a long way to go to convince her he was innocent. ''Considering what's happened since then, I wouldn't do it again, but I followed orders. I led my team to Area Fourteen, and then I returned to Area Thirteen to gather intel.''

''Those too were O'Dell's orders—you alone returning to Area Thirteen?''

''Those, too.'' Adam's voice went tight, and he fought the same sense of confusion he had fought then. Now, betrayal overrode it. ''No one was there. No support teams, no Omega team enemy—no one.''

''No one?'' Tracy straightened in her chair, her tone incredulous.

''No one.'' Adam bent down to inch a finger between his left ankle and the shackle. The damn thing dug into his flesh, making a sore spot. There was only one reason the shackles had to be so tight. Sergeant Maxwell was a masochist. ''I considered the absence of support and human resources significant. Something had gone wrong. So I radioed Home Base on a secure channel, reported it, and notified them that my team was in Area Fourteen.''

"Was the transmission acknowledged?"

"Yes," Adam said. "I received a 'Roger, Alpha One' response."

Keener still hadn't lifted her pen from the table to jot down any notes on the legal pad in front of her. Adam had mixed feelings about that. She did look thoughtful, though, chewing at the inside of her lip. But why didn't she ask any more questions?

While not elated by her lack of curiosity, in a sense, he admired her restraint. The woman might be an incompetent attorney, but she was a good listener, giving him the opportunity to disclose everything he wanted to disclose before bombarding him with questions. He liked that. He didn't want to like it, or anything else about her, but considering he had decided to trust her, finding some redeeming quality in her was a good thing.

He continued his disclosure. "A B-1 bomber made a pass over Area Fourteen and then circled back toward the base's flight line. For a minute, I worried that the bomber hadn't gotten the change of orders. That, not knowing there were personnel in Fourteen, the pilot would drop his load."

"Drop his load?"

She didn't have a clue. Not a clue. "His bomb, or load of bombs," Adam explained. "Live ordnance."

"Oh." Understanding flickered through her eyes.

God help him, she didn't even know what a *load* was and his life was in her hands? Adam grunted. He was in major trouble here. Major trouble.

"So the bomber flew by without dropping its ordnance."

"No, it dropped the ordnance, but not near my men. About five minutes after the run—ten since my radio call—my chemical alarm triggered. I checked and it was working properly so I tried to follow procedure and call it in, but my radio had blitzed out. Nothing I tried worked to repair it." He returned to the window, too agitated to sit. "I'll admit I didn't waste a lot of time on it. I couldn't. I knew I had to get to my men or they'd be exposed to whatever chemical had triggered the alarm. The wind was blowing southeast, somewhere between ten and fifteen knots—right toward them.''

In his mind, Adam slipped back to that time. Back to running through the dense woodland, fighting prickly underbrush, fallen trees from last year's Hurricane Ellie, the heat. God, the heat. It had to have been a hundred ten degrees inside that chemical gear. ''Before I crossed over into Area Fourteen, I got sick. My vision blurred. I had difficulty breathing, and my chest went tight. I figured it was heat stroke, and I tried to keep going. I *did* keep going.''

''So you got to Area Fourteen?''

''Yes.'' He rubbed at his neck with an impatient hand. ''At least, I think it was Area Fourteen. I was so disoriented, I'm just not sure.''

Skepticism clouded Keener's eyes.

He damned her for it. ''I was disoriented, counselor.''

''I see.'' She arched a doubtful brow.

''No, I don't believe you do.'' Anger rippled his tone. ''Not yet.''

She shifted in her chair and swept back her tangled hair with an efficient snap of her wrist. ''What made you think you were in Area Fourteen?''

This, Adam had hedged on deciding whether or not to tell her. Now, he knew he had been kidding himself, thinking he would have a choice. ''I saw a metal canister on the ground.''

Tracy leaned forward against the table. ''What kind of metal canister?''

''A bomb casing,'' he explained, his impatience with her ignorance putting a hard edge on his voice. ''I disregarded it as toxic because it didn't have the mandatory chemical warning label.''

''What label is that—exactly?'' she asked, still not lifting her pen.

Her blank legal pad mocked him. ''Chemical canisters

require a label. Either a yellow or a blue band around them. It's a visual warning that they're live ordnance, not training dummies.''

Absorbing his every nuance, she worried her lower lip with her teeth. ''So you disregarded this canister because it lacked the label.''

''Right.'' Adam stuffed a hand into his prison grays' hip pocket and stared out the window. ''I made it to my men.'' A mountain of regret and cold rage tore loose inside him. He fisted his hand in his pocket to bury it. ''They were all dead.''

Tracy paused. A thousand questions burned in her brain, but she refrained from asking even one of them. Burke needed a few minutes to regain control of his emotions. A blind man would realize he had been reliving the events as he described them.

He wouldn't like her noticing the slight shake in his hand, or the tremble in his voice. But he would hate to realize that she'd seen beyond his anger at finding his men dead and into his pain. Could he be that good an actor? Could anyone be so utterly convincing at faking that kind of pain?

As a survivor, she couldn't imagine it. But this wasn't about her, or her emotional response to loss. It was about Burke. And only God knew what he was and wasn't capable of faking.

She crossed her arms over her chest, not wanting to visualize the scene he had walked into out there. Not wanting to feel the shock she would have felt, the regret for the team, and for their families. For her, that would have been devastating. As devastating as learning Matthew had been legally drunk at the time of the accident, injuring her, killing himself, and Abby—a fact Paul, protecting her, hadn't disclosed. She'd been torn apart by it, mortified, and nearly destroyed. And from the vibes radiating from Burke, this incident hadn't been much easier on him.

When he appeared calmer, she urged him on. "Then what happened?"

"My men were dead, but they hadn't been hit by the bomb. There wasn't a mark on them. I figured whatever killed them had to be biological or chemical, and I remembered the canister," Adam said, clearly back in control. "I knew something way out of line had happened so I went back and buried the canister in a safe place."

A safe place? Obviously he didn't trust her enough to disclose the location. "Did being near the canister set off the chemical alarm?"

"Once it triggered, it stayed on. I reset it, but it kept triggering, so I can't say if proximity to the canister had an effect."

A shiver trickled through Tracy's chest. If what Burke said proved accurate, then the canister had to be live. What else would trigger the alarm? And if the canister was live and Burke had received a radio response, then Home Base had known the operatives were in Area Fourteen. If true, then Burke wasn't to blame, but the operatives' deaths had been deliberate. That made this incident no accident. It made it murder. But not murder by Burke.

But that was impossible. She shuddered. *Impossible!*

Burke's husky voice snagged her attention. "I passed out," he said from between his teeth, as if disgusted that he had succumbed to human weakness. "O'Dell—someone—must have laced my oxygen with something."

Convenient. And creative. "Why did you bury the canister?"

"I considered it prudent."

Standing at the window, he angled a look back at her that betrayed him, speaking volumes more than his words. He'd buried it because he hadn't yet tagged the enemy, or his allies.

"I don't remember anything else until I woke up in the hospital. People were calling me a traitor, and accusing me of deserting my men."

His resentment of that came through in his clipped

tones, in the stiff posture of his broad shoulders. So did his confusion. Tracy didn't trust it, or him. "Did you talk with anyone? Make any statement of any kind?"

"No, no official statements."

"None?" She couldn't hide her surprise. Surely the Military Police and agents from the Office of Special Investigations had attempted to gain statements from Burke. "Not even to the MPs or the OSI?"

"No," he reiterated. "But Lieutenant Carver talked to me."

"Who is Lieutenant Carver?"

"Colonel Hackett's aide," Adam said, reeking of his do-your-homework-Fluff attitude. "I'm told that my commander or his representative has to visit me at least once a month. Carver was it for August."

So Burke had read the facility's rule book. What wasn't noted in it was that, while the prisoner's commander or his representative did have to make monthly visits, his representative usually was a sergeant. "What did Carver say?"

"He lied. He said the team had been blown to hell and back by a bomb because I'd screwed up and led them onto an active bombing range. I saw their bodies. My men were not blown to bits. Their bodies were intact and unmarked." Burke grimaced, dropping his eyelids to half-mast. "Carver also informed me that I was facing a court-martial and a dishonorable discharge, and that the prosecutors would be seeking the death penalty."

"Why didn't you tell him about O'Dell's orders, or about the canister?"

Burke snorted, sounding almost amused. "I tried telling the truth about O'Dell changing my orders early on at the hospital. They called me a damn liar and said O'Dell had been off-duty all day. He wasn't, and Carver already had lied to me. Why waste my breath?"

Tracy puzzled through Burke's rationale. "No. Not wasted breath. You stopped talking because Carver and O'Dell both work for Hackett," she said, getting a fix on

how Burke's mind worked. "You didn't know which side
of the fence Carver sat on." *Enemy, or ally? When in
doubt, shut up.* She'd bet her bars that if asked, Janet
would confirm silence as one of their Intel drills.

"That, too." Burke's eyes glinted approval. "Until I
knew, the less said the better."

Tracy resented liking his approval, even as she wished
everything he had told her was true. Not for content—
he'd intimated multiple murders and a conspiracy, for
God's sake—but as a sign that Burke had proceeded in
trust and good faith and that he was being sincere. But
he wasn't. Somewhere deep inside her, she knew Adam
Burke was lying to her. "They say you deserted your
men because you got lost and led them onto the bombing
range instead of to Area Thirteen."

"I wasn't lost. I went to Area Fourteen because those
were my orders. I left my men there because those were
also my orders."

"Are you proposing that this incident was a conspiracy
which might, or might not, include Colonel Hackett and
Lieutenant Carver, as well as Major O'Dell?"

Burke slid her a hooded glare. "I'm not proposing anything. I don't know what the hell happened out there. All
I know for fact is O'Dell issued me orders, and I followed
them."

Burke wanted to say more. Sensing it, she encouraged
him to do it. "But . . . ?"

"But," he said, then hesitated before going on. "Everything that has happened since then proves—at least,
to my satisfaction—that I was set up to take a fall."

He believed it, Tracy realized. Every word of it. De-
lusions? Rationalization? He had to be suffering from one
or the other. Could mental instability be her legal hook?
"Set up by whom? For what purpose?"

Hands in his hip pockets, Burke turned to look her
straight in the face. "I have no idea."

Her skepticism again surfaced.

He must have noted it because he grabbed the chair

across from her, turned it around, and then straddled it, yanking the chains between his leg shackles tight. "I see your doubt. You don't believe a word I've said."

The absence of anger in his voice disturbed her. "You're accusing respected, high-ranking officers of murder and conspiracy, Burke. I'd be crazy not to have doubts. Wouldn't you?"

Adam frowned down at the table. A long moment passed, then he lifted his chin and met her gaze. "Look, you're a beautiful woman, but I think you're too young and idealistic to grasp how things work in the real world. I envy you your innocence—God, do I envy you your innocence—but I'd be a damn fool not to realize it could cost me my life. I need an attorney—"

"I'm your attorney." Something flickered in her eyes. Her face bleached white and she slapped a hand to her neck as if her heart had jackknifed straight up into her throat. "Too young and idealistic? Who gave you access to my Personnel file?"

That *had* come from her file. Verbatim. Adam rolled his eyes back in his head. "For Christ's sake, Keener. I'm in Intel."

Her face flushed. She flattened her lips to a slash and her hands into fists. "I'm not buying into this. But if I were, do you believe O'Dell acted on his own, giving you the orders?"

Adam draped his hands over the back slats of the chair, dipped his chin, and met her cool gaze. "No, I don't. Gus O'Dell doesn't have the brass to pull something like this. He'd never risk stepping on Colonel Hackett's toes."

"So you believe Colonel Hackett is also involved in this conspiracy?"

"Yes, I do."

Tracy stared at the bruises under Burke's left eye. What had been purple now had faded to green. Weighing all he'd told her, she cringed at the implications. Murder. Conspiracy. It had to be lies. All lies.

If called down, would Burke admit the truth? She doubted it, but she had to give him the chance. "Is that it, then?"

Wary, he nodded, his expression tense.

Finally, the man had behaved as a typical defendant. No rationalization or justification, but he certainly had blamed someone else. Major Gus O'Dell—and, by implication, Colonel Hackett and possibly Lieutenant Carver.

Madness. Sheer madness. But oh, so typical.

Burke's becoming predictable pleased her, relieved her. So why did she feel this shaft of disappointment stab her in the chest?

Not wanting to explore that, she forced her mind back to Burke's tale, to the plausibility of it. O'Dell? Maybe. Carver? Anyone's guess. But Hackett? No way. Definitely a screw-up on Burke's part, including Hackett in a conspiracy.

"Well." She folded her hands in her lap. "I have to say that your story sounds wild and creative. Very imaginative." She drew in a deep breath and turned the tables on him, preparing for anything. "But it can't be accurate."

Burke didn't bat an eye. "It's accurate."

"I don't think so." She disputed him with a tap of her nail against the blank legal pad. "Colonel Hackett is the problem," she explained. "He's ambitious, but respected and dedicated, and as I understand it, he's about to be promoted to command the Pacific theater mission. What on earth would motivate him to get involved in something like this?"

"Only he can answer that." Burke's accusing eyes glittered steel-gray. He didn't have to repeat his remark about her being too young and idealistic. It was etched in the lines of his face. "I never claimed to have all the answers, counselor. The bottom line is that there's a cover-up going on here. A huge cover-up. Whether or not you believe it doesn't change a damn thing—except that your doubt leaves everyone who stands to be hurt by this wide open for attack.''

"It leaves *you* open for attack.''

"Me *and* a country full of people who have no idea their own military is testing chemicals on them." Seeing confusion flicker through her eyes, he raked an impatient hand through his yellow-streaked hair. "You obviously don't get it.''

Wanting to snarl, she forced herself to smile. "Enlighten me.''

"Chemicals, counselor. They don't dissipate, or stay where you put them. They're airborne. And what hits the ground lingers for a couple of years. How many, depends on the type of chemical. The wind was blowing southeast that day. Do you have a clue what lies southeast of Area Fourteen?''

"No, I don't." God, but it grated at her to have to admit that.

"Base housing," Burke said from between his teeth. "You do know what base housing is, right? It's where the families of military personnel live. Many soldiers, their spouses and children. Do you get it now, counselor?''

If she believed any of this, that statement would have had impact. She'd be shivering with terror. Instead she felt enormously relieved that all of this was a lie. A chilling one, true. But then a lie meant to save a man from the death penalty would have to be chilling and terrifying, wouldn't it? "Why did you threaten two of the men on Alpha team?''

"I didn't.''

"Investigators say you did. That you killed them and sacrificed the other two men.''

"They lied." Cold rage shone in Burke's eyes. "Or someone lied to them.''

"It's always someone else's fault.''

"Only when that's the way it is, counselor." He grunted. "You still don't believe me.''

"No, I don't." She admired his tenacity. "But I will check for points of verification in your story. You mentioned several possibilities. The radio message—"

"You won't find it."

"If it exists, I'll find it."

Burke countered. "I radioed in on a secure channel."

"During an exercise," she added emphatically. "All transmissions are recorded during exercises—for strategical studies." She finally lifted her pen. "I'll also check for requisitions on the chemical alarm and gear."

"Environmental won't have them," Adam warned her.

She frowned. "They will, if they exist. General Nestler requires them to be filed on all chemical or biological resources. Basewide. Nothing moves without the paper."

Adam wasn't appeased. Irritated, he rocked back, crossed his chest with his arms, and tensed his muscles until they strained the seams of his sleeves. "Environmental will *not* have the requisitions," he repeated firmly.

The temptation to shout nearly choked her. "If they exist, they *will* have them, Burke."

"Damn it, woman. *Think!*" Adam balled his fist, pounded the heel of his hand against the back of the chair. The metal dented. "Only amateurs leave trails."

Afraid of provoking another violent reaction from him, she sat quietly and watched him.

Anger ebbed from his expression, and he lowered his voice. "Hackett has more years in the intelligence community than you and I together have in the service. He's got more clout than anyone on base, except General Nestler. And Nestler stays too immersed in getting his pet project contracted and funded to—"

"What pet project?" Tracy interrupted.

Adam scowled at her for being inept and uninformed. "Project Duplicity," he said. "Now can we get back to the point?"

"Which is?"

It took every ounce of control he could summon to not bellow. "Keener, you're a real piece of work."

"So I've been told." She didn't look at all offended. "Your point?"

He propped his hands on the table, stretching the chain between the cuffs tight, and then leaned toward her. "Let me lay this out for you in simple, easy-to-comprehend terms. You dig too deeply, you're going to ruffle feathers. You ruffle too many feathers, and you're going to wind up short a defendant."

"Exactly what are you saying, Burke?"

"I'm saying, within forty-eight hours of you nosing around like a little puppy, O'Dell and Hackett will see to it that I'm dead."

"Oh, please." Tracy guffawed. "Aren't you being just a little melodramatic? Who's going to kill you?" She lifted a hand heavenward. "You're in the hole, for God's sake."

"Yes, I am in the hole." He leaned closer still, until they were nearly nose to nose. "Open that closed mind of yours long enough to think, counselor. If you're going to murder someone, your victim being isolated makes getting to him damn convenient, now doesn't it?"

Tracy opened her mouth to dispute him, but the logic in what he'd said hit her. Without uttering a sound, she snapped her jaw shut.

"Finally, she sees the light." His exasperated breath warmed her face. "Check out my team's eyes."

"Excuse me?" Her brows arched, registering her confusion at the sudden topic shift.

"Their eyes," Burke repeated. "If my men were exposed to chemicals, then their eyes could show signs of mitosis."

"Mitosis?" Another I-haven't-got-a-clue response. No wonder he considered her inept.

"Fixed and dilated pupils." He refrained from calling her "fluff" again, she felt sure, only by an act of sheer will and determination.

A sneaking suspicion crept into Tracy, triggering her intuition and issuing her a warning. Burke hadn't pulled

that particular affliction out of thin air. And in it, she
sensed a grain of truth. The reports claimed his team's
bodies had been blown to bits, but Burke had seen the
bomber make the run and denied it; their bodies were
unmarked and intact. That, his specific reference to mitosis, and his tenacity had her sensing some truth in what
he had told her. If his men had been blown to bits, he
wouldn't be issuing her a challenge to check out their
eyes—unless he was deliberately misleading her.

He seemed too cocky and confident to be lying about
this. But what that meant, she wasn't ready to explore.
Not yet. "Why am I feeling this mitosis is extremely
significant?"

"Because it is extremely significant." Approval rang
in his voice. "Unofficial reports are that Project Duplicity
deals with the development of a chemical which causes
mitosis."

Tracy's stomach lurched and landed somewhere
around her kneecaps. She hated what she was hearing,
and what she was feeling. Knowing all she knew about
Burke, how could she consider believing a word that
came out of his mouth? How could she consider finding
any truth in what he was telling her—even a grain of it?
And how could she find the man appealing, much less
attractive? He was curt, rude, spiteful, intrusive into her
private life, and he was an accomplished liar. Physically
he was a work of art, even wearing prison grays. But,
dear God, he was a horrible excuse for a human being.

And yet, what he was saying about this mitosis in his
men would establish a direct link between the incident
and Laurel's god's pet project, Duplicity.

Good Lord, Burke wasn't just implicating O'Dell and
Hackett and maybe Carver. Now he was pulling General
Nestler into this. *Wait. Wait.* She focused on Burke. "*Un-
official* reports?"

He rolled his gaze. " 'Unofficial' doesn't mean inac-
curate, counselor."

"It doesn't mean accurate, either, or they would be official."

Tracy couldn't believe it. But Project Duplicity was Nestler's pet project, and while she would love to ignore that, she couldn't. She had to check this out. See if the project did involve a chemical that could cause mitosis. See the men's eyes. She had to do it. Because when she loaded everything on the scales, one thing became glaringly apparent and it refused to be ignored. That damn grain of truth.

Burke's men's bodies hadn't been blown to bits or he wouldn't have challenged her to check their eyes. What other part of his story was true, if any, she didn't know—yet. But she felt that grain's presence down to her bones, and it weighed a ton.

She'd have to tangle with Hackett and O'Dell. And with Nestler. Laurel's god. *Sees all, knows all.*

Dread raked through her. She was screwed. Screwed. Pure and simple. She'd never get promoted or be selected for Career Status. Hell, before this was over, Burke would probably get her dishonorably discharged right along with him—if not executed.

But what if Burke was right?

What if that grain of truth proved to be one of many grains, and chemicals had been released on unsuspecting soldiers and civilians?

While the grain of truth weighed a ton, doing the right thing and checking out that possibility weighed two. Since the accident, she had sworn off taking risks. Yet to face that eighty-year-old woman she would become in the mirror without more regret, now she had to investigate his claim and find out the truth.

And she had to do it, knowing that finding it would probably destroy her.

Chapter 5

Destruction can come quickly. It can bear down with the force of a hurricane for a swift kill. Or it can come slowly, creep up as innocently as a swollen river creeps up its banks until it overflows and floods, drowning everything in its path.

The first warning of Tracy's destruction crept . . . swiftly.

The morning after her discussion with Adam Burke, accidentally or intentionally through the base public affairs office, news of Tracy's assignment to the Burke case broke through base barriers and leaked to the outside world.

At seven-thirty A.M., the start of her duty day, the local media, via phone and fax, began hounding her for interviews.

By eight A.M., she had received the first phone threat.

The call had come from a woman who slurred as if she'd been on a week-long bender and regretfully had sobered up enough to have a monumental hangover. Now she wanted something, or someone, to scream at to take her mind off the pain. Tracy didn't take the comments personally, or worry about them.

The second call rattled her, but she gritted her teeth and sloughed it off. The man phoning her wasn't drunk. He was stone-sober, vulgar, and enraged that she would "dare to defy righteousness and defend Adam Burke."

A colorful string of character-assassinating expletives—against Burke and her—followed. Tracy hung up on the man, wishing her defense of Burke had at least been her own choice.

The third call scared the hell out of her. It came in not ten minutes before she had planned to leave for lunch.

"Keener?" the caller asked in a whispered rasp.

Male or female, she couldn't tell, but she felt the menace in the gravelly tone down to her toenails. The hair on the back of her neck stood on end, fear tightened her stomach, and she knew she would be looking back over her shoulder all afternoon. "Yes?"

"Burke is guilty. Get him off, bitch, and you both die."

Tracy stared at the phone in a terrified stupor. She shouldn't be shocked; Janet had warned her to expect this kind of reaction. Yet expecting to be threatened and experiencing it firsthand were two different things.

As she put the receiver down, Janet cracked open the office door. "I'm back—" She stopped mid-sentence and her smile faded. "Hey, you okay?"

Rattled from the bone out, Tracy straightened at her desk and nodded, wiping her clammy palm on the thigh of her skirt when her every instinct beckoned her to grab her locket with both hands and hold on tight. But Janet would notice that and she would worry. Neither of them needed that. "I'm fine."

Accepting her at her word, Janet lifted a white paper sack. "I brought you some egg rolls. Extra spicy. You don't want to go out just now. Reporters are swarming at the gate entrance." She walked in and dropped the bag on Tracy's desk. "So far, I think they're just locals."

Relieved that CNN wasn't crawling up her backside along with everyone else, Tracy inhaled deeply and caught a whiff of the spicy egg rolls. Her stomach had been growling for an hour and the food smelled like a slice of heaven. "Thanks." She reached in and pulled out an egg roll, pushing the call out of her mind. The paper sack crinkled, and she recalled Burke's first question. *Why had she been assigned?*

Considering their persistence this morning, the press had to be what had kept the case here for trial, just as Colonel Jackson had said. It made sense that the military would want to diminish publicity, especially considering Senator Stone, Mississippi's most powerful Washington representative, was up for re-election in November. He definitely would want to play down this incident, and being a prime force on the Armed Services Committee, he had the clout to have an impact. But why her? Why had Nestler specifically requested her to defend Adam Burke?

Janet dipped her chin. "So what's wrong?"

"Nothing you don't already know." No closer to an answer now than then, Tracy forced a smile to her lips and bit into the egg roll, wishing she had some hot mustard. "Just some clowns playing on the phone."

"Damn media hounds."

Tracy didn't correct Janet, or elaborate. The crank calls and threats would calm down and stop. The public had just buried four men; emotions were running high. In a few days, that part of this ordeal would blow over. Sad, when you got right down to it, but the public tended to have a short attention span. Once the initial flame of indignation burned out, apathy quickly followed.

Swiping her hair back behind her ear, Tracy swallowed the bite of egg roll. Too much cabbage in it for her taste, but she was too hungry to care enough not to eat every bite. "Have you had any luck on Burke's Intel file?"

"Not yet." Janet scrunched up her face. "It's a delicate matter. No one is eager to help him—not even the operatives whose backsides he's saved. But the team's funerals aren't over yet. The last one is today . . ."

Which meant that emotions were still raw and even Burke's strongest allies, if he had any, were still on hiatus. "What about the team?"

"I'm working on it. I had lunch today with Dr. Steven

Kane. He's the forensics expert who was supposed to autopsy the men.'' Her purse dangling from its strap at her shoulder, Janet leaned a slender hip against Tracy's desk. ''Indulge me a minute, okay? The romantic in me is in warp-mode, hormone overload.''

Tracy couldn't resist a smile. ''Go for it.'' She crunched down on another bite of egg roll.

''The man's a walking fantasy.'' Janet softly sighed. ''Brown hair and eyes, a profile that would do Adonis proud, and a give-me-your-heart-darling-you'll-never-regret-it smile.'' She pressed a hand to her chest. ''Be still, my heart.''

Seeing next week's heartbreak in the making, Tracy resisted an urge to roll her eyes back in her head. ''Did you ask him anything about the bodies, or just spend the entire luncheon visually devouring him?''

''I did both.'' Janet's eyes glittered. ''You're the only one around here who believes business and pleasure are a combustible mix. Personally, outsiders just don't have that special spark insiders do. I thrive on it.''

She did. But losing patience with waiting to find out what Janet had learned, Tracy urged her to talk. ''Well, while you were devouring and thriving, what did Dr. Kane say about the bodies?''

''They weren't autopsied.'' Janet dug in her purse, pulled out three packets of hot mustard and two of sweet and sour sauce, then dropped them on Tracy's desk. ''They were cremated.''

The bottom fell out of Tracy's stomach. ''Why?''

Janet cocked her head. ''Now, that I didn't ask.''

How could Tracy check out Burke's team's eyes if their bodies had been burned to ash?

She couldn't.

Had Burke known she wouldn't be able to do it? Is that why he had suggested it? Her gut instincts said no. He expected the evidence of mitosis would prove his credibility.

She should have gotten a stay order right away to pre-

vent the cremations from taking place until after she'd
had the bodies professionally examined. If she had known
Command was going to break normal protocol and not
do autopsies, she would have gotten the order. But no
one had bothered to notify her. Hell, why should they?
She was only the defendant's damn lawyer.

Fluff.

Burke's slur echoing through her mind, she ripped
open a packet of hot mustard. Her spirits sank even lower.
Maybe he had been right about Command and the assignment. Maybe with her defending him, the honchos
did feel assured of getting a conviction.

First the beating, and now this. Was she bent on
blowing his case to hell in a handbasket singlehandedly?

She squeezed her eyes shut. No way was she going to
drop the matter. No way was Burke going to look at her
through those icy dove-gray slits and make her eat dirt
for months because she hadn't found out about his men's
eyes. And no way was she going to look him in the face
and admit she'd failed . . . again.

She grabbed her purse and the egg roll bag, then
rounded the desk and stretched back to snatch up the
mustard. "I'll be back, Janet."

"Where are you going?" She followed Tracy to the
hall door. "The reporters—"

"I'll be on base." Tracy hiked up her purse strap and
yelled back over her shoulder. "I'm going to talk with
Dr. Kane."

The bodies might have been cremated, but someone
had to have seen them first. Someone had to be able to
answer her questions about their eyes. And God, but she
prayed that "someone" wouldn't include members of
their families. As Burke's attorney, she'd rather face a pit
of hissing rattlers than a single victim's family.

She walked outside, trying to remember where she had
parked that morning. Bypassing regular channels and going directly to Dr. Kane was a breach of protocol she
would probably come to regret, but it would save her a

ream of paperwork and a lot of time. And it wouldn't warn the prosecutor what avenues she was exploring in mounting her defense.

She spotted the Caprice. Two rows over, down three cars. Not that she honestly expected to discover that there had been signs of mitosis in the men. But just in case . . .

Odds were lukewarm at best, she figured, grabbing a note tucked under the wiper blade on her windshield. "What now?"

She checked her tires. They were between the lines painted on the asphalt. Uneasy, she slid into the front seat and then read the note, typed on clean white paper:

IT'S ARRANGED.
BURKE AND YOU DIE.

"It's *arranged*?" Tracy stared at the paper. Her hand began to shake and goose pimples peppered her flesh. Was this a threat . . . or a warning?

Four calls this morning from clients dropping her as their attorney because she was defending Burke. Reporters haranguing her by fax and phone. Three drunken or vulgar phone threats from crazies. This note had to be a threat. And it had happened here, no less. On base.

Had the whole world gone nuts?

No. No, it was anger. Frustrated outrage. They wanted her scared.

Well, they had succeeded. But she had given them that power over her. She wasn't one for taking risks, and that made her an easy victim. She hated being anyone's victim. Matthew had taught her that lesson, and Paul had reinforced it.

She couldn't control anyone else's actions, but she could control her own. She could refuse to give them the satisfaction of frightening her and take back her power. Fear could be healthy and keep her alert, but terror would stifle her, and being stifled would get her hurt. Operating in Intel's unfamiliar world, she had enough liabilities already. She didn't need any more. And why she had the strongest urge to run to Adam Burke for protection, she couldn't imagine. God knew that no man alive could be more dangerous than Burke.

The hospital parking lot was jammed. It was always jammed, on every base she'd been assigned to, or been sent to TDY. Though when on temporary duty, she seldom drove her car.

Tracy started looking for an empty space at the closest end of the lot, driving row by row. Whoever said a person could depend only on death and taxes obviously wasn't military. For them, there were death, taxes, personal crises at home while away on missions, orders to move to a new base at the worst possible time—usually right after finishing the last of the remodeling of the current home— and full parking lots at the commissary, the base exchange, and at the hospital.

On the third round of driving up and down the rows, she finally got lucky, though she had to wait for a black Volvo to vacate the slot—and it was located on the south forty, a long hike from the seven-floor building that was still rain-splotched from the morning shower.

The walk to the building seemed short compared to the one inside it. Down a long corridor, over to elevator B, which operated only on one side of the building, up to the third floor, then back across the mammoth building and down yet another long corridor.

By the time she reached Steven Kane's floor, her arches screamed, protesting against her black pumps. Buzzing saws and pounding hammers muffled the voices of the people shuffling through the maze, and Sheetrock dust tickled Tracy's nose. She cursed the construction still going on in the building. It should have been completed in May and, though September threatened, the fourth floor remained totally out of commission and parts of the other floors were still roped off with neon-orange banners and floor cones.

Finally, her winding through the bowels of the beast paid off. She tapped on Steven Kane's office door, swearing she would hike back to the car in bare feet. If a senior officer chewed her ass for being out of uniform, so be it. She'd get chewed in stocking-feet comfort.

The door opened. A man who fit Janet's dreamy description stepped out, wearing a black suit, white shirt, and a gray silk tie. The colors were wrong for him. Forest-green would have been a better choice. Then again, if he looked any better, he would have to be classified as a lethal weapon and kept in the vault under lock and key. Janet might even keep him around two weeks. "Dr. Kane?"

"Yes." Tucking his wire-frame glasses into his pocket, he came through the doorway, forcing Tracy to step aside, then headed down the corridor.

"I'm Tracy Keener," she said to his back, following him. "I've been assigned—"

"I know. You're representing Burke." Kane didn't slow down, much less stop to glance back at her. "Sorry, I'm in a hurry."

"One question, please." Tracy grimaced. He knew she intended to breach protocol and he clearly wasn't eager to be a willing participant.

In front of the elevator, she stepped between him and the door, blocking him from entering it. "The men on Burke's team. Did you see any evidence of mitosis in them?"

Kane reached around her and depressed the down button. "No comment."

Catching a whiff of his citrus cologne, she fought the urge to sneeze. "I'm not asking you anything that isn't documented and available to me," she persisted. Maybe if she had brought Janet along, he would have been more receptive. She had a way with men alien to Tracy.

The elevator bell chimed and the door slid open. Kane stepped around her, and then inside it. "Look, I'm sorry, Captain. But if you want any information on this, you're going to have to get it from Major O'Dell.''

Gus O'Dell, Colonel Hackett's assistant. The man Burke said had issued him the change of orders. Tracy stuck out her arm to block the elevator door from closing. ''Why?''

''Off the record?''

She nodded.

''Command's issued me a gag order. Major O'Dell is over at the simulator. You're welcome to ask him why I'm gagged, Captain. I didn't bother.''

She didn't imagine Dr. Kane would ask. Rule of thumb was, if you need to be told, you will be. If not, just follow orders. ''Which simulator?'' She knew of four on base.

''The one for gas mask and chemical training.''

The gas chamber. Figured. ''Thank you, Dr. Kane.''

He gave her that melt-your-heart smile Janet had talked about. It had no effect on Tracy whatsoever. She couldn't stop hearing Adam Burke's ''fluff,'' or seeing his mocking gray eyes.

Halfway to the gas-chamber simulator, Tracy accepted that her only hope of finding the truth was to somehow tap into Gus O'Dell and Colonel Hackett. Technically, investigating them was unethical. It could land her in serious trouble. They were superior officers with unblemished records—at least, according to their Personnel files. Did they have Intel files?

Now, exploring *that* would be risking even more problems. Besides, even if they had Intel files, there would be nothing of value in them or the OSI would have charged and arrested them.

Frustrated, Tracy passed a slow-moving Lincoln, and then steered around a slow curve. There had to be a way to find the truth. She slapped on her blinker and hung a left turn at the credit union, not knowing what to do or how to do it. Being outside her sphere of expertise had her about ready to gnash her teeth.

Janet would know.

She *would* know what was needed *and* how to get it done. Tracy waited for a white van to pass her, then made a U-turn and headed back to her office.

When Tracy walked in, Janet was sitting at her computer, keying in a brief. A lot about Janet mystified Tracy, especially her working as a legal assistant when she had such impressive credentials. She said she liked the work and the life-style she could live while doing it. Janet did seem happy, and that's what mattered most, so to each his own. "Can you spare me a second?"

"Sure." Swiveling away from the computer, Janet stood up and smoothed her sleek skirt.

Tracy entered her office, then closed the door behind Janet. "I need your help."

"I'm already doing everything I can on the Intel file, Tracy."

"No, it's not about that." This would go over with Janet about as well as marriage to an outsider. By her own admission, she was an in-the-system woman, all the way. At the credenza, Tracy fingered the leaves of her ivy. It was thriving, despite the lack of direct sunlight. "I don't know how to get it, but I need in-depth information on Major O'Dell and Colonel Hackett."

Janet's expression crumpled. "Oh, God."

"No, not Nestler," Tracy teased, trying to defuse the sudden tension between them. "Just O'Dell and Hackett — at least, so far."

Still tense, Janet lifted her hands, palms up. "Why?"

Her assistant was going to love this. Maybe enough to strangle her. "I can't say. It'd be a breach of confidentiality, and I gave my word."

Janet eyed her cautiously. "You could get copies of their Personnel files—"

"That's not deep enough, especially on Hackett." Here came the touchy part. Janet could report Tracy for this. Forget her promotion, she could get kicked out of the Air Force. She rubbed her locket. "The information I need won't be in any file. Or in writing."

"I see." Staring at Tracy's neck, Janet fisted her hands at her sides, her expression unreadable. "Then that leaves you one choice. A bug."

"A listening device?" Tracy clamped down on the locket, her sizzling nerves threatening to snap. "Surely there's another way. You're Intel-trained. Intel has to have other means. It can't just go around bugging people when standard files prove insufficient."

"I didn't say a bug was the only option. But in my opinion, it's the only one you're capable of pulling off. We're all home to unique talents, but covert operations isn't one of yours. No offense intended."

"None taken. I'm well aware that I don't have the nerves for this kind of work." Tracy thought over the option. She didn't like it. It felt kind of sleazy. But if it was her only road to the truth, then she had to do it. The part of her that hated taking risks rebelled, rejecting the idea, yet the words came out of her mouth anyway. "Okay, then. I need a listening device."

"Are you serious?" Janet looked at Tracy as if she'd lost her mind. "I was being facetious, Tracy."

"I'm serious. I need a listening device." Trying to hide her own mixed feelings about this, Tracy fingered her paperweight and looked back at Janet. "And I need to know how to use it."

Janet pointed a warning finger at Tracy. "What you need is a reality check." A frown creased her brow. "This is about Burke, isn't it? It is, isn't it?"

Tracy nodded. "It is."

"It's getting out of hand." Janet dragged impatient fingertips through her hair.

"It's been out of hand," Tracy countered. "Ask Adam Burke."

Janet glared at her. "Wiring someone is illegal. Don't you like practicing law? Good grief, you could end up in Leavenworth." Janet strode across Tracy's office. "Leavenworth? Did I say Leavenworth? Hell, Tracy, you could end up dead."

"I know the risks, okay? But I'm hitting red tape and brick walls at every turn. Dr. Kane is under a damn gag order, Janet. Why would Command gag him? Because something that shouldn't be *is* going on here, and whatever it is has cost Adam Burke his life."

"He's not dead, for God's sake."

"Not yet. But if the prosecutor is successful . . ."

"If he's guilty, then he deserves to die."

"*If.* That's the operative word here."

Janet rolled her gaze. "Everyone knows he's guilty."

"Then why the gag order? If there's nothing to hide, then why did Command issue it?"

"Kane's gagged from the press, just like everyone else on base except Public Affairs."

"Wrong." Tracy leaned toward Janet. "Dr. Kane is gagged from talking to me."

Surprise flickered through Janet's eyes. "But you're the defense attorney."

"Yes, I am. So why can't he talk to me about Alpha team's deaths?"

"I don't know."

"Someone is hiding something," Tracy said softly. "And, Janet. Burke might not be physically dead, but life as he's known it is over. Even if he's cleared in all of this, just being charged will follow him around like a black cloud. Intel won't touch him."

"He'll never be cleared." Janet rubbed at her forehead, crossed her arms over her chest. "But you're right. Even if he were, Intel won't touch him. It can't."

"So even if he's innocent, they've made him an outsider." The injustice in that possibility, slim as it was, had a tension headache coming on like gangbusters. Tracy rubbed at her temples. "If I have to step over the line to find out the truth, then that's what I have to do. You know I'm right about this. If you stood in Burke's shoes, wouldn't you want me to step over the line for you? Or are you going to stand here and tell me that when you had no other choice, you never stepped over the line?"

"Damn it." The stiffness drained from Janet's expression and her shoulders, and she groaned. "Why do I let you get me into these things?"

"Because you know I'm right. You've got highly developed instincts, and they're talking to you about this just like mine are talking to me."

Janet closed her eyes and shook her head. "Okay."

"You'll help me?" Tracy couldn't hide her surprise.

"I'll help you. But only with this—and I mean it." Janet plucked at a piece of lint clinging to Tracy's shoulder. "If I don't help, you'll try to pull this off anyway and screw it up."

She was protecting Tracy from herself. "Thanks."

"Don't thank me. All it means is we'll end up as cellmates in Leavenworth. Trespassing. Illegal entry. Violation of the Privacy Act. Infringement on the rights of a superior officer. Direct violation of the code on conduct. I can think of half a dozen more charges they'll dump on us without even thinking about it." Janet rolled her gaze ceilingward. "I've lost my mind. That's got to be it. Why else would I do something this stupid?"

Knowing the question was rhetorical, Tracy didn't answer. Janet had agreed because her instincts were alert and flashing the drill. *Duty first.* It was as simple as that. "If we get caught, I'll represent you."

"You shouldn't have any trouble at all." Janet grunted. "Just plead insanity. I *am* insane or I wouldn't consider doing this."

"Insanity it is, then." Tracy clasped Janet's shoulder. "But it's right."

"Right?" Janet guffawed. "It's illegal as hell."

"It's honorable—on a higher level."

"Be sure to put that in the jury instructions. Maybe they'll go easy and only sentence me to thirty years."

Tracy smiled, but Janet was right. They could end up in prison. Well, Tracy could end up in prison. She might get caught. Might be convicted. But she wouldn't be convicted of being afraid to risk all for the truth. She wouldn't be justly accused of lacking substance, of being fluff.

While Janet pulled strings to get the equipment, Tracy phoned Colonel Hackett's office and requested an appointment with him for that afternoon. He was a major wild card. If O'Dell had given Burke the orders and they hadn't originated with the gutless O'Dell, then Hackett was the logical originator—just as Burke had said.

Less than an hour had passed when Janet returned to Tracy's office with the equipment. The device was smaller than Tracy had imagined. It fit on her fingertip. And the tape and earphones for monitoring were about the size of a shoe box: far less cumbersome than expected, if every bit as daunting for what they represented.

Janet briefed Tracy on the equipment, on how to plant the device, gave her a crash course on the Intel rules and drills, and then strongly suggested Tracy put the taping equipment away from the office. When she left Tracy's office, Janet was still swearing she had lost her mind and insanity was her best defense.

Tracy practiced planting the device several times, and when she felt she could do it discreetly, she drove home and set up the taping equipment on a nightstand in her bedroom.

She finished with fifteen minutes to spare before her meeting with Hackett.

Staring at the headphones, she swallowed hard. A river of fear flowed through her. She was doing the wrong thing for the right reason. But if she were caught, her actions certainly wouldn't be viewed that way. She would lose everything. Yet if she didn't take the risks, then Burke would lose everything. She could sit in the wings and do nothing. Take the safe route. But she wouldn't like the woman it made her, and she doubted she could live with becoming that woman.

She tucked her hair behind her ear. If she failed and

got caught, under no circumstances would she implicate
Janet. Though he didn't know it, Burke had given Tracy
the tool to prevent her from doing that. Taking his cue,
she'd give only her name, rank, and serial number—and
never ask, but chance it that Janet would jump in and get
to the bottom of all this.

Tracy only hoped she didn't get caught and put Janet
in the position of having to decide whether or not to bail
her out, that the risks weren't futile, and she gained proof
of what had happened and why. Proof that Colonel Hackett was involved, as Burke believed.

But Hackett could be blameless. Innocent. And if so,
she was about to do him a terrible injustice. Yet Adam
Burke had been so sure . . .

She was putting a lot of faith in a man she didn't believe. But that grain of truth in what he had told her
would surface somewhere. Until then, she could only
move forward and pray to God her instincts proved right.

"I've got five minutes, Captain." Colonel Hackett sat at
his desk, wearing his infamous Jack Nicholas expression
of being interested but unconcerned. "What do you
need?"

By military standards, his corner office was plush, and
prime real estate. It was pleasing to the eye, decorated in
heavy oaks that shouted no nonsense would be tolerated
here, and forest-greens that whispered of dignity, discipline, and decorum. His executive desk stretched across
an expanse between two windows. A third window was
on the east wall. Tracy had an office with no windows,
only a mural of one, and it had taken two moves and
more jockeying than goes on at the Kentucky Derby to
get it.

She lowered herself onto his visitor's chair, the device
hidden in her palm. All she had to do was to remove the
paper tab and stick the device to his desk. But how could
she plant it out of clear sight with him in the room? That,
she hadn't practiced.

"Captain?" He looked down at his watch. "I don't mean to be rude, but I have a tight schedule today."

"I'm sorry, sir." As vice to General Nestler, Colonel Hackett's schedule had to be a bear. Everyone admired his ability to get things done. The man did have a marine's mentality: anything, anywhere, any means—for the Force. But he reputedly had a conscience that bent to the will of the country's best interests—as he, or General Nestler, deemed them.

Sweat trickled down between Tracy's breasts, and she felt the weight of her locket dangling from its chain. Doubt crept in. Was she doing the right thing? Looking at Colonel Hackett, she couldn't be sure. She offered him a smile. "I wanted to talk with you about Adam Burke."

"Tragic situation. I lost four good men." Appearing appalled by that, Hackett rocked back in his seat. "I hate to admit it, Captain, but I had high hopes for Burke. I thought he had potential. He did have a hell of a career going." Hackett stood up, then paced a short path to his office window and looked outside, clearly agitated at himself for misjudging Burke. "He taught me a valuable lesson." Hackett looked back at her, his intense green eyes shining regret. "You can never be sure about people, Captain."

She'd learned that lesson five years ago, and it nagged at her again now. She wasn't sure about Burke or about Hackett. She had to do this. "No, sir, unfortunately, you can't."

"A damn shame, that." He laced his hands behind his back, and gazed out the window.

Seeing no reflection of the office in the window, Tracy recognized her chance and seized it, reaching around the side of his desk nearest the wall. Her fingers bumped into a little gray disc, attached right under the lip of the desktop.

Oh, hell. Oh, bloody hell.

Someone already had bugged Colonel Hackett's office.

Chapter 6

Tracy hesitated. What should she do now?

Hackett seemed so devoted and yet something had to be out of whack with him or there wouldn't be a listening device stuck under the lip of his desk lid. Aside from her, who else would want to bug his office?

Do it! Do it now!

Instinctively reacting, she peeled off the protective strip, slapped the device to the wood beside the bug already there, and then straightened back in her chair, swallowing hard and ordering herself to calm down. He hadn't seen her move or he would have reacted. The man had extremely expressive green eyes, yet she'd noted no change in them. No, he hadn't noticed. God, but she hoped she wasn't doing him dirty.

Until she had seen that plant, she'd almost believed him too good, too devoted to be involved in any conspiracy, much less one as god-awful as Adam Burke had implicated Hackett in, but now she had doubts. Doubts and more doubts. Would they never end? "Yes, sir. It is a shame that you can't be sure about anyone."

The colonel again checked his watch. "What did you want to know about Burke?"

"Just some basics. Your perceptions and personal observations, more than anything else. Your opinion is highly respected at the JAG office and, I'm told, you strive for objectivity. That's rare in the Burke case, I'm afraid.''

"Even soldiers have emotions, Captain." With a weary sigh, Hackett returned to his seat. "Burke's actions hit them where they live."

"Yes, sir, they did." True, but did Burke actually commit the crimes? That was the question. Odds were, he had. Yet there was a seed of doubt, that grain of truth. "Colonel, please be frank. Would it be more convenient to discuss this when your schedule isn't so tight?"

"Yes, it would." Hackett looked relieved. "I'm due at a briefing with General Nestler."

His reaction alerted her instincts. He seemed too relieved for the reason to be just postponing a discussion about Burke. There had to be more to it. Tracy stood up. "I'll phone your secretary, then."

Hackett watched Tracy move to the door, interested but unconcerned. "That'll be fine."

"Thank you, sir." She walked out of his office clutching her notepad so tightly her fingers stung. Her heart hammered against her chest wall, and a sick feeling slithered through her stomach. Hackett *had* looked relieved. Not angry that Burke had failed him — odd, since the man reportedly denied failure in his men as an option—but relieved that Tracy hadn't pinned him down on specifics about Adam Burke. What had Hackett been expecting?

Obviously, worse than he had gotten. But who else had suspicions about him that were strong enough to warrant bugging his office?

That bug was damning evidence—at least, in her eyes. She hated to believe Hackett could be involved as Burke had said; hated it with a passion that surprised her. But she couldn't let that hatred bury the possibility that it could be true. Was Hackett involved? If so, to what extent? Or had Adam Burke lied? The second bug could be unrelated.

With luck, the listening device would ferret out the truth. It wouldn't provide any evidence admissible in

court, of course. No one could know it was there—*ever*.
But it could steer her in the right direction so she knew
what to look for and why she was looking for it, and that
search could produce admissible evidence.

Provided Colonel Hackett was conspiring and he
wasn't totally innocent.

Provided Adam Burke had told her the truth.

Provided Hackett didn't find the bug and have her arrested.

For now, she didn't dare speculate further; there were
too many unknowns. She could only move forward and
try to unravel the threads. Take Dr. Kane's advice and
visit Major Gus O'Dell. Maybe, just maybe, she could
stir up a little dust.

Half an hour later, Tracy drove down Hangar Row,
crossed the flight line, then passed the climate-controlled
hangar where tests determined planes' endurance levels.
The huge red-needle thermometer attached to the outer
front wall of the building read minus 28 degrees. They
must be running a safety check on icing—probably on
F-15s. About a dozen of them sat parked on the flight
line, and one had crashed in Greenland due to ice.

She parked and then entered the mammoth metal hangar housing the simulator chamber. O'Dell stood at the
far end of it, just outside the actual gas-chamber simulator, leaning against a wooden sawhorse, looking disgusted and bored with a group of simulator training
attendees. Other than the chamber and its control board,
a couple of fire extinguishers and oxygen tanks lined up
against the outer west wall, and spare masks and chemical
gear stowed on wooden shelves, the huge hangar designed to house several airplanes stood empty of equipment. What was that smell? Gin?

She cast a suspicious look at O'Dell, and walked over,
her heels clicking hollow sounds on the concrete floor.
He didn't look drunk, but he had been drinking. Red
rimmed his eyes and the sour smell of alcohol oozed from

his pores. He wasn't heavy—no one in uniform was allowed to be heavy—but he definitely bent toward the far side of acceptable limits on weight for a man five foot nine. His dark hair was threaded with gray, his features were sharp and angular, and his mouth appeared huge stretched open as he bellowed at some young lieutenant fitted out in chemical gear who looked a breath away from piddling on the floor.

"Why the hell did you hit the panic button, Harrison?" O'Dell shouted not a foot from the young man's flushed face.

"I couldn't breathe, sir."

"Well, excuse me, son." O'Dell waved a wide arm. "Did you hear that, men?" he shouted to the fifteen others, two of whom were women. "Lieutenant Harrison couldn't breathe." O'Dell harrumphed, then riveted a scathing gaze onto Harrison. "Well, now. Let's just stop the war because the lieutenant here can't goddamn breathe in his chemical gear." He again waved an expansive hand, his voice echoing, bouncing off the walls.

"Oh, wait. Wait." O'Dell touched a hand to his temple, then fostered a feral smile. "It's okay, Harrison. You don't *need* to breathe anymore because you're dead. You pushed the panic button, son. You killed yourself and all these other men, and you contaminated half the base. Now, isn't that a fine day's work you've done?"

The lieutenant did his best to sink through the ground.

Tracy wanted to rescue him; he looked like a lost, wounded puppy. But she knew better than to interfere. Not only would it tick off Gus O'Dell, her superior officer, it would make Harrison look even worse in front of his peers to be rescued by a woman.

Some things never changed. Men's egos ranked among them.

Had that been, in part, what had kept Adam Burke silent after his arrest? No. Not ego. Not with him. Even beaten and shackled, he'd retained his dignity. He was too self-confident to be intimidated. But being confident didn't make him innocent. He had to be guilty. Had to be.

O'Dell ranted himself out, and Harrison slunk back into the sixty-by-ninety-foot, metal-lined concrete chamber for another run at it.

When he was sealed inside, looking like a frog in his mask, O'Dell glanced at her. "What do you want, Keener?"

She didn't waste time on small talk. Already she had decided she didn't like Gus O'Dell, and she didn't want to give him the opportunity to return the disfavor. "Was there any evidence of mitosis in Burke's team members' eyes?"

"I have no knowledge of mitosis being an investigative finding."

O'Dell didn't so much as glance at her. He kept his gaze piniohed on the window in the metal chamber door. God help Harrison if he pushed that red panic button. "I understand you spearheaded that exercise, sir."

"I spearhead many missions, Captain." O'Dell nodded at one of the trainees. "Crank, get ready to haul Harrison's panicky ass out of there."

Tracy stepped into O'Dell's line of vision, and then smiled. "On that mission, did you issue Burke orders to separate from his men?"

"No, Captain, I did not." O'Dell looked past her shoulder, checking on Harrison through the window. "If there's nothing important to discuss, I'm a little busy at the moment."

A man's life. Nothing important? "Just a few more questions, Major. Please."

He let out an exasperated sigh and scowled.

Tracy backed up a step, until she realized he was still looking past her at Harrison. The lieutenant now lay prone on the chamber floor.

"Get him out of there," O'Dell ordered.

Crank reached for the chamber door.

"Wait!" O'Dell shouted, the color draining from his face. "Hit the green button!"

Crank stopped dead in his tracks. His eyes stretched wide and his Adam's apple bobbed three times. Hard. "Oh, shit."

A cold chill rippled through Tracy. She wasn't sure what exactly had happened, but their reactions proved everyone in the hangar had just survived a close call.

Crank turned to the control panel and depressed a lighted green button. When he then paused outside the simulator and monitored the second sweep on his watch, she figured it out. The chemicals inside the chamber were lethal. Pressing the green light triggered something to neutralize them and decontaminate the air. Crank had almost opened the chamber door without first decontaminating. He'd nearly exposed them all!

"Idiots." Under his breath, O'Dell muttered a curse. "What the hell can you do? You either treat them like two-year-olds or they screw up and contaminate the entire base."

"Sir?" Tracy intervened, weak-kneed and resisting the urge to rub her locket.

"What do you want now, Keener?"

"A rundown on events leading to Burke's arrest would be helpful."

O'Dell leveled her with a glare. "Burke screwed up, okay? He sent his men to an active bombing range rather than to the exercise area, and he got them blown up. He realized he'd screwed up, and he bugged out. He left his men to die, Captain, and they did. Now, what part of their deaths and his cowardice are you having trouble comprehending?"

"None, sir." Bristling, she forced herself to hold her temper. "I was just wondering—"

"What, Captain?" O'Dell asked, fairly shouting at her. *"What?"*

"Who found Burke?" He had said he'd passed out. No one was out there. Well, someone had to have been there or they wouldn't have found him, or the dead men. Yet in all the reports, there was no mention of who actually had found Burke, not one word, or what had prompted anyone to even look for him or his team in the first place.

"When he failed to respond to multiple radio transmissions, I sent in an excavation team," O'Dell said. "They pulled Burke out of Area Thirteen, and found the team in Area Fourteen. Well, what was left of them. They took a direct hit."

Tracy blocked visions of human carnage from her mind. "Was Burke conscious?"

"Of course he was conscious." O'Dell looked at her as if she were crazy. "He was running like hell, Captain, trying to save his lousy ass."

Stymied, Tracy wasn't sure what to say. She had hoped Burke had told the truth about being unconscious. But if O'Dell was being honest, then clearly he hadn't. "Why is Dr. Kane under a gag order?"

"You'll have to ask the general that."

"Thank you, Major. I appreciate your time."

He didn't acknowledge her. Tracy turned and walked toward the mouth of the hangar. At the left of its expansive door, she noted an elaborate alarm-system panel on the inside wall. With lethal chemicals on-site, not having a sophisticated alarm system would be a safety hazard. But considering what had nearly just happened in the simulator, it seemed to her that more internal hangar safeguards were also needed. No doubt one of the trainees would file a hazard report. Probably several of them would.

"Crank! Get me a phone over here." O'Dell's voice ripped over the barren floor and reverberated. "Now!"

Tracy stepped out into the sun. O'Dell sounded stirred up, all right. Stirred up, ticked off, and damn close to panic. And she'd bet her captain's bars he wanted that phone to call Colonel Hackett.

Adam Burke wouldn't call her "fluff" now. She

smiled to herself. Did he have an Intel rule or a drill for eating crow?

Adam stood before the phone in the activity room, flipping the quarter over and over in his hand, debating. Should he call her, or not?

Maxwell sat in the chair near the window, his thick arms folded over his chest. "You've got ten minutes left, Burke. That's it."

Adam didn't look the guard's way. *Damn it, just call her. Just do it.*

He lifted the receiver, dropped the quarter into the slot, and then dialed her home to avoid getting Janet. Keener would probably think he'd slipped over the edge, but what was the difference? Her opinion of him couldn't get any worse.

The phone rang three times. After the fourth, the answering machine picked up. Adam considered hanging up, but that warning knot in his stomach wouldn't let him. "Hi, it's me," he said. "I'm not sure why I'm calling you. Well, not exactly. This is going to sound kind of crazy, counselor, but my gut instincts are warning me you're in trouble. I guess I just wanted to see if you were okay. What the hell I could do about it if you're not, I don't know. But anyway, that's why I'm calling."

Definitely sounded like a fruitcake. He'd better explain. "I've got this feeling you're being threatened. I know it sounds like a line, but it's not." He toed the baseboard where it met the floor tile and shoved a fisted hand into the hip pocket of his prison grays. "I, um, learned the hard way to trust my instincts a long time before getting involved in Intel, counselor. A friend and I cut school and went vining. Do you know what vining is?" He'd better tell her, just in case. "Think about Tarzan, the vines he swung on to get from tree to tree. It was popular in my neck of the woods. Robin Hood escapes from reality, Georgia-style. When you're poor and on your own, you need those escapes. They keep you sane."

Why was he spilling his guts to her? She wouldn't give a damn.

Because she's in danger. You've got to warn her, or live with knowing you could have warned her and didn't.

"Anyway, my best friend, David, decided to vine." Adam's only real friend ever. "I had this feeling he shouldn't do it, but I knew if I said anything, he'd just balk and call me a coward, and then do it anyway, just to show me he could. We were at that age where image ranked more important than sense."

The dread Adam had felt then blanketed him now. "I kept my mouth shut. David grabbed the vine, bellowed a war whoop, and swung out. Midway, it broke."

Regret, the horror of watching his friend fall, again flooded Adam's mind. For a long minute, he couldn't talk. When he did, his voice sounded strained, thick. "He died, counselor. David died." And Adam had lost his best friend forever.

He gave himself a second to get past the emotions. He'd never before told anyone about David, or about the impact his death had had on Adam's life. "The point is, I knew he was in danger and I didn't warn him. Today, I got up with that feeling again, about you. So I'm calling. I don't know where the danger is, I wish to hell I did." Adam forked a helpless hand through his hair, despising the feel of the gummy yellow paint no amount of soap could get out. "Just . . . Just take care of yourself, okay?" He swallowed hard. "And when you can, let me know you're all right."

Why had he said that? Why did he care? The woman thought he was guilty. Adam slammed down the phone, then turned to Max. "I'm ready."

Tracy spent the rest of the morning doing her homework, pulling together background research on Major Gus O'Dell and Colonel Robert D. Hackett. When she had compiled a respectable amount of information to disseminate, she tucked it into an accordion file, then skated out and went home to go through it.

The house felt empty. She felt empty. It had been five years. *Five long years.* Wouldn't she ever get used to living alone?

The answering machine's red light blinked. At the end of the tiled kitchen bar, she tapped the button to listen to her messages, hoping not to hear any more threats. She'd maxed on them. Maybe Randall had called to apologize. "One can dream."

Instead, she found nine interview requests from various reporters, including CNN, and seven crank calls from threatening crazies. "Enough of this." Suffering all the abuse she could stomach for one day, she reached for the Stop button—and heard Adam Burke's voice . . .

His deep timbre conjured an image of him, leaning shoulder against the wall, phone to his ear, shackled, and she listened intently, noting the emotional inflections in his tone. They sounded strange coming from him. He'd been deeply entrenched in Intel for years. She would have sworn all that remained in him were Intel rules and drills, that he had no emotions left, just as Janet had said she had no conscience left. Of course she did, but those inflections in Burke's voice spoke volumes, and he painted a vivid picture of a young boy, arms braced at the fork of two tree limbs, watching helplessly as his best friend plunged to his death. It got to her—and it opened in her mind a side of Adam Burke she hadn't dreamed existed. One that drew her like a magnet. He too had suffered loss.

Had the survivor in him sensed the phone threats she'd received? The one in the note left on her windshield? He could be playing on her emotions. As an operative, he'd have the skills. Yet, survivor to survivor, this warning felt genuine. She lifted the phone and dialed the facility. Knowing she wouldn't be allowed to speak to Adam Burke, she asked for Sergeant Maxwell.

When he came on the line, she felt heat rush to her

face. Why should she be embarrassed? "Sergeant, this is Captain Keener. Will you please get a message to Adam Burke for me?"

"I suppose I could, yes, ma'am."

Tracy curled her fingers around the edge of the tile counter, then squeezed. "Please tell him that I received his message and all is well." When she saw Adam, she would tell him about the threats. He needed to know his instincts hadn't been off on this. He could continue to trust them. Though why he would worry about her when he knew she considered him guilty, she couldn't fathom. Yet he had. And she felt grateful. It'd been a long time since a man had cared enough about her to bother, and the call couldn't have been an easy one for a proud and angry man like Burke to make.

Maybe he wasn't quite the man she'd thought him.

Maybe he's suckering you into believing him.

"Is that it, ma'am?" Maxwell asked.

"Yes, Sergeant. Thank you." Again, her face heated. "And please thank him for me."

She scanned the rest of the messages. Nothing from Randall. Evidently her friend had joined the ranks of those who'd rather fold than fight. No great surprise there, just a tinge of disappointment.

Cradling the phone, she fixed herself a cup of tea, then walked down the hall into her bedroom. At the closet, she ditched her pumps and pulled on her Pooh slippers, desperately needing an attitude after this day from hell. Sitting down on her bed, she fluffed a pillow at her back, put on the earphones, and turned on the taping device to hear what, if anything, was going on with Colonel Hackett.

Guilt stabbed her. God, but she hoped she wasn't maligning the man, questioning his integrity. That second bug could be unrelated. It could have nothing to do with Burke. Yet, damn certain it had everything to do with him, she hadn't reported it.

Hackett's office was quiet. From the background noise,

he was there, but evidently alone. Mildly disappointed, she adjusted the headphones over her ears, then flipped open the accordion file and began reading the background data on him and O'Dell.

Hackett's career had been stellar. O'Dell's lacked panache, but he had proved to be no slouch. She made a few discreet phone calls, checking him out a little further. Most people were reluctant to talk to her because of her association with Burke, but when she got O'Dell's secretary, Connie Mumford, on the line, Tracy hit paydirt.

"Is this off the record?" Connie asked, sounding wary but worried and in desperate need of someone to listen to her concerns.

Tracy sipped at her tea. "It can be, if that's how you want it."

"I do." Connie dropped her voice to just above a whisper. "The major's never liked Colonel Hackett, but he's always respected him. Earlier today, he asked me for the colonel's phone number. I offered to put the call through for him, but the major refused. He called Hackett himself and requested a stat meeting. He was very upset at being put off until fifteen hundred hours."

Fifteen hundred hours. Three o'clock, Tracy translated, glancing at her watch. Ten minutes from now. "How upset was he?"

"I don't know. Nervous. Antsy, you know?"

"Nervous enough to knock back a strong shot of gin?" Tracy stared at the dresser mirror across the bedroom.

Connie hesitated, then answered. "Several. Partly because Colonel Hackett has high expectations. He's unyielding. Demands excellence, the major says."

Intolerant of failure among his staff. Tracy had heard that before, and again during an earlier call today with another source. "You said *partly*."

"The major knew the weasel would be at the meeting. He hates the weasel."

Tracy set her cup down on the nightstand. "The weasel?"

"Lieutenant Carver, Colonel Hackett's aide. The major says Carver is always in the shadows, never far from Hackett's side, watching and taking notes so Hackett can nobly kick ass. I don't know if that's true. I've only met the lieutenant once, and he seemed okay to me. Young and brash like most lieutenants, but that's normal, you know?"

"Connie, have you noticed any change in the major's behavior since the Burke incident?"

"Just between you and me, he's drinking more, but he's only talked about it once. It was close to quitting time, and only the two of us were still in the office. He was really upset, and he said he wished this whole Burke nightmare would just go away."

Tracy plucked a piece of lint from her nubby bedspread. "Don't we all?"

"I sure do," Connie admitted. "All this tension is getting to me. I don't want to end up on stress leave." She sighed. "I'm worried about the major, Tracy. I'm not crazy about him, but he treats me better than most of the bosses I've had."

He certainly hadn't treated the simulator-training attendees well. Tracy checked her watch. Three on the nose. "If I can help, or anything comes up you think I should know, give me a call."

"You will keep everything I said confidential, right?" Connie sounded worried, as if she had spoken freely and now suffered second thoughts. "I don't want it getting back to Colonel Hackett how the major feels about him. Life could get rough around here."

"It's confidential," Tracy assured her. "Call me if you need anything."

She hung up the phone and readjusted the earphones over her ears. Before they slid into place, she heard voices. Hackett was in his office. O'Dell was already with him, and talking.

"The longer it takes to get Burke* convicted and shipped off to Leavenworth, the greater the odds become that this situation presents serious problems.''

Tracy frowned at her reflection in the mirror. *What situation could present serious problems?* They could be talking about the press, budget funding—anything.

"May I be frank, sir?" O'Dell asked.

"Of course," Hackett lazily drawled.

"I've been passed over for light colonel, and the Phoenix board failed to get me promoted last year. Next year, I have to retire—unless I get RIF orders before then.''

Tracy listened intently. The Phoenix board made special attempts to get a select few promoted who had been passed over for promotion on the first go-around, and Reduction in Forces orders now were being handed down in record numbers. At the moment, no one was safe from them except pilots and doctors. The latter were still being offered incentive bonuses to stay in the service. But even with those bonuses, their pay lagged a long way behind that of comparable private employers.

Hackett cleared his throat. "I know your concerns about getting tagged, Gus. We've talked about it, and I warned you to prepare.''

"I have. My house is paid for, I've built up a respectable savings account, and a mutual fund IRA that will supplement my retirement check. I won't have to alter my standard of living at all—provided I get my retirement check. But if this Burke business blows up in my face, it'll screw me out of my retirement benefits.''

"What Burke business?" Hackett asked, clearly posturing.

"The exercise, Colonel."

"What about it?" Hackett's voice went hard. "Burke disobeyed a direct order, Major. He murdered my men. That's his responsibility, not yours, and certainly not mine.''

Aside from his firm tone, Hackett sounded baffled. As if he didn't understand how Burke's actions could cause O'Dell problems. Tracy was baffled, too. At face value, she sensed Hackett's sincerity, but her instincts told her

O'Dell hadn't been a willing participant in some aspect of that exercise. He seemed . . . almost drafted.

If he had changed the orders as Burke had said, then neither Intel nor the OSI would give a tinker's damn whether or not O'Dell had acted willingly. He'd acted. That alone would land him in Leavenworth.

And she also sensed Hackett, if involved, was far too ambitious to let himself become exposed. He would see to it Burke took the fall so none of his assistants would be exposed. Their exposure would taint him, and that the ambitious Hackett would never tolerate.

"Keener came to the chamber today, asking questions," O'Dell said.

Tracy's stomach furled, and she could almost see sweat beading above O'Dell's upper lip. "I think assigning her was, er, shortsighted, sir."

"General Nestler is never shortsighted, Major."

"But why her? Christ, Colonel, she's an idealist."

"Aren't we all?" Hackett responded. "If we worked in the private sector, we could make more money and have less demanding—and certainly less interrupted—lives. We could avoid the dangers inherent to our jobs. Yet we choose the military life. Why? We're idealists. Of course she's an idealist. She's one of us. We're all idealists, or we wouldn't be here, Major."

"She's pro-Force too, sir," a new voice added. "Colonel Jackson was emphatic about that."

Who was talking? Was it Lieutenant Carver? Connie had told Tracy that Major O'Dell expected the lieutenant to be at the meeting—in the shadows, near Hackett.

"Yes, she is, Lieutenant."

So it was Carver. Tracy twisted on the bed, folded her knees to sit Indian-style. All this time she'd thought being an idealist was a slur, but if Hackett's comments were a fair indicator, it was actually considered an essential asset.

"She's also openly stated her belief that Burke is guilty," Carver said. "And she's got a lot to lose by rattling chains, being up for promotion and Career Status selection.''

Hackett interceded. ''I'm sure the general felt she could handle this job or he wouldn't have requested her. This is a good opportunity for her to prove herself.''

''Don't you think, sir, that this case could do more than any recommendations to get her promoted and selected?''

''Yes, Carver, I do. And if she looks good, then her superior officers look good.''

A creak sounded. Tracy recognized it as Hackett rocking back in his seat. ''Gus?''

''Sir?'' O'Dell sounded hesitant.

''Are you trying to tell me something happened during this exercise that could cause Captain Keener to stumble?''

The colonel hadn't raised his voice, but his tone was no less intimidating for that. It gave Tracy cold chills, and she rubbed at her arms.

''Nothing that I'm aware of, sir.''

''Colonel,'' Lieutenant Carver interceded. ''If Major O'Dell feels Captain Keener is a potential problem, perhaps we should contact Burke and appeal to his sense of duty and honor.''

''No.'' Hackett barely gave the words time to travel to him before vetoing the suggestion. ''That would imply something that shouldn't have occurred had taken place.''

''Burke's not yet being adjudged is a loose end, Colonel,'' O'Dell said. ''The project goes up to Congress for funding in less than a week. Odds would be better if he'd been convicted.''

''That's an unreasonable expectation,'' Hackett said, then paused a long moment.

''Without that funding,'' Carver interjected, ''General Nestler isn't likely to support your Pacific assignment. It's a crucial factor in your career plan, sir.''

''I'm aware of my career plans, Lieutenant.'' Anger ripped through Hackett's voice.

''If Burke can't be adjudged before the project goes

up for funding," O'Dell said, "he's outlived his useful-
ness. Wouldn't you say so, sir?"

Tracy jerked away from the pillows and sat straight up,
plank stiff. *Murder?* Could they actually, by God, be discussing the possibility of murdering Burke?

"That's not our decision to make. A judge and jury
will decide when Burke dies."

Not *when,* Colonel. *If. If* Burke dies. Tracy grimaced,
though relieved. And what project were they discussing?

"As for the funding," Hackett went on, "I think the
captain might be useful."

In her mind, Tracy saw the colonel lighting one of his
cigars, despite the building being designated a smoke-free
facility. Only General Nestler would dare to object.

"No," Hackett said, sounding as if he were exhaling
a stream of smoke. "I think our needs would be better
met by taking a different tack with Captain Adam
Burke."

"What different tack?" Carver asked, sounding as
puzzled as Tracy felt.

Had Hackett done something wrong, or not?

"An alternative, men," the colonel said. "An alternative. Let's meet at the club for an early dinner to discuss it."

"Yes, sir," Carver said. "You have an Intel briefing
in fifteen minutes."

"Thank you, Lieutenant." Hackett grunted. "This
meeting is over, gentlemen. Dismissed."

Tracy listened to the shuffle of chairs, and then the
absence of sound. What exactly had she just heard?
Would Adam Burke have understood the conversation
any better than she had?

The kicker was, even if she repeated it and asked
Adam, she wouldn't be able to believe what he told her.
He was fighting for his life. The man would say anything.

Even as she thought that, she doubted it was true. Why,
she had no idea. Maybe because of those emotional inflections in his tone when he had called to warn her of

the threats, survivor to survivor. Maybe because he had
worried about her safety enough to call at all. Or maybe
because she was feeling a little less than nearly satisfied,
happy, and content, and the man was playing her emotions like a fiddle.

Just after dusk the next day, Tracy received the call.

Standing in her garden, knee-deep in muddy jeans and
fragrant rose clippings, and sucking on a finger she'd
pricked on a thorn, she snatched up the remote phone
from a wicker table and answered with a snarled,
"Hello."

"Captain Keener, this is Sergeant Maxwell at the facility. I'm sorry to bother you at home, ma'am."

Burke's guard. Tracy crooked her shoulder and neck
to hold the phone at her ear, then swatted at a mosquito
buzzing her cheek. "No problem, Sergeant. What can I
do for you?"

"There's no easy way to say this, but I, um, thought
you'd want to know as soon as possible." Dread laced
his tone, chilling her blood to ice. "It's about Adam
Burke. There's been a fire here at the facility, ma'am.
He's . . . dead."

Chapter 7

Tracy listened to what Sergeant Maxwell had to say, which unfortunately wasn't much. Details on the fire were, as yet, sketchy. She muttered something inane, and then got off the phone, her head whirling, her stomach revolting, and made it to the garden's wicker chair before her knees gave out. *Adam Burke dead?*

Good God, he couldn't be *dead*.

Numb all over, she stared sightlessly at the leaves rustling in the night breeze. How could he be dead? How could Maxwell not have gotten Adam out of solitary confinement before he had died of smoke inhalation? Had it been smoke inhalation? Or—*oh, please, God, no!*—had he burned?

Maxwell hadn't actually said, had he? God's truth, she'd been too stunned, she couldn't remember.

You dig too deeply, you're going to ruffle feathers. You ruffle too many feathers, and you're going to wind up short a defendant. Within forty-eight hours of you nosing around like a little puppy, O'Dell and Hackett will see to it I'm dead.

Shudders stormed through her. Hugging herself, she dug her fingertips into her fleshy biceps and rocked back and forth on her seat. Adam had predicted this, and he'd been right. What if he had been right about the incident, too? What if he had told her the truth? She had pushed O'Dell for answers to questions he wouldn't want asked about changing Adam's orders. But *had* Adam's rendition of the events been honest?

He worried about you enough to warn you. That tells you something about the man.

It did. A lot about the man. And that grain of truth in his story swelled to a pebble.

The possibility that Adam might have been honest had her temples pounding. Maybe he hadn't been imaginative or creative. Maybe there was a huge cover-up going on. Unthinkable, incredible, but maybe Adam was innocent.

Dying seemed too steep a price to pay to convince her of it, but she'd bet her bars he would go nearly that far to prove his point.

Within forty-eight hours . . . will see to it, I'm dead.

God help her, maybe she had gotten him killed.

Blame lay heavy on her shoulders, more oppressive than the walk through Cell Block D. Why had only Adam died in the fire? Maxwell had told her only the solitary-confinement block had been affected.

Only Adam's block.

An eerie feeling niggled into her anguish. Had the fire been accidental, or intentional?

She had to know. She locked up the house and grabbed her car keys.

By the time she drove to the facility, she was an emotional wreck and dead certain she had been directly responsible for Adam Burke's death. He had expressly warned her that her blatant inquiries would get him killed. Why hadn't she listened? Been more cautious, more discreet?

Had he been killed by Hackett and O'Dell? Had this been Hackett's enigmatic alternative?

The idea seemed absurd. Hackett's star was on the rise. He was Nestler's fair-haired boy, and according to Janet, he was about to be assigned a powerful command in the Pacific theater. O'Dell was on the way out, a scant step from retirement. At this point, he'd be a fool to risk his pension. Yet if the incentive were strong enough, would he consider it foolish?

What incentive could hold the appeal of his pension, benefits, and financial security? What could appeal enough to risk a long stint in the U.S. Military Barracks at Leavenworth?

Unable to think of an answer, she skirted the green and red fire trucks parked outside the facility's main entrance. Their spinning red lights cut sharply through the darkness, swirling god-awful color on the carnage. High-intensity floodlights were focused directly on the building. Firefighters battled the blaze with their hoses, but smoke and flames still engulfed the solitary-confinement block and belched roiling black clouds into the night sky.

Tracy stared at the charred tan brick, the molten and twisted lumps of what had been vinyl windows, the broken glass panes now soot-stained black. *Adam had been in there. He had died in there.*

Light from the fire crossed with that from the high-intensity lamps and illuminated Sergeant Maxwell, standing near an oak. Shock shone in his eyes.

Tracy approached him, certain he would be more receptive to her questions than the unit commander. He'd be more apt to find a way to blame the fire on Adam Burke.

She couldn't fault the commander. He had to have someone to blame. In situations where property was damaged, resources were lost, and people died, everyone always had to blame someone. If the unit commander couldn't offer up someone else, then blame would be assigned to him. If even remotely human, he would move mountains to avoid that.

Anxious and uneasy, Maxwell spotted her. His expression tightened.

She walked past a knot of gaping spectators over to him. "Thank you for calling me."

"Yes, ma'am." His face was smudged black, and the pungent smell of smoke clung to him.

Burning ash lifted sparks into the air and then flamed out. "Do you know what happened?"

He looked to a uniformed fireman reeking of authority for silent permission. On his sleeve, Tracy saw a "Chief" patch. He nodded, and Maxwell swung his gaze back to her, wiping his smutty forehead with a once-white handkerchief. Soot streaked across his brow. "We're not sure how the fire started," he said. "The inspectors think it was an electrical short in the air-conditioning circuit. That's confidential, ma'am."

"Of course." Smoke still billowed out of the building and the investigators already had deduced its cause? Odd, yet with advanced technology, not impossible. "The whole facility has central air-conditioning. Why did the fire affect only this block?"

"Each block has a separate unit."

"And only this one shorted out?"

"That's the inspectors' preliminary findings, yes, ma'am." A pointed look lit in Maxwell's eyes.

He wasn't comfortable with this deduction, either. It radiated from him as clearly as heat radiated from the fire. "When did you become aware that there was a problem?"

Maxwell dropped his gaze, clearly remembering her opposition to Adam's being beaten and not getting prompt medical attention. "The smoke detector went off," Maxwell said. "I was called to help break up an altercation between the Heavies. They're a group—"

"I'm aware of who the Heavies are, Sergeant."

"Yes, ma'am, I guess you would be." He rubbed at his neck. "I locked them down and then checked out the alarm. Truthfully, ma'am, I figured it was a drill. We've been having them all day, so I didn't ignore it, but I didn't panic. A fire drill has low priority when the Heavies are trying to carve out a fellow prisoner's guts."

Maxwell was clearly looking for absolution, and Tracy

gave it to him. "I agree." She toed her sneaker tip into the fine blades of grass. Even at this distance—a good two hundred feet from the building—heat had scorched the grass, and a thin dusting of gray ash blanketed it. "So you locked down the Heavies and then investigated the alarm?"

"Yes, ma'am. That's when I saw the flames. I notified the head of Security. We called it in right away and then evacuated the entire facility." He nodded to the prisoners standing in rows near the garden. "That's risky, but under the circumstances, we didn't have any choice."

Likely uncomfortable, standing there for hours, but at least the other prisoners were out of danger. "Seems prudent."

"It's standard procedure in potentially dangerous situations, ma'am." Maxwell stared down at the ground, and his eyes glazed. "Burke's cell block was under heavy smoke. The heat was incredible. I had an extinguisher but no protective gear. I tried, but I couldn't get to him, ma'am. I really tried."

She believed that he had. "No one is faulting you, Sergeant. I'm just trying to discern the facts for my final report so I can close out his file." *And hopefully find a way to live with the guilt of not protecting him. I didn't have to believe him to protect him.*

Maxwell's expression was mixed, as if he wanted to say something but knew it was wisest to keep quiet. Did his reluctance have anything to do with the fire chief standing only six feet away from them?

"I couldn't get to him." Maxwell's gaze drifted and lost focus. "No matter how I tried, I couldn't get to him. He burned bad, ma'am."

Tracy locked her knees to keep them from buckling. The note—*It's arranged. Burke and you die*—and Janet's words—*The man's crashed and burned, Tracy. He's going to fry*—ripped through Tracy's mind, and both took on a whole new meaning. Adam *had* crashed and burned and died. And she, the Intel novice, had gotten him killed.

The only man in her life who had protected her—or had tried to—with no strings attached, and she'd gotten him killed. Remorse swelled like a sponge in her throat.

When she could, she swallowed it down. "I'll need to see his body, Sergeant. To positively ID him."

"It's been transported to the morgue to avoid exposure." Maxwell shifted from foot to foot, clearly uneasy. "But I've gotta warn you. Burke burned beyond recognition, ma'am. Dr. Moxley had to request dental records to do the positive ID."

Randall? Surprise spiked up Tracy's spine. This swift movement through the system's required actions rated atypical, and from the worry in Maxwell's eyes, he knew it as well as she did. "Thanks, Sergeant. If you think of anything else, please call me. Day or night." She turned to walk back to her car.

"Ma'am, wait." Maxwell reached for the back pocket of his pants. "This isn't a good time, but I have the feeling there won't be one any time soon." He passed her a white envelope marred by his soot-smudged fingerprints.

"What's this?"

"Burke asked me to give it to you." Maxwell shrugged. "Seemed weird at the time. I figured he could give it to you himself. Now, though, I'm thinking maybe he knew. People do that sometimes—know they're gonna die, I mean. I swore I'd put it in your hands, so here it is."

"Thank you, Sergeant." Having no idea what was in the envelope, she nodded.

"Ma'am?" Maxwell's gaze grew intense and he dropped his voice to a whisper. "Something here don't feel right."

"I know, Sergeant," she whispered back, feeling it down to her soul.

She walked back to her car, an empty, sick feeling squeezing her stomach. Innately, she knew Maxwell was right.

Seated in the Caprice, she broke the seal on the envelope and pulled out a fistful of documents. She clicked on the dome light. A warranty deed on Adam's house, his car title, a hundred-thousand-dollar insurance policy, and a last will and testament.

She skimmed over them. The hair on her arms lifted. Her breath left her body. "Oh, Adam, why? *Why* did you do this?" How could he leave everything in the world he owned to her? Stunned, furious with him and with herself, she stuffed the papers back into the envelope—and saw a scribbled note.

Counselor,

If you're reading this, then I'm dead and you've gotten the envelope I left with Maxwell.

For the record, I haven't gone insane and it's okay that you didn't believe me. Sometimes I have trouble believing myself. I've left everything to you because you might need it. Convert all of it into cash right away. I mean it, counselor. Right away.

Unless I'm one-eighty out on this, you're going to have to disappear. This way, I know you've got the means to do it. Janet knows how to make it happen. She'll help you. Trust no one else, and be careful, counselor. I'm banking on you to survive and find the truth.

Adam

P.S. Don't waste time feeling guilty about me dying. You can't afford the luxury.

An affordable luxury or not, guilt buried her. While driving to the hospital, she reasoned through everything she could think of, speculated on more, and still the only thing in his note that made sense was Janet. She *would* know how to make a disappearance happen, and having worked Intel with her, Adam would know it.

Tracy pulled into the hospital parking lot, reluctant to

go inside. It had been five long years since her own accident and Matthew's death, since she'd given birth to
Abby only to have Paul tell her she couldn't hold her
baby because she too was dead. And Tracy had struggled
through them. She had accepted her loss, determined to
build herself a new life. But Adam's death made all those
memories fresh, ripped opened the wounds and left them
raw.

Back then, Paul had stepped in like a loving brother
and protected her, sparing her from having to identify the
bodies of her husband and daughter. But there was no
one to spare her from identifying Adam. She didn't love
him or believe him, though something odd was happening
in his case, but he had cared about her enough to worry
and to leave her everything he had, trying to protect her.
That changed her attorney/client perception of him. His
caring made this personal.

She'd never get through this. Not feeling this way.

Taking in three deep breaths, she gave herself a short,
firm lecture. *You have to do this. It goes with the job.
You owe him. It's the right thing.*

Repeating that litany to herself, Tracy headed toward
the basement morgue. Her heart chugged in her chest and
her blood beat at her temples. She might have to, but she
didn't want to do this. To be haunted by memories of
Matthew and Abby, of Adam. But the flood kept coming,
crushing down on her. Why did Adam's death bring all
of this back? Why had he had to bring up her past when
she'd finally buried her ghosts and managed to remember
more often than not only the good times? Why, after all
this time, did she have to suffer the pain of loving and
losing Matthew and Abby again? Why again, when God
knew it had nearly destroyed her the first time?

In the hallway, a brass-framed sign read Anatomical
Pathology. It was the morgue, identified by a diluted term
that spared the uninitiated from recognition and sent shivers scattering up her back because she wasn't one of
them. A numerical key-code lock bolted the blue metal

door. Angrily swiping at her damp cheeks, she knocked.

When Steven Kane opened the door, she stepped inside. "I've come to identify Adam Burke's body." Her voice shook. She hated it, but seemed helpless to steady it. "For my file."

He clasped her upper arm. "Tracy, you don't have to do that. Randall has already identified him by his dental records. It's definitely Adam Burke."

Relieved and yet suspicious, she insisted. "Thank you for trying to spare me, but I have to see Adam myself."

Dr. Kane's compassionate eyes softened even more. "Why?"

Because I might have killed him. Because this could be my fault. Because I heard him, but I didn't listen to him. "It's my job," she said lamely. She could take the forensics expert's or the pathologist's word. Either was permissible, but neither was acceptable. Not in Adam's case.

"For closure?"

"Yes." It was as good a reason as any, and better than any other she'd care to admit. "For closure."

Seeing far more than she wanted him to see, he moved to the row of silver door coolers recessed in the wall. He opened the second door from the left, reached in, and then pulled out the tray holding the white-sheet-draped body of Adam Burke.

"He's badly burned, Tracy." Clasping the corner of the sheet, Dr. Kane cast a worried look her way. "Are you sure about this?"

She wasn't sure about anything. Not anymore. Bracing herself, she curtly nodded, and Dr. Kane drew back the sheet.

All of her muscles clenched at once. Her heart throbbed, her stomach threatened to revolt, and she locked her knees to stay upright. A scream echoed through the chambers of her mind, sought release in her throat. She bit her lips until she tasted blood to keep it locked inside.

Unable to bear the horrific sight of Adam's charred

flesh another second, she looked away. "That's . . . fine," she finally managed on a wisp of breath.

Dr. Kane closed the cooler, and clasped Tracy's arm. Clammy and short of breath, she shamelessly leaned against him, needing his support. He led her into an adjoining room, an office filled with two desks and paintings of sailboats. A wooden-framed photograph of someone's kids sat on the desk nearest the door.

"Here." He held out a chair for her. "Sit down for a minute."

She collapsed on the chair and inhaled deeply, swearing she'd never forgive herself if she fainted. "I'm not fluff," she shakily insisted, having no idea why.

"No, you aren't." Dr. Kane's lips curved into a sympathetic smile. "Identifying a body is hard enough when it isn't mutilated. When it is, it's even more difficult."

"Yes, it is . . . difficult." It was hell. Sheer, unadulterated hell. As long as she lived, she'd never forget the horrific image, the burned smell.

When her heartbeat slowed to a gallop, she risked glancing up at Dr. Kane. No hint of condescension shone in his eyes, and she felt grateful for that. "When will you do the autopsy?"

"I won't." He held her gaze. "Command hasn't requested one."

Obviously, the fire could have killed Adam. But what if someone had put a bullet in his head or a knife through his heart prior to the fire? He could have burned posthumously.

And why that thought gave her comfort when it should scare the hell out of her, she had no inkling.

That was a lie. She knew exactly. Burning was a cruel way to die. Excruciatingly painful. Merciless. And she hated with passion the idea of Adam Burke dying that death. With that grain of truth nagging at her and her doubts about her responsibility in his death, she had to hate it. His warning and bequest had given her a rare glimpse of the real man. Of course she had to hate it.

"Are you okay?" Dr. Kane leaned away from her.

Certain she'd never be fine again, she nodded and then asked a question of her own. "Did you autopsy the men on Burke's team?"

"I'm under a gag order, remember?"

"I haven't forgotten," she said. "But I'm now looking at a dead client who might, or might not, have been set up to take a fall. That's confidential. I'm telling you because I want you to understand the significance of your answers. If I don't determine the truth about Adam Burke, he's going to be condemned as guilty forever."

"The evidence of that is overwhelming."

"It's not."

"He did it, Tracy," Dr. Kane insisted. "Look, it's common to feel guilty in situations like this, but dying doesn't make him a saint or exonerate him. Adam Burke committed those crimes."

Don't feel guilty. It's a luxury you can't afford. "But what if he wasn't guilty? What if it were you toe-tagged in that freezer? Wouldn't you want someone to ask the hard questions and find out the truth? If it were me, I would."

Dr. Kane looked away. A long moment later, he lifted a pencil from the desk. Twirling it, he avoided her gaze. "I'm not talking to you. In fact, you're not here. I'm alone, talking to this pencil. It's an antistress technique."

A bubble of anticipation burst in her stomach.

"The families refused to agree to have the bodies autopsied."

Yet another oddity. "What were the men's official causes of death?"

The doctor tossed down the pencil and glared at her. "For Christ's sake, Tracy, Burke led them onto an active bombing range."

So the men had been blown up—at least, they had been before they had gotten to Dr. Kane. They couldn't have been blown up before Adam had seen them or he wouldn't have told her to check out their eyes.

Trust no one else . . .

Dr. Kane could be paying her lip service. Tracy didn't push. There were other ways to find her answers about the team. "I want an autopsy done on Adam Burke."

"I can't do it." Regret filled Dr. Kane's voice. "If I could, I would. But I can't."

"Why not?"

"Command hasn't requested one."

"I'm requesting one."

"You can't." The doctor shoved the pencil back into a cup on the desk. "The order has to come from Colonel Hackett."

Terrific. Hemmed in by red tape again. "Why?"

"Because he was Burke's commanding officer and we already know what killed the man. An autopsy would be—"

"An unnecessary expense?"

"Frankly, yes. We're on a budget just like everyone else."

"But if Hackett requests an autopsy, then one will be done, correct?"

Dr. Kane nodded.

"Do you think he will make a request?"

"I'm sure he won't." The doctor looked away, to the children's photograph. "The colonel has already authorized release of the body to the family for burial. Chaplain Rutledge is contacting them now, notifying them of the accident and death."

"Released?" Surprise shafted through Tracy. Burke's body wasn't even cold yet. He'd barely been dead three hours. "Already?"

"Already," Dr. Kane said, still unwilling to meet her eyes.

He too thought this was extraordinary, though wild horses couldn't drag that admission from him. Tracy stood up. "Thank you for your kindnesses."

As she walked out of the morgue, she gave the cooler housing Adam Burke's body one last look. Had the men's bodies been intact when he had seen them in Area 14? When Dr. Kane had received them in the morgue? If not, what had happened to them between the time Adam saw them and they arrived at Dr. Kane's? The bomb had already been dropped, and there had been no reports of a second bomb. If those bodies had been intact on arrival at the morgue, then why hadn't autopsies been done on them? Why had the families refused? That didn't make sense. Unless the families were convinced that refusing would be in the country's best interests. That could have happened. After all, the men were Intel operatives. But why wouldn't Hackett request an autopsy on Adam immediately? His crimes were public, his case volatile. Hackett couldn't afford any speculation or uncertainty about Adam's death.

None of this felt right. Intuition or instinct, the feeling had engaged and it drummed out a warning: *Someone has a lot to hide.*

I'm banking on you to survive and find the truth . . .

Why hadn't Adam banked on someone else? Someone with the skills to do this right? He was Intel, for God's sake. He had to know people who were more capable. To her, Intel was an alien world. She was in over her head and drowning.

Tracy stepped out into the sultry night. She had failed Adam before and she feared she'd fail him again. How in heaven was she going to face his family and explain his bequest? She'd refuse it, of course, but they would still be hurt that he had excluded them. And how much was it going to cost her to legally insist his body be autopsied?

She stepped off the curb, down into the street. Did it matter? Whatever the costs, she had to pay them.

The woman in the mirror demanded it.

Chapter 8

It was after nine-thirty when Tracy got home.

The last thing she felt like listening to was the sound of airplanes flying a routine exercise mission from the base to Area Fourteen, firing loud gun blasts that had her walls reverberating and her windows rattling. But they were, and she was.

She showered, then put on her "attitude" Pooh slippers and her old flannel "comfort" robe, which necessitated knocking the air conditioner down a couple degrees. August nights were notoriously hot and humid in Grandsen, but tonight she needed the support more than the cool.

Knowing a cup, or even two, of Earl Grey tea wouldn't give her the courage needed to call Adam's family, she poured herself a healthy glass of Scotch and then sat down at the kitchen table with his file and the phone. His parents were her only hope of getting the autopsy done without further risks to her career.

The Scotch burned going down her throat and warmed the hollow in her stomach. When she'd consumed half, she read the names of Adam's emergency contact: his parents, Ruth and Gabriel Burke. Their address was in Georgia—Eastern time zone versus Tracy's own Central. It was late, but with the news of their son's death being so fresh, they would still be awake. Tracy had been awake all night, suffering through the inconsolable sense of loss.

I never even got to hold her. Not once.

Her throat tight, she gulped at her Scotch and forced thoughts of Abby out of her mind. Right now, she couldn't afford them. She lifted the phone, but hesitated to dial. God, but she hated to intrude on Adam's family's grief.

If you wait, you could be too late.

Adam's voice, nudging her. But he was right. Once he was buried, having his body exhumed could create a horrendous legal tangle and public stir. Worse, his family could have him cremated like his team, and then there would be no hope of ever having an autopsy done. As much as she hated intruding on his family now, she had to call. Surely when they understood the reason was to find out the truth about their son, they'd forgive her. What parent wouldn't yearn for the truth about their son?

Before she could talk herself out of it again, Tracy dialed the phone.

On the second ring, a woman answered. "Yes, what is it?"

Awake, irritated, and far from inconsolable. Her antagonism caught Tracy off-guard, and she stammered. "Mrs. Burke?"

"Who's calling?"

"Captain Tracy Keener. I'm Adam's attorney." Using his given name aloud seemed unfamiliar and strange.

"Haven't they told you yet? Adam is dead."

"Yes, ma'am. I'm aware of it." A sudden image of his charred body filled her mind, startled her. Shivering, she shut it out.

"Then what do you want?"

Everyone reacts differently to grief. Evidently, Ruth Burke reacted in anger. "I realize this is a difficult time, Mrs. Burke. I just wanted to offer my condolences."

"Don't waste them on the likes of him. Adam's always had a streak of bad blood. I warned him he would pay the price, but no one ever could tell him anything. He got what he deserved for what he'd done.''

This coldhearted bitch was Adam's *mother*? Tracy's nerves blistered. ''He wasn't adjudged guilty of doing anything, Mrs. Burke.''

''He would have been. It was just a matter of time. He never brought anything but shame to this family.''

No grief? No compassion? No loyalty? The woman's son was dead. Her own flesh and blood. Where in God's name was her grief? Needing fortification to continue, Tracy reached for her glass. ''I called to ask you to request an autopsy on Adam.''

''No.''

No? Tracy couldn't seem to recover from one shock before Ruth Burke belted her again. ''Why not?''

''We're having nothing to do with him. We haven't for years. I already told that chaplain so. He's handling the burial. If you want anything, you'll have to ask him.''

Good God, his own family wouldn't even bury him at his home or attend his funeral? What kind of hellish life had Adam had as a child? ''The chaplain can't request an autopsy. Only a family member can. It's essential, Mrs. Burke, to prove that the body is in fact your son's.''

''They've matched his dental records,'' she said without emotion. ''It's him.''

''But there is still the matter of whether or not he was alive at the time of the fire.''

''Dead is dead, Captain. You'll have to think what you want without any more proof. My husband and I have no intention of getting involved. Let the dead bury their dead, the Bible says. Adam shamed us in life, he'll not shame us again in death.''

Regardless of actions or accusations, Adam was their son. How could they justify treating him this way? How *long* had they been treating him this way? ''Does your attitude about this have anything to do with Adam leaving his assets to someone else?'' She couldn't bring herself to say ''to me.'' She tried, but she just couldn't do it.

"It's blood money. We don't want it—or him."

Sick. These people were twisted, and they damn sure weren't going to intercede. After talking to Ruth Burke, Tracy was relieved to hear it. She ended the call in a cold fury. If Abby had lived, Tracy never would have abandoned her. *Never.* How could the Burkes rationalize this cold and callous treatment of their own son?

Tracy mulled and muttered, downed the rest of her Scotch, and seriously considered having a second glass of it to calm down. But more depressants were the last thing she needed. Feeling desolate and alone, and more than a little pity for the boy Adam had been—and for the man he'd no doubt become because of it—she forced her mind away from family—his and hers—and back to what she could do for Adam. God knew he had no one else.

She glanced at the clock. Nearly eleven. Colonel Jackson wouldn't appreciate being awakened, but he was her last chance for getting an autopsy. Odds were against him supporting her, but she had to try. If she honored Adam's will, then she could request an autopsy. But she couldn't honor it, and in refusing to—which of course she had to do, even though the idea of everything he'd worked for going to his family made her nauseous—Jackson was her only option.

Swallowing hard, she dialed her boss at home. He answered on the third ring, sounding sleepy and grouchy at being disturbed. "Colonel Jackson, this is Tracy Keener."

"I've heard about Burke, Captain, and about your requesting an autopsy. No, I won't support your requisition."

He'd obviously expected her call. But who'd forewarned him? Dr. Kane? Sergeant Maxwell? Colonel Hackett himself? Jackson hadn't mentioned the bequest, so she doubted Maxwell had called him, though she felt sure Maxwell had read the documents before resealing the envelope and giving it to her. And it was too soon for Hackett to be running interference. Another couple of hours and maybe, but not yet. That left Dr. Kane.

Trust no one else.

She buried her disappointments. "May I ask why you won't support me on this, sir?"

"At midnight? No, you may not," Jackson said sharply. "Just let the nightmare end, Captain." He hung up the phone.

Just let the nightmare end? Tracy stared at the receiver, dumbfounded. How could it end? Without knowing the truth, how could it *ever* end? Didn't Adam, an officer with an unblemished record until now, deserve better than this? He'd served his country well for seven years. How could his country justify sacrificing him and *just let the nightmare end* before it found out the truth?

Tension knotted her muscles. Tracy rubbed at them. It was time to fall back and regroup. Get some rest. Then she'd think more clearly and escape this surreal dream.

She dumped her glass in the sink and then went to bed, slippers, robe, and all. The mattress sank under her weight, and she tugged the sweet-smelling coverlet up under her chin, curled her knees to her chest, and closed her eyes. In her mind, she saw Adam, sitting across the rickety table from her in the attorney/client room, again telling her he had learned the hard way not to trust anyone.

With his parents, she could certainly understand why. And yet he had come to trust her—at least to the extent of telling her his side of things and banking on her to find out the truth. Out of necessity, he'd had to trust someone. But he hadn't had to choose her. Amazing that he had, considering she'd already let him down twice by not anticipating the beating or getting a stay order to prevent Alpha team's cremations.

Now Adam was dead. And no one seemed to care.

She mentally walked around the wobbly table and cradled his head to her breast, stroked his shoulders, his broad back, that god-awful yellow stripe of paint in his hair, offering him comfort. "I care, Adam," she whispered softly over and over again. "I care."

He wound his arms around her waist, squeezed her hard, and feeling tremors ripple through his body, she held him tighter, doing her damnedest to soothe him and absorb his pain, to dissolve the emptiness inside him she knew from experience was clawing at his soul. And with him, for him, she mourned.

Sometime before dawn, the phone rang.

Blindly reaching through the darkness, Tracy snagged the receiver, then mumbled into it: "Hello." Her voice sounded scratchy and her head ached from crying herself to sleep. Whether she had cried for Adam or for herself, she wasn't sure. Probably both.

"Tracy, it's me—Paul."

She opened her eyes and stared at the shadowy ceiling. "What's wrong?" Her former brother-in-law still called often, but seldom during the middle of the night.

"I'm worried about you," he said. "The headlines on the Burke case are merciless."

So follow-up coverage on the case had spread from Mississippi to New Orleans. Well, it wouldn't be long until it went national. Probably by morning. Unfortunate, but predictable. Even more predictable was her suspecting Randall Moxley had phoned Paul and asked him to bring her to heel before she embarrassed them both. In that way, those two were just alike. "My defending Adam won't be a problem, Paul."

"Don't be naïve, darling. Of course it'll be a problem."

Her voice went deadpan flat. "Adam Burke is dead."

"Dead?" A deep sigh that could only be relief sounded through the phone. "Well, thank God for that. Did the other prisoners kill him, or did the bastard commit suicide?"

"He burned to death in a fire." She slammed down the phone, her throat thick, her gritty eyes filling with more tears. Even Paul, a tower of strength and comfort to her, had been totally devoid of compassion for Adam.

A man had died. No one knew for certain whether he was guilty or innocent, and yet all condemned him. He had been mocked, ridiculed, degraded, humiliated, and deserted by everyone—even his family. In light of that unpardonable cruelty, his guilt or innocence in his case suddenly seemed secondary, if not insignificant, and again she wept. This time, for him and for herself, and for the tragedy of what society had allowed itself to become.

Colonel Jackson seemed agitated.

He kept the JAGs' morning briefing abnormally short, and he didn't mention Adam or his bequest once, which disappointed the office troublemakers, Richard and Samuel, as much as it relieved Tracy. She'd awakened to a hellish downpour, and had had to fight the urge to crawl back into bed and pull the covers up over her head. Ted, sitting across the conference table and leveling a ticked-off expression on her head, made her wish she had just stayed in bed. What bone could he have to pick with her?

Colonel Jackson assigned a couple of new cases, then closed the meeting without his usual pep talk. He was either still ticked about her calling him so late last night and wanted to chew her out in private, or he was craving a cup of coffee as desperately as she was.

Swearing to kick the caffeine habit soon, she went back to her office, poured herself a cup of coffee, and then sat down with the morning paper, eager to see what the press had made of Adam's death. Maybe public opinion could force an autopsy. God knew, she'd exhausted all other options, unless she kept his bequest, which she just couldn't do. But odds were against the public helping. Like Paul, the public would be more apt to celebrate Adam's death.

The headline made her stomach flip. *Beauty Defends the Beast* . . .

Page one, no less. Tracy groaned. *Terrific.* She scanned

the rest of the paper but found nothing about the fire or Adam's death. Word evidently hadn't leaked out prior to press time. Should she rejoice, or mourn?

Mourn, she decided. Tomorrow's headlines would be even worse. The press would hear about his bequest, and Tracy and Adam's relationship—though it bore no resemblance whatsoever—would be touted as some kind of romantic tragedy. She'd be either crazy or a victim, and he'd be guilty.

Adam really had died. *Died.*

A deep ache sank into her, right below her breastbone. Everything in her wanted to just close the file and forget this case ever had happened. But she couldn't do it—regardless of Jackson's orders. Not even to avoid the inevitable mudslinging and professional repercussions.

She glanced at the phone. What the hell. Adam was already dead. If they had killed him, they couldn't kill him again. She was still vulnerable, but she had known the risks from the start. Enormous. And she would lose big, just as Janet had predicted. Her career. Maybe her life. But she owed Adam a debt, and she had to pay it.

She grabbed the receiver. Her palm clammy against the plastic, she dialed Gus O'Dell's number. Connie Mumford answered and put Tracy straight through.

O'Dell came on the line. "What do you want now, Keener?"

So much for civility. Forget courtesy. Well, she wasn't much in the mood for them, either. She wanted answers, damn it. "I went to the facility last night after the fire." She stared at her gleaming desktop. "I was surprised Adam Burke's body had already been moved to the morgue."

"Yes?"

Deliberately obtuse. Tracy resented that. "I learned at the morgue there's a Command block against him being autopsied. I'd like that position reconsidered."

"Why?"

Tracy used their own philosophy against them. "This

is a very visual case, Major. And it's becoming more visual as we speak. I don't think Higher Headquarters wants to risk the appearance of impropriety or a cover-up.''

He laughed. "I appreciate your concern for our reputation, as I'm sure Colonel Hackett will, but there aren't two people on the planet who doubt Adam Burke is guilty as hell. The press won't give us any trouble now.''

"Is that why Colonel Hackett refused to request an autopsy?''

"Actually, he didn't.''

"Oh?'' Tracy clamped down on the receiver. Dr. Kane had expressly said Hackett hadn't requested one and he had released the body to the family.

"General Nestler issued that order,'' O'Dell clarified. "Because of the possible negative impact and the explosive nature of this case, the general felt it wise to put this Burke matter to bed expeditiously. I'm sure you agree with the wisdom of his decision.''

"Yes, I do—theoretically.'' How could she disagree with the general? Truth was truth, and she did see the wisdom in his decision, but O'Dell's confidence in her agreement warned her a cover-up was definitely in hiding. "That course of action does seem logical, sir, but—''

"I'm glad you agree, Captain.'' Sounding amused, he cut her off.

That grated at Tracy, and she heard Adam's "fluff'' in her mind. "But I think—''

O'Dell interrupted again. "We strongly advise you to close your file.''

Tracy glanced down at the newspaper's headline and came face-to-face with the temptation to do just that. She dragged her thumb over the handle of her coffee mug. With these doubts festering inside her, could she just close the file?

No more so than she could just let the nightmare end. Not and live with herself.

Realizing she was opening a can of worms that would

probably prove lethal to her career, she stared at the paper. "We have to know what happened to him, sir. Beyond a reasonable doubt. Otherwise, the Air Force risks
similar situations in the future."

"Burke was a cold-blooded killer. A coward and a
traitor to his country and his men, Captain," O'Dell said
stiffly. "That's not a situation we face with monotonous
regularity."

"But it has happened, and we shouldn't risk it happening again needlessly. The country deserves our every
effort to prevent such incidents, and I'd be remiss in my
duty if I didn't do everything humanly possible to unearth
the findings and offer them for future strategic studies."

"I'm not happy to hear this, Captain. Your motives are
simple and pure, but they're also idealistic and misplaced.
Colonel Hackett and General Nestler will agree. We're
too close to the end of the fiscal year to be exposing our
underbelly."

Money. Why did so much that shouldn't, reduce down
to money? "But sir—"

"This was an assignment, not a crusade. Close the file,
Captain. That's a direct order."

Tracy stared at the newspaper until its black print
blurred. Her stomach soured and her chest tightened. For
the first time in her five-year career, she had no choice
but to deliberately disobey a senior officer's direct order.
That, or be forever haunted by Adam Burke and the guilt
of failing him yet again—without even trying to do the
right thing. "Thank you, sir," she said. "I appreciate
your time."

O'Dell hung up the phone.

Tracy slumped in her chair, certain hell was coming to
call. Worse, she'd summoned it.

That inauspicious beginning to Tracy's day set the tone
for the rest of it. By lunchtime, she had received messages for three more requests for interviews—word of
Adam's death was definitely out—and half a dozen more

phone threats from crazies who obviously hadn't yet tuned in to the news.

Janet breezed into her office. "Your appointment is in half an hour."

Raw-nerved and soul-weary, Tracy rubbed at her temples. With everything else, she had to put up with a headache, too? "What appointment?" Tension. It was tension.

"You need a little nurturing, so I booked you at Elegance for a facial. I'd have gone for the massage, too, but I wasn't sure your budget could stand it." Janet dropped a file on the desk, then turned back for the door. "Don't be late—and don't forget your checkbook."

More than ready to escape the office for a while, Tracy grabbed her purse. Leave it to Janet to realize before Tracy that if she didn't take time out to nurture herself, she wouldn't have anything left with which to nurture anyone else—including Adam.

The rain had stopped. In the parking lot, she straddled a mud puddle to get into her car, and that eerie feeling of being watched returned in full force. She covertly glanced around the lot, but noted nothing unusual. She had to quit letting the stupid threats get to her.

Putting them out of her mind, she keyed the ignition and glanced at the clock. Twenty minutes. Plenty of time to make it down to Elegance.

She left the base and stopped at the red light just outside the gate. Thankfully, the entrance/exit was free of reporters. Ahead, wooded reservation hugged both sides of the straight-stretch, four-laned Freedom Way. Just off its right shoulder stood a drainage ditch five feet wide. Swollen full, rainwater gushed through it.

With all of the signs of habitation behind her and the gray sky above her looking dreary and ready to split open and dump more rain, she felt isolated and vulnerable. Why couldn't she shake the sensation of being watched?

In a cold sweat, she again checked. Only one other car in sight: a blue standard-issue Air Force sedan. It pulled up behind her, and then stopped.

The traffic light changed. Letting out a little sigh of relief, she stomped the accelerator, chiding herself for letting empty threats get to her like this. People were just venting their anger. Nothing would come of them. Thank God she hadn't been so foolish as to report them to the OSI. That decision definitely had been right. Occasionally, threats went with the job. The last thing she needed to show the promotion board was that she couldn't handle the heat.

The threatening rain fell, splattering against the windshield. Tracy tapped the wipers on Medium, then checked her speed. Twenty-five in a fifty-five. No wonder the sedan whipped around her. She let it get a fair distance ahead of her, and then pressed on the gas.

The Caprice's hood flew up, blinding her.

Startled, she stomped on the brakes, slid on the wet pavement. Grappling for control, she turned into the skid, but the car didn't respond. It lurched off the road. Mud and loose gravel pinged against the undercarriage and fenders. The car fishtailed and slammed into the ditch, nose first. Water gushed over the hood, splashed against the windows. Tracy flew forward. Her seat belt snapped tight, dug into her thighs, her chest, knocking the breath out of her. Her forehead cracked against the steering wheel. Pain exploded inside her skull, and she screamed.

The car abruptly stopped.

Woozy, she shook her head to clear her vision. The Caprice had seated itself inside the muddy ditch. Water lapped at the car doors, and the ditch walls were too close; no way could she open the door to get out.

The window. She'd get out through the window.

Power windows.

The car wouldn't crank; the engine was submerged under frothy, gushing water. "Oh, God." Her hand shaking violently, panic clawing at her stomach, she again turned the key.

Nothing happened.

She had to get out of the car. One way or another, she had to get out, or drown.

Frantically searching for anything she could use to break the window, she found only the crumpled note, threatening her. Angry, outraged, she pulled off her pump, released her seat belt, and beat at the window with the heel of her shoe.

The window cracked. Safety glass. It didn't shatter.

She kept pummeling at the glass, urgently, hysterically, until she had hammered an opening large enough to crawl through, then tapped down protruding sharp slivers so she didn't spear herself. Rushing water slapped at the sides of the car, splashed inside, running in rivulets down the door panels to the floorboard and sloshed, already ankle-deep. More weight inside would cause the car to sink. The ditch was dirt; saturated mud was soft. If she didn't hurry, she would end up buried and unable to get out. She beat at the slivers, harder, faster, darting a panicky gaze toward the street, praying someone would appear and help her.

Where the hell was the driver of that sedan? He had to have seen her accident. Why hadn't he stopped?

Fear turned to anger. ''No one wants to get involved. No one cares about anything that doesn't directly affect them. Not anymore.'' Hearing herself shouting, she couldn't seem to stop. She grabbed the floormat, draped it over the opening, then dragged herself through the window, feeling the ragged, cracked glass scrape the mat against her stomach, her thighs. She tumbled out into the ditch, landing chin first in the muddy water with a hard thump.

Relieved, hugging the muddy ditch wall, she lifted her face to the rain, and laughed out loud. She'd done it! She'd gotten out!

Thunder crackled. Lightning streaked through the sky, striking a tall pine not a hundred feet from her.

She had to get out of the water. Crawling on her hands and knees, sliding in the mud, fighting the force of the gushing water, the steep slope of the ditch, she worked her way around to the car's hood—and snagged her finger on raw metal. It stung. A bright streak of blood zagged down her index finger. What had cut her?

The hood latch. Its dull metal gleamed shiny, and it was scored.

Someone had deliberately weakened her hood latch.

This had been no accident.

Chapter 9

It had been a day from hell and, from all signs, a night from hell would follow.

An Air Force standard-issue blue sedan like the one that hadn't stopped at Tracy's accident sat parked across the street in the dark shadows between the street lamps. She stared out at it from between the slats in her living room window's blinds. Who was watching her? Why?

Maybe Colonel Hackett had discovered the bug in his office.

No, if he had, she wouldn't be watched. She'd be arrested. And she'd been tempted to but she hadn't reported the accident or the threats to the OSI or the base MPs. Maybe that decision hadn't been wise. What if she ended up dead before learning the truth about Adam?

Unless I'm one-eighty out . . . you'll need to disappear.

A cold chill shimmied up her spine. She crossed her chest with her arms and rubbed hard, again missing the perk of having a man in her life. If Adam were alive, would he be there for her now? She'd bet her bars that Adam, unlike Randall, wouldn't be a fair-weather friend and desert her at the first sign of trouble.

That was a safe bet. With his family and ex-wife? No way would he cut and run. The man had been bred, born, and had died in mountains of discord and political adversity and still he had called to warn her because he had been worried and had left her everything he had. Adam would have been there for her. But he was dead.

Dead.

Just before dawn, the sedan pulled away from the curb and disappeared down the street. Exhausted from the all-night vigil, Tracy still had no idea who was watching her. She checked and double-checked the locks on the windows and doors, then crawled into bed and collapsed against the pillows, again thinking of Adam.

He would be different from Paul or Randall. Supportive, but not pushy. Intense, but dependable in all things. What he'd done for her proved that. Guilty or innocent, the man knew how to make a woman feel special. Tracy tucked the covers up under her chin. Had he ever felt special? Loved? He hadn't with his family or, according to Janet, with his ex-wife, Lisa. It seemed the worst cruelty a man could suffer, to die feeling unloved.

Tracy closed her eyes and imagined him in bed with her, holding her, making her feel safe and protected, and her stroking him, making him feel loved. At least once, everyone should feel loved. They whispered back and forth, talking of everything and nothing, sharing childhood secrets and fears and desires. Feeling his strong arms around her, his warm kisses arousing her, making her feel desirable and wanted, she drifted into her dreams.

What now? Tracy stepped into her office and closed the door.

Janet's perfume smelled subtle, but the woman seated at Tracy's desk clearly had raising hell on her mind, and Tracy would prefer the entire JAG office didn't hear it. "Whatever it is, break it to me gently." She stuffed her purse into her bottom desk drawer. "I survived the night from hell, but I'm still shaky."

Glaring at her, Janet tossed a stack of messages down on the desk. The pink slips scattered. "You got six phone calls this morning. Six. All threats." Worry twisted Janet's expression and she propped a hand on her slim hip. "How long has this been going on?"

Bloody hell. Plopping down on the chair Janet vacated, Tracy stared at the ivy on her credenza. It needed water; its leaves were drooping. "Since the day after I got the Burke assignment."

"What?" Janet screeched.

Tracy darted her gaze toward the door. "Will you calm down before you have Jackson committing both of us to a mental hospital?"

"Calm down?" Janet dumped a glass of water into the ivy's brass bowl. "I should wring your neck."

"Now look who's slinging threats."

Janet whirled around on her. "These are serious, damn it."

"I know that now." Tracy swiped her hair back from her face and sipped at a steaming mug of strong coffee Janet had placed on her desk. "I knew after the car accident yesterday."

"*Car accident?*" Janet's jaw gaped and her knees folded under her. Fortunately, she was standing right in front of Tracy's visitor's chair. "I think you'd better start at the beginning—and don't leave anything out."

Tracy told Janet about the accident, the threatening calls, the sedan parked in front of her house all night, and about the sensation of being followed everywhere she went. "I have no proof of that, but—"

"Instincts become attuned to these things." Janet rubbed at her cheek. "Intel rule is to trust them."

Grateful for the support, Tracy nodded. "Then I got up this morning and found my garden had been destroyed." Her chest went tight. "Every single blossom, sickled down."

"I'm sorry." Empathy filled Janet's eyes. "I know it was your special place."

"Yeah." Tracy dragged in a steadying breath. "And Anderson's Garage called right afterward. The Caprice is totaled." Maybe she should have told the police about the hood latch being scored.

"Have you called your insurance carrier?"

Tracy nodded. "I directed all inquiries to Anderson's Garage." If they disclosed the weakened hood latch, then she'd pay the elevated insurance premiums now. If not, she'd suffer the pangs of conscience for delaying that disclosure until after the Burke matter was settled and the threats stopped. Then she'd make restitution and pay the difference in premiums. No sense in giving the promotion board or selection committee anything else to hold against her. They had plenty of fodder already. "I came in hell-bent on reporting all of this to the OSI."

Janet dipped her chin and looked up at Tracy from under her lashes. "So, are you going to?"

"I don't know. I'm torn." Tracy swallowed down some hot coffee, inhaled the steam rising from her cup. "I've made zero progress at uncovering the truth about Adam, and reporting all of this could keep me from ever finding out anything. But I'm angry. I feel . . . hunted." *And as alone in the world as Adam must have felt.* Tracy didn't fear living her life, but she did fear living it alone. She hated it with conviction. "Damn it, I don't know what to do."

"Adam?" Janet cocked a wary brow.

"That is the man's name, Janet." It couldn't be wrong to want to matter to someone, to want someone to matter to you.

Janet rubbed her lower lip with a hot-pink nail decorated with a silver stripe, but didn't comment further. Grateful, Tracy considered trying to explain, but she'd dreamed of making love with the man, and considering Janet felt strong ties to the team members he supposedly killed, she'd never understand. Wiser to move back to safer ground. "If I file the report, once the OSI hears Burke is involved, they won't be any more receptive than any one else has been, and the promotion board will definitely add 'unable to handle pressure and intense situations' to their 'too young and idealistic' listing of my flaws."

Janet turned thoughtful. "The selection committee won't be any less harsh, either."

"My feelings exactly." Tracy grunted and set down her coffee cup. "Even Paul has been riding my back, telling me to get out of the line of fire."

"He just wants you to come back to New Orleans."

"Hell will freeze over first, and he knows it." She'd lost her family there. Every street corner held too many memories. "But he's still gearing up to do some major interfering. After a while, you pick up on the signs. Paul is wonderful, but he tends to dominate." Adam had been right about that, and it had played a part in her joining the Air Force.

"Don't feel guilty for not wanting him to run your life, Tracy. You loved Matthew, but he's dead and you're not. You have every right to go on—without Paul's interference."

"I know." She pulled out her secret fear and exposed it. "It sounds unappreciative, but at times I think his attempts to protect me are actually attempts to control me."

"Considering he didn't get into government contracts until after you did, which gave you no choice but to transfer out, I'd say that's a distinct possibility."

"Maybe he didn't understand the conflict of interest."

"Oh, please. The man runs an empire," Janet said without heat. "He just doesn't want to let go."

That didn't feel quite right, yet something in Janet's assessment struck a chord. "He's an intelligent man. Why can't he understand?" Tracy let her gaze slide away, to the window mural on the south wall. "Sometimes you just can't go back. Some hurts just cut too deep."

"You're all he's got. Maybe he's afraid you won't need him anymore." Janet grimaced. "Whatever you do, don't get noble and marry the man. You'll never love him, and you'd be miserable married to a man already married."

"Paul isn't married."

"Yes, he is. To Keener Chemical."

Janet had Tracy there. Nothing mattered to Paul more than the family business. Nothing. She turned the topic. "So do I report these threats?"

"If you do, you'll lose more than you'll gain." Janet looked annoyed by that. "Burke is dead, Tracy. His own family won't even attend his funeral. I vote you let it go. All of it."

"I wish I could. God knows it would make my life easier, but I can't."

"Because it's not right?"

She knew Tracy too well. "Because he was a soldier, and many times during his service to this country, he put his life on the line. Finding out the truth is a matter of honor. Adam died branded as a coward and a traitor, but we don't know for fact that he was either. We don't *know* it, Janet."

"Honey, even if Adam Burke was as pure as fresh-fallen snow, he'll still be dead. Clearing his name won't change that, but it could get you murdered. Whoever is behind this isn't playing games. They've been warning you, but if you don't listen, they'll get serious. Dead serious."

"I don't even know if all of this is being done by one person. The incidents and threats could be unrelated."

"They could be, but why stake your life on it?" Janet walked to the office door, then grasped the doorknob. She looked down at it, not back at Tracy. "I don't have many friends. Lots of acquaintances, but few friends," Janet said softly. "I don't want to lose you."

"Me, either." Touched, Tracy smiled. "How did you know Adam's family won't be at the funeral?"

"Chaplain Rutledge called. We chatted." Janet shrugged. "The service is tomorrow at two." Fear lit the depths of her eyes. "Don't go to it, Tracy. There'll be hell to pay."

She hated worrying Janet, but how could Tracy not go? She could have been responsible for his death. His family wouldn't be there, and she seriously doubted any of his coworkers would be. "I'll consider it."

"In other words, you're going." Janet grimaced. "Damn it, it's that nobility thing again, isn't it?"

"No." Tracy admitted the truth. "It's not."

"Then what is it?"

"Guilt," Tracy said on a whisper. "And regret."

Chapter 10

Rain spit down on the black canopy hovering over Adam Burke's coffin.

Tracy stood in the wet grass, to the left of his bronze casket. Chaplain Rutledge, a thin man about forty wearing the vestments of a Catholic priest, stood at its top, his dark head bowed, his glasses slipping to the end of his rain-soaked nose, his expression suitably solemn.

There was no honor guard. No U.S. flag draped Adam's coffin. No guns saluted, no planes flew an honorary flyby. No wreaths on wire stands littered the ground under the canopy, or spray of flowers rested on the barren top of his coffin. There were no flowers at all, except for the single white rose in Tracy's hand. And there were no mourners.

Not a single soul stood at his grave, weeping because Adam had died and he would be absent from their life.

Those entrusted by his family to arrange his final resting place hadn't seen fit to bury him in a veteran's cemetery, or even in the veteran's section of Peace Cemetery; the only cemetery in Grandsen. He had been denied even that—*without being adjudged.*

That injustice sickened and saddened Tracy, leaving her feeling as bleak as the dreary weather. She looked down the long rows of white crosses and tombstones, holding her umbrella closed at her side, squeezing its handle. Pity swelled inside her. Pity for Adam, and anger at everyone who had let this happen.

Her eyes stinging, the back of her nose burning, she bowed her head and silently swore, *I will find out the truth, Adam Burke. I swear, I will.* And then she prayed for peace; for him, and for herself. Prayed that in learning the truth, she would prove the fire had been accidental, that Adam hadn't been murdered because she hadn't taken his warning seriously. And she prayed her hands wouldn't forever be stained with his blood.

A cold gust of air chilled her skin. Her thoughts tumbled back five years, to the night of her accident. She should have realized Matthew had had too much to drink; she had been stone sober. She had no excuse for not realizing it. None. And he and Abby had died . . .

"Ashes to ashes . . ." The chaplain committed Adam's soul to God, and finished with a whispered, "Amen."

Tracy stepped forward and placed the single rose on top of Adam's coffin. A tear dripped down her cheek.

Surprise flickered through Chaplain Rutledge's eyes. He stepped away, to the edge of the canopy. Rain slanted under its edge, soaking him from the knees down. "Captain Keener, why are you weeping?" he asked, his voice soft and gentle. "I understood that you didn't know Adam Burke well."

She stepped over to him, a knot of tears in her throat. All afternoon, thoughts of Matthew's and Abby's funerals—funerals Tracy hadn't attended because she'd been hospitalized—had tormented her. She hadn't been there at the cemetery to mourn them, just as no one had been here to mourn Adam Burke. Why she had mentally tied her own family to a man accused of the most heinous crimes, she had no idea, and yet she couldn't seem to sever the two. "He's been condemned in everyone's eyes, and yet no one knows whether or not he's guilty," she told Chaplain Rutledge. "His own family turned their backs on him—his country, too. And if he wasn't guilty, he deserves better."

"As I suspected." Chaplain Rutledge held his Bible in front of him with both hands. Not as a shield between them, but as if it were a cherished, familiar friend. "Your being here had nothing to do with the money."

How had he known about Adam's bequest? "I can't keep the money."

"Oh, but you must keep it." He glanced around the cemetery, down its winding gravel road, and then looked back at her. "At Adam's request, I arranged for the preparation of those documents, Captain. What he did was his choice, and he made it."

She cocked her head to look up at him. "Do you know why?"

Clearly thoughtful, the chaplain touched a hand to her arm. "No, I don't. But I'm certain he had his reasons, and we should respect them." The chaplain's gaze softened. "For whatever comfort it might bring you, know that the One Who matters most knows the truth, and He hasn't condemned Adam unjustly. No truth escapes the light, Captain. Faith and hope shall flood even the darkest crevice, and the truth shall spill forth like sunlight and shine."

As those words left his mouth, the chaplain blinked, then blinked again, as if he'd stumbled onto some grand realization. He gently squeezed her arm. "That's why you're here, Tracy. You're Adam's sun."

A tingle streaked from her arm to her heart. *She* was Adam Burke's sun? But she'd failed the man repeatedly. She lifted her gaze to the chaplain's, suffering a twisting, almost painful, urge to pour out her fears about failing Adam, her regret, and that she had likely caused his death.

Trust no one else.

She bit down on her lips, ashamed to admit the truth aloud and to find solace in silence and reason from Adam to not have to admit the truth. But even without the advice in his note, living with these feelings was painful enough. She couldn't admit this aloud, either; she wasn't that strong.

The rain pounded a staccato beat against the vinyl canopy. "Tracy," the chaplain said, elevating his voice to be heard above it. "Expand your thinking. Forgive yourself for the wrongs you believe you've done this man, and focus now on what you can do for his memory."

"Thank you, Chaplain." She opened her umbrella and noted he hadn't brought one. "I'll walk you to your car."

Chaplain Rutledge offered her a gentle smile, looped his arm through hers, and then began walking across the grass to the gravel road, toward their cars. "That *is* why you're here, Tracy. To be Adam Burke's sun."

The rain sprinkled against the side of her face and gravel crunched under her shoes. "I wish he'd chosen someone competent."

"He did." The chaplain stopped at the door of his car. "You follow your heart."

Her convictions, yes. But her heart? She stared at him, long and hard. It would take some time for her to absorb all he had told her and yet she had no trouble absorbing the feelings that had come with his words. The truth hadn't yet spilled forth from the dark crevices. But it would, through her —if she dared to follow her heart.

Oh, that was asking a lot. So much. Too much.

"If you'd like to talk, you can reach me through the base chapel," Chaplain Rutledge said, getting into his car.

"Thank you." Tracy backed up a step, and watched him drive away.

When he rounded the first curve on the winding road, she turned toward her rental car—and saw a blue sedan. It sat parked beneath an oak limb that encroached over the road. Through the thick leaves, she saw a man behind the wheel.

Her heart thudded hard. Had he been following her? This was the third time she'd seen a standard-issue sedan. She couldn't say it was the same one—they all looked alike—but determined to find out who was in this one, she left the gravel path and cut across the grass to the car.

Stopping a safe distance away from the driver's window, she tilted her umbrella back and looked inside. Gus O'Dell.

If Adam had told the truth, O'Dell had changed his orders and he'd have a storehouse of reasons for not wanting her to investigate further—and for following her. A cold chill slithered up her back. "Major," she said, the heels of her pumps sinking in the soft mud. She pulled the left one loose. It made a sucking sound, and she glanced down. The shoes were ruined. "Why didn't you attend the service?"

His sour expression didn't change. "I have no respects to pay, Captain."

Rain pelted her hip. She shifted the umbrella to block it. "Then why are you here?"

"Just verifying the bastard's dead and buried." O'Dell's gaze hardened. He draped an arm loosely over the steering wheel, and his tone turned bitter, accusing. "Why are you here?"

She swallowed back an angry response. "Oh, I don't know, sir. Maybe because I'm his attorney and he wasn't proven guilty. Or maybe because concepts like compassion and mercy and forgiveness appeal to me. Or maybe I was just curious and I wanted to see who would stand up and give the man the benefit of doubt. That is one of the principles we military types fight for, isn't it, sir?" She grunted and lifted a hand, knowing she was going too far; knowing it, but unable to stop herself. This treatment of Adam cut too deeply into her beliefs. "And I did see, didn't I? No one. Not one single person gave Adam Burke anything. Not the benefit of doubt, not mercy, and certainly not compassion. Says a lot about us as people, doesn't it, sir?"

"Yes, it does—for our collective good judgment and

our lack of tolerance for those who mock the very things we fight to defend.''

"Don't I wish. But I believe indifference is more accurate.'' Tracy lifted her chin. "You know, I can stomach people being for or against the man based on beliefs. But indifference?'' She let out a little grunt. "Indifference is the worst insult of all.''

O'Dell's expression became grim. He keyed the ignition, and the engine roared to life. "I suggest you get your emotions under control, Captain. Some clients deserve your righteous indignation, but Burke wasn't one of them.''

Before she could remind O'Dell that every American wronged was worth righteous indignation, he stomped the accelerator. The sedan swerved down the road, its spinning tires spewing gravel that stung her shins. Refusing to let the likes of Major Gus O'Dell reduce her to rubbing her locket, she crossed an arm over her chest, and muttered, "Sanctimonious bastard.''

Scrutinizing him until O'Dell drove out of sight, she returned to her car, still seething.

Someone's watching.

The familiar sensation crept through her. Goose bumps peppered her skin. What had alerted her senses this time? Chaplain Rutledge and O'Dell had left. Except for her, the cemetery was deserted.

No, it's not. You're being stalked.

Her hands shaking, she locked the doors and cranked the engine, knowing her instincts were right.

Chapter 11

Bone-picking time evidently had arrived.

Ted leaned against the frame of his office door, his arms akimbo, his expression stony.

Bloody hell. She didn't need this. Not today. And never from Ted.

He'd entered the Air Force on a direct appointment, which meant *with* Career Status, and he was definitely on the promotion fast track. He'd made major below the zone, and according to Janet, he'd make lieutenant colonel early, too. Ted suffered no worries about his military longevity.

Envy slithered through Tracy. She tamped it. Ted didn't mingle much, but his professional sagacity had earned him esteem, and since she'd bailed him out of a touchy situation with an irate contractor threatening to sue because he'd lost out on a project bid, Ted had gone out of his way to be nice to her. He felt he owed her, but he didn't. She'd just been doing her job: protecting the interests of the United States.

What had him steamed at her?

He waylaid her in the hallway outside his office. "Did you go to Burke's funeral?"

The troublemakers, Richard and Samuel, rode hard on Ted's heels. "She did," Richard answered. "She's tracking cemetery dirt all down the hall." He forked a hand through his curly blond hair. "Are you nuts, Keener?"

"Only when provoked." She tried to pass them, but standing shoulder to shoulder, they blocked the entire hall.

"You're making us all look bad." Samuel laid a glare on her that could melt iron. "Burke was a coward. You had no business going to his funeral."

Are you really going to take this? Fluff.

Remembering Adam's taunt got to Tracy in a way none of the JAG officers' jabs could get to her. She stiffened and focused on Ted. "I'm Adam Burke's attorney, and I went to his funeral because I felt it was right. Are you forgetting the man wasn't adjudged guilty?"

Richard grunted. "Christ, Keener. Do you have to witness a murder firsthand to believe one happened?"

"I need indisputable evidence. And before you condemn a man, you're supposed to need it, too." She wheeled her gaze from Richard back to Ted. "Ironic, isn't it? All three of you devote your professional lives to preserving freedom, and yet you feel so damn righteous in snatching it away. Is it something you ration out when the mood strikes you?"

Samuel glared at her. "Any of us could have been tagged for this assignment, but you're going too far. Burke made a mockery of everyone in uniform, and you're idolizing him. You're making us all look like bleeding-heart idiots."

Bleeding-heart idiots? She chilled her voice. "You disagree with what I did. Fine. But I suggest you exercise caution in judging me. Someone might come along and hold you up to your own standards, and I don't think you could stand the scrutiny."

Angry and treacherously close to exploding, she pushed through their human barricade and strode into her office. *Damn it. Why do I let them get to me?*

"I heard," Janet said from her desk. "The office politics will be sheer hell."

"I know, I know. You told me so." Because the crimes had been committed against fellow officers, the

JAGs took her attending Adam's funeral as a personal slight. "And you were right. I'll be eating dirt for months," she said in Janet's general direction, then stepped into her office and slammed the door shut.

She slumped in her desk chair and buried her face in her hands. "Self-righteous jerks. Pompous—"

Her office door creaked open. She schooled her expression, and looked up.

Ted strode in, looking ready to commit murder. "I want to talk to you."

Tracy straightened in her chair. "If you've been selected office spokesperson to read me the riot act for calling you three down on the carpet, save your breath. You damn well deserved it."

Ted stuffed his hands into his pockets. "You're stepping on my toes, Tracy."

"Be grateful I'm not stomping on them." She glared up at him, unwilling to back down. "That little attack out in the hall was inexcusable, and you might recall that I've saved your toes a couple of times, too. I don't expect your gratitude for doing my job, but I damn well expect a little latitude. How dare you criticize my actions? Especially when you don't have a clue in hell why I'm doing what I'm doing, and you haven't even bothered to ask."

The starch left Ted's shoulders. "Look, I was out of line, okay? I was pissed about something else, and I just unloaded." He stuffed his hands in his pockets and stared at her, locked in some mental debate. "I shouldn't say anything about this, but it's because you've saved my toes that I have to." Worry flooded his eyes. "You're in real trouble, Tracy."

"What are you talking about?" And why did she have this awful feeling she was going to hate it?

"We both know the Burke case assignment was a by-name request from General Nestler, and Burke left you his entire estate. What I know and you don't is why Nestler tagged you to defend Burke." Ted lifted his gaze from the star paperweight to her. "An officer specifically asked Nestler to assign you, Tracy. I was in the office and heard the general's call firsthand. He didn't solicit the officer's recommendations or request suggestions. That's significant, considering the officer was Colonel Hackett."

"Hackett?" Burke's boss? Surprised, Tracy stilled. "Why would he care?"

"That, I don't know." Ted braced a hip on her credenza, brushing against the ivy leaves. "But he *never* does anything without a reason."

What reason? What did this mean? "So Hackett's request is why I'm in real trouble?"

"No." Ted shifted his weight. The credenza's legs creaked. "You're in real trouble because you're stepping on my toes."

Tired of riddles, she elevated her voice. "How the hell am I doing that?"

"By sticking your nose in my project."

She lifted her hands. "What project?"

Ted's jaw snapped tight. "I know you're damn good with contracts on cutting-edge technology, and that if it weren't for your brother-in-law bidding on so many projects, you'd still be doing them. But he is doing them, and you're not. I'm counsel on Project Duplicity, and I'm telling you to keep your nose out of it. You'll cost me making light colonel below the zone."

"A man is dead and you're worried about making lieutenant colonel early? Get a grip, Ted." Resentment and disappointment flickered in his eyes, and the truth hit her like a sledge to the back of the head. "There's a connection between Adam Burke's case and Project Duplicity. That's what you're telling me."

The resentment faded. "I'm not telling you anything except that you're stepping on my toes and I don't like it. You're exceeding your authority, Captain."

Ted pulling rank? How atypical. How interesting. "A

man's reputation is worth the excess, Major. Live with it. Better yet, help me find out the truth.''

"I can't." The anger leaked out of Ted's voice. "Things are happening here that you don't understand."

"Obviously." She rocked back. "Enlighten me."

He scowled at her. "I'd have to breach security, and you know it. You're not the only JAG with ethics."

"Of course I'm not. But tell me, Ted." She softened her voice. "Just what are you afraid I'm going to find out?"

Their gazes met and locked. A tense moment passed. Then, without a word, he turned to walk out of her office.

Damn it. "If you want me to stay off your toes, you'd better tell me how my case connects to your project. I won't be held responsible for crossing a line I can't see."

He glanced back at her, worry pulling the lines in his face taut. "I don't know how they're connected. But if you try to figure it out, know going in that you'll be risking a lot more than just your career."

She nearly fell out of her chair. "Are you threatening me, Ted?"

"I'm warning you." His eyes turned solemn. "Friend to friend."

That knocked the wind out of her sails. He was project counsel and he honestly didn't understand the connection himself. This wasn't a case of "I could tell you but then I'd have to kill you." Ted *didn't* know.

Trying to key in on what he sensed, she began quizzing him. "Is Project Duplicity ready for funding?" Weeks away from year-end, it had to be close, if not waiting in the wings for its turn at bat before Congress.

"Everything has been ready for a couple months except the clinical-study findings."

"Cutting it kind of close on the timing, aren't they?" If not ready by fiscal year-end, Congress wouldn't consider funding the project for another year.

"There was a snag," Ted said. "But the program manager says it's cleared now. I expect the studies in the next couple of days.''

"I see," Tracy said, wishing she did see. What was the connection? She could question Ted on the project, but it was classified. Pushed, he might or might not tell her, but he would resent it. Shoe on the other foot, so would she.

Ted stared at the door, his back to her. "I can't tell you what you want to know. I can tell you I have a bad, bad feeling about this.''

Sharing his bad feeling, she watched Ted walk out the door.

Certain she was coming down with a cold, Tracy pored over Adam's file and everything she could legally examine on Project Duplicity. Unfortunately, there wasn't much. Just the log assigning Ted as counsel and his hours spent on the project.

Someone rapped on her office door, then immediately opened it. Janet.

She walked in talking. "Colonel Jackson's gotten word you went to Burke's funeral. He wants you to report to his office now.''

"Terrific." Tracy permitted herself a groan. "What next?''

"Hey, where's your locket?" Janet pointed the tip of her pencil at Tracy's neck.

Tracy reached for it, but her locket was gone. "Oh, God." She sneezed. "I know I had it on at the funeral." Had she lost it there? "I've got to find it, Janet. I *need* that locket.''

"Go placate Jackson." Janet passed Tracy the tissue box. "If the locket's here, I'll find it.''

Feeling naked, vulnerable, Tracy swiped at her nose with a tissue and left the office, dreading the coming confrontation with her boss. Scared stiff that she had signed her own career death warrant, she ignored numerous nasty looks coming her way from the other JAGs. Evidently Samuel and Richard had been busy spreading the news through the whole damn building.

She stepped into the colonel's outer office, wishing she'd changed her shoes. Even furious, Jackson would notice the mud.

His secretary, Peggy, a neat freak equal to the colonel himself, ushered her into Jackson's inner sanctum without so much as a courtesy greeting. Tracy supposed her silence adequately expressed Peggy's disdain.

"She's here, Colonel." Stepping aside, Peggy darted Tracy a reprimanding look.

Ignoring it, Tracy faced the colonel. "You asked to see me, sir?"

"Yes, I did."

He didn't suggest that she sit down which, if she hadn't already been expecting it, would have been her first clue that she was in for a class-A ass-chewing.

"Well, Captain Keener." He leaned back in his chair and folded his arms across his chest. "It appears you've been busy."

"No more so than usual, sir." No way would she respond specifically to such a general remark. He might not yet know just how busy she had been.

"Let me make this simple," he said. "The Burke case is closed. You've been issued a direct order, as I understand it, to close the file. You've elected not to do so. Since I didn't personally hear that order, and mine wasn't expressly stated as a direct order, I backed you, but let it suffice to say that the men upstairs are not happy."

She wasn't exactly thrilled herself. "Sir, I think—"

"You'll think, Captain," he interceded, his face blotching red, "what I order you to think. Do you realize how Burke leaving you his entire estate makes this office look?"

So much for Jackson's compassion. "I can't be held accountable for his actions, sir. Only my own. And I've done nothing wrong." She shifted on her feet. "Aren't you interested in why he left everything to me?"

Jackson looked as if he wanted to shake her. "It's a tactic to make you feel guilty, Captain. Obviously it worked, or you would have had better sense than to go to his funeral."

Tracy stared at him, defiant. "You realize you're ordering me to brand one of our own as guilty without knowing for fact he committed any crime."

Jackson scowled. "Look, Keener, off the record, I agree with you. But you're ticking off some powerful people who can end both our careers. Either way, Burke's is already over. I've backed you until now, but this is it. A direct order. Close the file and forget it, refuse the bequest—and clean up your damn shoes."

Offended, Tracy bristled. But through her resentment, she saw the truth. He feared Hackett and Nestler.

Tracy understood that fear. Hell, she felt it herself. But she wouldn't lie and say she would stop investigating when she knew in her heart she wouldn't. "I'll take care of the shoes right away," she said. "Sir, may I say something?"

Frustrated and clearly out of patience because she hadn't responded to his direct order with a simple "Yes, sir" agreement, Jackson nodded.

"When I became an officer, I made a commitment. If I fail to follow my convictions, then I lose far more than a promotion or selection for Career Status. I lose my self-respect." She swallowed down a lump lodged in her throat. "That's all, sir. I just wanted you to know."

He slid her an exasperated, earnest look. "Why are you in the Air Force, Keener?"

She gave him a crooked smile. "For the money, sir."

"Right." He grunted. "We're *all* in it for the money."

No professionals joined the military for the money—not unless earning half or less what they could earn in the private sector was their goal. Their reasons ran deeper, flowed over into the ideals of what the country was all about. Things like patriotism, honor, duty—they weren't concepts, they were a chosen way of life.

Looking torn between shaking and hugging her, Jackson nodded. "Dismissed, Captain."

Tracy left his office, praying her knees would hold her up long enough to get her back to her office. Not only did she feel the onset of a horrendous head cold, she had just subtly warned Colonel Jackson she wouldn't obey his direct order, and he hadn't pulled rank on her.

But he could pull rank on her. At any time, he could. An idealist she might be, but she wasn't stupid. And Jackson *would* pull rank on her—the first moment he felt threatened.

Chapter 12

Tracy went home in a black mood.

She slung her uniform blouse on her bed. Not only had she been chewed out, humiliated, and shunned by the other JAGs and their support staff, she'd ruined her new pumps, and she and Janet had failed to find her damn locket.

How was she supposed to deal with anything without her locket? She ditched her skirt, tossed it beside her blouse. It wasn't just that the locket was the last gift Matthew had given her before he'd died, what was in it could never be replaced.

The doorbell chimed.

Standing in her bedroom in her bra and panties, she grabbed the first thing within reach—her flannel robe. Tugging it on, she headed down the hallway. So what if whoever was at the door thought she was certifiable for wearing flannel in August?

Peeking through the peephole, she saw Paul Keener standing on the front porch. His resemblance to Matthew had always been strong, but now it seemed even more so. For a moment, she couldn't breathe. *It's not him. It's Paul. Paul who dominates out of love—even if it drives you crazy.*

A smile curved her lips and she twisted the deadbolt. When it clicked, she pulled open the door. "Paul." She lifted a hand. "Why didn't you tell me you were coming to Mississippi?"

The corners of his mouth curved. He caught her in a bear hug and touched a warm kiss to her cheek. "Ah, Tracy." He pressed a kiss to her forehead. "It's good to see you."

"Careful." She pressed a restraining hand to his chest. "I'm catching a cold."

"It's worth it." He squeezed her tighter. "I've missed you. Talking on the phone once a week isn't the same as seeing you."

Past his shoulder, she saw a white limousine. Leave it to Paul. It wouldn't occur to him to drive himself. Still smiling, she pulled away, and he let her go. He looked so much like Matthew—a blessing and a curse that comforted and disturbed her. Black hair, blue eyes that twinkled whenever he looked at her; a strong face, not angular so much as subtle with quiet strength. She let her gaze drift down to his navy suit, snowy-white shirt, and silk tie. As usual, not a crease out of place. "You look wonderful."

He let his gaze drop from her robe to her bare feet. "You look . . . interesting."

Self-conscious, she felt her face flush hot. "I was changing out of my uniform. It's been a day from hell."

"Ah." He slid her a commiserating look. "You'll need to talk about it, then."

He knew her so well. She'd always worked through her troubles by talking to Matthew. She hadn't expected him to resolve her challenges, only to listen. After he had died, Paul had slipped into Matthew's role. "Let me grab some clothes, and then we'll have a good visit. I'm eager to hear how things are with you."

"Don't change." He loosened his tie—about as informal as Paul Keener ever got. "Let's sit and you can tell me about your day." He suddenly became serious. "I want to talk to you, too."

That was the second time today she had heard that

statement, and if the contents of this talk mirrored those of the first, she swore she'd scream until her lungs gave out.

In the kitchen, she opened the fridge door and peeked inside. "Would you like a beer?" Why was she antagonizing him? He was adorable and good, but a snob who preferred wine.

"A beer sounds . . . interesting." He stood in the doorway and watched her open two bottles, and then pass one to him. "Red Dog?"

She shrugged and walked back to the living room, then sat down on the sofa. "I wanted to give it a try."

He sat down beside her, and took a small sip of beer. From his grimace, he hated it. "It's not bad."

His smile made her suspicious. "Did you drive over from New Orleans just to talk to me?"

"No. I know you're sensitive and I'm respecting your independence, even if I do miss seeing you." He patted her hand. "I'm here on business. One of my project bids."

Glad to hear it, she moved her hand from his under the pretext of taking a sip of beer. Cold, it soothed her raw throat. Why did his simple pat on her hand strike her as a condescending gesture? Surely she was being overly sensitive. "So what did you want to talk to me about?"

He shoved aside an issue of *George,* then set his beer down on the coffee table. The end table's lamp slanted mellow light over his chest, shadowing his eyes. "I'm worried about you."

"Why?" She knew why he should be worried, but he didn't know. Or did he?

"You went to Burke's funeral, Tracy." Paul clasped her hand tightly.

She pulled her fingers free. "Randall asked you to come, didn't he?" Of course he had. She could choke Randall for this.

"He called, yes. But business brought me here." Paul

again captured her hand. "Don't be angry with Randall. He was worried."

"He's overstepped his bounds. We're not even friends now." Hell, she didn't even like the spineless cut-and-run jerk anymore.

"That doesn't mean his concern isn't genuine."

"I don't want his concern." After her last phone conversation with him, she didn't want anything from Dr. Randall Moxley except space. Lots of space—between them.

"I know you're experiencing trouble over this Burke case. And unless you stop pursuing the matter, I'm afraid you're bound for more." Paul gave her hand a gentle squeeze and let her see his worry. "Tracy, you're all I have left. I want you safe and happy. I care about you."

Oh, he was catching her at a weak moment. At a time when she felt as alone as Adam must have felt most of his life. Knowing her locket wasn't there, she reached for it anyway. "I'm doing what I have to do. That's all."

Paul let a smooth fingertip trail down the line of her jaw, temple to chin. "You don't have to do anything. Let me take care of you. You should be dressed in silk and living at Woodwind, not wearing flannel and living cramped in this little house. I can give you everything you want."

He couldn't give her what she wanted most. Not unless he could raise the dead. She wanted her daughter. And to find the truth for Adam. But she couldn't say those things to Paul. And she couldn't admit, not even to herself, how tempted she was to just crawl under his wing and allow him to shelter her. For five years, life had been hard, rife with challenges. Who wouldn't be tempted to escape? Yet his comment about her robe and her house irked her. True, the house was a matchbox compared with Woodwind Manor, but it was her home now, and she loved it in a way she'd never loved Woodwind. Wealth was all Matthew had ever known, and she'd loved him enough to tolerate it, but she'd never adjusted and felt at home at Woodwind.

She'd come to hate the place and Matthew, too, for dying and leaving her. And for Abby. But with time, she had worked through that anger and, more or less, had made peace with it. On occasion, she still had a hard time when she recalled the accident, especially during the holidays. Honestly, holidays were a bitch. But she could never marry Paul or live at Woodwind Manor again. "I love this house. It's mine."

He let her see the apology in his eyes. "I only meant that you deserve more. I'd give you everything, if only you'd let me. And I'd protect you from all this ugliness—"

"This ugliness is life, Paul." Loving and hating him for what he offered her, she rubbed at her temple. "What you're describing is an ivory tower, and I'm no princess. I'm just a woman trying her best to put together a life that offers some fulfillment. I want to contribute something worthwhile. Is that so hard to understand?"

"No, it's what makes you special." He stroked her arm, rubbed tiny circles at the base of her nape, under her hair. "Please don't be angry with me for caring."

"I'm not. Really." She should be, but she couldn't be angry with Paul. He'd been good to her for too many years. A constant in her life when there were no others. She looked into his eyes, eyes so like Matthew's. So different from Adam's. "Most women would love what you're offering me, but—"

"Don't say it. You could be happy, if only you'd give me a chance." A gentle look softened his eyes and he stared at her mouth. "Let me prove how good I can be to you." He bent his head to kiss her.

Slightly repulsed, she backed away.

Paul sighed. "You're my family, Tracy. You belong at Woodwind. Why won't you marry me, and let me take care of you?"

"I belong here." She steeled herself against the pain

in his eyes. "I love you as much as Matthew loved you, and I'm grateful for everything you've done for me. But I'm not in love—"

"Stop." His expression turned solemn and the fine lines at the corners of his eyes deepened. "You're my brother's widow. My only family. I need you as much as you need me. Being in love isn't relevant. Loving is. I love you, and I only want what's best for you."

She was all that Paul had left of Matthew. Tracy finally understood, and her heart ached. God, but she didn't want to hurt him. "You're a wonderful man with a good heart, and those qualities are so rare." Adam would understand what she was saying. After suffering love's absence his whole life, he'd definitely understand. But this was Paul, and he'd never grasp her meaning. Still, she had to try. "You deserve someone who loves you and is in love with you, too. That's what makes a marriage magic, Paul. I can't give that to you. It's just . . . not there."

Hurt clouded his eyes, and she squeezed his hand. "Please try to understand. What you're offering sounds like heaven. But it's not right for me. I know that in my heart, Paul. And because I do, I have to refuse you and do what I think is best for me. You want to protect me, but I need to protect myself."

The lines in his face hardened, his expression turning as grim as his voice. "I will give you anything, everything you want, and you still won't change your mind?"

The man offered her the moon and had the money to provide it, but Tracy couldn't marry him. "I can't. It wouldn't be fair to either of us."

"I won't say I'm not disappointed, but I understand. It's too soon. We'll discuss the matter later." Paul stood up and then walked toward the front door. "For now, please consider heeding my warning about the Burke case. I might not be your husband yet, but I am your brother-in-law. I don't want you to get hurt, and I'm certain Adam Burke can destroy you, even from the grave."

Bloody hell. She'd failed again to close the marriage

issue permanently. Tracy couldn't hold off a frown. "Why do you feel so strongly about the case?"

Paul's eyes glittered. "When you play with fire, darling, you get burned."

He strode down the sidewalk to the street. His driver opened the limo's door, and Paul ducked inside. But even when the door shut and he disappeared behind the dark tinted glass, she felt his anger at her lingering on the porch. Strong, almost smothering her. And it frightened her in a way nothing about Adam Burke ever had.

Leaning against the doorjamb, she watched the limo glide down the street. *When you play with fire, you get burned.* Had Paul referred to her, or to Adam?

The cold Tracy thought she'd been getting turned out to be the flu.

She sat at her desk, wishing she had stayed at home that morning, wishing her head would stop throbbing, and her stomach would stop revolting. The only saving grace was her certainty that she would have to feel better to die.

Clammy, miserable, she cleared her desk, then buzzed Janet to tell her she was skating out.

Ignoring the intercom, Janet burst into Tracy's office, her eyes so energetic they threatened to throw off sparks. "Sergeant Phelps just called."

Her stomach began rumbling again. Tracy fought it. God, but she hated throwing up with a passion. "Who is Sergeant Phelps?"

"He's a friend of Sergeant Maxwell's who works at the hospital in the emergency room."

"Okay." She'd talked with the head of the ER, but he'd told her nothing that would help. Woozy, she resisted the urge to rest her head on her cool desk. "Why is this significant?"

"Phelps said he overheard you discussing Burke with his boss in the ER, and what his boss told you worried Phelps. So he talked it over with Maxwell, who vouched for you and told Phelps to call and tell you about it.''

''Tell me about what? What worried Phelps?'' Nothing about the meeting with Phelps's boss should have aroused concern, much less worry. It'd been an exercise in futility. But maybe Phelps knew where Adam had been brought in from and could resolve the dispute. Adam said Area 14, O'Dell said Area 13.

''Phelps wouldn't give me any specifics. He said when it's safe to meet you, he'll call.''

What was Tracy supposed to make of that? So far, he'd told her nothing, except that he had overheard her conversation with his boss. ''Fine,'' she said, again fighting the urge to throw up.

''Unless you've taken up smoking pot, you've got a fever. Your eyes are glazed.''

''It's the flu.''

''Well, what the hell are you doing here? Trying to get me sick? Go home and go to bed.''

Tracy grabbed her purse. ''I'm on my way.''

Chapter 13

When it's safe to meet, I'll call. When it's safe... I'll call. When it's safe...

Curled up in bed, the tip of a thermometer sticking out of her mouth, Tracy remembered Janet telling her about Sergeant Phelps, the hospital worker friend of Maxwell's who had called with information on Adam's case. The puzzling message Phelps had forwarded to Tracy replayed over and over again in her mind. *When it's safe to meet, I'll call.* Safe for what?

The phone rang.

Tracy pulled the thermometer out of her mouth, read it—101—and considered just letting the phone ring. She'd gotten three crank calls already this morning, and it wasn't yet noon. But it could be Janet phoning with word from Sergeant Phelps. Tracy tapped the TV remote's Mute button and mumbled into the phone, sounding as god-awful as she felt. "Hello."

"Keener, this is Colonel Jackson."

He felt threatened; she could hear it in his voice. *Bloody hell.* "Yes, sir."

"I just got off the phone with Colonel Hackett."

Oh, boy. She grabbed the covers and wadded them in her fist.

"He was not happy, which means I am not happy."

Which means soon I won't be happy. She rolled on her

side, barely resisting the urge to bury her head under her pillow.

"Colonel Hackett is threatening to have you court-martialed."

Court-martialed? For going to a funeral? Tracy looked at the empty pillow beside her and saw Burke's Personnel file. His photo lay on top. *Don't believe it, fluff. He's bluffing.*

"According to Hackett, General Nestler's pet venture goes to Congress for funding in a few days. I can't stress too much the importance of that contract being funded, Captain. The project will impact not only the military but the civilian community. It's a matter of national security, and I heartily recommend you avoid any further action that could jeopardize it, or Hackett won't have to court-martial you. I'll do it myself."

This was the second time allusions had been made that connected Project Duplicity and Adam. First Ted, now Colonel Jackson. "Excuse me, sir, but I don't see the connection between this project and Adam—"

"Of course you don't. Get your idealistic head out of the clouds, Captain. Your zeal is commendable, but your shortsightedness is appalling. Bad press makes obtaining that funding doubtful. Cease and desist all interference now."

The connection was the fear of bad press keeping Duplicity from being funded? "Sir—"

"Shut up, Keener," Jackson shouted, losing any semblance of composure. His breath hissed through the phone line. "I understand your position. I understand your views on duty and honor. Hell, I share most of them. We've talked about this before, but it's clear you aren't in the loop. Accept it. And hold these thoughts. Burke cost the Air Force millions. He stained the reputation of every man and woman wearing a uniform. He elected to forget his pledge to his country to serve and protect. He put his own safety first. He killed four men. And he got exactly what he deserved."

"He deserved to be judged," she said, tight-lipped. "He deserves the truth."

"He was judged, and he got the truth," Jackson shot back. "Burke was guilty, Keener. I believe it. General Nestler, Colonel Hackett, and Major O'Dell also believe it. If we're all convinced, then that should be enough to convince you. You're a junior officer with limited knowledge on this. My last word on this is a question. Do you have the best interests of this country at heart?"

Tracy squeezed her eyes shut. Jackson was cold, logical, and convincing. But he seemed too cold and logical to be honest. Her nerves on edge, her instincts hummed. She lifted Adam Burke's picture, heard his "fluff," and again closed her eyes. "You know I do, Colonel."

"Fine," Jackson said. "Screw up again, and I promise I'll come down on you so hard you'll think you're experiencing the wrath of God." Jackson slammed down the phone.

Tracy jumped. Her ear ringing, she rested her chin on the butt of the receiver and stared into Adam Burke's photographed eyes. She'd made a vow. Now, the value of her word would be tested.

Jackson would crush her. Did she trust herself, the system, and her convictions and keep seeking the truth, or did she fold under pressure like the gutless wonders?

Expand your thinking, Tracy. "*Faith and hope shall flood even the darkest crevice, and the truth shall spill forth like sunlight, and shine. That's why you're here, Tracy. You're Adam Burke's sun . . .*"

Remembering Chaplain Rutledge's words, Tracy lifted her chin and spoke to the photograph. "I won't fold, Adam. No matter how rough or dark it gets, I won't fold."

Janet breezed into Tracy's house through the back door, carrying a white paper sack. "I come bearing food—and advice."

Tracy swiped at her red nose with a tissue, shut the

kitchen door, and tightened the belt of her heavy flannel robe. God, but she couldn't get warm. Her fever had to be raging. "Forget the food. My stomach's at war, and it's losing big. What advice?"

"Sit down while I nuke this chicken soup." Mindful of her nails, which today were lacquered red with a gold star tipping each one, Janet rummaged through the kitchen drawers, and pulled out a spoon. "You look like hell."

"I feel worse." Tracy pulled out a spindle-backed chair and sat down at the table. The sun slanting in through the window above the sink had her squinting— and finally figuring out why Janet was a fanatic about her nails. When in Intel, she couldn't wear them long or decorated. She couldn't do anything to draw attention to herself. Intel people strove to fade into the woodwork. The nails were Janet's locket: her symbol that she now had the freedom to choose.

Janet poured the soup into a bowl, splashing a little on the white-tile counter, then slid the bowl into the microwave and set the timer. When it started humming, she fisted her hands at her sides and her expression turned thunderous. "I know I said I wouldn't, and getting involved isn't any smarter today than it was before, but if you're still interested, I want to help with Adam's case."

That, Tracy never would have expected. "Why?"

"Seeing how the JAGs reacted to your going to Burke's funeral . . . well, it hit me."

"What hit you?" Tracy asked, totally confused. "You expected them to be upset."

Anger and resentment burned in Janet's eyes. "It hit me that Burke might not be guilty. He probably is, but he might not be. He might just have been doing his job, like all the rest of us. And if this happened to him, then it could happen to someone else. It could happen to me."

"Yes, it could," Tracy admitted. "I need you, but I've got to warn you. Helping me won't win you any popularity contests. I've hit more blocks and brick walls than there are at the facility, and I've been issued direct orders to 'close the file and let this nightmare end' by O'Dell and Jackson. I expect looking for the truth will probably cost me a promotion, status selection, and my job. It could cost you yours, too.''

''If I lose my job for finding out the truth, then screw it. I don't want to work there, anyway.''

Satisfaction warmed Tracy inside. But Janet couldn't walk into this without knowing everything. ''You should know too that Adam left everything he had to me.''

Her eyes stretched wide. ''Whatever for?''

''He thought that unless he was one-eighty out, I'd need to disappear. In fact, he said you would help me. That I shouldn't trust anyone except you.''

''Me?'' Surprise flickered through Janet's eyes. ''Why would he suggest me?''

''I suppose because you'd worked together. He knew your capabilities and he knew I trusted you. He said you would know how to make a disappearance happen.''

''True, but he also knew I thought he was guilty as hell. I'd think he'd suggest someone who believed he was innocent.''

Tracy lifted a hand. ''Such as?''

''Mmm, good point.''

Regret laced Tracy's voice. ''He knew I thought he was guilty, too.''

''And he still tried to protect you?''

Tracy nodded.

''Don't you find that odd?''

''Very odd, unless he was innocent.'' Tracy tilted her head. ''Well, still willing to help?''

Janet paused a second, digesting, then slowly nodded. ''I'm in.''

Tracy smiled. Janet knew the risks and was willing to sacrifice for them. Maybe the whole world wasn't going down the tubes. Maybe a few people were left who still cared about more than just themselves. ''Grab a pen. There on the counter, by the grocery list.''

When Janet appeared ready, Tracy reeled off a list of instructions. "Find out what Adam was wearing when the excavation team pulled him out of Area Thirteen. Verify it was Thirteen not Fourteen. Begin running down any chemical gear requisitions—alarms and personal protective gear—and see if you can get a copy of the readiness exercise tape, or at least a transcript of it. Adam said Home Base acknowledged his radio transmission with a 'Roger, Alpha One' response."

Janet tapped the point of her pencil against the pad. "Anyone in particular at Environmental you want me to check with on the requisitions? And what about the timing? A week either side of the exercise?"

"A week should be fine." Tracy swallowed hard and debated. If she told Janet whom Adam had accused, she might bail out, and Tracy desperately needed her expertise. But if Janet was going to bail, better that she do it now. "And, no. No one special to contact. But several special someones to check on." Being totally honest was the right thing. Risky, but right. "Check on Major Gus O'Dell. Lieutenant Carver. Colonel Hackett." Tracy's voice went whisper-soft. "And General Nestler."

"*Nestler?*" Janet's jaw gaped. "Oh, dear God."

Tracy waited a moment for Janet's shock to settle. A swift current of tension permeated the room. Feeling it down to her bones, Tracy stiffened and waited.

Janet stared at her a long minute. When she wadded a bit of her gray silk skirt in her fist, Tracy knew that the possibility of the two of them having to go up against the big guns hadn't escaped Janet. Resolve slid down over her face like a mask. "I'll get started right away."

"Great." Tracy almost sagged in relief. She wasn't cut out for covert work, and she'd have to be a lot more discreet than before. Adam had died. She didn't want another death on her hands. Janet's, or her own.

Janet reached for the phone, checked for a tap. It was clean. "Go take a bath. You'll feel better. I'll make a couple of calls and reheat the soup when you're done."

"Sounds good." Tracy left the kitchen.

Thirty minutes later, when Tracy returned to the kitchen, Janet had gathered a lot of data. "Any word on the Home Base tape?"

"Nothing conclusive," Janet said. "Environmental verified it. There is a thirty-second blank spot."

That *could* have been Burke's transmission and Home Base's "Roger, Alpha One" response. "Was the blank spot before the bomb was dropped?"

"Yes, just before it. And there's more," Janet said. "Environmental called back a few minutes ago. Brad Meager, the guy who handles chemical requisitions, says an alarm had been reported faulty and sent out for repair the day of the Alpha team incident."

The hairs on Tracy's neck stood on end. "Who reported it?"

"Gus O'Dell," Janet said. "The alarm could have been diverted from repair to him."

Implications were building, but they weren't conclusive proof. "It could have been," Tracy agreed. "But was it?"

That was the question they had to answer to have the first bit of concrete proof Adam hadn't lied.

The microwave's bell chimed. Janet removed the steaming bowl of soup, set it on the table, and then passed Tracy a napkin and the spoon. "You eat, I'll talk."

Just the smell had Tracy's stomach grumbling a protest. "I don't think I can."

"Do it anyway," Janet said. "Trust me, honey, you're going to need the strength." She headed back to the counter and put on a pot of coffee. "By the way, who's driving that blue sedan parked across the street?"

"It's back?" Tracy rushed to the front entry, and then peeked out through a gap in the miniblinds' slats. A blue sedan, Air Force standard-issue, sat parked across the street, down two houses. Her heart sank. "I've seen one several times, including at my accident. The jerk didn't

stop. I'm not sure who's been driving them, but O'Dell
was in one at Adam's funeral.''

"Well, O'Dell isn't driving this one," Janet said. "I
didn't recognize the man."

Tracy stumbled back to the kitchen, feeling weak and
queasy. "Hell, it could be anybody. Maybe the OSI.
Jackson threatened to have me court-martialed. Hackett
is on the warpath, and O'Dell is right there with him.''

Janet grabbed a mug from the cabinet and filled it with
hot coffee. "Threatening phone calls and notes, someone
messing with your car, and now you're being followed . . ." She sat down at the table across from Tracy.
"I realize you're sick, but I figure you're bent on contin-
uing this investigation regardless of who is on the warpath or any court-martial threats. Am I right?''

Tracy hadn't told Janet about the note. How had she
known about it? Had it been a warning, not a threat? One
from Janet? Unsure, Tracy considered lying, but this was
Janet, and Tracy trusted her. She nodded. "You're
right.''

Janet put down her cup. "Then it's time to get smart.''

"What?" Tracy sipped at the soup. It burned going
down her throat and hit her stomach as spicy hot as if
she had swallowed a quart of jalapeño peppers.

"You're in dire need of a little strategic Intel and career warfare advice.''

"Career warfare?" Tracy lifted the spoon. "I hate
even the sound of it.''

"You don't have to like it, just be good at it.''

"I'm all ears.''

Janet took a drink of her coffee, then wrinkled her
nose. "When's the last time you ran some vinegar
through your coffeepot, for God's sake? This stuff tastes
like it was boiled for a week in a cauldron.''

"I didn't know you were supposed to." Tracy
shrugged and took another bite of soup. It didn't burn
going down nearly as much as the first bite.

"Now you do." Janet tilted her head, then spent the

next two hours briefing Tracy on operative drills, rules, and tricks of the Intel trade she'd picked up over the years on making discreet inquiries, handling rental cars, checking cars and houses for bombs, and a multitude of other incidental helpful hints for one wanting to survive. "Got it?"

Tracy's head swam. "I'm not sure. Covert methods just don't come natural to me."

"Of course not. Even kids have to learn to lie, Tracy. When you get down to brass tacks, this is no different— except for the reasons making it necessary, of course. You've made a point of living your life walking the straight and narrow. Now, you have to tiptoe out of the sun into the shade a little. It's not going to feel natural or comfortable without experience. The actual art of the craft is, well, an art. It has to be learned just like every other kind of art."

"I'll do my best."

"That's all any of us can do. I wouldn't have given you this little crash course, but you'll need it. I don't want you to get hurt." Janet frowned and dumped her coffee in the sink, looking uncomfortable. "By the way, Randall called the office three times this morning."

"He's trying to make nice." Tracy sipped from her cup. "I chewed him out for recruiting Paul to put pressure on me." The man was a pig, cutting and running and then calling Paul.

"That explains it, then. He doesn't often sound humble. I suggest you let him grovel a while. It's good for the soul."

"Groveling is good for his soul?"

"Not his, darling. Yours." Janet grabbed her purse and briefcase. "Eat, and then go back to bed. I'll check your window and door locks on my way out. These threats have me edgy. So does that sedan."

"Me, too."

"Wanna stay at my place for a while?"

"No, thanks." She dabbed at her chin with her napkin.

"I won't be frightened out of my own home."

Janet nodded knowingly, then went to check the locks.

Tracy sipped soup from her spoon. These days, it seemed she couldn't win, and Adam had nothing else to lose. Four men were dead and everyone wanted someone to blame. Adam was convenient, particularly now that he was dead. But dead or alive, how could any of them, especially Randall—he was a doctor, for God's sake—not care if an innocent man was falsely accused?

Provided Adam is an innocent man.

Her stomach twisted, rioting. Adam would care. She knew it as well as she knew she was going to lose her lunch.

She made it to the bathroom just in time.

After rinsing her mouth, she wobbled her way back to bed. The closed blinds at the windows made her bedroom dark. Physically sick and sick at heart, she clicked on the bedside table lamp.

A thick file folder lay on her pillow.

Her heart thumped a staccato beat. Burke's Intel file. Janet had to have left it here when she'd checked the window and door locks. Damn, she was good. Tracy could never swear under oath where she'd gotten the file. "Smart, Janet. Very smart." Tracy settled back against her pillow and opened the file.

Within minutes, she was engrossed—and impressed— and terror-stricken. Some of his missions had been life-threatening, some near-suicide. All had been dangerous enough to turn hair gray, and there were a lot of them. For Adam, endangering his life had been just another day at the office.

She admired that, but she didn't like it. The reason why glared at her. Motivation in his case. Would a man who routinely risked his life performing missions for his country commit the crimes against his country that Adam had been accused of committing?

She mulled over the possibility and her eyelids grew heavy, then heavier. She needed sleep but fought it, want-

ing to keep reading about Adam. He really was a re-
markable man . . .

Startled awake by the phone, Tracy jerked, scattering
the papers from Adam's file that had been spread across
her chest. She fished for the receiver and found it buried
in her tangled bed coverings. "Hello."

"Tracy Keener?" a man asked.

"Yes?" Her worry alarm sounded. The man was a
stranger; she didn't recognize his voice.

"It's safe."

When it's safe to meet, I'll call. Sergeant Phelps, Maxwell's friend from the hospital's emergency room.
"Where and when?"

"Right away," he said. "Fourth floor, rooftop patio."

She didn't have to ask what building. She knew he
meant the hospital.

"They lied to you, Captain." He sounded shaky, extremely agitated and nervous. "And I think they're lying
to everyone else, too—including me."

Chapter 14

For security reasons, the lights remained on around the clock in the hospital waiting rooms. Tracy had learned that bit of trivia on a former case, and tonight, she was glad to see the policy in effect. She was worried enough about making this meeting with Phelps without having to do it locketless *and* in the dark.

Still under construction, the fourth floor was deserted and eerily quiet. Orange tape and floor cones blocked off the staff elevator, new carpeting lay uninstalled in rolls against the walls, and with every step, her sneakers lightly squeaked on the concrete floor. The wallpapering was half-done, and signs taped to the door frames warned: Wet Paint.

The fumes and paper paste burned her nose. Twitching it, Tracy stepped inside what would be the nurse's station for Four North and scanned past a low row of white cabinets to a tinted glass door, leading outside. A halogen lamp burned there, slanting light across the concrete floor and up the six-foot-high stucco walls. Clearly, this was the rooftop patio.

A red sign with white lettering that read "Automatic" was stuck to the tinted glass at eye-level and a sensor camera had been attached to the wall above the frame. She stepped closer, in front of the sensor's electronic eye, but the door didn't open. Maybe it wasn't yet operative.

To the left, she spotted a light switch on the wall. Was

it for the overhead fluorescent, or for the door? It could be either. In case of a lock-down, the hospital had to have a way to deactivate the motion sensors. Yet if it was for the overhead lights, turning it on could summon Security. Taking the risk rattled her, but what other option did she have?

Sweat beaded at her temples. Before she could talk herself out of it, she flipped the switch.

The door slid open.

Blowing out a breath she hadn't realized she'd held, she rubbed at her stomach. Her muscles were still in knots about coming here. It was definitely stupid on Janet's Smart-Factor scale. She stepped halfway outside. A chill wind hit her in the face. About thirty by twenty feet, the patio was as deserted as the rest of the fourth floor. The only things out there were two white metal tables and matching chairs, and an urn-type ashtray—an odd thing to see at a hospital these days. It probably wouldn't be there postconstruction. Too many lawsuits to risk having smoking areas anymore. Was there a camera above the outside of the door as well as inside it? She looked up, spotted one, then stepped out into the sultry night.

The door slid shut behind her.

Wobbly from flu and nerves, she sat in a chair facing the door, hoping Phelps hadn't changed his mind and coming here hadn't been a mistake.

Minutes trickled by. Twenty of them. Sick and uneasy as hell, she accepted it. Phelps was a long shot that hadn't panned out. A no-show. Something, or someone, had scared him off. As spooked as he had been on the phone, it wouldn't have taken much. Damn it. Couldn't she get a single break in this case?

The door opened. A small man about forty, balding and wearing thick black glasses, stepped outside, wearing a white uniform and sneakers. ''Captain Keener?'' he whispered.

''Yes.'' She stood up.

''Don Phelps.'' The wind lifted his collar, blowing it

against his neck. ''Sorry about the timing on this. I had to be sure it would be safe. I've got a wife and two kids counting on me.''

''I understand. This is a touchy case and getting involved in it carries a lot of risks.''

Phelps nodded emphatically. ''Max tells me you'll protect me as a source.''

Sergeant Maxwell, the guard from the facility. ''I will.''

''All right, then. I don't have long—I told them I had to run down to the lab—so let me get to the point. I was working in the ER the night they brought Adam Burke in. He was out cold—clearly drugged—though that wasn't put into the records.''

''Why would it be omitted?'' If Burke were on drugs, wouldn't that strengthen the case against him?

''It shouldn't have been. That's what made me sit up and take notice. My boss personally took care of Burke. That's unusual, too. He normally sticks to the administrative side of things. I got drafted to assist him with Burke. I'm an orderly, but we were swamped that whole night. Lots of patients complaining of chest pains and nausea.''

Chest pains and nausea. Two of the symptoms Adam had claimed he'd felt before passing out in Area Fourteen. ''Were the patients mainly military members?''

''No, ma'am. It was strange. We see a lot of chest pains here—high-stress jobs, you know? Especially around fiscal year-end. But we don't usually see it happening to kids. That night, I'll bet we had a dozen kids in here, complaining of chest pains.''

A coincidence? Her instincts ruled against it. But how in the world could it be proven? She'd have to work on that. ''That does seem strange,'' she told Phelps.

Nodding, he braced a foot against the wall, leaned back, and lit a cigarette. ''Anyway,'' he said, exhaling, ''when you asked my boss what Burke had been wearing when they brought him in, I happened to hear you. I also heard my boss's answer.'' Phelps grimaced and the wind slicked his thin hair back from his face. "He lied to you, ma'am. Burke wasn't wearing standard BDUs. He was wearing chemical gear. His face was bare, but his skin had indentations consistent with the markings of having had on a chemical mask until just before he'd been brought into the ER."

Tracy's heartbeat kicked up a notch. "Did you see the mask?''

"No, ma'am. Only the marks on his face."

"How did Burke arrive here?"

"The records say by ambulance, but a Black Operations team brought him in. I recognized some of the operatives from training."

"Where was he brought in from?" Asking couldn't hurt, though she didn't dare to hope.

Phelps drew on the cigarette, and shook his head. "Sorry, just the bogus report on that."

"Why would your boss lie and withhold information about Burke?"

"I don't know." Phelps rubbed at the back of his neck, extremely uncomfortable. "The only thing that makes sense is that someone told him what to include and omit from his notes."

"Is he a gutless wonder who'd rather fold than fight?" she asked.

"Frankly, yes, ma'am." Phelps let his foot scrape down the wall to the floor. "But if you ask me that openly, I'll deny it."

Career warfare. Tracy was beginning to understand what motivated it. "If you were to speculate, what else would you deduce from your boss's actions?"

Phelps looked her straight in the eye. "I'd deduce that someone higher up the chain of command doesn't want the truth to come out. Everyone thinks Burke is guilty. I admit I did, too. But the boss lying, well, it got me to wondering. And then when Burke supposedly died in the fire—''

"Supposedly?" What was that about? Burke was dead. There was no *supposedly* to it.

Phelps again checked to be sure they were alone on the patio. "Hospitals are the same as everywhere else. They're full of gossip. And rumor has it, the corpse of a homeless John Doe found over in Area Fourteen disappeared from the morgue the same night Burke died in the fire."

Tracy's nerves sizzled. She wanted to believe it, for Adam, but could she? "If that's true, wouldn't word of it have been made public by now?"

"They say the hospital board and the OSI are keeping it quiet because of all the bad press lately. They figure if this got out, it'd raise all kinds of questions."

"Ones no one wants to answer." That grain of truth in Burke's story grew stronger, ran deeper inside her. And bad press would lessen the odds for Project Duplicity being funded. But why refuse to autopsy Burke, then? Raising doubts, maybe. Like Janet had said about discreet inquiries. Give people a reason and their imaginations don't run wild. The fire was the reason, and it was obvious. Do an autopsy, and you raise doubts.

Phelps took a drag from his cigarette, and then stabbed it out in the urn. "The hospital board is extremely conservative, if you know what I mean."

"Yes, I do." She did know, from Randall. "Sergeant, you said they found John Doe in Area Fourteen. What killed him?"

"I don't know, ma'am. The body disappeared before the autopsy. But I saw it, and there wasn't a mark on the man."

Tracy almost feared asking her next question. "Could it have been chemical poisoning?"

"I'm not a doctor, but I've had some chemical training, and I wouldn't rule it out."

"Did you happen to notice John Doe's eyes?"

"Ma'am?"

"Did you see his eyes?"

"No, ma'am. I didn't."

"What about the children's eyes? The ones treated that night for chest pains?"

"Can't say I noticed anything unusual, but I'll check the records."

"Thank you." A bubble of tension swelled in her belly. "Sergeant, do you think someone substituted John Doe's corpse for Adam Burke in the fire?" Oh, God. This was too far out.

"No way. There'd have to be cooperation between the facility, the hospital, and Higher Headquarters. I can't see any of them agreeing to do it—not with the damage to the facility."

She had to agree. It involved too many people, too much property destruction, and it raised too many red flags that couldn't be ducked. Most emphatically denying the possibility was Adam Burke himself. His face had been plastered on the nightly news and in the newspaper. If he were alive, someone would have seen and recognized him.

John Doe probably had been a vagrant with the bad luck of wandering into Area 14 at the time Alpha team had been killed. Or maybe . . . Could he have been hired to dispense the chemicals and somehow contaminated himself?

Something sailed over the stucco wall. It thudded against the inner wall, and then rolled over the concrete into the light, pouring out smoke.

Startled, Tracy jerked. It resembled a hand grenade, and it had a yellow band.

Chemical and biological resources require a yellow or blue band, to warn people they're live, not training dummies.

Adam's instruction replayed in her mind. She snatched her purse from the table.

"It's chemical!" Phelps ran for the automatic door.

Tracy ran behind him, doing her best not to breathe.

"It won't open!" Phelps beat at the glass with his fists. "Damn it, why won't it open?"

Terror rocketing through her veins, Tracy looked back at the lethal smoke.

They were trapped.

Chapter 15

Phelps panicked. He bent double, hyperventilating. "Let's scale the wall!"

They were four floors up. Scaling the wall was a stupid idea. The smoke thickened, snared between the high walls, burning Tracy's nose, stinging her eyes. They had to get out of there. "Try not to breathe," she said, scanning through the haze.

Why, of all times, did she have to be sick and weak *now*? Phelps was too terrified to move. If they were going to get out of there—without going over the wall and free-falling four floors—she'd have to find the way.

Her purse strap snagged on a chair arm. It was metal, heavy. It could work. She dragged the chair over, heaved, slammed it against the door.

The glass shattered.

Her arms stung up to her elbows. "Phelps, let's go."

He hugged the wall, fingers spread, body stiff enough to snap. Shock. The man couldn't move. "Sergeant, move your ass!" she shouted. "That's a direct order!"

Back scraping the wall, he slid toward the door. She grabbed his sleeve and shoved him through the opening. As she crossed the threshold, her instincts nudged her, and she glanced over. The wall switch that controlled the door's automatic sensor had been turned off.

Someone had deliberately locked her and Phelps on the

patio. That chemical bomb had been meant to kill them.

Her heart catapulted, stuck somewhere in her neck, and she held tight to Phelps's sleeve, dragged him into the hallway. Finally, he seemed to get his legs back.

They ran down the long hall, legs pumping, sneakers squeaking in tandem. A stitch caught in her side. Tracy clutched at it and came to a dead stop at the staff elevator door. Sweating profusely, weak to the brink of collapse, she slumped against the wall and gulped in deep breaths of uncontaminated air.

Phelps stopped beside her, pale and shaking hard. "Who did you tell we were meeting?"

"No one." The stitch in her side eased. She wiped at her sweat-soaked face. "You?"

"Not a soul." He pivoted to look at her. "Who could have done this?"

Had her phone been tapped? Phelps's? She stared at the orange floor cone, certain she was about to throw up again. This time, not from flu but from knowing someone damn well meant for her to die out on that patio—and she might have.

They had been exposed; no ifs, ands, or buts about it. So had portions of the hospital. Thankfully, being under construction, the immediate area was empty of people. But what chemical was it? How far did its reach extend? She didn't know, but she had to find out—now.

"Captain, who do you think did this?" Phelps asked again.

"Someone with access to chemical bombs who didn't want either of us to survive the meeting." Damp hanks of hair clung to her sweat-dampened face. "Unfortunately, how-to instructions are available everywhere. It could be anyone—legal or crazy, in or out of the system."

Lingering here wasn't wise. Whoever had turned off that switch could still be around. She moved toward the elevators, cautious, watchful, alert. "We need to get checked for exposure." From all she had read, it was probably too late, but there was a chance the unknown chemical wasn't lethal. A small one, but a chance.

"Not here." Phelps's voice pitched to a screech.

"Somewhere, then." Tracy passed the elevator door, then peeked down the adjacent hallway. Empty, thank God. Phelps had a point. In light of what he had told her, either of them going to this ER would be giving his boss, if so inclined, a license to commit murder. That gamble, she wasn't willing to take.

Dr. Kane popped into her mind. So did Randall.

Figuring Randall was the lesser of the two evils, she decided to go to him. Someone had to warn the hospital of the exposure, and it sure as hell didn't appear Phelps had any intention of doing it.

She passed a window. Dawn was breaking. Randall always came to the hospital before dawn, but she doubted Dr. Kane was here. He didn't strike her as the obsessive type.

Phelps paused at the elevator. "I'm going to Saint George's. You wanna ride with me?"

"I think it's better if we split up." Tracy had more to do. To retrieve and report the bomb.

Worry flicked through the sergeant's eyes. "Don't be long. This exposure is serious."

He knew her plans, but had no intention of becoming involved. After what they'd just experienced, she couldn't fault him. She'd like to, but he had children to think of, a wife. He had a life outside of his work. "I won't. You go on now."

Looking relieved by her dismissal, he stepped into the elevator.

When the door slid shut, she retrieved the bomb, praying whoever had flipped the switch had long since gone, and then headed for the stairwell. As rotten as she felt, the idea of being closed in on an elevator just after being locked out on a patio aroused more claustrophobic feelings than she'd ever experienced—walking through Cell

Block D. And right now she felt too damn fragile to fight them.

Midway down the first flight of stairs, she paused to rest. Footsteps sounded above her.

Gripping the iron banister, her knobbed knuckles scraping against the rough wall, she looked up, strained to hear any sounds. Nothing. And no shadows on the white walls or the concrete steps. The stairwell was as silent as a tomb.

Doing her damnedest to get a grip on her fears, she snaked through the maze of corridors down to the pathology lab. Someone was really trying to kill her. Not warning her off, like before, but trying to kill her. God, what a hard concept to grasp. Everything in her wanted to insist it was a mistake, the product of an active imagination, of too much TV. But rationalizing was a good way to wake up dead. Weakening her Caprice's hood latch had been a warning. This bomb was definitely attempted murder. And if the chemical proved lethal, murder.

Her murder!

Shivering, she entered Pathology. Randall sat on a stool at his lab desk, his white-coated back to her. "Randall." Her voice sounded as weak as a beggar's, and scared and just sick enough, she didn't care if he realized it.

"Tracy?" Clearly startled to see her, his blond brows shot up on his forehead. "What are you doing here?"

Feeling an intense urge to be held, to feel safe for a moment, she locked her arms around his waist and hugged him hard.

Surprised by the demonstrative gesture, he lifted his arms around her. "Hey, what's happened to you?"

She told him about the bomb.

His hands trembling, he cupped her chin and checked her eyes. "No signs of mitosis, but I'd feel better if Steven Kane took a look. He's far more experienced." Randall reached over the lab desk and grabbed a phone.

After a brief conversation, he hung up. "Steven's on his way."

"Good." Tracy's mouth felt desert-dry. "Could I have a glass of water?"

"Better not, until we're sure you're okay." Randall led her to the stool he'd vacated.

For all he had done wrong before in her eyes, in this, he was responding exactly right. "I appreciate your help." As soon as the words left her mouth, doubt filtered into her mind. Would he help her if he knew her meeting had been about Adam? She doubted it, but she had no intention of finding out.

Randall patted her arm. "Just relax, okay?"

"Okay." Someone was trying to kill her, and she was supposed to relax? She began sweating. Whether from the flu, fever, or exposure to the chemical, she had no idea. Within minutes, her mind fogged, her vision fuzzed, and more and more disoriented, she latched onto the lab desk for stability. Symptoms, she realized. All the symptoms Adam had described feeling out in Area 14. "Randall, what if I've contaminated you?"

"You rest until Steven gets here. I'll go decontaminate. We have a chamber."

The smells in the lab sharpened, pungent and strong. Her stomach rebelled, pitching and grumbling, and her neck felt too weak to hold up her head. A strong wave of nausea rolled up to her throat. Fighting it, she rested her head on the cool lab desk and closed her eyes.

The next thing she knew she was awakening to voices. Randall and Steven Kane conferring, sounding as if they stood at the far end of a long tunnel. She tried to open her eyes, but her eyelids felt leaden. She couldn't seem to lift them. God, she was tired. So . . . tired.

When she next awakened, her mind had cleared. Had her fever broken?

"Tracy." Dr. Kane gave her one of those special smiles Janet had raved about.

Unmoved, Tracy straightened on the stool, stiff and

sore and achy all over. The fever hadn't gone, and her tongue felt as big as a boulder. Why was she hearing Adam's "fluff" in her head now? "You aren't wearing protective gear."

"It's not necessary." Dr. Kane frowned, clearly worried. "The bomb wasn't chemical."

Tracy feared believing him. "But it had a yellow band."

"That surprised me, too. But it was a dummy. I ran the tests twice, just to be sure."

She grabbed a paper towel from a stack at the far end of the lab desk and dabbed at her damp forehead. If Adam's men had been killed with a supposed dummy, and she'd been threatened with a dummy someone had tagged as live, that opened the door on some scary possibilities. Someone could be substituting live chemical/biological ordnance for dummies. Could be abusing the bands. Someone could be committing treason.

Dr. Kane snagged her attention. "From all we can determine, you're fine except for a strong case of the flu. Definitely no mitosis."

Enormously relieved, she again posed the question she'd asked him the night she'd identified Adam's body. "Was there evidence of mitosis in Burke's men?"

"Tracy," Randall interceded. "I asked Steven here to help you, not to be interrogated."

She ignored Randall. "Was there, Dr. Kane?" Knowing Phelps would never again risk involvement, she asked a second question. "The night of the Alpha team incident—the children treated in the ER for chest pains. Did they have symptoms of mitosis?"

"No, of course not," Randall said sharply, clearly tense and irritated.

"Dr. Kane?" she persisted. "Did they? Any of them?"

He looked away.

"Tracy, that's enough." Randall raised his voice. "Between the flu and this scare, you're jumping at shadows. No one had mitosis, okay?"

She swiveled her gaze—and saw the truth in Randall's eyes. He was lying to her.

A frown knit his brow, and his hand trembled on her cheek. "Who did you meet up there?"

"That's confidential," she said without heat, still reeling. Why would he lie to her? Why?

"It's important, Tracy," he persisted, softening his voice.

"It's still confidential." She backed up a step, out of his reach. "I would tell you if I could, but I can't. Not without breaching security and ethics."

Dr. Kane dragged a fingertip over his temple, decidedly uncomfortable. "Well, I'd better get back to my office. I'm glad you're okay, Tracy."

"Thank you," she said stiffly. "I appreciate your help."

He nodded, then left the lab and closed the door.

"Tracy." Randall sounded determined. "I'm worried about you, and so is Paul. He called me last night looking for you."

Her ex-brother-in-law, it appeared, still hadn't accepted that she was going to live her life her way—without his dominating interference, or his help and support. She admired his willingness to sacrifice a loving marriage to care for his brother's widow. But, damn it, she wanted to stand on her own feet, and on her own merits. Sooner or later, Paul had to accept it—hopefully, before his refusal to accept it drove a permanent wedge between them. "I'll call him."

"Soon, I hope." Randall slid her a look laced with reprimand. "Paul is a powerful man with a lot on his mind. He really doesn't need you adding to his worries."

Tracy would take offense, but Randall happened to be right. Not that she had asked Paul to worry. But they were family. Worrying and family come as a package deal. And running Keener Chemical was a heavy load. Paul had chosen to carry it; he could hire a CEO to manage it at any time, yet his father had built the Keener family business from nothing, and Paul was protective of family and family assets. As long as he lived, no one else would ever make decisions affecting Keener Chemical. How that would have worked out if Matthew had lived, Tracy had no idea, but she would bet her bars it would've created friction between the brothers eventually. Before Matthew had died, she'd noticed early warning signs.

Sliding off the stool, Tracy eased her purse strap up on her shoulder, eager to get home and into bed. "Thanks for helping me, Randall."

He nodded. "I wish you would reconsider and tell me who you met. Someone else should know, Tracy. This shouldn't be taken lightly."

"I'm not taking it lightly. You can rest assured of that."

"Whatever you're doing, it's clearly dangerous. You're stepping on toes."

He sounded like Ted. "I've explained already. I can't tell you." He understood security and ethics. Why was he being such a persistent pig about this?

"What if next time you're hit with more than a warning? God forbid, but you could end up dead, and no one would have any idea where to even start looking for your killer."

He suspected she was in mortal danger and his main concern was obtaining the identity of the person she'd met so that if he did kill her, Randall could inform the authorities. She stared at him, frighteningly close to blowing her stack. How disgustingly inadequate. Damn cold, too. Randall could use a few lessons from Adam on how to treat—

She halted that thought, unwilling to finish it. "I won't breach ethics or security."

"I'll keep it confidential. I swear it." Randall grasped her upper arms. "Professional ethics are fine and security is essential, but not at the expense of your life."

She went stone-cold inside. He was manipulating her. Deliberately trying to frighten her. Did he think she was too dull to pick up on his tactics? "I appreciate your concern, but I can handle this."

Before he could respond, she left the lab, still seething resentment. She'd vowed never to ask Randall for anything, yet she'd gone to him for help. That was okay, considering the hospital had been involved, but she'd choke to death before asking him for anything again. Friends don't damn lie to friends. Or manipulate them.

She walked outside. Away from the lab's strong smells, she felt better. Daylight had come, but the sun was in hiding. The sky streaked gray and the air smelled of rain.

In the parking lot, she stopped beside a white Lincoln. What car had she driven here?

That was the problem with switching cars so often. Though after the hood-latch incident, Janet's advice to do it was too wise to ignore. A Mercury, Tracy recalled. Dark-colored.

It took all the energy she had left to locate the rental car and fish her keys out of her purse. When she rounded the back end to the driver's side, she stopped. Deep scratches gouged the burgundy paint down to the metal. Scratches that read: "Burke's Bitch."

"Terrific. Just damn terrific." Using Janet's techniques, Tracy checked out the car for explosives, and found nothing. She got in, and then slammed the driver's door shut. The rental company would charge her a fortune for this.

Angry, sick, and exhausted, she drove home, a thousand questions running through her mind. Why had Randall, the slug, lied to her? Not decontaminated her in their chamber, too? Who had pulled the stunt with the smoke bomb? Was someone substituting dummies for live ordnance or abusing the bands? If so, who? Worse, why? They had to be black-marketing ordnance, and that truth terrified her.

She pulled into her driveway, suffering a serious sinking spell, then crawled out of the car. "Okay, you've maxed." True, that. Even her teeth hurt. "Down some medicine, sleep, and then attack this logically."

The rain started before she reached the back door, and she got that nebulous, uneasy feeling of being watched. She looked toward her ramshackle garden, but saw no one there. Still, she rushed her steps to get inside.

"You're getting paranoid, Keener." She closed the door, clicked the deadbolt into place.

Dumping her purse on the kitchen table, she filled a tall glass with orange juice from the fridge. Her sinuses were stuffy and her head throbbed, and she longingly remembered the days when Matthew had been home to greet her. She supposed all the threats had acted as triggers, bringing him to mind so often these days. Taking a long, cold drink from the glass, she wondered about Adam. After his divorce, had he ever walked into his house and resented it being empty? Survivor to survivor, she'd bet her bars he had—often.

She walked down the hallway to her bedroom, tossed her clothes into a heap on the bedside chair, and then put on her PJs and robe and her Pooh slippers. If ever she needed an attitude, the time was now. That bomb could just as easily have been live. She could just as easily be dead.

Dragging one foot in front of the other, she wobbled to the bath and, hip to the vanity, pulled out the flu medicines from the cabinet over the sink. She hated to take them—they made her drowsy—but she had to do something. Between the medicine and steaming her sinuses, which threatened to explode at any second, maybe she'd feel human enough to get some sleep. Lord, did she need sleep.

She downed the meds, then filled the bathroom sink with steaming hot water and shut off the faucet. Seeing spots before her eyes, she slung a towel over her head, then bent low and sucked up the steam.

A few minutes later, the water cooled. She debated adding more, but the medicine was working its magic, and she could barely keep her eyes open.

A thud sounded. Somewhere distant.

She stilled, and heard another. *Someone was in the house!*

Straightening, she reached for the towel draped over her head. Strong fingertips cinched down on her neck, forced her forward, burying her face in the water. The splash soaked her robe.

Fighting the restraint, she swung out, but swiped only air. Stomping, kicking, she still failed to connect with flesh. Weak, tired, and slow from the medication, she threw her weight backward, hoping to knock her attacker off-balance. Her face came up, out of the water. Sputtering, she gasped in deep lungfuls of air. The attacker pinned her arms at her sides, tied something around her neck to hold the towel in place. She slumped back against the vanity. Even suffering an adrenaline rush, terrified she'd be murdered, she lacked the strength to fight.

Her attacker lifted her, then carried her out of the bath. By his strength, she knew she was being kidnapped by a man. He took her outside. They were leaving and she was too drugged to stop him, too weak and groggy to even protest. Where was he taking her? Her face at his chest, she felt his heart thump against her cheek. Jesus God, he was going to kill her and she was going to sleep through it.

Chapter 16

Tracy's head throbbed. Her whole body throbbed and ached.

Her kidnapper dumped her in the back seat of a car—at least, she assumed it was the back seat. Scrunched on her side, she felt vibrations. The engine was running. She fought panic, and failed. Wordlessly, he bound her arms and ankles. The ties weren't tight, but just feeling them around her wrists and ankles reminded her she was restrained, and that infuriated her. When the car door slammed shut, she risked reaching out. No steering wheel or dashboard. Soft velour fabric. Had to be the back of the front seat. The towel tied over her head, she didn't dare to shift positions. As it was, breathing air through wet terrycloth was a challenge.

The front door shut and the man stomped on the accelerator, pinning her back against the seat. The tires screeched and grabbed on the wet pavement. He was crazy, driving this fast in the rain. He must be going seventy miles per hour.

Her stomach lurched with every bump, every turn, every swerve. The rain beat against the car. It had cooled down outside, but inside, in her robe and Pooh slippers, it was plenty warm—and yet her teeth began to chatter. It wasn't nerves, though she was terrified, and she refused to feel inferior because of it. It was the flu. And from the odd feeling in her head and the sweat soaking her body, she supposed that her fever had broken. So why hadn't her stomach calmed down? Oh, God, if only he would stop the car for a minute. Just for a damn minute.

She suffered the jarring as long as she could, trying her damnedest to muffle her moans and mewls against her arm. But not being able to see, the wet towel plastering against her nose with every indrawn breath, only added to her nausea.

Whose toes had she stepped on hard enough to warrant being kidnapped? She hadn't found concrete evidence conclusively proving anything Adam had told her. The bomb at the hospital had been a dud—clearly a warning, just as the car's hood latch had been a warning. Whoever was behind those incidents didn't want her dead, they wanted her to stop investigating. This was different. Far more serious. And for the life of her, she couldn't imagine who would initiate it, or why. O'Dell or Hackett wouldn't consider her that great a threat—unless . . . Had she stumbled across something and failed to recognize it as significant?

The bands around her wrists snagged on her robe button and jerked tight. Silk? *You should be draped in silk . . .*

Paul?

No, absolutely not. He was domineering, yes. But he'd never do this to her.

Whoa, Tracy. Wait a second, girl. He rebelled against your leaving him even after you joined the Air Force. He got Keener Chemical involved in government contracts exploring new technology, too. And he did everything humanly possible to get you not to defend Adam—even promised you the moon to get you to marry him.

True, but Paul cared about her. She was all the family he had. He wouldn't do this.

Not even to scare you into coming back to him?

She refused to believe it. He wouldn't.

Then what about Randall? He lied to you. And he wanted to know who you met at the hospital. Why, do you think, was it so important to him to know?

No idea, but Randall wouldn't do this. Kidnapping her wasn't on his list of goals and it certainly wouldn't advance his career.

Her kidnapper continued to drive like a demon from hell. She needed to consider other possibilities, but she was so sick to her stomach, she couldn't think anymore.

The car hit a bump and a too-common wave of nausea rolled up from her belly. She had no choice but to alert her kidnapper. "I'm going to throw up. You've got to stop the car. *Please.*"

"Two minutes," the man said, speaking his first words to her.

Finally, the car stopped. The back door opened, and then he helped her out. She wanted to shake off his hands, but she was too jelly-kneed to stand without his support.

Behind her, he untied the rope circling her neck, lifted the towel from over her head, and then untied her hands. The rain had stopped, but the sky remained a dull dark gray. She wanted to look to see who the man was, but she didn't have time to even glimpse him. Two steps from the car, she bent forward, leaning low to the ground, and threw up.

When her stomach had emptied, she saw that she was crouching in a weedy patch of sand. Her legs were shaky, her face flushed hot and damp, her skin clammy cold.

"Flu, or nerves?" The man pressed a blessedly cool handkerchief against her forehead.

"Flu," she said through trembling lips, then opened her eyes—and saw Adam Burke.

Adam. "Oh, God." Her heart hammered, threatening to burst through her ribs. "You're alive."

"For the moment." He frowned at her. "Feeling better?"

A flood of emotions gushed through her at once; she didn't know which to feel. Happy or sad, afraid or relieved. Should she rejoice or mourn? He was alive; she hadn't caused his death. But he'd kidnapped her.

Anger. More than anything else, she felt anger. It swelled in her and erupted. "What the hell do you think you're doing, pulling a stunt like this?"

"I'd say you're feeling better." He gave her forehead a final dab with the handkerchief and then grasped her arm. "I hate to rush you, counselor, but standing out in the open isn't in our best interests."

"It's six in the morning, for God's sake. Who do you think is going to bother us?"

"It's nearly four in the afternoon. You slept a while. I suspect, due to the flu medication you took." He kept walking, urging her toward the car. "If you give me your word you'll behave, I won't tie you back up. I don't want to, I know you're not well."

She debated. She couldn't get away from him, so she'd bide her time. "I promise."

Looking relieved, he helped her into the front passenger seat. "It reclines, so you can stretch out, if you'd be more comfortable."

"You're concerned about my comfort?" She grunted. "What a novel concept coming from a man who tried to drown me in my own bathroom sink. You abducted me from my home."

"You chose not to disappear. It was necessary."

"Why? Better yet, necessary for whom? Certainly not for me."

"The men trying to kill us might disagree. In fact, I'd bank on it." Adam slammed the door, then walked around the hood.

Trying to kill us? She stared at him, moving past the front fender to the driver's door. The swelling was gone, and he looked like his Personnel file photo again, except for the tension in him now that had been absent then. Still, he was gorgeous. Crazy as hell for pulling this stunt, but gorgeous. "Why do you still have that yellow streak in your hair?"

"I've been a little busy. Haven't had time to dye it."

He got in the car, shifted into Drive, and then pulled out on the dirt road, kicking up a cloud of dust that could be seen for a mile. "For the record, I didn't kidnap you to hurt you."

"You expect me to believe that? You tied my hands and ankles. You covered my head with a wet towel and tied it around my neck with a rope."

"I didn't."

"Don't damn lie to me." She glared at that god-awful yellow streak disappearing under the collar of his black shirt.

"It was silk scarves."

"Whatever!" she shouted at him. "You tied me up."

"I saved your life."

"So you kidnapped me to save my life? You expect me to believe that?" She stared at him, incredulous. "It's the most absurd thing—"

"When you got back from the hospital meeting with Phelps, two men were in your house. I seriously doubt they dropped in for a friendly visit."

Tracy thought back. She had heard two distinct thuds. Adam disarming the men? "How did you know about Phelps, or that I'd been to the hospital?"

"Someone turned off the power switch to that automatic door, counselor. Do you think that person wasn't waiting inside, just in case you managed to get back in?"

"The bomb was a dummy."

"The man waiting was real."

"What man?"

"The one I knocked out and stuffed in a cabinet at the nurses' station—Phelps's boss."

"So you've been following me." Why that calmed her down, she had no idea. Burke was the worst possible kind of adversary. He had nothing left to lose.

The rain started again, and the interior of the car turned as dark as night. He flipped on the headlights, then glanced over at her. The lit-up dash cast an eerie green shadow on his chin. "Yes, I've been following you. So has Lieutenant Carver, and at times, Gus O'Dell.''

Hackett's aide and O'Dell—*and* Adam? No wonder she'd had strong sensations of being followed. ''Are you crazy? You're supposed to be dead. How did you fake the dental records?''

''I didn't fake anything.'' He scowled at the road. ''For a while, though, I wondered if I had slipped over the edge. Then they targeted you, and that convinced me I was still sane.''

Randall obviously had lied about the dental records. But on whose orders? ''How did you get out of that fire?''

''The power went out in the cell block. My door opened. I heard this man's voice in the dark. He told me to get out of the cell block fast, or die. I got out.''

''Who was he?''

''I didn't ask. When you're smelling gasoline and being offered a chance to survive, you don't ask, you just take the chance.''

She braced a hand on the door's armrest and turned in the seat to stare at him. ''I'm not buying into this. I want the truth. All of it. Right damn now. Kidnapping is a federal offense—''

''You'd rather I had let those two kill you?''

She grimaced. ''How do you know they intended to kill me?''

''If they were coming for coffee, I would think they would ring the doorbell. I'm certain they wouldn't break into your house, packing weapons. I'm no strategic expert, but even for me, the picture was clear enough.''

Could that be true? Bristling, she glared at him. ''So why do you care about me?''

''Frankly, I need a witness.''

''To what?''

''The truth. I'm going to prove I'm innocent. You're going to know it.''

''If you expect me to thank you for dragging me into this, you can forget it. You scared the hell out of me.''

"I don't expect anything from you, counselor, or from anyone else. I just didn't want to see you wake up dead."

A cutting survivor remark, straight from the heart. Why did hearing it sting? "So you kidnapped me to save me?" She couldn't believe that. And yet, like his original disclosure, it held a ring of truth. She had heard those thuds.

"To save you and to prove the truth." He swerved left onto another dirt road. "I've never lied to you, counselor. Now I mean to prove it to you. There *is* a conspiracy going on. How high up the chain of command it goes, I don't know—yet. But I suspect it involves General Nestler, and I mean to find out."

Tracy shook her head, closed her eyes. "Damn it, Burke. Faking your death and kidnapping your attorney isn't a way to prove anything except that you're insane."

"I'm not insane, I'm determined. I will prove the truth." His eyes shone intensely. "And you're going to help me."

Shock streaked up her back, tingled at the roof of her mouth. "I'm not your partner, for God's sake. I'm your hostage. Why in the name of heaven would I help you?"

"Because you want the truth, too." He drove to a blue sedan, parked on the side of the road, abruptly stopped, cut the engine, and then opened his door. "Come on."

A glare streaked across its windshield, yet the sedan was obviously empty. "Where are we going?"

"To the other car." Adam must have seen her worried look; he smiled. "It's okay. I planted it here. They'll come after us, and when they do, I'd rather not be in the same car."

Tracy didn't move. "Were you driving the sedan parked outside my house?"

"No, that was Carver."

"What about when I had the accident?"

"Would I leave you in a ditch?"

"I don't know. Would you?"

His lips flattened to a slash. "No."

"Then who did?"

"O'Dell." Adam unsnapped his seat belt. "Let's go."

"I don't think so." She didn't move an inch. "You stole that car, Adam."

"I don't steal."

"Do you have a requisition for it?" Please. Did the man think she was stupid?

"I appropriated it," he said defensively.

"You stole it."

"I did not." He raked a hand through his hair in frustration. "What the hell is the difference?" He shot her a glare that had her legs shaking again. "Look, I'm trying to be reasonable, counselor. You're coming, one way or the other. I'll leave the choice to you. Do you want to walk, or be dragged?"

He meant it. Only a fool would believe he didn't. "I'll walk."

When they were seated in the sedan, she strapped on her seat belt. "You're going to be in Leavenworth a long time for this, Burke. A long time."

"That's a fluff comment, counselor." He rolled his gaze. "I'm not guilty, and I did not fake my death."

A frown knitted her brow. "Then who did?" If he said Randall, to hell with it. She'd just faint. She'd had all she could take, and Adam already considered her fluff and incompetent. A little faint certainly couldn't worsen his opinion of her.

"I suspect Hackett. Maybe O'Dell."

That intrigued her. "Why would they fake your death? They want you dead and buried and your case closed." Jackson's "wrath of God" ass-chewing attested to that.

"On paper," Adam said. "But they don't really want me dead. At least, not yet."

"You're not making a bit of sense."

"I'm making perfect sense." He slid her a "Think, woman" look. "If I were really dead, then I couldn't be accused of committing more crimes. And if I had remained imprisoned, I wouldn't be free to commit more crimes."

True on both counts. "So the man who burned—"

"I'm not sure yet," he said. "There's a rumor at the hospital about a missing corpse. It doesn't seem probable, but I'm checking it out."

John Doe. Betrayal swam through her, leaving bitterness in its wake. "Randall identified your body by your dental records. He lied."

"I'm sorry, counselor," Adam said, sounding sincere. "But yes, he did."

Tracy squeezed the door handle. "This doesn't fit. He's so image-conscious. So terrified of his board disapproving his every sneeze. Why would he falsely identify you?"

"I suspect he was ordered to do it."

"That's no excuse. A lie's still a lie. He preaches ethics, but the sorry bastard lied."

Adam cocked an eyebrow. "I thought you were having an affair with that sorry bastard."

"We were once friends. That's all." If someone had issued Randall orders to falsely identify Adam, was it such a huge mental leap to suspect that someone also had ordered the substitution of John Doe's corpse? It could have happened. But what about all the egos and powerful players in between? The hospital and the facility? "I don't get emotionally involved."

"Not since Matthew, eh?"

She had no intention of answering that. None. Fear cracked open a new wound inside her. "Exactly what crimes do you expect O'Dell and Hackett to commit and blame on you?"

"That, I don't know," Adam said, clearly irritated that he hadn't figured it out. "But I'm betting there will be more of them, unless they're stopped and exposed, which is why we—"

"*We?*" She cut in. "Oh, no, Burke." She swiped her hand down the front of her robe, tugging it closed over her knees. "There's no *we* in this."

"I need your help."

That admission mentally knocked her on her backside. "You kidnap me, and you actually expect me to help you?"

"Not only do I expect it, counselor." The damn man smiled. "I demand it."

Chapter 17

Light faded to darkness. With it went some of Tracy's fear and indignation. Adam obviously hadn't kidnapped her to kill her or she would be dead.

Actually, she thought, leaning against the car door, her face pressed against the cool glass, he'd taken the risk of exposing himself as still being alive to help her. And the two distinct thuds she had heard from her bathroom explained the new scrapes on his knuckles.

Who were those men? Why were they in her house? The thought of them being there and her not knowing it petrified her.

She glanced over at Adam from beneath her lashes. He'd been driving all day and into the night and yet he didn't look tired. Dark stubble shadowed his jaw but he appeared alert, watchful. Dangerous . . .

The dirt road narrowed. Tall weeds slapped against the car fenders, and a trickle of fear slid through her chest. She didn't like fearing him—not after she'd risked her career and her life trying to unearth the truth for him. Not after she'd attended his funeral and had mourned him. Not after she'd read his Intel file and had learned of his disastrous childhood and his short but equally disastrous marriage. And especially not after she'd identified with him as a survivor and had dreamed of making love with him two nights in a row.

Obviously Adam had never known unconditional love.

If he had, they might not be in this situation now.

"You're awake," Adam said. "Feeling better?"

She was. Maybe he had scared the flu right out of her. Whatever the reason, she would accept the blessing and be grateful for it. "Yes."

"Your fever broke about an hour ago," he said. "You slept through it."

"I always sleep through fear." She bristled at the lie.

"No you don't. You drink Earl Grey tea, wear that flannel robe and your Winnie-the-Pooh slippers. And you pace the floors a lot."

A denial on her lips, she looked down and saw twin smiling Pooh faces sticking out from under the hems of her PJs. Heat rushed up her neck to her face. The man knew her better than she thought, more than she would like.

"I stopped and bought a cooler and some drinks."

Looking down, she saw a small ice chest on the floorboard near her feet. She rubbed at her stomach. "I don't think I'd better try a whole drink just yet."

"I didn't get juice. They had concentrate, and you only drink freshly squeezed."

How had he learned so many intimate details about her?

The man's Intel, dummy.

Uncomfortable, she turned the tables on him, twisting on the seat to face him. "Why did you risk exposing yourself to help me?"

His eyes shone approval. She hated liking that; she really did. He realized she had come full circle and now accepted he had kidnapped her to save her life.

"Maybe I didn't want to be blamed for your murder."

Tracy dismissed that fluff remark. "More likely, a dead man can't commit murder. If they want you alive to commit more crimes, then they wouldn't let it be known you're alive until after the crimes are committed. Otherwise, you'd be hunted down and tossed back into the facility. You wouldn't be available to blame for anything.''

''Very astute, counselor.'' Adam drank from the can of Coke, then offered it to her.

Wanting a sip, she shook her head. ''Better not. I'll make you sick.''

''I'll risk it.'' He passed the can over.

She took it and drank a small swallow, careful not to touch the can with her lips. ''You didn't answer my question. Why did you help me?''

His knuckles on the steering wheel went white and his jaw clenched. Conversely, his voice went whisper-soft. ''You attended my funeral.''

''Good God, you had the impudence to attend your own funeral?'' She passed back the Coke. ''Why would you take such a risk?''

His fingers brushed against hers on the can, and he held them there. ''You don't believe I'm innocent. I know it and you know it. Yet even after I was supposedly dead, you kept looking for the truth.'' He pulled in a breath, as if savoring that knowledge. ''No one has ever sacrificed for me before.''

Exactly how closely had he been monitoring her? ''Sacrificed?''

''I know what it's cost you, counselor. Jackson's holding you personally responsible. Still, being threatened with disciplinary proceedings hasn't stopped you.'' Adam shifted on the seat, plainly uncomfortable. ''Maybe that's just the way you are, and it's common for you, but what you're doing isn't common for me.''

''Life's been hard on you.'' Touched, Tracy's heart softened toward him, awakening feelings she had never thought to feel again. Feelings she didn't want to feel. Feelings she feared. She reached for her locket, found her neck bare, and then remembered it wasn't there. She'd lost it, too.

Beside the narrow road, a flock of doves lifted from the tall grass and took flight in the night sky. Adam watched them, a frown knitting his brow. "I don't need your pity, counselor."

"You don't have it." She let her hand slide over his face. His five-o'clock shadow rustled against her palm. She liked the sound. "I wasn't making a commentary, just stating a fact."

Adam glanced into the rearview mirror, stiffened at the wheel, then slammed his foot down on the accelerator.

Tracy's head banged against the headrest. "Damn it. It was just a simple comment. You're taking it kind of hard, aren't you?"

He rolled her a "fluff" look. "They've found us." He nodded for her to look behind them.

A cloud of dust spewed out behind their sedan. Through it, she saw headlights, about three hundred yards behind them. Her heart seemed to stop, then tripped and shot straight up into her throat. "Who is it?"

"I don't know. Probably the men from your house."

Weeds beat at the sides of the car, at the windows. Hating the noise, fear smothering her, Tracy darted her gaze back, then forward. "There's a crossroad." Was she really trying to help him get away from them? She was making herself an accessory, for God's sake.

"I see it." He waited until the last second, then hung a sharp right.

Another crossroad lay just ahead, at the top of a small rise. "They're still coming," Tracy said, her voice elevating.

Adam swung left, drove a short distance on the pothole-infested road, hitting puddles. Muddy water splashed against the car, the windshield, obscuring his vision. He drove headlong into the weeds, beyond them into a field of corn, and then cut the lights. In the dark, the car bounced over rows, its frame creaked and groaned, and Tracy's stomach ricocheted between her chest wall and her kneecaps. She grabbed the dash in a death grip. Her hand stung and her arm ached up to her elbow. The car suddenly halted. In a cold sweat, she wheeled her gaze to Adam. "Why did you stop? Do you want to get caught?"

Ignoring her, he cut the engine, then turned in the seat and looked behind them.

She could just see herself trying to explain this to Jackson. Forget any promotion or status selection, she'd be doing time in Leavenworth with Adam Burke. "You've lost your mind."

"Maybe." He didn't so much as glance at her.

Sounds of their pursuers' approach filled the car. Tracy's nerves snapped tight. Oh, God. They too had turned left at the last crossroad. Any moment, they would pounce on her and Adam. Would they turn them in to the authorities? Not likely. Not if they wanted him available to commit more crimes. But then why chase him? Maybe just observing. That seemed logical. Adam wouldn't be killed; they needed him, provided he was right about all of this.

But they could kill you, and blame him for your murder.

Panic choked her. "We can't just sit here."

"Shhh." Adam lifted a finger to cover his lips.

She glared at him, then looked back. God, had she ever in her life been this scared?

A black two-door whizzed by without even slowing down.

Tracy swallowed a groan. "Do you think they saw the bent weeds where we came into the field?"

"I don't know." Adam turned back into his seat and cranked the engine. "But we're not hanging around to find out."

He backed out of the field at an angle. The car bumped and rocked over the rows, threatening to jar her teeth loose and get her stomach started up again. "For God's sake, Adam, take it easy."

"Sorry." He answered as if by rote, then pulled onto the dirt road and headed back in the opposite direction.

When he pulled back onto a semismooth surface, she

quit kidding herself. The tremble quivering through her had nothing to do with the car or surfaces, it had to do with fear. She wrung her hands to still them.

"Calm down, counselor." Adam gently squeezed her hands. "If they saw us, we'll know it soon enough."

"Excuse me for being nervous. I'm new at this business of having people run me out of my house and chase me at speeds only demons drive, trying to murder me."

"Experience doesn't make it easier to handle," Adam said calmly.

Rubbing the back of her hand with the pad of his thumb, he obviously hadn't taken offense, and he happened to be right. Experience wouldn't make this easier to handle. She looked over at him. Being in Intel, he probably faced this type of thing often. Even when reading his Intel file, she hadn't thought about the realities of his job. That had her feeling ashamed. She'd rested under his protective wing, like the rest of the country, and she'd never—not once—stopped to think about what that cover protected her from, or what he and others like him had to endure to offer her that protection. "What does make this easier?"

"Nothing."

"Nothing?" Hating the sound of that, she frowned. "There has to be some positive way of dealing with the stress."

"You just do it." He shrugged, glancing at the rear-view mirror.

"That's it?"

"That's it." He stopped at the main road, then took the four-lane highway, heading toward Jackson, farther and farther away from Laurel.

Tracy watched the road behind them a full fifteen minutes, but the black two-door never appeared. "I think we've lost them."

"For now." Adam reached into the cooler near Tracy's feet, pulled out two sodas, and then handed her one. "Unless I'm way off base about this, they'll be persistent."

That prediction had her popping the top on a can of soda, wishing it were a stiff shot of Scotch that would settle her nerves. She took a long drink. It felt good going down her throat. She must have swallowed a ton of dust. *Way off base?*

She thought of his note, his bequest, and guilt flooded her. Survivor to survivor, he'd done all he could to protect her. True—she recalled the bathroom-sink dunking—some of his methods sucked dead canaries, but he had been effective.

And she'd been ungrateful—and unwilling to give him even the benefit of doubt. "What exactly is your way-on-base theory?"

"Do you really want to know?" Adam put on his blinker, passed a pickup truck with a rusted-out back end, and then whipped into the right lane behind a green van with a bumper sticker that read, "America, Love It or Leave It."

"Yes, I do. You kidnapped me, Adam. I think you at least owe me the truth." How much did she owe him? Her life? At least that benefit of doubt. Lights from a small shopping center shone up ahead on the right.

"Let me think about it." He turned in at the store, parked facing the plate-glass window of City Drugs, and then turned off the engine. "Can I trust you to stay in the car and not run for the first phone to turn me in?" He pocketed the key in his jeans.

She looked straight into his eyes. "Maybe."

"Damn it, counselor, I need to know I can trust you on this. Can I?"

"I don't know. That's as honest as I can get."

He got out of the car, rested a hand on its top, then bent down to look back inside at her. "Unless you want to walk into City Drugs in your robe and Pooh slippers, I suggest you put some effort into inspiring a little more confidence."

"I'm not going to lie to you, Adam. I won't."

He leaned his forehead against his arm and stared at

her. Light from inside the store streamed across the car hood and, in it, she saw the lines of his face harden, his body stiffen. He stared at her without a word, hard and deep, as if doing his damnedest to see straight into her soul. "I trusted you with the truth once. That was hard to do, counselor, but I haven't regretted it. So I'm going to trust you again and hope you don't disappoint me. If you do, know that you could get us both killed. I'm only alive as long as I'm not a major liability." He softened his voice. "I'm not ready to die yet. And I'm not ready to watch you die."

Having no idea what to say, she kept quiet.

He let out a little sigh and headed into the store, his jeans hugging his lean hips, a baseball cap hiding the yellow paint streaking his hair.

She looked at the storefront. He'd parked right by a pay phone, as if baiting her to use it. Oh, but she should. She really should. If she did, she might just save her job and herself a stint in federal prison.

So why aren't you moving? Why not just get out of the damn car, walk the ten steps to the phone, and call the base Operations Center, the OSI, the MPs, or even the local authorities?

Still, she didn't move.

Okay. Okay, so something is going on. Something big. But are you convinced Adam is innocent? No. Of course not. So why don't you save your neck and turn him in? Let the authorities handle this. They know how to do it without getting killed.

But would they do it? That was the question that had her staying in her seat, staring through the plate glass into the store. Adam walked up to the cash register. He didn't so much as glance outside to see if she was still in the car. Reaching into his back pocket, he pulled out his wallet and paid for his purchases. What was he buying?

Hair dye. To cover the yellow paint.

You're being stupid. Go! Call before he comes out! Hurry!

She gripped the door latch, ready to pull. Adam set something else on the counter at the register. A bottle of juice. Orange juice. *For her.*

"Damn you, Adam Burke." She squeezed the metal tight and then released it. "Damn you to hell and back for making me care about you."

He returned to the car with a plastic bag, reached in, pulled out the juice, and then passed it to her. "You didn't do it."

"I considered it." She took the bottle, then twisted off the cap. Pressure escaped it with a little hiss.

"But you didn't do it," he insisted.

"No, I didn't do it." She could admit it, but not while looking at him. She stared at the bottle. What was the difference? He already thought her incompetent, fluff. What could it matter if he added "fool" to his list of her flaws?

"I'm glad, Tracy." He pecked a kiss to her temple.

Stunned, she spilled orange juice down his chest.

His eyes twinkling, he straightened the tilted bottle, but he didn't say a word about her soaking him, Actually, the man looked damned pleased with himself. Not sure how she felt about that, she warned him, "If you call me *fluff*, I swear I'll dump the rest of this over your head." She lifted the juice bottle.

The corner of his mouth twitched. "You asked about my way-on-base theory."

She nodded, still reeling.

He, conversely, appeared calm and collected. "I'm nearly positive all of this is tied to Project Duplicity."

Duplicity. That snapped her to. "General Nestler's pet project?"

"Right." Adam pulled out his keys, started the motor, then pulled out of the shopping center. A muscle in his jaw ticced, as if he really didn't want to say something he felt he must. "Do you know that a privately owned chemical laboratory is the sole-source selection in the potential contract for the project?"

A sole source was a one-on-one agreement between the government and a supplier source. No competition. No bids on the project. In this case, a chemical company. But why would Adam fear knowing that would upset her? He did fear it; she sensed it as clearly as she felt the juice slide down her throat. "No, I didn't know. But sole-source projects are common, especially when they deal with new technology." Other than what Adam had told her, a mention from Colonel Jackson, and Ted accusing her of stepping on his toes, she knew nothing about Project Duplicity. Security on it was damn tight.

"This sole source is rumored to be developing a derivative of sarin, a deadly chemical agent." Adam stared out at the road through the windshield.

Why was he deliberately avoiding looking at her? "Yes?" She was missing something. Something vital that Adam wanted her to comprehend without him having to disclose it. What, she had no idea, but it had her uneasy. Actually, it had her sweating bullets.

He slanted her a resigned look. "Your ex-brother-in-law owns a chemical lab, counselor."

"Paul?" She grunted. "Now you think Paul is tied up with O'Dell, Hackett, Nestler, and Randall, and they're all responsible for what happened to your men in Area Fourteen?"

"It's possible."

Anger shot through her. "It's not!" Paul wouldn't murder men. He'd been wonderful to her. Domineering and interfering, but wonderful.

"It is possible," Adam insisted. "Since you joined the military, Paul has become involved with government contracts. Don't pretend you don't know it. You were reassigned from working contracts because of that conflict of interest."

"By my own hand," she informed Adam. "I requested reassignment."

"Bottom line is you were reassigned due to Keener bidding on government contracts."

Tracy stilled. "So he's involved with Project Duplicity? Is that what you're telling me? And he's somehow involved with what happened to you?" She couldn't believe it. Didn't want to believe it. But could it be true? Paul had sworn he would never get involved in government contracts and then he had done it—after she had become an expert in that field. She'd had to start over. Could he be using this project to make another manipulative attempt to control her?

"He *is* involved with the project," Adam said. "The jury is still out on whether or not he's involved with what happened to me and my men. But we're going to find out."

Tracy swallowed a bitter lump in her throat, watched the highway signs as they sped by them. She didn't want to know. She really didn't want to know. Paul had been there when she'd most needed him. He was all the family she had left. He couldn't, wouldn't, get involved in murder or treason. He just damn *couldn't!*

You're Adam Burke's sun.

Again Chaplain Rutledge's words ran through her mind, and tears stung her eyes. Her vision blurred and she blinked hard. Matthew and now maybe Paul, too. Was every man in her life destined to betray her?

Adam was right; they did have to find out. Because no matter how much pain Paul's involvement would cause her, or how much relief determining his innocence would bring, it would cause her even more pain to know Adam could be innocent and yet be deemed guilty because she lacked the courage to look for the truth. The woman in the mirror would condemn her the rest of her days. And justly so.

More fearful than she had been the day she'd gotten out of the hospital and it had hit her like a sucker punch to the stomach that she had to go on with her life alone, she whispered softly, "Yes, we have to find out."

Chapter 18

They drove east.

At nine P.M., Tracy figured she had kept quiet long enough. She was angry with Adam. Angry because he had frightened her in her home, because he had raised doubts in her mind about Paul, and because he made her feel things for him she didn't want to feel. And that anger had her lashing out. "I realize I'm your captive, but I'm only human. I'm tired, hungry, and I want a bath." Since her fever had broken—she still swore he had scared it out of her—she had felt clammy. She needed a shower in the worst way, and a shampoo. Her tangled hair had dried in clumps. No self-respecting cat would even drag her in.

"Sorry." The damn man laughed. "I'm not trying to make you uncomfortable. We just needed to put some distance behind us."

"That's another thing," she said. "Where are we going?"

"Greenland."

"Greenland?" she fairly shouted. "We can't go to another country."

Adam glanced her way. "Greenland, Mississippi. It's about five more miles. Can you wait that long?"

Not wanting him to see her relief, she turned flippant. "Would it matter if I couldn't?"

Regret flickered through his eyes. "Not really."

Not at all surprised, she dropped him a curt nod. "Five miles will be fine, then."

He smiled. Not with his mouth, but with his eyes.

She hated it. Hated the good feelings it aroused in her as much as she hated liking his approval. Yet Adam hadn't had much to smile about in his life and that she had dredged one out of him brought her a secret pleasure she couldn't deny, not without lying to herself. She didn't happen to like that, either. Contrary, she frowned at him and looked out the side window.

They drove the rest of the way in silence.

Adam took the Greenland exit, then drove down to the Lucky Pines Motor Lodge.

When he turned in, Tracy had to stifle a groan. The paint was peeling off the wooden building, exposing weathered gray wood. The metal "Office" sign, suspended from a square of angle iron, hung crookedly, dangling by a length of chain attached to one eyebolt. The other side's chain hung loose, dragging the ground. Cottages had been staggered haphazardly across the lot, and nearly every vehicle in sight was a mud-splattered pickup truck, parked in red dirt and knee-high weeds. "Are we staying here?" It looked like a joint with hourly rates.

"Unless your rich husband left you an estate in the immediate vicinity."

"Matthew didn't leave me anything," she said before thinking. Adam's surprised look put her on the defensive. "We were too busy getting through law school to worry about wills."

As soon as the words left her mouth, she regretted them. Not because of how Adam might take them, but because they made her think. Until Adam had come along and left her his bequest, had risked exposing himself to protect her, and had bought her orange juice, she'd really believed that about Matthew and wills—that they'd been too busy for him to think about protecting her. But now, she wondered.

"This place isn't fantastic, but it's not as bad as it

looks.'' Adam passed the office and drove around to the back of the main building.

"Lord, I hope not.'' Amazing, but the place had security lights and a rear parking lot. When he backed into a slot near a secondary exit and turned off the engine, Tracy knew he had been here before—and that he had known their destination before he had kidnapped her. "What rooms are we in?"

His expression turned sheepish. "Room twelve."

The bottom dropped out of her stomach. "You expect me to share a room with you?"

He blew out a sigh that threatened to topple the pines. "How many times have you heard of a victim's quarters being separate from their abductor's, Tracy?"

He'd used her name. She liked the way it sounded, even now. Compared to his accusatory "fluff" and his sarcastic "counselor," who wouldn't like it? But she still, more than ever before, hated liking anything about him.

"Grab the cooler, will you?"

She'd like to grab it, and swing it into his gut. "Why not?"

He opened the car door, preparing to get out. "Look, you can make this easy or hard, it's up to you. I'd prefer easy, but I'm up for either."

"You're forgetting that you're a willing participant in this venture, Adam. I'm not."

"I'm not forgetting anything," he insisted. "If whatever is going on here comes to pass, a lot of innocent people are going to die. I'm especially not forgetting that."

She might be crazy for being attracted to the man, but she still recognized the truth when she heard it, and about this, Adam was being honest. "What do you mean?"

"Let's go inside. After you shower, we'll talk about it. It's time you understood the scope and potential impact of all of this."

His words filled her with dread. The only redemption

was that speaking them had him looking as grim as she felt.

She grabbed the cooler and followed him inside.

The room was large, and not as bad as she had expected. Two double beds took up most of the space. A table and two chairs fitted into the far corner, and a dresser hugged the west wall. A television sat atop it, bolted down, of course. The wood was cherry. No burn marks ruined the shiny surfaces, and from the gloss, it appeared the place was clean. That was a comfort. She'd expected a roach motel with cracked ceilings and had instead gotten a rustic but quaintly comfortable room.

"You grab a shower." Adam set down his gear. "Clothes are in the closet."

She spun around and stared at him. "You brought me clothes?"

"I didn't think you'd want to run around in your PJs for the duration."

It was a thoughtful gesture. But the bitch in her reared its nasty head, refusing to allow her to show any gratitude. "Just how many times have you been in my home?"

"Several."

"Several?" She planted her hands on her hips.

Ignoring that outraged gesture, he adjusted the air conditioner, located below the window. "Can I trust you to stay put?"

"You're leaving?" Now why did the prospect upset her? She *had* lost her mind. Totally.

"*Hungry* was one of the items on your list, right?"

It had been. "I'll stay put." Where did he think she'd go? They were out in the middle of nowhere and he had the car keys. No doubt the Lucky Pines didn't allow long-distance phone calls, and her calling card was at home in her purse.

He looked deeply into her eyes for a long moment, and then nodded. "For the record, when you elected not to call the authorities at City Drug, you ceased being a hostage—at least, in my eyes. I'm going to trust you, Tracy. Please don't disappoint me again."

She didn't have to ask what he meant by that "again." She'd blundered already, and it had cost him dearly. He'd been beaten, his team had been cremated—both because she hadn't been doing her job. Yet he hadn't kidnapped her for revenge, but to protect her and to prove the truth. What kind of man was he really?

The kind who had implicated Paul in all of this. She didn't fully grasp the ties, not yet. But before they left this room, by God, she would. If she had to grill Adam until daylight, she would understand all of this.

When he'd gone, she looked in the closet. The clothes weren't hers. He'd bought them. She checked a couple of labels. How had he known her size?

Deciding she'd prefer not to know, she looked through the clothes. Basic, but suitable. Why would he bother?

You cared enough to try to find out the truth. Sacrificed . . .

"Whatever." Discomfited, she jerked open the top dresser drawer and found a white oversize T-shirt. It'd do. She pulled it out, and headed for the shower, trying not to think about him choosing clothes for her. "For God's sake, Keener. It's no big deal." She glared at her reflection in the mirror. "Anyone in Intel knows how to grab essentials when on the run."

She finished showering, then stepped out of the tub and dried off. *You didn't turn him in. Accept it. After this stunt, you'll probably lose your freedom, your career, and maybe your life.*

She met her own gaze in the mirror and refused to cower. She'd handle whatever came just as she'd handled grief. One day at a time. And when that had been too hard, then one hour at a time. And when that burden had become too heavy, then one minute at a time. If she got down to second by second in this, then so be it. But she would *not* fold.

She turned out the light, then stepped into the room.

The lamp on the table between the beds was turned on, casting a soft amber glow throughout the room. Adam was back, with food, and it smelled like heaven.

"I hope Chinese is okay." He wadded up a white sack, then tossed it into the trash.

She looked at the table. He had even remembered hot mustard. Her heart softened toward him a little more. "It's fine."

He turned to smile at her, stilled, and let his gaze drift down from her head to her bare toes.

She felt like an idiot, standing there in a T-shirt and Pooh slippers. Sitting down at the table, she cocked her head. "How did you know my size?"

His eyes twinkled mischief. "Intel encourages intense observation."

"Uh-huh." She pursed her lips, then grunted. "More likely, experience at gauging."

He lifted her fork, then pressed it to her hand. "Let's eat."

While they dug through white cartons of sesame chicken, lo mein, and egg rolls, Tracy watched him. He never totally relaxed. To most people, he would appear relaxed, but a tense alertness in him warned he was ready. At a moment's notice, he could attack or defend. Considering someone was trying to kill them, that comforted her, but it worried her, too. For him. That constant, added stress couldn't be healthy.

"I've been thinking about what you said about Paul." She twirled her fork in the carton of lo mein, certain it would be kinder to her fragile stomach than the sesame chicken. "I just can't believe he would get involved in anything this crooked."

Adam paused eating, dabbed at his mouth with his napkin. "Why not?"

"Gut feeling." She munched down on a bite of egg roll, loving the spicy taste. "When my husband and daughter died, I was in the hospital. You know that, of course. And you know Paul handled all of the arrangements for their funerals, including identifying their bodies. Until I fully recovered, he took care of everything, including me." She tilted her head, swiped her still-damp hair back from her face. "For my security, he even offered to marry me. I can't see a man willing to sacrifice himself to protect his brother's widow doing something so . . . so—"

"Illegal?"

"Actually, *despicable* is what I was thinking." She dipped her egg roll into the hot mustard, then swiped it through a puddle of sweet and sour sauce. "It just doesn't fit."

Adam leaned a forearm against the table. "I think it fits better than you realize. What man offers to marry a woman unless he wants to spend his life with her?"

"One who wants to protect her. Who feels it's his responsibility. I'm all the family Paul has left now."

"Sorry, not good enough." Adam clicked his tongue. "Paul could take care of you without marriage." Adam took a bite of egg roll, chewed, and then swallowed it, clearly thinking. "Did you ever date Paul, Tracy?"

Her face went hot. "Once. Then I met Matthew, and we knew we belonged together."

"And Paul, being a loving older brother and a superior human being, stepped aside without any ill feelings. He probably encouraged you and Matthew to get together. Love is rare, you can't squander it, and all that rot, right?"

Exactly right. Exactly. She swallowed a bite of lo mein that suddenly seemed too big for her throat. "I realize it sounds hokey, but it's true. And if I'd let him, Paul would have taken care of me financially without marriage. So that doesn't mean he wasn't sincere."

Adam frowned. "This doesn't absolve him, counselor. Actually, it makes his involvement more apparent."

She stabbed her fork into the carton. "How in heaven do you get that from this?"

Adam reached over and touched his napkin to her chin.

"Hot mustard," he explained. "Alone, I don't. But answer this for me. When Matthew died, Paul inherited everything, right? I'm assuming he did since you said you inherited nothing."

She nodded. "He did."

"And then Paul asked you to marry him. You refused and joined the military. But it wasn't until then that Paul began negotiating for government contracts, which cost you your job in your chosen field. Or did he begin bidding before you went into contract law?"

"It was after I specialized in contracts. But I don't think Paul would jeopardize Keener Chemical's reputation by going after government contracts just to punish me for refusing to marry him, Adam. That is where you're going with this, isn't it?"

"It's exactly where I'm going."

"Why? His proposal was a noble gesture. He wanted to protect me. That's all."

"I don't think so. I think Paul wanted you for himself. He's wanted you all along. And when you preferred Matthew, and then Matthew died, Paul decided to try to step back into your life as your husband. That's what he's always wanted."

"I don't want to believe that."

"I know," Adam said, spearing a piece of sesame chicken. "But it makes sense."

It did. She couldn't meet Adam's eyes.

"Maybe deep down, he resented you for preferring Matthew."

"I never saw any evidence of that."

"Doesn't mean he wasn't feeling it. Haven't you ever refused to say what you really felt?"

That too made sense. It also made her unsure who to fear. On the one hand, she owed Adam for protecting her against the two men in her house—something her fair-weather friend Randall wouldn't have done. But on the other hand, it had been Adam who had kidnapped her and put her in jeopardy. Worse, she was strongly attracted to the man, and growing more so. Crazy beyond belief, considering she still had more than a few suspicions that he was guilty of treason, of being a coward, and inadvertently, a killer.

Unable to eat, she dropped her fork into the carton, then shoved it away. "Adam?"

"Mmm?" He looked up from his chicken to her.

"What about this derivative of sarin makes it worth all of this?"

He swallowed a drink from his canned soda. "Sarin's been around since the forties, Tracy. But just recently it's become a hot product in chemical-warfare circles. It's a dual technology."

A shiver skidded up her spine. "Civilian and military applications?"

Adam nodded. "Intel believes Iraq used sarin against Iran and, in the civilian sector, terrorists used it in a Japanese subway attack at rush hour. If they had applied it properly, they would have killed thousands. You can bet they won't make that application mistake again."

"So it's the terrorist aspect that has the military worried."

Again, Adam nodded. "It's only a matter of time before some fanatic blitzes the New York subway system or the Atlanta airport."

"You said the terrorists applied it improperly. What are its long-term effects?"

"We don't know." Adam's eyes went from solemn to somber. "Sarin's typically lethal."

"Oh, God."

"It doesn't dissipate, Tracy. It contaminates everything it touches, including the land. Four years after exposure, properties are still evident."

"This is serious." Grim possibilities plagued her mind.

"More so than you think." Adam too shoved away his food, as if he also had lost his appetite. "In quiet circles, it's being said that this derivative, retrosarin, is far less expensive than sarin and ten times as lethal."

Cheap and effective. "A terrifying combination," she said. "And exactly the mix the military looks for when procuring."

"Tracy." Adam's eyes grew serious, solemn. "It could wipe out entire cities."

As if that disclosure weren't enough to turn her hair gray, she sensed an "and" coming and braced for it, praying she'd be disappointed.

"And," Adam continued, "retrosarin *is* Project Duplicity."

Chapter 19

A shadow fell across Adam's chin and he didn't meet her eyes.

Tracy absorbed the shock. Perhaps learning retrosarin was related to Project Duplicity shouldn't have surprised her—Adam had been connecting the two for some time—but it did. Because of Paul. Her stepping on Ted's toes hadn't upset him *with* her so much as *for* her. Ted knew Paul already had cost her the work she loved with R & D. Now he worried that Paul was interfering with her career again on Project Duplicity. But Paul? Involved in a conspiracy?

That was more than she could absorb. Her insides quivered and her hand shook. She stared down at the lo mein, at the sesame chicken's sauce congealing against the inner sides of the carton. "Adam?" Her voice unsteady, she forced strength into it and lifted her gaze to meet his. "Is this connection between Paul and Project Duplicity suspicion or fact?"

Regret shone in his eyes. "It's fact."

As if physically struck, she stiffened, trying to absorb that, too. She squeezed bits of her T-shirt in her fists beneath the table ledge, not wanting Adam to see how much this upset her. "Have you, um, taken this up the chain of command?"

"Taken what up the chain? My word that retrosarin killed my team? Where's my proof, counselor?" Frustra-

tion filled Adam's voice, tightened his jaw, and he pushed
back from the table. "Duplicity is Nestler's pet project.
His baby. Have you forgotten that?"

"No." She evidently hadn't made herself clear. "I
meant, have you taken your suspicion that there's a connection between what happened to you and your men and
Project Duplicity up the chain of command? Have you
reported it to the OSI?"

He walked over to the window. The air-conditioner
blew a stream of air up over him, plastering his shirt to
his chest and ruffling the plastic drapes at the window.
"I've been cautious." He rubbed at his neck with a weary
hand. "Informal, anonymous reports only." He looked
back at her. "I'm not sure what good it's done. The problem is hard evidence. I don't have anything irrefutably
tying the two together. Why they would kill my men just
doesn't make sense, and until it does, I won't find the
evidence."

The lamplight shadowed his back, catching on the yellow stripe painted on his hair, but Tracy still saw the
truth. She was growing more convinced by the moment
that Adam had told her nothing but the truth. "What kind
of evidence could there be?"

"I don't know." He glanced back at her, as if afraid
to hope she believed him. "I've driven myself nearly
insane thinking about it, but I haven't come up with anything solid."

Tracy thought back to her days of working with this
type of program, back to program managers, contractors,
and bids on potential contracts. Proof. What would a
chemical company need as a basis for obtaining a contract
on a new dual-technology chemical—

A conversation with Ted came to mind, interrupting
her thoughts. A mention of Project Duplicity and its being
ready for funding. "Adam, what about Duplicity's clinical studies?"

"What?" He walked back toward the table and sat

down on the bed nearest her, that ridiculous yellow stripe
in his hair mocking her.

"The clinical studies," she repeated, her stomach flut-
ters growing more intense. The puzzle pieces were starting to fall in place. "Before Paul or anyone else could
get a contract, they'd have to show the potential of their
product. Even to get approval to develop a prototype he'd
need some kind of clinical study. Being the sole source
doesn't exempt the company from that requirement, and
I know the study was holding up Project Duplicity from
going to Congress for funding."

"How do you know that?"

"Counsel told me there had been a glitch, but it had
been rectified."

"Counsel?"

"Ted," she said. "He's counsel on the project,
Adam." What she was about to suggest horrified her.
"Could your team have been their clinical study?"

Adam's eyes gleamed. "This might be it, counselor."

She reached over and clasped his arm. "It's worth
checking out."

He pressed a hand atop hers, his fingers warm, his palm
rough and gentle at once. "Definitely, though the idea of
them using my team as guinea pigs makes me sick."

"It makes you angry," she amended. "Me, too. But
they had to have the studies, Adam, and as twisted as it
may seem, they might well believe the end justified the
means."

Adam stared at her. "God, I hope not."

"It wouldn't be the first time." He stood too close.
"People get so caught up in things they feel are necessary
that when something threatens them—in this case, the
project—they sacrifice from a sense of duty and honor.
They consider it noble."

"Like the suicide missions."

"Right. Those involved don't see them as suicide missions, they see them as accomplishing the mission. Getting the job done. Preserving the ideal."

His eyes warmed.

She should let go of him, pull her hand back, but it felt good to be touched and to touch again. She had buried the ability to touch her emotions along with Matthew, or so she'd thought until Adam dropped into her life. Now they were rioting.

"We'll get started on this tomorrow. It's late," Adam said, his voice thick. "We'd better grab some sleep."

She pulled back her hand, mildly disappointed and swearing to herself she wasn't. She tossed the remnants of their dinner into the trash can. "Which bed do you want?"

"You call it." At the dresser, he picked up the hair dye he'd bought at City Drugs.

"I'll take this one." Her face warmed at choosing the one he had just vacated.

Walking to the bathroom, he didn't look back. "Fine."

Tracy crawled into bed and plumped her pillow. She didn't fear him. But maybe she ought to be scared witless considering what she had read in his Intel file. Adam had performed so many missions with survival odds of less than two percent, it startled her. He also had been given just about every award, honor, and medal the service offered soldiers. But men who put their lives on the line as he had over and again just didn't kidnap and kill their attorneys—even if they had nothing left to lose. They just . . . didn't. He was proving a point. Trusting her because everyone else in the world had abandoned him, including his sorry family.

He had taken a leap of faith, trusting her to want the truth badly enough to give him the benefit of doubt. And by not turning him in at City Drugs, in a small way, she had taken a leap of faith. But was that token gesture really one worthy of his trust?

"Damn." His muffled curse sounded from the bathroom.

She looked toward the bath. Light inched out from a crack under the door, slanting a wedge on the dull carpet.

"Damn it." Adam cursed again; this time, not so quietly.

Tracy cocked an ear, switched on the bedside lamp. "What's wrong, Adam?"

"Nothing."

That was the biggest something of a nothing she had ever heard. She turned from her side onto her back. Ah, the hair dye. A smile teased at her lips. She tossed back the covers, eased to the bathroom, and then lightly tapped on the door. "Need some help?"

"I can handle it."

There was a "Please, help me!" buried in that remark. She twisted the cold metal doorknob. "Are you decent?"

"More or less." He swung the door open.

A laugh threatened her. Knowing he would be offended, Tracy swallowed it down and bit her lips to keep even the hint of a smile from her face. Adam had slung dark brown hair dye all over the bath. Nothing had been spared. Not the walls of the shower, the tile floor, the sink, or even the skylight overhead. "Good grief, Adam."

He glared at her, his hair spiked with brown foam that stained his ears, his forehead, and a streak on his bare chest. "The directions said to rub it in."

"Into your hair, not the next county." She grabbed his arm and tugged, urging him to sit on the closed toilet seat, but he didn't move. "I can't reach. Sit down and I'll help. In case you haven't noticed you're a little taller than me."

He folded his knees, bumping into her thigh. "I've noticed."

Oddly pleased by that remark, Tracy lifted a towel from the chrome rack near the tub, then inched between his spread knees and draped it around his shoulders. "Where are the directions?"

"Hell, you mean you don't know any more about this than I do?"

"Is that a backhanded way of asking if I dye my hair?"

She cocked a brow. "There are gloves attached to the directions, Burke. They keep you from getting dye stains on your hands."

"Oh." He nodded toward the sink. "Over there."

Tracy pulled on the gloves, not sure whether to clean him up first or finish applying the hair dye. Probably the dye, she figured. The clock was running and it was oxidizing. She worked the color into the yellow streak first. The paint would be resistant to the dye; it might not penetrate. Then she worked the color through the rest of his hair. It was thick, soft. Appealing.

Her breathing shallowed, and Adam, she noticed, hadn't said a word since she'd first touched him. "There." She stepped back. "How long does it stay on?"

"From when I started, or now?"

"From now," she said, hoping there wasn't ten minutes' difference between the two.

"Twenty minutes." He checked his watch.

"Good. Let's get this mess cleaned up before we end up paying for wall paint and only God knows what else."

He stood up. The bath was crowded with both of them in it. Tracy tossed him a wet washcloth, amused that he seemed as comfortable standing in front of her wearing jeans, a towel, and hair dye as he had been when wearing his shirt or his prison grays. His wrists still bore scabs from the shackles. And angry at seeing them, she wondered how long he would carry the internal scars from all of this.

He stretched for a spot on the ceiling and bumped into her. "Sorry."

Tracy stilled. Facing her, he stood so close that heat radiated from him, and despite the dye, the most pleasant smell lingered on his skin. Distinct. Masculine. Heady. She looked up at him, saw him looking down at her. A burning lit low in her belly, suffused her. He wanted to kiss her, and she wanted to be kissed. She didn't want to think about belief or disbelief, didn't care about problems or challenges or careers. She just wanted to touch him.

Lifting her hand, she pressed her fingers against his broad chest, relished the feel of his fine hair grazing against the pads of her fingertips. God, but she loved the feel of him. Hard and soft at once. "Adam?"

Adam didn't move. He knew only too well what he wanted from her, but what did she want from him? She beckoned him with her eyes and pushed him away with her hand. Which signal did he follow?

He'd be crazy to let this attraction between them develop. He didn't need a lover, he needed an ally. And yet this was Tracy. The woman who had damned the costs and attended his funeral. The woman who didn't talk courage, but lived it, seeking the truth. The woman who had convinced herself she no longer had a heart a man could touch, and then cried for him.

Cried . . . for him.

His heart in his throat, he caressed her arm, elbow to shoulder, letting his hand glide over the soft cotton sleeve, letting all he felt for her shine in his eyes. He wanted her to see it. To see everything. To know everything. To understand that he wanted her, and he had wanted her since he'd first seen her in the attorney/client conference room when he had been beaten, shackled, and shamed. As emotional now as then, he warned her, and himself. "This probably isn't smart."

"Probably not. Certainly not." She raised onto her toes, leaned into him, breasts to chest, and offered him her lips.

"Tracy." He whispered in a tone half prayer, half plea, claiming her mouth.

Gentle and tender, their lips mated, searching and exploring. No simple kiss, this. This kiss stripped souls bare, ignited bodies. It made promises, offered solace, asked for forgiveness. And it humbled. Oh, God, how it humbled. He had dared to think that what they were feeling was just a physical attraction, that it couldn't touch anything deeper in him because there was nothing left to touch deeper in him that his family and his ex-wife hadn't already destroyed. He thought he'd been protected. Safe. He'd been wrong.

He was neither. Yet with Tracy's mouth on his, with her hands cruising over his back, his shoulders and sides and ribs, he didn't want to be protected or safe. He wanted to be loved.

She broke their kiss and looked up at him, her confusion shining in her eyes.

Panic struck his stomach. "Don't say you regret it, Tracy. Please." He hated the pleading he heard in his own voice.

"I won't," she whispered. "I don't." Then she kissed him again. Harder. Hotter.

And unable to resist, Adam kissed her back, unleashing all of the emotions he had choked off since his arrest, his divorce—since childhood. The anger and fury, the disappointment and bitterness, the shame, and Tracy still gave, soothing him, accepting what he offered, returning his fervor with steadfast gentleness until the bad mellowed and drained away, leaving only the good. Tenderness seeped into his touch, his mouth, and she held him tighter.

And when the kiss ended and she sagged against him, squeezing him as if he were a treasure she didn't want to lose, he knew he was lost. That simple gesture torched a flame of hope inside him that he feared and craved down to the marrow of his bones. How could he open himself up to the pain of loving again? Especially now? Especially with Tracy?

With Tracy, how could he not risk it?

Love hadn't wandered his way before, and he doubted it would again. He'd learned young that love is rare. A gift he'd hungered for his whole life, and it had eluded him.

Her breath warm on his neck, she reared back, certainty burning in her eyes. "I don't want to have sex with you, Adam."

His chest went tight. "I don't want to have sex with

you, either.'' He didn't. He wanted to make love with her. God, did he want to make love with her. But she had known love before, and so he doubted that was what she had meant. He could seduce her—her physical reaction to him proved it—but he didn't want to take from her. He'd taken too much already, had made too many choices for her, and that truth had guilt stabbing him like a knife. Knowing he had cost her plenty and he could, and probably would, cost her even more, twisted the blade and cut deeper.

He backed away to the sink and turned on the water. ''I'd, um, better get this stuff off.'' He couldn't look at her. One glance, one hint of a glance, and his resolve would slide right down the drain with the hair dye.

She stood in the doorway for a long moment, watching him, then softly sighed and went back to bed.

His knees nearly folded. He rinsed the dye from his hair, pulled the towel up over his wet face, and stared at his reflection in the mirror, reminding himself of the thousand reasons he would be out of his mind to finish what they had started. When he considered himself convinced, he went back to the bedroom.

Tracy heard his footsteps and closed her eyes. She lay still on her side, calling herself forty kinds of fool. She'd kissed him, survivor to survivor. He was her captor and proving a point. He didn't care about her beyond that, and she didn't want him to, not really. She didn't want to invest emotionally. Certainly not with a man who wouldn't recognize love if he was slugged with it. Not with any man.

And yet Adam had made her feel things no man, including Matthew, had ever made her feel. She'd loved Matthew enough to marry him, but he'd never made her feel like this. Never like this . . .

Yet Adam had snubbed her, too. He'd turned away. Had he been suckering her along so she wouldn't turn him in? No, he couldn't be that manipulative. It wasn't in his eyes.

Desperate men commit desperate acts, fool.

Oh, shut up.

Adam turned off the lamp on the nightstand between their beds. He didn't take off his jeans. For some reason, that surprised her. Shuffling covers and punching his pillow, he settled in his bed. Did he snore?

"Are you asleep, Tracy?"

Should she answer him? "Not yet."

"Thanks for helping me with my hair."

"You're welcome." She smiled and cranked open one eye. Faint moonlight slanted in the window from between a gap in the plastic drapes. "Did the color cover the paint?"

"Yeah, it did." He sounded pleased.

"That's good." She was happy for him. The streak had to eat at him. Seeing it every time she looked in a mirror would drive her insane. She should stop there, but her heart wouldn't let her. "It never should have happened. I, um, owe you an apology for that, Adam. I should have expected that they might beat you and I didn't. I'm . . . sorry." It sounded so lame. It *was* lame.

"It wasn't your fault."

"Yes it was. I know how things work at the facility. I should have anticipated it, and I would have, but I was too self-focused and—"

"You didn't beat me, Tracy." He raised up on one elbow and an arc of moonlight swept across his shoulder. "They did. Let the blame rest where it belongs."

Forgiveness. So easily given, and yet so hard to accept. She swallowed hard. "Thank you," she said in a shaky whisper, wondering how he had found the courage to forgive even now, when so much had been stolen from him.

"I want you to know something."

Turning on her side, she pushed down the edge of her pillow and looked over at him. It was too dark to see anything more than his silhouette, but she still felt his gaze on her. "What?"

"I trust you." He grunted. "That shouldn't seem like such a big deal to say, but I've been working up the guts to do it for half an hour."

His frankness surprised her. She had read his Intel file cover to cover. She knew the type of missions this man performed. He faced terrorists one-on-one, infiltrated enemy temtory to gather intel, dealt with people the rest of the world was only too happy to forget existed. Adam had more courage in his big toe than she had in her entire body. And yet he'd had to work up the courage to tell her he trusted her. She closed her eyes and savored his words, knowing his family had made them hard for him to admit to himself, much less to her.

His voice dropped a notch, strained. "Do you think one day you'll trust me?"

Her heart contracted, clenched as if he had squeezed it in his fist. She wouldn't lie to him. He deserved better. "I'm working on it."

"That'll do for now." He let out a sigh and rolled over onto his back. "Can I ask you another question?"

Not sure if she wanted to open up any more doors between them, she hesitated. But then she recalled his leap of faith, and she refused to be a coward. "Sure."

"When I went into the store to buy the hair dye, why didn't you report me? I know you considered it, but why didn't you do it?"

She could be kind or honest, but not both. Honest won. "I did seriously consider it," she confessed. "But then you bought me orange juice."

"What's that got to do with it?"

"About as much as me going to your funeral."

"Oh."

"I know. It's a fluff answer, but it's true."

"It's not a fluff answer."

Her heart tripped, then hammered. "Really?"

"Really."

One little word, yet it meant more than she could say. "My instincts tell me there's truth in what you've told me. I'm not convinced you're innocent, Adam. But I'm dead certain you're not guilty.''

"Now that's a fluff answer.''

"It's not.'' She grunted into the darkness. "Okay, so it doesn't make a lot of sense. But I know what I mean, and it's not fluff.''

"You want hard evidence.'' He sighed and stared at the ceiling. "There's a part of me that is really pissed at having to prove I'm innocent—I won't lie about that. But the soldier in me understands. It still resents, but it understands.''

She rubbed the soft cotton pillow slip between her forefinger and thumb. "I'm sorry.''

"For what?'' He sounded surprised.

"That you're having to go through all of this.''

"I'm sorry I'm dragging you through it with me. If I had a choice, I wouldn't.''

She believed him.

"I could damn the system, or anything else—and I probably will before all the dust settles. But not right now.'' He rolled toward her, stared across the empty space between their beds. "I got into some trouble back when I was a boy. Nothing serious, but it was a wake-up call. I was thirteen and, I thought, invincible. I stole a basketball from a neighbor's kid.''

"We've all done something like that as children, Adam.''

"Not to the police chief's son.'' He laughed, low and deep. "Good came out of it, though. The chief took me down to the station and called my parents. They refused to come get me. I'd gotten into trouble on my own and I could get out of it on my own, they said. I think their reaction shook the chief up. He wasn't quite sure what to do with me. It took a little while, but he decided how to handle it.''

"What did he do?''

"He blistered my ears with a lecture fit to reform a murderer and then locked me in a cell for half an hour.

I thought I'd be stuck in there forever. When he let me out, he warned me that if I didn't turn my life around, I'd end up in a cell forever.''

''Good grief. That's a little extreme for stealing a basketball.''

''It was perfect. One of the nicest things anyone's ever done for me.'' The hint of a smile etched his voice. ''I owe him a lot.''

''What? How can you be grateful for that?''

Adam explained. ''While I was in the cell, I accepted that I couldn't rely on anyone else. I was responsible for myself and for the type of person I became. I took stock and accepted facts. I stopped drifting through life and blaming others for the way things were, and I started building the life I wanted to live.'' Adam sighed. He'd done well, too, damn it. Until now. He'd kept his pact with himself on becoming the type of person he wanted to be. He'd thumbed his nose at temptation and stood fast. He could take solace in that. Others had fallen. But he'd stood fast. ''It hasn't all worked out as planned,'' he confessed. ''But I didn't put the screws to my men, my country, or to myself.'' He looked over at Tracy. ''Someone put the screws to me.''

''What exactly do you mean?'' She kicked the covers off her feet.

''I was allowed to survive the incident only so I'd be alive to take the blame for causing it.'' God help him. He was crazy about a woman who wore Pooh slippers, even to bed. ''They thought I'd slash and sever.''

''Slash and sever?''

''Cut and run.''

Chapter 20

The truth hit Tracy between the eyes. He *had* been allowed to survive—the incident *and* the fire—so that if the truth should be unearthed, he would be available to take the blame. Bloody hell. "With the charges hanging over your head, of course Hackett, et al, thought you would cut and run. Who would dream you'd risk the death penalty to come back to clear your name?"

"I wouldn't have. But then you got involved and things got complex."

Damn it, no. He couldn't have come back for her. She had to be reading him wrong. "Does Hackett have the kind of clout it would take to arrange arson at the facility?"

"He could. He's got contacts worldwide," Adam said. "General Nestler definitely does."

Overwhelmed, Tracy lay silent. What if Nestler was involved? Then Adam would be going toe-to-toe not with a single senior officer but with a whole damn group of them. They had the clout, and the odds. "Adam, why didn't you just disappear?" He was Intel-trained like Janet, only he had a lot more experience. If she knew how to make someone disappear, then certainly he did.

"Three reasons," he said, sounding hesitant to reveal his rationale. "Even believing I was dead, you kept seeking the truth, and you were being stalked for your dedication to finding it."

"What's the third reason?" she asked, hoping she didn't regret it. Two of three reasons had been because of her. She loved and hated knowing it. Feared the responsibility of it.

"It was a matter of honor."

That could mean anything. Devotion to country, the Force, a sense of duty. Anything. "Could you be a little more specific?" A breeze danced through the pines, slanting shadows and moonlight through the window.

"I had to watch over you."

"Why?" Three for three. Her heart strummed. If not for her, he *would* have disappeared.

Avoiding her eyes, he paused, and his voice dropped to a mere whisper of sound. "You cried for me, Tracy."

And no one else had. The depth of meaning that held for him stole through her chest, and tears stung her eyes, made her throat feel thick. She curled on her side, her knees to her chest, and fisted her hand at her chin, rebelling against an intense urge to weep.

As if realizing how emotional they both had become, Adam cleared his throat and turned the topic. "You know, we've got a lot of implications but no hard evidence. I want the truth as much as you do—maybe more. The question is, how do we find evidence?"

Lying in separate beds in the dark, they discussed possibilities, dissected them and the implications, and in the space of a breath, she confessed knowing about Adam's past and calling his mother after the fire, trying to get the woman to demand an autopsy. "I can only imagine how much your parents hurt you over the years. But I'm sure it's been a lot."

"Early on, yes. But after a while, I stopped letting them." He let out a self-deprecating laugh. "Of course, my ex-wife picked up where they left off, until I stopped letting her, too."

"I'm curious about her."

"My mother?"

"No. Your ex-wife." Tracy couldn't fathom him allowing a woman to get close enough to him to hurt him. Not after his parents. And yet his ex obviously had or he never would have married Lisa.

"She was beautiful, sweet, and gentle-natured," he said matter-of-factly. "She wanted to love me. At least, I think she did. But she just couldn't."

Tracy felt a catch in her heart. "You are lovable, Adam."

"It was the job," he said. "In theory, she wanted to be married to an Intel officer. She just didn't like the reality of it. The secrecy of the missions, me being gone so much—all of it."

"That's a common problem." Tracy had heard it again and again at the JAG office. Spouses tired quickly of the job coming first and family taking a backseat to duty. Wearied of military members leaving abruptly, unable to say where they were going or when they'd be home. And they resented having to handle alone all of the crises and problems that inevitably cropped up at home during their members' absences. The base offered counseling services and a family liaison to assist, but many spouses hesitated to air their family's personal laundry, unsure how it might impact their members' careers. They suffered in silence. Some endured the trials without bitterness, some with it. Some kept on enduring, and some cut and ran. Lisa had cut and run.

"I thought we could work through it," Adam confessed. "When you marry into Intel, it takes a while to get used to the way things are. But she didn't make the transition."

The change in his voice had Tracy frowning. Why had it become so hard-edged? Was he still in love with Lisa? Or just still resentful that she too had left him? "What happened?" Tracy shouldn't have asked; it was too personal. But done was done. Would he answer her?

"I came home from a three-month TDY in the Pacific and found her playing house with another man."

It didn't take much imagination to visualize that scene,

or how it had crushed Adam. Reaching out and trusting someone had to have been hell for him, yet he had done it, and she had betrayed him. Why had she had to betray him? It wasn't fair. Not after what he'd been through. His marriage had been just one more kick in the teeth. One more scar on his heart.

"It didn't get ugly," he said. "I just left and never went back."

And he had never risked trusting a woman again—until now. She knew it as well as if he'd said it. Even after Tracy had failed him, he had risked trusting her. The courage that had taken on his part staggered her, and it melted what resistance she had left to keeping him out of her heart. "I wish you could have had a happy marriage, Adam."

He slid closer to the edge of his bed, closer to her. "Does anyone?"

"I did," she whispered.

"I'm sorry he died."

"So am I. Matthew was a good man. You would have liked him."

"I'm sure I would have."

Tracy slid over to the edge of her bed, scrunched her pillow, and stared across the empty space between their beds to Adam. "I wish I could have gone to his funeral, and to Abby's." Tracy admitted aloud what she had kept secreted inside her for five long years. "I've accepted Matthew's death, but at times, I still struggle with accepting my daughter's. Living with it, I mean."

"Why?"

"Because she wasn't allowed to live before she died. That seems so . . . unfair."

Adam reached over the space between them and covered her hand on the mattress with his. "You were only five months pregnant. The odds were stacked too high against her."

"I know." Tracy swallowed hard against her anger at that truth. "But losing her will always hurt."

"I'm sure it will," Adam said simply. "You loved her."

Tracy had loved Abby. Immensely. Deeply. Totally. She always would. "What really offends me is when people say things like 'Oh, you're young. You can have other children.'" A tear slipped to her cheek. Why had she let Matthew drive? *Why?*

Understanding sounded in Adam's voice. "One child can't replace another. You'd love other children as much as Abby, but you'd never love her less for loving another child."

A second tear trickled down the path of the first. She loved Abby but she hadn't protected her. Her child, her responsibility, and she hadn't protected her. A sob caught in Tracy's throat.

Adam came to her, sat down on the side of her bed and held her, closing his arms around her shoulders, sweeping her back with his hand. She'd never before seen such tenderness in him, and it touched her in places she'd forgotten she could be touched. She was supposed to be a woman who refused to love, who refused to care too much, and yet in his arms, with her face against his bare chest and his heart beating against her ear, she realized that while she had been refusing to care, she had been more than slightly crippled. She'd been lonely, lost, and empty. So empty, and absent from life.

Adam tightened his hold on her, buried his face at her neck, and pressed a kiss to her damp cheek, to her temple. "You're not fluff, Tracy."

She wrapped her arms around his bare sides, her elbows brushing against the waist of his jeans, and looked up into his eyes, determined to take the plunge her heart had been urging her to take since she had first read his Intel file. "No, I'm not fluff, Adam," she whispered. "And you're not guilty."

He swallowed hard, bobbing his Adam's apple, and gently squeezed her, thanking her for her belief in him in a way no words could describe. "I have to prove myself to you,'' he whispered shakily, his hands on her unsteady. "I have to know that at least one person in the world believes in me and knows I'm innocent.''

I am worthy of belief. I am innocent. I am worthy of being loved . . .

Unspoken, and yet all of those feelings were there for her to feel in his touch. So was his desire that she be that one person. She saw it, heard it in the tremor of his voice, felt it in the grip of his hands and in the pounding of her heart. She wanted to give him the words, but she couldn't, so she kissed him instead. Poignant and tender. Survivor to survivor.

"It's been a long time since anyone cared so much about me.'' He nuzzled at her neck, pressed his nose against her skin. "Even longer since I've cared so much about anyone.''

Tracy stilled, rattled by the wealth of feeling in his words, by the impact of his tenderness and his kiss. "I do care, Adam,'' she confessed. "I hate admitting it, and I hate it that I'm more attracted to you than I know is wise, but I do care.''

"I know.'' He smiled at her. Not a happy smile, but one tinged with sadness, as if he knew exactly what she meant because he felt the same way.

"You'd, um, better get to bed.'' She pulled away from him.

He didn't move from the edge of her mattress. He smoothed her hair back from her face. "I'm sensing guilt. I don't like it.''

"It's not guilt. It's knowing that loving and losing hurts. No one's eager to feel it once, much less more than once.''

"So this isn't about guilt or having sex, it's about being afraid of loving and losing.'' Insight trembled in his tone. "What haven't you accepted about loving and losing, Tracy?''

"Abby's death.'' God, had she actually said it out loud? "It haunts me.''

"I'm sorry."

She could have kissed him. No absolution. Only empathy because she'd screwed up and they both knew it, acknowledged it, and accepted it. "Me, too. I hate it when people tell me it was an accident, that I'm not to blame."

"You were her mother. Of course you feel blame. You'd feel responsible for whatever happened to her whether or not it's logical or you actually deserved the blame. That's how maternal instincts work—when you've got them. Some mothers don't."

His mother hadn't. So how come he understood exactly how she felt? But right or wrong, guilty or blameless, none of that really mattered. "I should have noticed that Matthew had had too much to drink to drive. I was Abby's mother, it was my job to protect her, and I didn't. That's indisputable, the bottom line."

"No, it's not," Adam countered. "There are times when you screw up and you just have to forgive yourself for it. It's damn difficult to love yourself enough to do it. Forgiving someone else for their mistakes is always easier than forgiving yourself for your own. But you either do it, or it eats at you forever. It haunts you. That's the bottom line." Adam pecked a kiss to her forehead, then moved back to his own bed and settled in. "It takes a hell of a lot of strength to let go, Tracy."

A few minutes passed in silence, and if Adam were smart, he'd let the silence go on, but he was crazy about her, as much as he was capable of being crazy about anyone, and, when it came to her friend Randall Moxley, Adam didn't give a damn about being smart. He cared about Tracy getting hurt. He had to at least try to warn her. "Tracy?"

"Mmm?"

"Be careful with Moxley, okay?" Once, Adam had feared she was working with Moxley, selling new program technology. Now he wondered how he ever could have believed something like that of her. But he hadn't really known her then.

"What do you mean?"

Maybe he shouldn't have said anything, but it was too late now. Pandora's box had been opened. "He's an arrogant ass who's overly worried about impressing the hospital staff and not nearly worried enough about your safety."

"True—about the hospital staff," Tracy agreed. She'd have to lie to refute Adam and she had the feeling he had been lied to more than enough.

Flat on his back, he folded his arms beneath his head. "I bet he gave you hell for defending me."

Tracy guffawed. "Who hasn't?"

Adam debated, then decided. He either trusted her, or he didn't. He'd come too far to go soft now. "Janet Cray."

"Janet opposed. Strenuously."

"No she didn't." Adam sighed. "She gave you space to make your own decisions and then tested the strength of your commitment and conviction."

Tracy sat straight up. She left her bed, came and stood over him. She'd trusted Janet—*trusted her*. No. No, not Janet. She wouldn't have done that to her. Fisting her hands at her sides, Tracy glared down at Adam. "Are you saying Janet betrayed me?"

He looked up at Tracy, his eyes solemn. "I'm saying she didn't betray you. She's the only one who's been more worried about you getting hurt than keeping herself safe."

What had Janet done? Something that could be perceived as betrayal; that much was clear, but what? Confusion churned in Tracy. Nothing was what it seemed. No one was *who* they seemed. Since Tracy had entered the Air Force, she'd led a simple life. She'd worked; she'd had to deal with the blow of giving up her first love of consulting on leading-edge technology because of Paul's involvement in military contracts. She'd built herself a life alone, one centering on her work, her home, her garden, and she'd found a measure of peace. She hadn't been satisfied, happy, or content, but considering all she had dared and lost, she had been only a little more than slightly crippled. Now, everyone seemed bent on taking even that from her, on severely crippling her.

And she was angry. Furious. Outraged. She had lost all she could lose. She'd lost everything. And she'd started over—alone. *Alone!* And still that hadn't been enough. Life still had to take more. And that frightened her. People were trying to kill her, for God's sake.

The urge to scream or cry warred in her, and Tracy battled them both, glaring down at Adam. "If Janet didn't betray me, then what exactly are you telling me?"

The sheet was draped over his chest. He wadded the edge of it in his hand. "I'm telling you that she's been in touch with me since I left the jail, Tracy."

"What?"

He sat up. "She only let me know you were in serious trouble for disobeying a direct order and not closing out my case file."

Grapevine-attuned, Janet knew a lot. But how had she known Adam was alive? How had she known where to find him—how to reach him? *Why hadn't she told Tracy?*

"That's it?" Tracy asked. Janet had been in Intel. Had been? *Was.* Once in, always in, regardless of where you're stationed, your position, or your official status. Janet hadn't left Intel. Maybe it wasn't her primary duty anymore, but she still remained in its ranks. If anyone would know about Adam, it would be her. She'd worked with him before, and—the truth rang clear—Janet believed him innocent. "She told you as a means of protecting me?" That was the most obvious deduction. But nothing was as it seemed, so was it the right deduction?

"Yes." Adam dragged a hand through his hair. "Look, I know this is hard for you. All of it. You didn't buy into the program, you were drafted. They forced you to defend me and get involved. Like I told you before, if

I could do what needs to be done without you, then I would.''

"But you can't.'' Innocents would die. Her chest went tight with fear. They were confronting some powerful people. She could end up dead—and probably would, if she crossed those powerful people, which she had no choice but to do. Still, it was the right thing. "I'm a military officer, Adam.'' She lowered her gaze to his chest so he couldn't see how deeply upset she was. "I *did* buy into the program.''

Going back to her bed, she stopped at the foot of his. Fear wasn't a sign of weakness, it was a sign of good sense. She was afraid, and strong enough to admit it. Crossing her chest with her arms, she looked over his feet up to his face. The soft T-shirt bunched over her ribs, beneath her arms. "Adam?''

"Yes?''

Her mouth incredibly dry, she licked at her lips to moisten them. "Would you hold me for a while? Just until I get used to the idea of someone trying to murder me.''

Adam couldn't believe his ears. She wanted him to hold her? She was turning to him to feel safe? Surprised she'd let anyone see her this vulnerable, that she'd chosen him, touched him too deeply to speak. He tossed back the covers, and opened his arms.

Tracy scrambled over the foot of the bed and nestled against his chest. Feeling her tremble, Adam's heart wrenched, and he wrapped his arms around her. Didn't the woman know he could never refuse her anything?

She's getting to you, Burke.

He heard his conscience, and acknowledged it. Yeah, she was getting to him. Hell, she *had* gotten to him.

He stroked her tangled hair and massaged the knots of tension from her neck. The urge to make love to her hit him hard and hot and deep. He clamped his jaw and buried it. That time would come, but it wasn't now. She had come to him for protection, to feel safe in a world that had turned upside down and unsafe. For respite from the ugliness and fear. What was happening was hard for a realist. Tracy, with one foot planted firmly on the ground and one just as firmly in the clouds, was an idealist who believed she was a realist, and that doubled her agony. She had watched her husband and daughter die and, weighed down by misplaced guilt, she'd pulled herself up by the bootstraps only to have her ideals stomped on again. And that, Adam hated most of all.

The woman who had cried for him had been hurt too much, and now she faced more danger. She deserved all of the good life had to offer. Every damn bit of it. Not pain and fear. He tightened his hold on her, listened to her ragged breathing, and silently vowed to protect her, to prove his theory that Paul Keener was working with Colonel Hackett and Major O'Dell—and probably General Nestler—in a conspiracy to corrupt Project Duplicity. Adam would expose them all—including Laurel's god.

Any soldier with sense feared Nestler. His clout ran right up the chain of command, cruised through the Pentagon, and rolled straight on into Congress. But Adam would cross him. He'd cross anyone, do anything to anyone to protect Tracy and find out who had killed his men—or he'd die trying.

Forfeiting his life was highly possible. Adam didn't need the bean counters' stats to deduce that his survival odds ranked less than his typical mission's two to ten percent. But to stay true to the man he'd become the day his parents had abandoned him in that jail cell, he had no choice. He was used to risking his neck, and to doing his job knowing his competency would impact a nation. He could handle those pressures. But— He looked down at Tracy's sleeping face, at her arm slung over his chest and her knee wedged between his thighs, and his heart turned over in his chest. But he was not accustomed to working and risking or impacting Tracy's life.

In knowing all she had done for him, he had fallen hopelessly in love with her.

God help them both.

Chapter 21

Adam rolled out of bed, rousing Tracy.

Jarred awake by his hand at her shoulder, she cranked open her eyes, fuzzy and confused. Why was he waking her? It wasn't even daylight yet. From the bathroom light, she saw his finger pressed over his lips. Grasping his motion for silence, she nodded.

He pointed to the bathroom door and stepped back to let her get out of bed. "Hurry," he mouthed, clenching a blue shirt in his hand.

Tracy grabbed her slippers, snagged a change of clothes he had put on the dresser for her, and then joined him in the bath, giving him a what's-going-on look he'd have to be dead to miss.

"We've got company," he whispered, sliding his arm into the sleeve of his blue shirt.

"You want to run?" Appalled, she clutched the bundle of clothes to her chest.

He fitted on a shoulder holster and gun. "Consider it a strategic retreat to regroup." He shoved the door shut. Under his thumb, the lock snapped into place.

Tracy dropped a slipper on the floor. Fretting, resigning herself to running, she snatched it up and stuffed it back into the bundle. "How are we supposed to get out of here?" There was only one exit—the door where company was trying to enter.

Adam looked up.

"The skylight?" Her eyes stretched wide and she whispered a shout. "You've got to be kidding. I'm not athletic at all, Adam. How am I supposed to—"

Before she finished her question, Adam had the skylight open, the bubble punched out, resting against the roof, and Tracy suspended midair. "Drop those damn slippers and stretch."

"No." She needed them. *Oh, how she needed them.* "Oh, God. I can't do this. I haven't worked out since OTS." Officer Training School had been five years ago.

"This is no time to digress or debate, counselor. Stretch."

A muffled scrape sounded in the bedroom. Tracy sucked in a sharp breath.

"One more and they'll pop the deadbolt and be in the room," Adam warned her. "Hurry!"

"I'm trying, damn it," she whispered, exasperated at the effort of lifting herself through the opening. She tossed the slippers and clothes out through the hole, then heaved.

Suffering a flailing kick to the chin, Adam grimaced. He planted her foot on his shoulder, then cupped her backside, and shoved.

Cursing a blue streak between gasps, doing her damnedest not to scream, she catapulted up, then rolled onto the roof.

Adam turned on the shower, hooked the skylight's opening edge, twisted his shoulders to diagonal corners, and then hoisted himself up, scraping his back and banging an elbow on the lip of the frame. On the roof with Tracy, he crouched and closed the bubble over the opening, then swiped at the roof grit clinging to his hands. "Come on."

Tracy didn't budge; just sat there with her fingers splayed on the rough shingles, certain any movement would send her tumbling to the ground. For the first time, she understood exactly the terror Phelps had felt on the rooftop patio when he'd thought they'd have to scale the wall.

"Tracy, we've got to go. Now."

"I'm a lawyer, for God's sake. My sense of adventure consists of writing a dynamic brief. The idea of running across a roof appeals to me about as much—"

"As a bullet between your eyes?" Adam suggested with a scathing glare. "That's your choice, counselor." He grabbed her arm and tugged. "Move it."

Swearing she would not faint, she would not heave, she would not whimper, Tracy crawled. She couldn't stand up on the roof, the pitch was too steep and her legs were too wobbly. The gritty shingles scraped at her knees, her palms, and her heart roared, threatening to explode. The coward in her wished it would, and she could die without having to suffer. But Adam, damn him, wouldn't let her die. He grasped her hand, yanked her to her feet, then pushed her toward the edge of the roof. Tracy looked down. It was only a one-story building but, *dear God,* the grass looked miles away.

"See that car?" Adam whispered, pointing through the dark toward a security light. "The red one, over there— three rows out, fourth car from the end?"

She nodded, too paralyzed by fear to talk. Men's voices sounded inside their room below. Whoever had been trying to get in had done it. In minutes, they'd find the bath empty and come out after them.

"Get to it," Adam said. "Go. Go. Go."

He had to be joking. Had to be. "How?"

"Jump."

"*Jump?*" The man had lost his mind.

Adam pushed her.

Tracy hit the ground with a hard thump that knocked the wind out of her. Before she recovered, Adam landed beside her on his feet, dropped to a roll, and then stood up. He rushed over to her, still a motionless heap on the ground. "Tracy, let's go."

Aching like the dead, she pulled herself to her feet,

gathered her slippers and clothes, and then dogged his heels to the red car, swearing she'd murder him as soon as they were safe. He'd actually, by God, pushed her off the roof.

On the far side of the parking lot, two men in military uniforms examined the car Adam had driven here. Were they MPs? She strained to see the patches on their uniforms, but couldn't. The shadows were too deep.

Clutching her bundle of clothes, she slid into the car, scared and angry, her scraped knee throbbing. She rubbed at it, and roof grit rolled off her shin and pattered on the vinyl floor mat. "Jesus, Adam. Now you're adding grand theft auto to the list of charges against you?"

"It's not stolen." He locked the doors.

"Why didn't the dome light come on?"

"I disabled it." He shoved at her shoulder, forcing her to fold over. "Get down."

Her face slapped flat against the seat. "You planted this car here. Like you did the other one on the dirt road."

"For God's sake, Tracy, be quiet."

"Why? No one can hear us in here." Lord, she was nervous. Babbling again.

He hunched over her, shielding her body with his. "Stay down."

"Why would someone break in on us?" Still babbling, but whispering. That would have to do. No way could she stay silent through this. And why was the parking lot so busy at three in the morning? Ah, the bars had just closed. The activity would help, but at any moment they could be seen and recognized. "I don't get it. Can't they decide if they want you dead or alive?"

"Identify 'they.'" Adam scanned the parking lot, sweat beading on his brow. He eased a key into the ignition, removed his gun from the shoulder holster and put it on the seat beside him. "It's obvious now that we're dealing with more than one group of adversaries, counselor."

"It is?" She wasn't a mental slouch, but she certainly wasn't following his line of thought.

Adam nodded. "We're alive. The attackers left us a way out. Hackett and O'Dell are professionals. They wouldn't have done that."

Peeking up over the door, she looked out the window. The security light shone down on a white Lincoln parked three slots away from them, and a second car moved slowly down the row behind them. When it braked under the light, she saw the driver clearly. "Adam," she said in a barely discernible whisper. "It's Lieutenant Carver."

Carver motioned through his window to the two men making mincemeat of Adam's abandoned car. "Let's go," he called to them out the window, and then raised the glass. The men rushed over, got in, and Carver sped out of the lot.

"Hackett," Adam suggested. "Carver would do anything for him."

"He wouldn't let you go," Tracy said. "Hackett doesn't want the truth out, Adam, and he knows now you're going to expose it. No, Hackett isn't behind this. Not if he's responsible for the incident with your men."

A blue sedan circled the lot, then passed by their car. In the light, Tracy saw Major Gus O'Dell driving it, and in her mind, more puzzle pieces shifted into place and interlocked. "Adam, what if someone close to Hackett and O'Dell discovered the conspiracy and opposed it? Could the opposer be running interference for us?"

"Possibly." Adam kept his gaze firmly fixed on O'Dell.

So did Tracy. O'Dell parked then headed directly for the abandoned car. He looked in through the windows, then pulled something out of his coat pocket, and walked to the motel entrance. Shiny metal glinted in the light. He was going to their room. With a gun. She had no illusions about what he intended to do once he arrived there. O'Dell meant to kill them both. Her and Adam. *It's arranged. Burke and you die.*

Had Carver known O'Dell was coming for them and protected them?

Tracy gasped. "Adam, I'm sure I'm right about this. Either Carver has found out about the conspiracy and opposes it, or he's been recruited to help expose the truth."

Adam cranked the engine and shot out of the parking lot, leaving half the tires on the asphalt. "If so, who recruited him?"

Tracy didn't hesitate. "General Nestler."

"Logical—if Nestler isn't working with Hackett and O'Dell. But he has to be. Hackett needs Nestler's support to get that Pacific assignment."

"Maybe Hackett has a compelling reason to cross Nestler. Maybe one more compelling than the Pacific assignment." Tracy tugged on her Pooh slippers.

"Maybe. But if Nestler knew, opposed or not, he'd have to order a formal investigation." Adam frowned at her feet. "And for the record, no shoes can give you the power to do what you need to do. It comes from inside. You've got the tools, Tracy. Trust your gut, and use them."

Maybe one day, she would believe that and she wouldn't need the slippers anymore. But that day, by God, wasn't today. "Right now, I need all the attitude I can get—from any source. So back off about my slippers."

Several hours passed without incident, and Tracy unsnapped her seat belt. She normally would have considered unbuckling crazy while barreling down the highway at seventy miles per hour. But their circumstances weren't normal, it was daylight, they were on a straight stretch of road, and she was sick of feeling like a nut case for riding around in just a T-shirt.

She hitched her jeans up over her hips and then zipped them, bumping her elbow on the door. Her arm stung up to her shoulder, and she rubbed it. Adam hadn't spared her, or her panties, so much as a glance, and that pricked at the woman in her—until she followed his line of vision up the four-lane highway leading back to Laurel and saw what had his full attention. Carver drove in the left lane just two cars in front of them. Goose pimples peppered her flesh. "Adam."

"I see him." Adam eased his foot off the gas pedal, and the car slowed down.

When Carver didn't follow suit, Adam relaxed. "What you said about Hackett and Nestler holds merit, counselor."

She had said a lot. Actually, she'd babbled like an idiot ever since they'd driven hell-bent-for-leather out of the Lucky Pines, complaining about the scrapes on her hands and knees, the grass stains on her T-shirt. She'd vented her anger at him for pushing her off the damn roof, and for his insisting it had been necessary or they'd still be standing there: an assessment probably true, but which she'd denied—emphatically. And she'd speculated on everything from O'Dell's intent to murder them to Nestler's involvement. What *specifically* was Adam referring to? Having no idea, she waited for him to enlighten her.

"Project Duplicity is Nestler's pet. He wouldn't want it corrupted," Adam said. "But he does want it funded."

Tracy fished a bag of potato chips off the backseat, opened it, then pulled out a palmful of salty chips. "Okay, Nestler wants his project funded, and he needs clinical studies to get it."

Adam snitched a chip, then crunched down on it. "Hackett gets those studies and he solidifies Nestler's support for his promotion, to head the Pacific theater mission. That's the wild card. Hackett runs the readiness exercise and ruins the project's odds for funding and he knows Nestler is going to ship his ass to Iceland or some other outpost. He's not going to the Pacific. That's a given. So why would Hackett risk ruining Nestler's project's odds?"

"Maybe he didn't expect what happened to happen."

"Or maybe he did. He's ambitious, counselor, and Nestler writes his OERs. Nestler would play out every eventuality, which means Hackett would, too."

Tracy followed Adam's line of thought. Nestler writes Hackett's Officer Effective Reports, therefore he largely governs Hackett's next promotion and assignment. Hackett screws Nestler and ends up in no-man's-land. "It's hard to imagine Hackett crossing Nestler, then. Unless he stands to gain more than he'd lose by crossing him."

"What could he gain?" Adam lifted a hand from the wheel. "Hackett blows the promotion and he's subject to RIF orders."

A mandatory exit from the Air Force. "With those risks, I don't know what would motivate him. But I think our finding out will prove significant." Tracy bit down on another chip. She was missing something very basic in all of this. What, exactly, eluded her. But it was there.

The road became bumpy; expansion joints reacting to the heat. Adam switched lanes, now trailing far behind Carver. The back end of the lieutenant's car was barely visible.

Easing his grip on the steering wheel, Adam snatched another chip from Tracy. "Hackett is in this up to his eagles."

"I'd bet my bars on it," Tracy mumbled. "The puzzling part is General Nestler. Which side of the fence is he on?"

"I'm not sure. I think he's on the right side, until I weigh in Hackett and his promotion. Then, it only makes sense that Nestler's also corrupt."

"Not if he recruited Carver to run interference." Her mouth dry from the salty chips, Tracy longed for a drink. "Unless Nestler's gotten what he wants from Hackett and now he's hanging him out to dry."

"Could be." Adam blinked, then blinked again. "There's one way to find out."

Tracy rolled her eyes back in her head. "Why do I

have the feeling this means more of your covert stuff and you're including me in it?''

"Because it does, and I am." He spared her a glance, then returned his focus to the road. "Changed your mind about me being innocent?"

"No, I haven't." She frowned. "But I'm your lawyer, damn it, not your Intel partner. I know diddly about covert operations, especially about ones involving conspiracy against our own. I could do more damage than good, and I hate all of this . . . this . . ." Words failed her.

"Fear, counselor," he said. "It's called fear. That's what you hate. But like it or not, you are part of the program, remember? You took an oath. It's not convenient right now, but you can't only keep that oath when it is convenient and you know it. Otherwise, you wouldn't have done any of what you've already done."

He was right. Shame had her face hot. "Bloody hell, Adam, only a moron wouldn't be terrified. I know the law, okay? I don't know how to perform covert missions that could end up getting me and you and a hell of a lot of other people killed. The responsibility terrifies me. Damn right, I'm scared. I'm scared stiff." Feeling better for having unloaded, she shifted her shoulders, trying to slough off some tension. Her insides felt as if a swarm of bees were having a field day in them.

"You think getting Intel training keeps you from feeling fear? It doesn't, Tracy. You just function anyway. In spite of it."

He made sense. You'd have to be inhuman. "Okay, but you're trained, and you can rely on your training. On honed instincts. My instincts are honed to the intricacies of the law."

"Maybe when you get down to it there isn't a lot of difference."

"Maybe. I'll have to think about that." She glanced at Adam. "You said there was one way to determine which side of the fence Nestler sat on. What is it?"

Adam looked her right in the eye. "Retrieve the canister I buried in Area Fourteen."

Tracy didn't like this. Not at all. "We'd have to break even more laws." And this time, she'd be a participant. She'd be an accessory.

"Yes, but we need the canister to analyze its contents. If it has retrosarin in it, then we've got a direct link between Paul Keener and Gus O'Dell, and General Nestler."

Laurel's god would bury them both without even breaking a sweat. "I can't just waltz into Area Fourteen, and neither can you. Technically, you're dead, but I'm not. I'm AWOL, Adam." Being absent without leave left her open for court-martial, for demotion and dishonorable discharge, for God's sake. "And facts are facts. I may believe you, but I'm still your hostage."

Hurt clouded his eyes. "Have I treated you like a hostage? Have I harmed you in any way? Didn't I explain that you were about to be killed, counselor? And didn't I tell you that you stopped being a hostage when you didn't turn me in at City Drugs?"

Tracy squeezed her eyes shut. He had been good to her. Hell, he'd saved her life. And she'd been looking for a way out. A safety net that would absolve her from wrongdoing. Human of her, but oh, so wrong. She who prided herself on doing the right thing had done him yet another grave injustice. And she had hurt him. She cared for him, and she still had hurt him, trying to protect herself. Her eyes burned. "I'm sorry, Adam. It's the fear. I was wimping out."

He didn't look at her. "Do you still doubt me?" His voice sounded deceptively soft.

Be honest. She lowered her gaze to his hand, gripping the steering wheel. His knuckle had blanched white. "I want to, because not doubting you forces me to accept that we have traitors in uniform, and I can't stand the idea of that. But I don't doubt you," she confessed.

"Deep down, I know you wouldn't kill, sacrifice, or abandon your men."

"Thank you." Adam breathed again. He hadn't realized that he had stopped breathing, waiting for her answer, but he had. Covertly glancing her way, he saw tension lining her face. She didn't like what she had just done—wimping out—and she had realized that her feelings for him had strengthened, deepened. From all signs, she didn't know what to make of that.

Neither did he. A part of him, the stupid part willing to open himself up to being hurt again, was elated. He loved her, and she was the first woman since Lisa that he'd cared enough about to make him consider trusting again. And yet another part of him, the wise part, knew the odds ran high that her caring for him could ruin her life. That part of him hated knowing her feelings for him had strengthened. He wanted her safe, not in danger, and anyone who went to this much trouble to build a conspiracy wouldn't let it just fall apart. They would do whatever it took to protect their interests.

He could have left Tracy out of this and she never would have known him, much less come to care for him, but she had refused to stay out of it. In her babblings, she claimed she wasn't an adventuress, that she was a coward. She wasn't. When no one else in the world had cared that he'd "died" falsely accused and had been tagged as guilty without a trial, she had cared. Enough to put her job and her peace of mind on the line. Maybe she hadn't known then she would be risking her life, but she had realized it long before Adam had kidnapped her, and she'd still persisted, rattling cages, looking for the truth. A coward?

No. She was one of the bravest women he'd ever known. And—he glanced down at her slippers—one of the most vulnerable. But pointing out that vulnerability would be a tactical error; she wouldn't appreciate it. At least, not yet. "I need your help, Tracy."

Tracy stilled, stared at him. Such a simple statement,

but the feelings it carried would blast mountains, or melt hearts.

"Not because you're a hostage, but because you want to help me stop them from unleashing retrosarin on the country and because you believe it's the right thing to do."

Any words but those and she might have been able to refuse him. But still stinging from the shame of her cowardice at wanting to hide behind his kidnapping—an act of mercy, not violence—she couldn't. She had to choose. Should she trust him? Or not?

It was that simple. That simple, and that complex.

She shoved her hair back from her face and met his gaze. "All right, Adam. I'll help you."

Chapter 22

"Grandsen?" Tracy stared at Adam, certain the man had lost his mind. *"We can't* go back to Grandsen."

A hot, phantom wind ruffled over her face, through her hair. Sitting on the hood of the car, she shifted her weight and rolled her gaze to the blue "Rest Area" sign. "In case it hasn't occurred to you, we have no place safe to go there. We can't go to my house, we certainly can't go to yours, and the VOQ isn't likely to send out a welcome wagon to greet us." The visiting officers' quarters were definitely off-limits.

"Just drink your drink and stop worrying." He leaned against the front fender and toed the sandy red dirt. It clumped on the toe of his sneaker. "I've got things under control."

"Sure you do." Tracy plunked down the drink can and slid up, letting her legs dangle over the fender. "That's why you're up on all these charges, and you're doing your damnedest to add new ones to the list every time I blink."

Adam propped a hand next to her thigh and glared at her. "I didn't expect my own team to screw me, counselor. Would you?"

She wouldn't. "No, but that doesn't mean we can just drive out to Area Fourteen and dig up the canister. It's a sealed area, Adam."

"Bombing ranges are always sealed areas. But Fourteen isn't locked in a vault, it's surrounded by a fence. Just a fence.''

She crossed her arms over her chest. ''I'll bet my bars it's guarded.''

''Maybe.'' Squinting against the sun, he stared at her lips. ''I'd give it fifty-fifty odds.''

''More like a hundred percent.'' She grunted and swatted at a mosquito buzzing near his ear. ''If that canister has retrosarin in it, whoever put it there is going to be looking for it.''

''I'm sure they've searched extensively for the canister.''

''Which means they've either found it, or they're still looking for it.''

''Maybe they can't find it and that's why Carver warned us O'Dell was coming to the Lucky Pines,'' Adam said, the side of his hand brushing against her thigh. ''Maybe Carver thinks we'll lead him to the canister.''

''Then why let us fall behind? Wouldn't he have glued himself to us on the road?''

''Not if he felt confident we'd retrieve the canister. He'd give us the space to do it.''

Logical. Carver had no need to interfere. ''So Nestler still could be working with Hackett or against him.'' Tracy couldn't resist. She looped her arms around Adam's neck, buried her forehead against his chest, and sighed. ''I really want Nestler to be on the right side in this. I really do, Adam.''

''He might be.'' Adam lifted her chin, stared down at her. ''We'll have to keep playing the cards we're dealt and see.'' Pain flickered through his eyes. ''But we won't give up on him until we know for sure.''

Like everyone, including her, had given up on Adam. She nodded solemnly, wishing he would kiss her, calling herself forty kinds of fool because she really wanted his kiss. ''No, we won't give up on him. Not until we know for certain.''

Satisfaction burned in Adam's eyes. He let the backs of his fingers brush against her cheek, hooked her chin and bent toward her, then touched his lips to hers, kissing her as if she were fragile and he feared she would break. In his arms, she felt many things, but fragile wasn't among them. She felt afraid, offended at the wrongs done to them both, angry and confused at all the deceit, and ticked at Adam for pushing her off the roof. And she felt desire. It had been so long since she'd truly desired a man. Since she'd hungered to touch and be touched. Not since Matthew. And yet with Adam it was all so . . . different. With Matthew, she had been young and caught up in the wonders of first love. She'd wanted all of the things most women want. The magic. The romance. The passion. But that was before she had experienced the agony of loving and losing. Before she'd learned that loving unconditionally can devastate and destroy. That love is joyous, but nothing in the world could cause a woman more pain and suffering.

Now, she knew all of that and more, and yet she found herself craving the chance and taking it. Falling in love with Adam Burke wasn't wise. Risking all that suffering again was insane. She was not an adventuress or brave and he'd never love her, but for now, she was his candle in the window. Yet if she wasn't careful, when he walked out of her life, he'd be walking out with her heart. Then what would she have left?

He separated their mouths. "Did I do something wrong?"

Already anticipating the pain to come, she gave him a negative nod, and not wanting to delve into this—the man read her emotions far too easily—she turned the subject, sounding too breathless to hope he wouldn't realize the effect of his kiss. "So what's the plan?"

He stared at her a long moment. "We go to Area Fourteen and dig up the canister."

She scooted off the edge of the car's hood. Her feet

on the ground, she swatted at the dust on the seat of her jeans. "Should we wait until dark?"

"I considered it, but I don't think traipsing around in the woods at night is a good idea." He slid into the car.

Tracy got in on her side. "The woods in the light of day is god-awful enough. But at night? No, thank you."

"Maybe you are fluff." His eyes twinkled an appealing contradiction. "How did you ever get through survival school?"

"I'm a lawyer, Burke. My survival schools were on contract negotiations and military law. And at those, darling, I am not fluff."

"Point made, counselor. You can knock off the killer glare."

She glared harder. The damn man smiled, and she recalled what he had said about retrosarin. That it didn't dissipate. "Adam, how are we going to retrieve the canister? If it's live, then—"

"Exposure risks. Yes, I know." He shrugged enigmatically. "I've got it under control."

Yet another trust test. Why did it always come back to that with him? Why couldn't he just tell her how they would be protected? Why did he have to test her again and again?

Because he'd been betrayed? Maybe. More likely, he still considered her fluff.

Or maybe because you can't disclose what you don't know.

Her heart softened, and it was all she could do not to reach out and caress him. He was protecting her. Again.

They drove another two hours, then Adam turned off at the Laurel Air Force Base exit. Another thirty miles of wooded reservation land lay between them and the base, but they were less than ten minutes from Area 14.

A cold chill arced through her back and fear squeezed her in a death grip. What would they find out there?

* * *

Adam pulled off the highway and onto a dirt road. About forty meters in, he turned left on a trail of ruts in the dense undergrowth, and then stopped the car in a clump of pines. "We go in from here on foot."

Tracy resisted a groan by the skin of her teeth. Another of his "fluff" looks she didn't need. She felt shaky enough about this already.

They stepped out of the car and Adam went around, got some gear out of the trunk, then began burying the car with fallen branches and clumps of weeds.

Tracy followed his lead and helped him. When they were done, she cast the lump a critical look. "It's not going to fool anyone."

"It's not supposed to." Adam wiped the sweat from his brow with his sleeve. "It's supposed to keep anyone driving down the road from spotting the car. No one would bother searching this area on foot. It's too close to the main road."

He made sense. And too hot and sweaty to decide whether or not to resent it, Tracy cupped her hand at her brow to block the sun from her eyes and watched him.

He hiked the straps of two black bags over his shoulder. "Ready?"

Dread dragging at her belly, she nodded.

An hour later, she was hot, sweaty, sick of sultry air and the baking sun. She was also tired of dogging Adam's footsteps, even with the view of his jean-clad backside in motion enticing her. She swatted at yet another bug. "Damn mosquitoes."

"They're sand fleas," Adam said, not bothering to look back at her.

She tripped over the roots of an oak. "Damn it."

He glared back at her. "Look, I realize you're not overly fond of the woods, and you're not an adventuress, but could you pipe down? If you're right and there are people out here looking for the canister, I'd prefer not to tell them an hour in advance that we're here, too."

"Sorry." Another bug was doing its best to eat her

through her sleeve. She slapped at it. "I'm not used to this covert stuff, you know. I'm—"

"A lawyer," he interrupted, sounding exasperated. "Yes, I know, Tracy."

Succinctly reminded to be quiet again, she hushed and glared at his back. It was different for him. He'd been trained in Intel. He'd been to survival school, and a lot of others, to build specialized skills. He probably liked the woods. She hated them. Give her courtrooms; that was jungle enough for her. And her little backyard garden. Not this sliver of bug-infested hell.

"Veer this way." Adam crawled over the half-rotten trunk of a fallen pine.

"Why?" The way was clear straight ahead. Tracy started to defy him just to show him she could, then decided that was stupid. The hallowed halls of the military judicial system were her playground. This was his turf. She lifted a leg to hike over the tree trunk.

Adam assisted her, set her down on the ground beside him, and looked back to the path.

A rattlesnake slithered to its nest.

"Oh, God." Tracy felt her knees buckle.

Adam held her up, and smiled. "It's okay, counselor. We're going this way."

Damn straight, they were. Way, far away, from the snake. "Um, Adam, what other kinds of wildlife might we find out here?"

His eyes twinkled. "Honey, you don't want to know."

She swallowed hard. "I was afraid of that."

He pecked a kiss to her cheek, then stepped away, and started walking.

They trekked for hours. Tracy cursed the relentless sun. The muscles in her legs burned, her feet throbbed as much as her head, and she jumped at every twig snap, fearing another snake—or worse. Why hadn't Adam just told her what else they might encounter in the way of wildlife? Then her imagination wouldn't be in overdrive.

He stopped suddenly in front of her.

So attuned to placing one foot in front of the other and just walking, Tracy stumbled into his back. If he called her fluff, she swore she'd just turn around and march right out of this hellhole. She'd warned him she'd be lousy at this.

He dropped the black bags without a word. "We're coming up on Area Fourteen."

Coming up on it? "Where have we been?" They'd been hiking for three miserable hours.

"In the safety zone." Adam dropped to a squat and unzipped one of the bags. "Here"— he passed her a suit of clothing and a pair of gloves—"put these on."

Tracy recognized the clothing from the gas-chamber-simulator hangar, when she had gone to see O'Dell. The shamefaced lieutenant had been wearing it. "Chemical gear?" her voice shrilled. "Where in heaven did you get chemical gear?"

"I appropriated it." He put the suit on, passed her the headgear, then put on his own. "Quit glaring at me and put on your gear, okay? I didn't save your neck to get you killed before you can prove I'm innocent and expose whoever is guilty." He clamped a black cube to his belt.

"What is that?" Putting on the gear, she nodded toward the cube.

"A chemical alarm." He depressed a button that distinctly clicked, arming it.

"Adam, I know damn well you didn't get clearances or file any requisitions with Environmental for this equipment. How did you get it?"

He shot her a sly smile. "Anyone with a little ingenuity can get around the requirements, counselor. At least, for long enough to perform a quick recon mission."

"Reconnaissance mission, my eye." She folded her arms over her chest, half admiring him, half wanting to choke him. "Sergeant Phelps from the hospital got it for you, didn't he?" Phelps could file the requisitions for a trauma medical exercise without raising a single eyebrow.

"No he didn't."

An ally in Environmental? Perhaps, Tracy thought. Or perhaps an ally in Tracy's office. One who formerly worked with Adam Burke in Intel. Janet?

Not asking Adam proved challenging, but to avoid yet another "Trust me" response, Tracy stifled herself, and put on the gloves. The less she knew about this, the better.

With not an inch of skin exposed, Adam started hiking again, and within minutes, Tracy admitted she had been wrong. She hadn't been in hell before, but she was in it now. The chemical gear was heavy and hot. Sweat soaked her back, trickled down between her breasts, drenched her hair and burned her eyes. And she was furious. "You realize that by 'appropriating' this gear, as well as your fistful of other charges, you'll be tried for theft and unauthorized use of controlled government property." The mask muffled her voice.

"If I'm caught, I will," he said, sounding just as croaky as she had. "And for kidnapping you—which are all more reasons you have to survive." He shoved at a low-slung branch encroaching on the path and held it until she passed and stood even with him. It snapped back, rustling the leaves. "I'm going to need a hell of a lawyer."

He thought she was a hell of a lawyer? Her heart contracted, slowing a beat and then racing out of control. She looked beyond the mask's frog-eye lens and into his eyes. God help her. She had done the most stupid thing, on a long list of stupid things, in her life.

Knowing it was insane, that he'd never love her, she'd fallen totally and completely in love with Adam Burke.

Chapter 23

Adam pointed to a dense spot where the undergrowth appeared crushed. "I passed out here."

Tracy frowned. It did appear that something had fallen there, but surrounded by miles of woods and brush, how could he know this was the exact spot he had fallen? "Are you positive?"

"I'm positive," he said in his "Trust me" tone. He took off, following an erratic path.

Skirting a spiny bush, she followed him, not at all convinced. He paused to finger broken branches and examine hollows in the uneven ground. She saw the tracks he picked up on, but only after he had found them. If his Intel file hadn't proven it, this venture would: Adam was very good at his job. He definitely had not gotten lost or terrain-disoriented the day of the incident.

"I put on the chemical gear here." He stopped and looked back at Tracy. "And this is where I got dizzy. See the jagged ruts in the dirt?"

Tracy squatted down for a closer look at the ground. "It is more disturbed than what we've seen so far." She squinted against the sun, up at him. "Can one person staggering around leave this much evidence?"

"Sweepers," Adam said, approval shining in his eyes.

Resenting the gloves that kept them from touching skin to skin, she grasped his outstretched hand and straightened her knees, standing up. "What are sweepers?"

"People who clean up messes in missions that have gone sour. Black Operations, Tracy."

Even sweat-soaked, her skin prickled and chilled. Everyone in uniform had a healthy respect for, and a fear of, Black Ops.

Adam walked on. She followed, becoming more adept at seeing the signs. Just to her left, the leaf-strewn ground looked scraped. "You staggered here."

"Yes," Adam confirmed. "I suspect O'Dell laced my oxygen supply with disabling drugs, and here's where I was when they kicked in full force."

She sucked in a sharp breath.

Adam must have understood her concern, because he quickly reassured her. "Don't worry. I checked out this equipment myself. You're breathing pure oxygen."

Grateful he had checked, she nodded, determined to keep a tight leash on her fear. It threatened to build to volcanic proportions. "Your being drugged is consistent with Sergeant Phelps's comments."

"Is that what he told you on the rooftop patio?"

"Yes." She reiterated the conversation with Phelps, and then told Adam about Randall and Dr. Kane checking out her and the device. "It looked like a grenade," she said, realizing she was back to babbling. "But it was just a smoke bomb."

"No." Adam disagreed. "It was far more than a smoke bomb, honey."

Honey. She liked hearing the endearment, even if she hated what Adam had attached to it.

"It was a warning."

She kicked at a stone, watched it tumble under a squat bush. "I know."

"Careful. Don't risk tearing the gear." He grunted. "That bomb must have scared ten years off your life."

"At least ten," she confessed, not feeling at all weak for the admission. When he walked on in front of her without a word, she stared at his back. "What? No smart-ass 'fluff' comment?"

He shrugged. "I'm thinking maybe sometimes fluff is good."

The alarm at his belt beeped.

Adam stiffened. "Whatever you do, don't take off any of your gear."

Her stomach lodged in her throat. "What is it?"

Adam looked at the cube-shaped device. "Low-level chemical exposure."

Each word struck her like a surprise left hook to the chin.

"Without testing equipment, I have no idea what kind."

Somehow, she found her voice. "But it is lethal."

"Or unrecognized."

"So it could be retrosarin."

He nodded. "Let's get the canister and get out of here."

Minimizing their exposure sounded great to her. "Which way?"

"There." He pointed past a patch of wild berries to the base of a sprawling oak. "Between the two protruding roots on the south side."

Adam dug up the canister. It was painted like camouflage BDUs and Jeeps used in combat. Just the sight of it made her sick to her stomach.

"It's definitely a nerve-agent dispenser."

"But it doesn't have the yellow or blue band."

"I told you it didn't, and that's why I originally discounted it."

He set the canister into the black bag, which was lined with some kind of strange-looking fabric she didn't recognize. Hoping that lining kept the chemical from spreading—Adam had said it had airborne capability—she watched him zip the case. He smoothed the ground and then spread dry leaves over the hollow where the canister had been. On finishing, he stood up and swiped his gloved hands, knocking off the loose red dirt. It sprinkled to the ground, grains pattering against the leaves and the toes of his combat boots.

When he looked at her, no tenderness shone in his eyes. Worry flooded them. "The canister triggered the alarm, Tracy." He manually silenced the terror-inducing beep. "It's definitely not a smoke-filled dummy." His voice shook. "It's live."

Tracy didn't want to believe it. Gus O'Dell, a major in the Air Force—the same Air Force she proudly served—couldn't, *wouldn't*, have done what it appeared he had done. She didn't want to believe Colonel Hackett, an ambitious but highly decorated officer, had sanctioned—or had planned—such a heinous crime against a team under his command—*his own men!*—against the Air Force, the country. Against Adam. Oh, they had speculated on it, but doing so in safety felt a lot different from considering it while standing on a bombing range dressed in chemical gear, hearing the damn alarm sound, and seeing the lethal canister with her own eyes.

The canister. Hope flared in her chest. "Couldn't this be a different canister, Adam? Maybe it isn't the one involved in the incident with your men."

Adam paused, clearly frustrated and regretting what he had to say. "Look around you, honey. What do you see?"

Blue jays chirped in the trees overhead, and she scanned the area. "Woods. Bugs. Birds. Leaves. Dirt. Bushes. Trees."

"Exactly," Adam said. "This is an active bombing range, right?" When she nodded, he went on. "So why don't we see any evidence of bombs?"

There hadn't been. In all their walking through the range, there had been the snake, tons of squirrels and birds, and lots of pits in the ground where previous bombs had in fact fallen, but there hadn't been one single sign of a bomb canister. Had they all exploded? Maybe only specific types of chemical canisters remained intact when detonated. Maybe the other intact canisters had been collected for study—or to hide evidence. "Bloody hell."

"We can prove this is the right canister." Adam lifted the black bag. "All we have to do is have the trace contents examined."

Sick at heart, Tracy nodded. "Discretion would be wise, don't you think?"

"Most definitely."

"I swore I'd never ask Randall for anything ever again. He's a liar, but he has lab access."

"No."

"Why not?" Tracy had the feeling Adam was keeping something from her about Randall. Something vital she should know. He had warned her to be careful around Randall. Adam wouldn't do that without reason. When he didn't answer her, she became sure of it, and persisted. "Why not, Adam?"

He looked at her through the mask. "I have legitimate doubts about the good doctor's integrity that go beyond his falsely identifying my body."

If he'd belted her a right jab, he couldn't have shocked her any more. "What kind of doubts? Are you thinking he substituted John Doe's corpse for you in the fire?"

"I have no proof of that, and I already told you, I consider it unlikely. Too many people would have to be involved. Intel rule is strive for simplicity."

"Then what doubts are you talking about?"

"Randall is under an unofficial OSI investigation, Tracy. This is confidential, but under the circumstances, I feel justified in telling you—provided you keep it in the jurisdiction of attorney/client privilege."

"I will."

"Unofficially, concerns have been raised that the doctor could be passing along to hostile parties technical information that renders obsolete new technology either in production, or soon to be contracted for production."

"*What!*" she shouted, unable to restrain herself.

"Randall?" Seeing Adam nod, she sputtered. "But that's absurd. The man is obsessed with his image and goals and with appearances. He doesn't rock boats. He's terrified of displeasing the hospital board. I can't believe he would dare something like that. Good God, Adam. You're talking treason."

"Yes, I am."

Treason? Randall? Impossible. Just . . . impossible. "If the OSI had reports of this, Randall would have been arrested on suspicion. Then they'd work to discern the truth."

"If the OSI had a *formal report,* then they would have arrested him. But they don't," Adam countered. "What they've got is an unofficial, informal hypothetical situation intimating that it might be beneficial to the interests of the United States for the OSI to monitor a 'potential situation' and obtain clues to Moxley's identity. He wasn't specifically named, Tracy."

But those clues made his identity apparent—which is why Adam had warned her to be careful around Randall. Oh, God. And she'd been friends with the slimy slug.

The urge to hang Randall on suspicion herself burned strong in her belly. But she couldn't think about this now. She was too angry to be reasonable, much less objective or fair. She dipped her chin to the black bag holding the canister. "Since Randall is out of the question, how do we have the contents verified?"

"We don't," Adam said, watching her cautiously. "You do. You take the canister to Dr. Kane and have him run the tests."

"Me?" Surprise streaked up her back.

"You have to do it, Tracy," Adam insisted. "I'm dead, remember?"

"Almost." A man's voice sounded off Adam's left shoulder.

Swallowing a gasp, Tracy looked up and saw not one man, but four soldiers. They weren't military; none wore any rank. But they all were dressed in traditional BDU fatigues. They all had black-grease-smutted faces.

And they all stood legs spread apart with M-16s leveled on Tracy and Adam.

Chapter 24

Tracy looked to Adam for direction. Maybe he had been in this position often, but she had only looked down a gun barrel a select few times in her life—during training—and she'd never had one, much less four, aimed at her. What did she do?

Adam lifted his hands.

She mimicked him, noticing his gloves. Why was he sliding his foot?

They were wearing protective gear. The gunmen weren't. The area was contaminated. Adam wanted her to stall. Whatever chemical had triggered the alarm wouldn't affect them, but it would affect the gunmen. Yet it had been a low-level warning. Did that mean the chemical was lethal? Debilitating? Oh, how she hoped it meant debilitating. Otherwise she would have to battle with her conscience about whether to tell the men about the exposure.

That, she decided, was going to be a battle anyway. They pointed guns at her, but that didn't absolve her from doing what was right. She wouldn't be responsible—or held accountable—for their actions. Just for her own. That was scary enough.

The eldest of the four men, about forty, had gray hair and the coldest eyes she'd ever had the misfortune to see. The others deferred to him. One had called him Reuger.

"Let's go," Reuger said. He motioned with his

weapon, swinging the tip of its barrel deeper into Area Fourteen.

Adam began moving, slightly dragging his right foot. Leaving a trail he could easily follow out of here, she suspected. Walking beside him, she deliberately dragged hers, as well, and considered bumping into the bushes. No. No, she couldn't. The branches could prick her gear and render it useless.

Reuger led the way. Tracy walked sandwiched between him and Adam, and Reuger's men brought up the rear. What kind of heartless animal would put men in a contaminated area unprotected?

The same heartless animal who had sacrificed Adam's men?

Fifteen minutes elapsed. Then ten more. Tracy's nerves threatened to shatter. Who were they? Where were they taking them? And what were they going to do with them once they got them there?

Obviously they were interested in more than just the canister or they would have shot and killed her and Adam where they'd found them. And just as obviously, low-level exposure didn't kill quickly or the men would already be dead.

"Slow down," Adam silently mouthed.

Seeing a fallen branch, Tracy deliberately stumbled over it. She fell to the ground, clasped her leg, and cried out. "Oh, God, my knee. Adam, I think it's broken."

Reuger slid her a frosty glare, then leveled Adam with an icy one. "Carry her."

Adam helped Tracy to her feet and then lifted her in his arms. Wrapping her arms around his gear-clad neck, she looked through the mask and saw his approval shining in his eyes. Worry filled her own. How were they going to get out of this?

"Pick up the pace, Captain Burke," Reuger ordered.

Ironic, Tracy thought, as they moved deeper and deeper into Area Fourteen. She had refused to call Adam by his title, yet a gunman probably intending to kill them afforded Adam the respect she had denied him. God, but she regretted that.

"I can't go any faster," Adam said. "She's no light-weight."

Snidely preferring "no lightweight" to "fluff," Tracy looked at him through her frog-eyed mask, and saw the twinkle in his eye. Even terror-stricken, if she hadn't known it before, she would have realized at that moment she had fallen in love with him.

Adam stopped. "I have to tie my boot."

Reuger retained his unflappable calm, but his men lacked his discipline and grumbled. "Quit stalling, Burke."

The others murmured their agreement, and Adam had the impudence to look affronted. "Who are you?" he asked Reuger. "What do you want from us?"

Reuger didn't deign to answer either question. "Tie your bootstring, Captain. We have a lot of ground to cover before dark."

Adam must have realized he wouldn't get answers to any questions because he didn't ask any more. He again lifted Tracy in his arms. She felt almost guilty now that she hadn't been more inventive with her injury. They evidently had a long way to go, and Adam had to carry her. Fine for her, but taxing on him. He didn't seem winded or taxed, but the man was human. He had to be feeling the strain.

Adam squeezed her, warning her to look at him. She met his gaze and he blinked rapidly. What was he telling her?

He elbowed the alarm at his belt. He had silenced it before they had been intercepted, so it hadn't beeped . . . His intent hit her. The alarm—chemical exposure. The blinking—mitosis.

She glanced over Adam's shoulder at the middle one of Reuger's men, walking five feet behind them. His pupils were dilated.

So were the other two's.

Mitosis.

And they were sweating. Tracy and Adam were, too, but they were wearing the hot gear. These men were suffering the effects of the chemicals. And they held M-16s on her and Adam. Should she warn the men?

Her logic told her no. The men would kill them. They were on the wrong side of this conspiracy, and they had to be stopped. But her conscience rebelled. No matter who they were or what they were doing, they had lives, families, people who loved them, and that part of them—regardless of the wrongs they had done, or had yet to do—deserved to know that they were about to die. But would it be kinder to let them die unaware? Or to give them the opportunity to come to terms with death, to settle things in their minds?

"Adam," she whispered. "We've got to warn them."

"They'll kill us."

"What's all the conversation about?" Reuger stopped under the shade of a wild magnolia, turned back, and glared at them.

She let Adam see the pleading in her eyes. The mask encumbered, but it didn't hide the truth. The chaplain's voice rippled through her mind. *No truth escapes . . . You're Adam's sun.* "Please, Adam. We have to live with this. We'll do no better, be no better than them."

Adam stopped on the path and set Tracy down to the ground. The men stumbled to a halt behind them, and Reuger swiveled the M-16, aiming at Adam. Tracy's heart rocketed and fear oozed from her pores. *God, please don't let this be a mistake. Please!*

"It's about chemical warfare," Adam told Reuger. "You've been exposed."

Reuger grunted and rolled his gaze. "The area's been swept. It's safe."

"It's not safe," Tracy insisted. "Look at your men, for God's sake. Don't you see their pupils? Don't you see their sweat?"

"We're all sweating, Captain Keener. It's extremely warm out here."

"They're staggering, and you're swaying on your feet." He was. "A dilation and fixation of the pupils of the eyes is called *mitosis*. That, the sweating, the dizziness, the tightness in your chest—all of those things are symptoms of chemical poisoning. It was a low-level exposure, or you would already be dead."

Reuger bolted his gun, loading its chamber. "Are you telling me that my men and I are going to die, Captain Keener?"

She stiffened, terrified to admit the truth, but even more terrified of living the rest of her life knowing she'd lied to a dying man. She couldn't control their actions, but she could control her own—provided she had the courage to do it. "I'm afraid so, yes."

Adam stepped between her and the gunman. Reuger slumped back, against the magnolia's trunk, shaking its leaves. He fingered the trigger of his weapon, glared at them, his fury turning to shards of ice in his eyes. "He lied."

The first of Reuger's men collapsed on the ground. Within moments, the other two fell beside him. A heartbeat from hysteria, Tracy bent over them and looked up at Adam. "Is there anything I can do? Anything?"

"I'm sorry." Regret shone in Adam's eyes. "There's nothing."

A moan crawled up her throat.

"Give me your gear." Reuger jabbed the barrel of his weapon against Adam's ribs.

"It won't do you any good. You've already been exposed. The chemical is inside you and nothing will help. You'll only be taking me with you."

Reuger dropped to his knees. Red sand splattered, spraying their gear-clad shins, and his weapon dropped to the ground with a dull thud. "He lied. The son of a bitch lied."

Tracy swallowed hard. "No authorized entity, or anyone in their right mind, would send you out here without protective gear.''

''He said it was safe. It'd been swept and was safe.''

Adam looked at Reuger. ''He was wrong. Maybe someone lied to him. Or maybe he wanted you and your men dead.''

''Who is your boss, Reuger?'' Tracy moved next to Adam.

But Reuger couldn't answer. None of the men could answer. Clutching at their chests, they writhed in the dirt, convulsing.

Unable to bear watching this, she looked at Adam. The horror she felt was mirrored in his eyes.

His men had died this death. Men who had pledged themselves to duty. Who had taken their oaths of honor, loyalty, and protection into their hearts.

Men who had been betrayed by their own.

The chemical didn't differentiate between good and bad, between evil and honor, it just killed. Those good men had died. And so too did these men. Reuger stared up at the sun through unseeing eyes. Her heart in her throat, Tracy swept a gloved hand over his face, lowering his eyelids.

Adam said something; she heard him, and yet her emotions blocked her comprehension of his words. He wrapped an arm around her shoulder and pulled her close to his side, turning her away from the bodies. ''Come on, Tracy. Let's go.''

Tears blurred her eyes, but she stumbled alongside him, down the path back to the car. ''Why couldn't Reuger have redeemed himself, told us who he'd worked for?'' she asked herself more so than Adam. ''Why couldn't we stop this before more people died?''

''Some people can't be redeemed.'' Adam lifted her over the trunk of the fallen pine, then set her back on the ground. ''Some have no use for redemption.''

''How could anyone have no regret?'' She stopped under the shade of a huge oak and stared at the sun-dappled ground. "They'd have to lack a soul."

"Or to believe they're doing what's right."

Like Reuger. She walked on, retracing their trail, her steps even heavier now than when they'd created it. "And when they learn they're not doing what's right, then they suffer regret," she said softly. "They suffer knowing, 'He lied.'"

Tracy stared at the black bag containing the canister, her mind reeling from witnessing firsthand the horrible deaths the men had suffered, from knowing Adam's men had died that same death during an exercise. An exercise, for God's sake. A supposedly safe and protected strategic study.

She hugged her chest with her arms, resentful and grateful for the gloves, the chemical gear. Without both, she and Adam too would now be dead.

"We're ready, honey."

She stumbled into the car, her rioting emotions making her heart race. "Do we have to keep on this gear?"

Adam slid her a worried look and fastened her seat belt. Her hands didn't seem to want to work inside the gloves. Nerves. It was nerves.

"Yes, we do," Adam said, as the car's engine purred to life. He drove out of the woods, back to the dirt road. "We can't take it off until we decontaminate."

She didn't even want to think about that. Trust him, he'd said. So she had, and she would. He knew what to do from here. She'd just go along for the ride and do her best to pull herself back together. Men had died, and seeing it rattled her to the core. Shook her so deeply she couldn't tell where all the turmoil started or stopped, only that it filled her.

The steady, cold blast from the air conditioner helped settle her down, and it made wearing the gear tolerable physically. Emotionally, Tracy couldn't wait to get the damn stuff away from her skin and out of her sight.

She stewed for half an hour, but recognizing Freedom Way, the road to Laurel Air Force Base with the rain-swollen ditch that almost had become her watery grave, she panicked. "Adam, where are we going?"

He looked over at her, his inner turmoil as evident as her own in the flat slash of his mouth. "To a safe place."

"On base?" Fear scattered up her spine. "Are you crazy? You're dead and I'm AWOL. We'll get arrested at the gate."

"Trust me, Tracy."

Trust him? *Trust him?* Her life had become a living hell since he had been insinuated into it. She was in love with him, though she wasn't crazy about the idea, but that didn't make her stupid. "This is a mistake. A big mistake. There's no place on base that's safe for us."

His jaw went tight and he flicked a wrist, switching the recirculating air up a notch. "We're going to the gas-chamber simulator. We can encapsulate the canister there, before we expose half the county, and dispose of the contaminated chemical gear. The bag holding it now is only safe for twenty-four hours."

"You *are* crazy," she said before she could stop herself. "Adam, for God's sake, be reasonable. We can't just walk into the simulator."

"We don't have any choice. If we don't encapsulate the canister, then we contaminate the general populace. Do you want them to die like the men in Area Fourteen? Like my men died?"

"No, of course I don't." Shuddering at the thought, she stared at the ceiling of the car, not knowing what to do. "But walking into the simulator? We'll be recognized."

"*We* aren't going. *I* am. And I won't be recognized."

He would. God help her, he would. And then he would be killed, or put back in the facility, and then Hackett would know Adam wasn't going to quietly disappear. Another accident would happen, only this time Adam wouldn't escape. "Why the simulator?"

Adam braked at the traffic light, then looked over at her. "Because we can't just throw that gear in the trash. It's contaminated, Tracy. Our disposal choices are limited. The simulator has facilities appropriate for handling biohazardous equipment."

"So does the hospital," she countered. "Our odds of being caught there are lower."

"But our risks of the gear being mishandled are greater," he insisted. "I won't take this stuff to a place where people are already weak and sick. I can't do that." He spared her a glance. "Besides, the car's interior is contaminated, too. The hospital can't handle it. The chamber can."

He had a point. Several. The biohazardous waste hospitals dealt with wasn't in the same spectrum as the contaminated waste they had. And the car would fit in the chamber—barely, but it would fit. "All right. But I'm going with you."

The traffic signal changed. A guy driving a white Corvette ran the light. Adam waited until the intersection was clear and then stepped on the gas. "You're not going—and don't bother arguing with me on this."

"I will bother." Seeing the guard shack at the base gate ahead, Tracy gripped the door handle and squeezed the cold metal.

"Look, if I get caught, they'll either kill me or put me back in the brig. I need you out here. Someone has to be left on the outside who has the guts to expose the truth."

Adam, dead? She couldn't bear the thought. Couldn't make herself consider it. He was being realistic—she knew that, and she saw the wisdom in what he was saying. She didn't like it, but she saw it. "So where are you taking me?"

"To a safe place," he said, clearly relieved she wasn't going to argue with him anymore.

"A safe place?" The guard shack was close now. Two more cars in front of them, and then they would either be admitted, detained, or shot. The tension had sweat trickling down between her breasts. "On base?"

"On base," Adam confirmed, sunlight slanting through his window and across his lap. "There's a special place for Intel people. You won't have a lot of comfort, but you will be safe."

The guard waved the first of the two cars through the gate, his gun holstered. And then the second car. Adam pulled to a stop beside the shack. The man walked out and, on seeing the chemical gear, his eyes widened.

Tracy went board-stiff. He had recognized them. *Oh, God. What would he do?*

He hesitated a scant second that seemed to drag on a lifetime, then sharply saluted and waved them through the gate.

Adam stepped on the gas pedal. On clearing the guard shack, he sighed.

Stunned, Tracy couldn't move. "Adam?"

He cupped her hand fisted in her lap. "It's okay, counselor. We're in."

"Yes, but why?" She looked at him. "For the hundredth time, Adam, I'm AWOL and you're dead. That guard recognized us, I know he did."

"You're right, he did. Otherwise, he would've stopped us."

"You *knew* he would recognize us?"

"Tracy, any terrorist worth his salt can get a suit of chemical gear. If he hadn't checked us out, I'd be furious, and I'd be back there chewing his ass."

"But you're dead, Adam."

He gently squeezed her hand. "I'm Intel, honey. I've been dead before."

She stiffened as if she'd been slapped. "So the guard thought all of this, your arrest and the charges—everything—was just another mission?"

"Possibly," Adam said. "Most likely, he hasn't decided what to think. Not yet. But he's a trained professional. He won't risk blowing my cover for fear he'll blow my mission."

Tracy closed her eyes, quietly groaning. "I'm not cut out for Intel work, Adam. I'm really not. I just don't have the nerves for it."

When Adam didn't respond, she supposed he had surmised the same thing. That irritated her. She refused to feel inferior about this; she was a lawyer, not an Intel officer. And she was a good lawyer. Damn good. Even Adam agreed on that.

In silence, he drove past the credit union and base exchange, then on past the hospital to an isolated part of the base on the far side of the flight line. In the airport overrun's wooded bumper, he pulled off the road and stopped.

Woods on one side of them and freshly mowed weeds on the other, Tracy looked at Adam, confused. "What are we doing here?"

"This is the safe place."

"An empty lot?"

"It's not empty, counselor." He opened the car door, then got out and led her not into the lot, but across the street, into the woods.

She wasn't sure but she thought she saw the hint of a smile curving his lips. If she didn't love him, she would have given him hell for that smile. She might just do it anyway. After she murdered him for pushing her off that damn roof. Her blasted knee still ached from that fall— and from all the tromping through the woods. That hadn't helped it any. She'd seen men die, for God's sake. She'd been through hell, and she wasn't interested in games.

Between the trunks of two ancient magnolias, Adam stooped low to the ground. What he did only he knew, but a faint whirring sounded and an opening appeared in the grass. Tracy looked down into it. Concrete steps, a metal handrail—it looked like a stairwell. "A bunker?" She swiveled her gaze to Adam. "Here?"

He nodded. "Get inside. I can't leave the car parked here."

"But—"

He rolled his eyes back in his head. "Tracy, this isn't a time for discussion. Get in the bunker. Go straight to the decontamination chamber. It's right at the foot of the stairs on the left. Strip and leave everything but your skin in there. Everything." He didn't wait for her to answer before going on. "You'll find what you need. I'll be back as soon as I can."

Fear exploded inside her and she clutched at his arm. "What if you don't come back? What do I do then?"

He stepped closer, touched a blunt fingertip to her masked face and let it trail down her cheek. "You bury me again, honey, and then you find out the truth."

Oh, God. Her muscles clenched, her chest ached. A jumbled mass of feelings whirled in her heart, her mind, but she couldn't speak. There were too many feelings and no words to convey them all. No mind could comprehend them all.

"I know. Me, too." Masked, he dropped a mock kiss to her lips, then released her. "Stay put here until tomorrow." He nodded down the stairwell. "Go on. Hurry now."

She stepped down the concrete stairs, then paused. "Be careful at the simulator. There's an elaborate alarm system. The panel is on the inner wall, just to the left of the hangar's main door."

"I know."

"I should tell you that I planted a bug in Colonel Hackett's office."

"You did?" Surprise trickled through Adam's voice.

She nodded. "One was already there, Adam. Did you plant it?"

"No, but I'm glad to hear someone else has strong suspicions about Hackett, too."

Disappointed, she stared at him. He was clearly antsy to get going. "Adam?"

"Tracy, I've got to hurry. The car . . ."

"Come back to me," she said in a rush, then swallowed hard. "I've buried too many people I care about already."

He cupped her face mask with his glove, and his voice turned tender. "I'll try my best, counselor."

Afraid she might never again see him alive, Tracy stood there, greedily drinking in everything about him, until the opening between them slid closed. And then she gave her emotions their due. She slumped down on the cool stairs, and cried.

The bunker wasn't at all what Tracy had expected.

She left the decontamination chamber birth-naked and, outside it, picked up a towel from the stack on the end of a wooden bench. Wrapping it around her, she then explored.

No one else was there; the stillness and lack of noise made that apparent. The walls, ceiling, and floor were constructed of concrete, and the long hallway branched off into two smaller ones that looked more like window-less apartments. Fire extinguishers hung on the wall every twenty feet. A big concern down here, she supposed, entering the second apartment.

Space being at a premium, none was wasted. A double bed and chest rested against the outer wall. A bathroom, stocked with personal supplies, lay on the left, and a kitchenette with a table, two chairs, and a small refrigerator was to the right. There was no stove. Two cabinets near the table were stocked with food. She opened the fridge. The things she would find in her kitchen at home filled every shelf.

Glimpsing an upright metal locker on the other side of the bed, she walked over, then opened its door. Some of her own clothes hung on the metal rod, including a complete uniform, and beneath them, on the floor of the locker, sat her own shoes.

Adam had planned well. He had known before he had kidnapped her that he would eventually be bringing her here. Recalling Reuger and his men, she amended that thought. Adam might not have known, but he had prepared for the possibility. Nice asset in a man.

She glanced at the wall clock near the door leading to the hallway. It was huge; a school clock with large black numerals and a red sweeping second hand. Two o'clock. How long would it take Adam to encapsulate the canister, dispose of the gear and car, and get back here?

That depended on whether or not he ran into complications.

Denying that he would, she swiped her hair back from her face and returned to the closet. Her body had dried, but the stench of Area 14 and all she had witnessed there clung to her skin. She needed another shower. She needed to do *something* to feel clean again.

Reaching for the hangers, she grabbed a pair of jeans and a T-shirt, doing her damnedest to not let fear sink its talons into her. It proved challenging. Adam was again putting his life on the line. He could be caught. Killed at any time.

He was innocent—of course he was innocent. But being innocent wouldn't keep him alive.

She crunched the shirt in a tightfisted grip. Why hadn't she come to terms with loving him before he'd had to risk his life again? Whether it was the situation or true feelings—feelings this strong have to be real—she should have told him. He'd had so little love in his life. He would have known. Now she might never again have the chance to tell him.

No. No, that wasn't possible. He would come back. He would. She jerked up a pair of sneakers from the bottom of the locker.

A gold locket fell out onto the white floor.

Her locket.

Her heart wrenched and she let out a little moan. She fell to her knees, lifted it by the chain, and then opened it. Abby's photograph as a newborn. Tears burned Tracy's nose, her eyes, and spilled down her face. She thought she'd lost the photo forever, and—

An uneasy shiver slithered up her back.

She hadn't worn these sneakers since before all this started with Adam. She and Janet had searched high and low, and they had deduced Tracy had to have lost the locket at the cemetery.

Adam had been at the cemetery; he'd told her so. He had found her locket.

And after already giving her everything he had to give, her very life, now he had given her back all she had of her daughter.

"Oh, Abby." Tracy gently fingered the photo, as if caressing her daughter's face, feeling the ache of losing her as if it had only just happened. She'd never dared to dream she would love anyone again. And she hadn't, until Adam. "I always lose everything I love, and I'm so scared I'm going to lose him, too."

She rubbed the edge of the gilded locket, letting her fingertip trace its rough rim. He could die and never know she loved him. She wasn't sure it would matter to him, but it mattered to her. She squeezed her eyes shut. "It matters . . . to me."

He had to come back. He had to get through this, and come back to her. He deserved to know. After all the hell in her life, she deserved at least one last chance to tell him.

Life isn't fair. You know what you deserve and what you get can be poles apart.

"Shut up," she told her conscience. "He'll come back. I know he will. I believe it." She sniffled and put the locket on, hearing its little catch slip into place, feeling it nestle in its familiar place between her breasts. Tears swelled and fell down her face, and fear's talons clawed her hard. "Oh, bloody hell." She gave in; cried until her head throbbed—for Abby, for Adam, for herself. Cried and prayed, letting all her fears and hopes pour out, until she had nothing new left to say. Then she showered, just standing under the stream of water, letting it spray her head and sluice down her body until her tears stopped,

DUPLICITY   277

her mind emptied, and the hot water turned cold.

Emotionally and physically drained, she turned off the tap, toweled dry, and dressed in the fresh jeans and T-shirt. Then, she waited. And waited. Sitting at the kitchen table, then sprawling across the bed, she watched the clock, and waited some more.

By nine P.M. her nerves had frayed. Something had gone wrong. He wasn't coming back. He had been caught, or killed. If Hackett or O'Dell had found Adam, he was surely dead.

The red light above her door flashed, and a quiet alarm beeped.

She darted her gaze to it. Heavy footfalls sounded in the corridor, outside her room. Someone was here.

She sprang to her feet, unsure what to do. Should she step into the hallway and see who it was? Stupid idea. What if it wasn't Adam? What if it was someone else from Intel with access to the bunker? What if it was Hackett? O'Dell? Nestler? *Please, not Nestler.*

Oh, God, how she wished she could run and hide. But hide where? In or out of the bunker, there was no place to hide. There was no refuge.

She had no alternative but to face this head-on. And her instincts, fully alert, shouted that she would fare best by retaining an element of surprise—provided whoever was out there didn't already know she was here. Maybe they did. Maybe they'd come to get her.

Resolved to confront them first, Tracy turned the knob and opened the door.

Chapter 25

Adam paused outside the bunker's decontamination chamber. Tracy's chemical gear lay folded on the floor in the corner next to the wall. Relieved to see it there, he again heard her voice. *Come back to me, Adam. I've buried too many people I care about already . . .*

Either she didn't realize she'd fallen in love with him yet, or she had and she was fighting it. Considering her past, she was probably fighting it. God knew, he was. But he felt it in her touch, saw it in her eyes. It awed and humbled him. And it scared the hell out of him. She didn't trust him. To a point, yes, but past it? No way. He did trust her. It was love he didn't trust.

He walked on, into the first apartment. Seeing no signs of life, he turned and headed for the second apartment. Did she love him because of their situation, or because she just loved him? He had to be out of his mind for daring to hope she loved him, but God, he wanted it to be true.

As he rounded the corner, she stepped into the hallway, hugging a fire extinguisher and aiming it at him as if it were an M-16. "Stop right there."

He looked up at her face. So much emotion: relief, joy, gratitude. The magnitude of it struck him like a swift kick in the stomach.

"You're okay." She dropped the canister. It thudded against the tile floor, and she ran to him, closing her arms, hugging him as if she were trying to crawl inside him. Shaking hard, she buried her face at the crook in his shoulder. "Oh, Adam. You're okay."

Her heart thumping against his chest, he wound his arms around her. "I'm fine, honey," he whispered, stroking her hair.

She reared to look up at him, a smile on her lips and in her eyes. "You look tired—and you smell like soap."

She'd been crying. And worrying. Her eyes were still red, and tension radiated from her. He hated it. He wanted her happy. She'd given him more than anyone else in his life. "I showered at Environmental and made a few simulator adjustments." Before she could ask what adjustments, he kissed her long and deep and with every intention of kissing her until the last of her fears melted.

When she threaded her hands through his hair and let out that sexy moan that turned his mind to mush, he forced himself to separate their mouths. He could get used to this. To coming home to Tracy. This wasn't home, and she wasn't his, but for the moment, he could pretend both. Dangerous, tempting pretenses he had never experienced before and innately knew he never would again, but ones he'd hungered for all his life. He wanted to feel what it was like, being loved. If only for a short time.

He loved her. And he wanted her in ways he had no right to want anyone. Not with this conspiracy hanging over his head. Yet he couldn't stop wanting her, or needing her.

Needing her? He *needed* her? Loving created *needs*?

The realization shocked him, frightened him in ways facing an armed enemy couldn't. He had sealed off his heart to needing anyone a long time ago, long before Lisa. He'd had to cancel out his emotions to survive, and he'd had no problem keeping them canceled out until now.

But—the truth surfaced—he hadn't canceled them out; he'd only buried them, just as he'd buried the canister.

She burrowed against his neck. "Did you have any trouble?"

He considered telling her the truth, then decided against it. She'd worry herself into oblivion. He hadn't expected to run into Gus O'Dell at the chamber. O'Dell hadn't seen Adam, but it had been a damn close call. If not for Lieutenant Carver's timely intercession—the second time he'd run interference for Adam—O'Dell would have tagged him. He'd play hell missing the car parked inside the chamber. "No." Adam looked down at her. "No trouble at all."

Her smile widened. "I was a little worried."

She'd been sick with it. He hated and loved that. Few people had wasted their worrying on him. The urge to tell her he loved her hit him hard, but the timing was all wrong. "We need to talk for a minute before you go to the lab and get Dr. Kane to analyze the canister contents." The thought alone made Adam wary. And until he felt comfortable—at least, reasonably so—he couldn't allow himself to speak of his feelings. Much of his Intel training had honed his instincts and those instincts had saved his ass too many times for him to ignore them now. He might love and trust Tracy, but he also feared her. Personally and professionally.

She stepped away and crossed her arms. "Talk about what?"

"About what I expect will happen." He walked around her and then sat down at the table. "About us."

Her smile faded. "I think I'd better sit down for this."

When she settled on the chair across from him, he laced his hands atop the table. "I've been in Intel a long time, and I've seen next to nothing happen and it sour missions. I know Intel isn't your world, but you need to know that when things go wrong in it, people die. Not just the bad guys. The good ones, too. And innocents. Men, women, kids—no one is protected."

"I understand, Adam. I've witnessed death firsthand. You reconcile yourself to doing your best and then let it go. The good guys don't always wear white hats and sometimes, no matter how hard you try, you fail.''

"You can't just know it.'' He watched her carefully, assessing her reaction. "You've got to accept it. To know going in that you might fail, and you might not come out. Those aren't just words, they're reality.'' His eyes scorched her. "You could die.''

"Yes, I could.'' She dipped her chin, stared at the tabletop. "I understand the risks. A lot of people could die.'' Tilting her head, she looked back at him. "I don't know if I've got what it takes to do this right. I'm out of my comfort zone—that I do know. Everything is different here. Perspective blurs the rules. I can't promise not to screw up, Adam. But I'll do my best.''

Satisfied with that, he nodded and clasped her hands in his. "Now, about us.''

"Adam, wait.'' She licked at her lips. "I know we've said we care for each other, and I do care about you. A lot. But I have to be honest. Some of what I'm feeling stems from a deep-seated need to protect you.''

Wasn't it normal to want to protect someone you love? Pain flashed through her eyes, and gave him insight. "You're afraid because you couldn't protect Matthew and Abby?''

"I'm afraid because during all of this, I've come to know you. I don't mean through your files, though that's a factor, too. I mean you, inside. And I'm very attracted to all the good I see in you.''

The need to self-protect put a bite in his tone. "Hormones have a way of clouding vision, counselor. Don't mistake them for feelings that aren't actually there.''

Was she doing that? Maybe. Maybe not. "Point taken,'' she said. "I'll admit my hormones are active around you; you're a gorgeous man. But there's more to this than that.''

He chewed at the inside of his lower lip. "We're involved in a volatile situation, honey. Trained or not, proximity and pressure impact your emotions.''

Extremely astute man. "That's part of it, too," she admitted, more than a little flustered because he seemed bent on not letting her say what she wanted to say. "Look, I don't mean to make you examine feelings you might not be in the best position to examine right now. But when you left me here, I did a lot of thinking, and the thing that bothered me most was I hadn't told you how I feel about you."

He tensed and his expression turned grim: sure signs he wasn't yet ready to hear that she loved him. "I care a lot, Adam," she substituted spontaneously. "And I'm grateful."

"For what?"

"I didn't think I could care this way about anyone again. You proved to me I can, and I do." Now what had she said wrong? His expression had turned rock-hard. "Is that a problem?"

"No."

Terrific. Teeth-pulling mode, and he wasn't looking directly into her eyes, either. "Adam, what's wrong?"

"I'm crazy about you."

"And that upsets you?"

"Hell, yes, it upsets me." He glared at her. "I trust you, and yet I'm wary of you going to Dr. Kane." There. The truth. It hadn't been something he'd wanted to do, but he had gotten it out in the open where they could discuss it. She would probably be ticked, or worse, hurt, but just maybe her reaction would give him the insight needed to make the right decisions. He *had* to make the right decisions. Too much was at stake to make any wrong ones.

"Why are you wary of that?" She sounded genuinely baffled.

He could tell her, but he damn sure couldn't look at her while he did it. He lowered his gaze to the oak table. "Because you could tell Kane or Randall Moxley the truth. That I'm alive and I kidnapped you. You could turn me in."

"What?" She jumped to her feet, outrage radiating from her every pore.

Clearly ticked to the gills, and hurt. Regrettable but, damn it, these concerns were too important to just dismiss. "I'm sorry, Tracy, but you could turn me in. That's a fact. And considering the price you could pay for aiding me, you'd be a damn fool not to do it."

"You sorry son of a—"

"Wait." He held up a hand, then stood up. "Don't kill me just yet." He lifted her fisted hand from her side and rubbed the back of her fingertips with his thumb. "I don't believe you would do it, but you turning me in to save your own neck is a viable consideration."

"It most certainly is not. I gave you my word." She glared at him, trembling with rage. "Killing you for pushing me off a roof—now that's a viable consideration."

"Are you still pissed about that?"

"Bloody hell, Adam. My knee still feels like a basketball."

He glanced at it. Barely swollen at all, and no bruising. "Your knee's fine. Can we get back—"

Her jaw snapped shut. "I might kill you, but I won't turn you in, okay?"

"It wasn't an unreasonable fear, Tracy." He forced himself to look into her eyes. His voice softened. "You feed the good in me. You make me believe there are people who will sacrifice and pay the personal costs for the greater good. You live that belief, Tracy. You do, and it touches me. You touch me." He closed his eyes, lifted her hand to his forehead, and held it tightly. "And I'm going to go on from here, believing that you won't betray me."

Solemn, she stared straight into his eyes. "And hoping I don't disappoint you?"

"Yes." Hard to admit, but he couldn't tell her any less than the truth.

She didn't say anything. But she didn't pull her hand

out of his grasp, either. That was a good sign, wasn't it?

"Have I done anything to make you doubt me, Adam?"

"No." He'd been afraid she would feel that way. "Nothing. It's not you, not really. It's me. And Moxley."

Her brows shot up. "What's Randall got to do with this?"

"Directly? Nothing. But you have been friends, Tracy, and he lied about me and about my men. They weren't fatalities of a typical bomb."

"Randall *and* the coroner lied." After what Tracy had seen in Area Fourteen, she had no doubts of that. Was there anyone who wasn't involved in this damn mess?

"Yes." Too agitated to stand still and disclose the rest to her, Adam shoved his hand into his jeans pocket. "I told you Intel has strong suspicions about his integrity, Tracy."

She stared up at him. "And about mine, due to our association, right?"

"Right." Adam leaned back against the counter, not at all surprised by her frank assessment or her acceptance. She was bright; he had known she would see the implication and his cause for concern.

"And what about you?" She leaned a shoulder against the wall beside the fridge. Its motor whirred softly, and ice cubes plunked down from the icemaker into the bin. "Do you consider me guilty by association?"

"If I did, you wouldn't be here." He was being equally frank. "But I'd be a fool not to realize that sending you to Kane with the chemical canister is a risk. You're a career officer up for promotion and selection who—as you've often reminded me—currently is AWOL. It's not unreasonable to think you might decide you'll come out on top of the heap by reporting all this to the OSI and letting me fry by myself. So I'm asking you straight-out, Tracy, and I'll believe whatever you say. Are you going to turn on me? Are you going to advise the OSI that I'm still alive and gathering evidence on the incident? If you do, Hackett will know I'm a liability. One way or another, he will silence me. You'll be out of danger, and I'll be dead. If I'm dead, Tracy, I can't come back for revenge against you. You'll be safe.''

She stared at him long and hard. "You're right. But if I did any of that, then the conspiracy would succeed. Hackett and O'Dell, and Paul and Randall—and Nestler, if he proves to be on the wrong side of this—would all get away with what they've done. People would die, Adam, and I would have to live with knowing I had let them.''

He didn't give her a second's reprieve. "Yes, you would.''

Tracy straightened from the wall, then walked over to him. Standing so close she felt his body heat seeping to her through his shirt, she looked up into his eyes. "I want the truth. I want them stopped.'' She pressed a hand to his chest, let her fingertips glide down to his ribs, then back up to rest over his heart. "I'll never betray you, Adam. I swear it.''

He clasped her upper arms and gently squeezed. "I didn't mean to hurt you, but you've got to understand. I've gotten to know you, too, and I see what's beneath the great body and beautiful face. You're principled, Tracy. Honor means something to you. But all of my life, I've been kicked in the teeth by everyone I've ever trusted. Every single person. With a track record like mine, I'd be a damn fool to expect anything different from you.'' He let his chin sink to his chest, pressed his forehead against hers. "But I do hope you'll be different.''

He pulled in a ragged breath and met her steady gaze. "I want you to believe in me. I want to know that deep down in your stomach, you're sure I've done the right things. I want your trust and your faith, Tracy.'' About to continue, he stopped, unable to admit the rest to anyone but himself. He wanted her love. More than anything else, he wanted her love. "Hell, I don't just want those things from you, I need them. Don't you see? My needing anything from you makes you as dangerous to me as Hackett and O'Dell.''

Reeling, Tracy did see it. All of it. Adam's fear and uncertainty at leaving himself professionally and personally vulnerable. His hope that she wouldn't betray him as everyone else had, that she would prove different. She saw herself. Her promotion, her Career Status selection, her current AWOL status. She was being hunted down by a powerful superior officer—maybe a group of them— who had tentacles and the clout to use them to end not only her career but her life. And she was on a collision course with an opposing, unknown entity who well might be her ex-brother-in-law—a man she'd trusted for five hard, long years. Paul might be an unwitting victim. But he might also be an active participant. Of course Adam asked himself if he was sane or crazy as hell for trusting her. Hadn't she asked that of herself?

Maybe she was a fair share of both—sane and crazy. And maybe that was okay. But she had no right being hurt because he doubted her. Not when she herself had doubts. So she said the words he'd often spoken to her— and prayed they had the same effect. ''Trust me.''

''I said I did.''

''Not with your head, Adam.'' She touched his chest. ''In here.''

''I do.''

And that scared him most of all. *You're Adam's sun.* The light to flood all the dark crevices inside him, to gain freedom from the past, yes. And to love. Grasping Chaplain Rutledge's true meaning had her almost giddy. She lifted Adam's hand and cupped it to her chest, over her heart. ''I trust you, too, and I have faith in you. In here.''

He blinked hard and his Adam's apple bobbed three times. She wanted to kiss him. But that would complicate his thinking. She wanted to be straightforward. This wasn't about confused emotions or intense situations, or even about physical attraction. This was about character.

His and her own. She backed away. "I'd better get going."

Adam glanced at the clock and his demeanor changed to professional. "Dr. Kane's on duty now." Adam pulled the keys from his jeans pocket and passed them to her. "Look for a brown Jeep in the Maintenance parking lot, on the other side of the flight line. Third row."

The red car had been contaminated. He'd left it at the simulator. He passed her something—a listening device. Looking at it against her palm, she felt a cold shiver creep up her backbone. "What, um, do you expect me to do with this?"

Adam met her gaze, hard and unyielding. "I expect you to see him and plant it in Randall's office."

"What for?"

"He's on duty tonight. When you take the canister in, he's going to cut and run. Don't ask how I know, I just do. You stay in this job long enough and you get gut feelings. I've got a gut feeling. And when Moxley runs, we've got to find out to whom he runs, and with what information. We still don't know how he connects in all of this."

She had tried convincing herself that Randall had only followed orders—for the greater good—tried denying that he was up to his lab coat on the wrong side in this, but she couldn't play ostrich anymore, and her instincts shouted that Adam had gotten verification of it. "John Doe burned in the fire at the facility, and Randall planted his body there, didn't he, Adam?"

Surprise showed in Adam's eyes. Regret followed. "Yes, honey. He did."

Randall fooled her. How had she not known what kind of man he really was? How could she have been so blind and stupid and dull? "Was John Doe really already—"

"He died at the hospital," Adam said. "Sergeant Phelps verified it and proved that Moxley confiscated John Doe from the morgue."

"With whose approval?" She'd sincerely thought this

possibility too complex. That it would have involved too many people in too many places to be plausible. When she'd talked with Phelps, so had he. Now she learned he'd proven otherwise. That not only was this plausible, it was fact. And that evidence of how many people were involved in this conspiracy scared and sickened her.

"I'm not sure, but I suspect Colonel Hackett arranged it," Adam said. "Phelps tracked back to O'Dell, then got stymied."

Something about this felt wrong. She nodded at Adam, even more angry and disappointed that she'd been taken in by Randall. Why couldn't anyone just play straight anymore? Why did everyone put on multiple faces to confront the world, and wear another in private?

"I'm sorry, Tracy." Adam's voice turned soft. "I know this hurts."

"It does." She shrugged. "He once was a friend, I thought, safe. Only now I find out he wasn't safe at all, and being wrong about him rattles my faith in my judgment."

"You can handle this."

"Yes, I can. But I damn well resent having to handle it. I hate it, Adam."

"I'm glad." Adam pecked a kiss to her lips. "Now, get going. I'll be here, waiting."

She walked to the door, again thought of telling Adam she loved him, but again decided against it. He'd only just accepted that she wouldn't betray him. From there all the way to being loved was too big a gulp for him to swallow down in a single dose without choking.

"Make sure you're not followed on the way back."

"I'll do my best." She dropped the listening device into her pocket. *Dear God, please let my best be good enough!*

Tracy entered Randall's austere and empty office with mixed feelings. Her trusting and believing in Adam was sane. Her playing at being a spy was crazy as hell. What did she know about it? True, Janet had given her a briefing on career warfare, on Intel rules and drills. And those same concepts did in ways parallel those in Tracy's job. That gave her a little confidence. Planting the listening device in Randall's office couldn't be any more challenging than it had been in Hackett's, but was planting it the right thing to do?

She'd agreed to do it, but now that she was here . . .

Stop it. You made a commitment. Randall lied. He crossed the line. Just do it.

Adam hadn't had to protect her from the men trying to kill her at her house, nor had he been forced to prove the truth to her. He'd done those things—everything—because he had wanted to do them. He'd trusted her, when anyone else in his position wouldn't dare to risk trusting anyone. And he wanted to trust and have faith in her, to feel certain she would be fair, and committed to seeking the truth. They needed to know how Randall connected. Who had ordered him to lie about the dental records? To substitute John Doe? She could not recall Randall ever mentioning knowing Hackett or O'Dell. They couldn't be his connection in this. It just didn't fit. Of course planting the device was right. Of course it was.

The door opened behind her. She slapped the device to the underside of Randall's desk, backed away from it, and then turned toward the door.

Randall walked in, saw her, and smiled. "Well, this is a surprise."

Considering she was AWOL, she supposed it was a big surprise. A huge surprise.

"I thought you were still down with the flu." He walked over to his desk and sat down. "Glad you're feeling better."

He didn't know she was AWOL.

How could he not know? She had racked her brain all the way from the bunker to the hospital for an explanation that wouldn't add to Adam's list of charges, had come up with a tale of her being kidnapped by Reuger and his men, and there was no need to explain anything. Randall had no idea she was AWOL.

Did anyone know?

If not, great. If so, then should she feel grateful, or insulted? "I'm feeling a lot better," she said, hearing his intercom buzz.

"Sorry, I've got to get this." Randall reached for the receiver. "Dr. Moxley."

He listened for a moment, and then frowned. "I'll be right there." He hung up the phone and stood up.

Tracy nearly panicked.

"I've got to get down to the ER," he said. "Can you wait here for a few minutes?"

"Actually, I'm here to see Dr. Kane. I just dropped by to see if I could use your phone."

"Sure." He headed for the door. "Come back by after your appointment with Steven. Maybe we can sneak in a cup of coffee."

He wanted to grill her. His curiosity burned in his eyes. "I'll do that," she lied.

Randall walked out and shut the door. She paused a second, making sure he didn't come back, and then reached for the phone. Her hand shook badly. Was Adam listening to her every word already? She dialed and then waited, hoping it would be answered.

"Hello."

Thank God. Tracy squeezed her eyes shut. "Janet, it's me."

"Where the hell are you?" she whispered, muffling her voice.

"I'm okay. Confused as all get out, but okay."

"I know it was a shock, learning the way you did, but it was necessary, Tracy. Honest."

What was she talking about? Ah, Tracy figured it out. Janet's warning Adam that Tracy was in trouble. "I'm not upset." She glanced at a stack of files on a file cabinet behind Randall's desk. One tagged "Keener Chemical" caught her eye. What in the world would Randall be doing with a Keener file? She pulled the folder out. "I saw Randall. He didn't know I was AWOL."

"No one knows," Janet said. "I covered for you. You're home with the flu."

I'm not AWOL! Stunned, Tracy couldn't take it in. "Thanks, Janet. For everything." Maybe, if fate smiled on her, she would come out of this with her reputation and her career intact—and if it was damn gracious—with Adam, too. Could fate be *that* gracious? "I've got to go."

"Keep in touch, and let me know if there's anything I can do."

"I will." Tracy hung up the phone, staring at the contents of the Keener file. One sheet of paper was inside. One.

Randall Moxley's résumé.

Chapter 26

Tracy had stashed the black bag containing the canister at the nurse's station on the fourth floor. She might be an Intel novice, but she knew the value of caution.

After retrieving it from the cabinet where Adam had stashed Phelps's boss the night of the rooftop patio incident, she walked directly to Dr. Kane's office, cursing the maze the construction made of getting there and the Sheetrock dust tickling her nose. Were the workers making any progress at all?

Randall stood in Dr. Kane's office, talking with him. Her biggest surprise on seeing him there was that she felt no surprise. From the time she had seen curiosity gleam in his eyes, she had expected him there, and sorry jerk that he was, he hadn't disappointed her.

Dr. Kane stood up and extended his hand. "Hello, Captain Keener."

She shook his cool hand, hoping the forensics expert in him would be receptive to her request. She was reluctant to ask him anything with Randall there. Although appalled, after she thought a moment, she realized it made sense. If he were to cut and run, as Adam had predicted, Randall would do so immediately after hearing her request, and the listening device planted in his office would inform Adam.

Dr. Kane, like General Nestler, was a wild card who could go either way. He could agree to help her, or deny her request and report her. If he chose the latter, she would soon be doing hard time at Leavenworth. God, but she hated subterfuge. With passion and conviction. "Hi, Dr. Kane."

He motioned to a soft leather chair, his glasses reflecting the bright fluorescent light. "Randall tells me you wanted to see me."

"Yes." Smelling lab chemicals, she sat down and set the black bag on the floor near her feet, then glanced from Randall to Dr. Kane. "I need to know the contents of something. I'd appreciate your running an analysis."

He hiked a hip on the corner of his desk, draped an arm on the knee of his brown slacks. "For a case?"

"Professional, not personal." She nodded. "And important, or I wouldn't ask."

"No problem." He offered her a reassuring smile that would have had Janet's hormones in warp-speed, mate mode. "What exactly are we examining?"

"A canister." Tracy swallowed hard.

"Like one you would find full of flour on the kitchen counter?"

"Not exactly." Oh, God. She really didn't have the nerves for this kind of work. The knots in her stomach had knots. "More like one you would find on an airplane, containing a bomb."

"A bomb?" Dr. Kane's voice was pitched high and the glasses he dropped into his lab pocket clanged against a pen.

She nodded, hesitant. Well, hell. If you shoot for brass, you're never going to hit gold. "I suspect we're going to find a form of sarin," she said, watching Randall from the corner of her eye. His face bleached white.

"Christ Almighty, Keener." Dr. Kane dropped onto his chair. The group of file folders in his hand fluttered, rustling. "What are you trying to get me into here?"

Seeing him mentally shunning her, she pleaded with him. "Look, I realize this situation is . . . delicate." God, what an understatement. "But it is—"

"It's more than delicate. You're talking chemical warfare, Captain. Unauthorized chemical warfare, no doubt."

"You're right. It is unauthorized." Her mouth went stone-dry. "But if you don't help me, a lot of people could be hurt—military and civilians."

Randall's face still lacked any color, and he blinked a hundred times per minute. "I, um, have to get back to the ER."

Before either she or Dr. Kane could utter a word, Randall was gone, and Tracy's hope for his innocence died. She hadn't wanted to believe the worst about him, but his reaction proved Adam right; Randall had cut and run. He was involved in more than falsely identifying Adam, lying about the team, and smuggling a corpse to the facility. He was in this conspiracy up to his eyeballs and guilty as hell. And she would bet her captain's bars that he hadn't gone to the ER, he had gone to make a phone call—*please, God*—from his office.

"Captain." Dr. Kane recaptured his voice, and her attention. "I'm not clear about what's going on here, and truthfully, I'd prefer not to be briefed."

"I agree, Doctor." He couldn't tell what he didn't know. "It's safer for you."

He lifted the glasses back from his pocket and then fitted them on his nose. "Technically, in a situation like this, I'm supposed to contact Environmental and General Nestler immediately."

She answered him with a frankness that surprised even her. "If you do that, you could be signing my death warrant."

Dr. Kane didn't so much as blink. "I'm getting the feeling you mean that literally. Tell me I'm wrong."

She smoothed a hand down her jeans. The rough fabric was as irritating to her roof-grit-sore palms as to her ragged state of mind. "I can't."

He studied her a long moment, clenching the files in his hand. The folders rumpled and creased. The urge to rush him into deciding had her fidgeting. She bit her lip to keep her mouth shut. He had to draw his own conclusions without coercion. But, Lord, if he didn't do it soon, every nerve in her body was going to shatter.

"Okay." He rubbed at his chin, tossed the files onto his desk. "Okay. I'll run the analysis first, and then decide."

Tracy nearly slid to the floor in relief. "Thank you."

"Don't thank me yet." He accepted the bag holding the canister. "What I'll do afterward depends on what I find here."

She would think of some way to handle this and not put them all in even more jeopardy. She *had* to think of something.

"The analysis will take some time." Dr. Kane stood up. "I'm assuming you want to wait for the results."

She nodded. "I'd prefer to assist you."

A frown creased the skin between his eyebrows. "If this is sarin, it's deadly."

"Yes, I know."

"I don't suppose there's any sense in asking how you came to possess this canister, or this encapsulation carrier case." The speculative gleam in his eye vanished and his hand shot up. "No, don't answer that. I don't want to know."

Tracy wouldn't have answered him anyway, but she appreciated his reluctance to know any more than was necessary for him to do what he had to do. In fact, she blessed him for it.

"All right, Captain. You can assist," he said. "Come with me."

Three hours later, dressed in chemical gear, Dr. Kane looked over the lab table at Tracy, his expression grim. "We've got confirmation."

"What is it?" The muscles in her back and neck screamed, protesting her bending double over the table for so long. She twisted to loosen up. At least wearing the heavy gear in the lab was more comfortable than it

had been out in Area Fourteen. After that hellhole, almost
anywhere would be a breeze—except Leavenworth.

He hitched a hip against the edge of the table. "It's
not sarin."

"It isn't?" Surprised, she stared at him through her
mask.

"No. But it is an unknown derivative of it. We haven't
seen it before." His gloomy tone clearly conveyed that
he grasped the gravity of the situation. "This is stronger
than sarin. A lot stronger. It's odorless, colorless, and
lethal."

"As suspected." *Ten times as strong and as lethal.
Cheap and effective.*

Dr. Kane rolled his shoulders, stretching out a kink,
then wrinkled the bridge of his nose, as if he longed to
rub it but couldn't because of the mask. "We don't yet
know the long-term effects of sarin, and now we've got
a derivative of it to worry about."

Adam had been right. Retrosarin. *Oh, God. Retrosarin!*
And Paul had created it. "What do we know about
sarin?" she asked Dr. Kane.

"Not enough." He secured the canister, then turned to
walk out of the lab, motioning for her to follow. "Right
after the Gulf War, we burned a pit of ammunition. It
turned out to have chemicals in it—sarin. A respectable
number of our own troops suffered extremely low-level
exposure. Because of what happened in the war—and
after sarin was improperly applied during a terrorist attack
on a Japanese subway—several research projects to study
the long-term effects of low-level exposure to the chemical are now in the works. The problem is that, until those
incidents, there were no long-term effects. Typically, a
minuscule amount of sarin kills."

He stepped into a decontamination chamber and waved
her inside. "There is an antidote—a type of bleach—but
this derivative is substantially stronger. That antidote
won't be effective."

No antidote? If Paul created this monster and didn't

create an antidote, she'd kill him herself. The chamber door slid closed. "Is there any possibility that the sarin antidote might be strengthened and be effective?"

"I'd bet against it." He pushed the controls to begin the decontamination and, when the red light on the control panel came on, he sat down on a tile bench that ran end to end inside the chamber. "At one time, the United States stockpiled sarin, but controls have tightened. It was developed in Germany, and it isn't difficult to produce, by any means, but it has to be manufactured in a lab. My guess is this derivative does, too."

A lab. Like Keener Chemical's lab. Tracy's heart sank. *Oh, Paul. What in the name of heaven have you done? Why? Why have you done this?*

She sat down on the bench beside Dr. Kane. There wasn't conclusive proof Paul had sanctioned or participated in the exercise that had killed Alpha team but there was no denying his involvement any longer. No room for hope. Paul had to be up to his eyeballs in this conspiracy.

Reuger and his men flashed through her mind. Had they worked for Paul? He would want the canister retrieved. When Hackett and O'Dell failed to find it, it seemed logical Paul would initiate his own search. He had too much to lose by not locating it and hiding the truth. Keener Chemical—his life and pride, his family business.

He's already married to Keener Chemical. Janet had said it, and she'd been right.

Dr. Kane sighed. "I'm still not clear about what exactly is going on here, but I'm up against the wall. This derivative is extremely dangerous, Captain. In the wrong hands, it could wipe out entire communities."

A bell sounded, and Tracy swerved her gaze to the control panel. The light was green. She stood up, stripped off the chemical gear, leaving on her jeans and T-shirt, then sat back down.

Dr. Kane slid her a wary look. "I see that you've done this before."

She tugged down on her shirtsleeve. "You don't want to know."

"Right." He grimaced. "Anyway, I have no choice but to report this to Environmental and General Nestler. I can't wait any longer, not knowing what I know."

Nestler. The wild card who could be a good or a bad guy. Was she totally insane for holding out hope that he proved to be good? "I understand, Dr. Kane. But please, for your own protection, retain a sample of the derivative. Hide it somewhere safe and tell no one about it—*no one*. Not until you hear otherwise directly from me or Captain Burke. If we survive this, we're going to need it as proof. If not, you'll need it to develop an antidote right away."

"Burke is alive?" Shock flooded Dr. Kane's eyes.

Tracy nodded. "And risking his life to protect the rest of us."

Dr. Kane swiped a hand through his hair, ruffling it. The brown strands caught the light and shone gold. "Are you saying this chemical is already in the wrong hands?"

She didn't answer him. "When you notify Environmental and General Nestler, it would be wise for you to simultaneously notify nonmilitary officials."

Her trepidation hadn't escaped him. "Any particular nonmilitary officials?"

"I suggest the governor, your state senators and representatives, including Senator Stone, the EPA, and the head of the Senate Armed Services Committee. Stone serves on that committee, so that will give you a little protection."

Blowing out a ragged breath, Dr. Kane nodded. "I'll do that, Captain."

"Thank you." She meant it sincerely.

"Don't." He stood up. "I may not know what this is all about, but I know you're risking yourself for the rest of us as much as Captain Burke. I owe him an apology."

"Oh?"

"I convicted him without a trial." Dr. Kane's stern expression softened, and he looked chagrined. "I'm grateful. Please tell Captain Burke, and tell him I'm sorry.''

Maybe the bad guys didn't always wear black. Maybe some did wear blue uniforms. She lowered her gaze to Dr. Kane's white lab coat. But maybe some of the good guys still wore white. ''I will. Keep the canister encapsulated until Environmental picks it up.''

''And a separate sample in a safe place until you or Captain Burke tells me otherwise.''

''Right. Just in case.'' She didn't have to say ''in case I fail.'' Dr. Kane was a clever man. He knew it; she saw it in the way he looked at her. As if he were looking at a woman he feared would soon be dead.

Tracy couldn't resent his reaction. It was honest. And truthfully, she felt those same fears. She didn't have clout or a position of authority over the suspects in this case. She didn't have covert-operations training or years of experience in the field to draw from. Hell, she didn't even know who all of the players in this conspiracy were, much less their positions. Each of those shortcomings presented her with an opportunity to fail and gave her opposition the advantage. But she did have something they didn't. Something in addition to a burning desire for justice and the truth.

She had Adam.

''Captain?''

Leaving the lab, Tracy stopped and looked back at Dr. Kane. ''Yes?''

''The mitosis in the team you asked me about. It was there.''

So the men hadn't been blown up. Their bodies had arrived at the hospital intact. Tracy swallowed hard. ''And the children?''

Dr. Kane nodded. ''Them, too.''

Tracy parked the Jeep in the Maintenance lot. Sure she wasn't being followed, she returned to the bunker.

Adam opened the door from down below and stood

waiting on the steps, looking as relieved as she had felt
when he had returned from encapsulating the canister and
disposing of the chemical gear.

He hugged her hard, and she sagged against his broad
chest, relaxing for the first time since she had left him
there. He felt safe; solid and sure. She could get used to
this. So used to this. So easily.

When he loosened his hold, she looked up at him. "We
got it. It's an unknown derivative of sarin. And Randall
was extremely obvious, Adam. I also discovered he had
sent a résumé to Paul at Keener Chemical." And seeing
it had humiliated her. Infuriated her. Randall's friendship
hadn't been genuine. She had been a means to an end, a
solid contact between Randall and Paul. "He wanted a
job, and from all signs, he got it."

Adam sent her a consoling look. "Moxley's an arrogant ass and a stupid man."

Rhetoric or not, Adam's words soothed her wounded
ego, and she smiled up at him. "Thank you."

He looped an arm around her shoulder, and walked
down the steps to the apartment. "Dr. Kane cooperated?"

She nodded, then filled Adam in on specifics. Midway
through, she saw she had only half of his attention and
chided him for it. "I risked my neck and you're not even
listening?"

"I am." He pointed to his ear. "Moxley's on the
phone. He called Hackett—I suspect, right after he
learned you had the canister—but the colonel was in conference with General Nestler so they've just connected."

"Nestler and Hackett?"

"No, Moxley and Hackett." Adam walked over to a
piece of complex-looking taping equipment that hadn't
been on the dresser earlier, and then pressed a green button.

"That settles it." Hackett's voice filled the bunker
apartment. "Cancel Captain Keener."

"Excuse me?" Randall's tone spoke volumes. Incredulous topped the list.

"Shut her up, son," Hackett reiterated, as if speaking to an errant child. "She's a liability we can't afford."

The blood drained from her face and her insides turned to ice. Tracy sucked in a sharp breath. Adam curled an arm around her shoulder, offering silent support.

Randall cleared his throat. "I trust that all interested parties approve of this option."

"They do." Hackett's voice dropped, lethally soft. "And Moxley, don't question my authority again. It'd be a shame if your activities somehow became public knowledge." Hackett ended the call without waiting for a response.

Adam turned the machine off. "You okay?" He rubbed at his neck, as if uncertain what she needed.

"No, I'm not okay. I'm mad as hell, Adam. I'm not hurt, or even mildly surprised." She rubbed at her locket. "I'm just mad as hell."

Adam smiled, infuriating her. He chose the most godawful times to smile. "Randall uses me to get in with Paul Keener, implicates me with the OSI in matters that make my integrity questionable, gets involved up to his earlobes in a conspiracy that risks national security, lies about you and your team, agrees to kill me, and you're smiling?"

"I'm happy."

She scowled at him, tempted to throw something. "Happy?"

Adam sidled closer, draped his arms over her shoulders, and stared into her blazing eyes. "You came back to me."

That simple admission knocked the wind right out of her sails and the indignation right out of her heart. "Of course I came back. You knew I would."

"I hoped you would." He stroked her cheek with the pad of his thumb.

"Because you didn't want to be out on this god-awful limb alone?"

He gave her a slow negative nod.

"Why, then?" She hooked her hands on his sides,
where his soft blue shirt met his jeans.

"It depends." He fingered her T-shirt at her shoulder.

Honestly, sometimes talking to the man was like pulling teeth. But he had good hands. Their warmth seeped
through the soft fabric and heated her skin. "On what?"

"On why you came back."

He needed reassurance. To know he was needed. "I
see."

"Do you?"

She nodded and stepped closer, until they met breasts
to chest. "I had to come back because, fluff that I am,
Adam, I trust and believe in you."

"Is that it?"

Her ego still smarted from Randall's antics and now
Adam pushed, demanding to know where he stood in her
heart. "I care about you, Adam. I told you I did."

"How much?"

"Pardon me?" Pushing *and* wanting his pound of
flesh.

"How much do you care about me? A little? A lot?
Enough to last a day or two? A month?" He turned se-
rious, so serious her heart fluttered against her breastbone.
"Enough to last . . . longer?"

A lifetime. He'd wanted to say it; she sensed it as
clearly as she sensed his touch. But he feared they didn't
have a lifetime, and so he had compromised. "I think,
longer."

"How much longer?"

"I don't know." She tamped the exasperation edging
her tone. "Life doesn't come with guarantees. You think
you have someone for life and one day you wake up and
find him dead. There are no guarantees, Adam, so I don't
know how long I'll care. I just know how I feel now.
And now, I care."

He smoothed back her hair, leaned toward her, and
rubbed their noses. "You're as afraid of love as I am,
Tracy Keener."

"Damn right, I am. Love can chew you up and spit you out. It can suck you dry." It could and had. And—*oh, God, please!*—she didn't want to hurt that way again.

"What about joy? Contentment? Peace?"

"What about them?"

He stroked her cheek with his thumb. "I'm told love can bring those feelings, too. In your experience, is that possible, counselor?"

"Yes." She curled her fingers into the flesh at his sides. "But then it only hurts more."

He frowned down at her, confusion in his eyes.

"When it ends."

"Matthew." Adam cupped her head and pulled her against his chest. "He didn't want to die and leave you, Tracy."

"He might have." She lifted a fingertip to the placket of Adam's shirt, ran her fingertip between the third and fourth buttons. The soft fabric brushed against the backs of her fingers.

"He didn't," Adam insisted. "He had no choice."

"I know," she said. "In my head, I know. But my heart says he should have fought harder to live. I felt . . ." She let her voice trail off. The words sounded too ridiculous to speak.

"Abandoned?" Adam suggested.

Surprised at his insight, she looked up at him.

"Do you still love him, honey?"

Her answer mattered to Adam; she could see it in his taut expression, feel it in his whipcord tension. "Love lives on." She cocked her head. "Funny, I hadn't really understood that until now. But I have accepted his death, and I'm not in love with him anymore. I haven't been since the night of the accident."

"So why do you keep his photo in your locket?" Adam nodded to the chain at her neck.

"I don't. It's Abby's." She blinked hard, then looked at him. "You had it all that time and didn't look inside?"

"It was private."

Honorable. She smiled at him. "I can't tell you what it means to me to have this back. It's the only photograph I have of her."

Adam felt a tight hitch in his chest. A child born and died in less than a day, but not forgotten. Never forgotten. He would have loved Tracy for that alone. She would have made a wonderful mother. Devoted. Caring. She wouldn't have demanded respect, she would have earned it by example, giving it to her daughter and nurturing her.

"Adam, where did you find my locket?"

He blinked away memories of his own mother. "In the cemetery, after my funeral."

"That's where Janet and I thought I lost it. Thank you for giving it back to me."

"I debated long and hard," he confessed. "I thought it was Matthew's photo." He touched a sweet kiss to her lips to apologize.

Pressing a hand flat against his chest, she frowned. "Are you jealous of Matthew?"

"Should I be?" Adam asked, his hands tensing.

"No. My heart's big enough to love both of you— providing one day you'll let me into yours." Tracy already had let him into her heart, but she feared admitting it, except to herself. What would happen to her after this was over? If they survived and Adam realized what he felt for her was gratitude, not love? Her heart couldn't bear one more good-bye, one more tear. Worse, one more lie. Not in the name of love. Matthew had promised her forever. He'd given her ten months and one day, and a lifetime of regret because she had let him drive that night. Knowing Adam feared the pain of family, why was she opening herself up to heartache again? He had promised her nothing at all.

"Tracy?"

She opened her eyes, met his gaze, and saw his desire and passion, his unspoken promises of caring and devotion, of—

"I care about you, honey."

Her heart wrenched, leaped, urged her to admit that she loved him. But her head refused, reminding her that he was an intense man in an intense situation. A man likely transposing one emotion for another. "Oh, Adam."

He kissed her; tiny pecks of kisses, long and luxurious ones, and she returned them, imparting her own, wanting him in every way a woman wants a man when he's touched her heart. Nestling into the curve of his arms, languishing in the heat stirring between them, she felt the fire inside her ignite and flame and spread until it consumed her.

By silent accord, they undressed, eager to touch skin as they had touched hearts, and when they stood naked, Tracy openly admired him, loving the look and smell of his lean body, the quiver of his muscles responding to her slightest touch, the feel of him wanting her, the tremor in his hands on her body, as unsteady as her own.

Facing her beside the bed, he laced their fingers, their heated bodies close, brushing with each indrawn breath. "You're sure about this?"

She nodded. "More sure than I've been about anything in a long time. I adore you, Adam. And I love how you make me feel."

With pure male relief, he groaned, and fell back on the bed, bringing her with him. And there, he adored her, lovingly caressing her skin, whispering all the tender words she ached to hear, and when she thought she'd die from the heat he created in her with his hands, mouth, and tongue, he came to her, joining their flesh, their spirits, their hearts.

Tracy had made love in the innocence of youth, in the blush of first love, but that had been before she had known the costs of loving. This was different. She feared it because, this time, she knew those costs. She knew the pain and suffering, the ache and loneliness and emptiness, of loss, and she had to choose to willingly risk that pain for this joy. She didn't want to do it. It had hurt so much. But this was Adam. Adam who had risked his life, and now his heart. For her. *For her.* He might not have given her the words, but he'd proven his feelings through his actions and deeds. He loved her.

And she loved him. Opening herself to the possibility of pain, to the joy, she opened her soul to him, terrified and soon elated at setting her emotions free. He whispered her name on a shuddering sigh, and she loved him, meeting him stroke for stroke, touch for touch, kiss for kiss; heart, body, and soul.

And when they came and she rested against him on the tangled sheets, she stroked his chest, amazed and humbled at what they had shared, awed and inspired at the wealth and depth of feelings for him still in her heart. The fire between them had been satiated for now, yet the flame burned on. And deep inside her most secret self, she knew it would burn forever.

Chapter 27

Tracy munched down on a potato chip.

Stretched out on the bed and scrunching his pillow, Adam smiled at her. "Do you always eat potato chips after making love?"

Sitting back against the headboard, her knees bent, her feet flat on the bed, she drew the sheet up over her breasts, tucked the bag of chips between her knees, and then swiped at the tip of his nose. "Only when I'm thinking."

The lamp on the bedside table slanted warm amber light over the side of his face. His eyes clouded. "Tracy, tell me you don't regret loving me."

"No, no regrets." Understanding his need for reassurance, she licked the salt from her lips. "Actually, I was thinking about the conspiracy."

"Oh." Disappointment flooded his tone.

Pleased at hearing it, she let the hint of a smile curve her mouth. "I was thinking the sooner we get this cleared up, the sooner we can go on with our lives."

"Good point." He raised up on an elbow to snitch a chip from the bag nestled between her knees. "Hackett, O'Dell, and Moxley are definitely on the wrong side of this. It appears grim on that front for Keener, too. But Nestler still troubles me."

"Mmm," Tracy mumbled, then swallowed. "Because

of Sergeant Phelps, we know Janet is more deeply involved than we believed, too.''

''All she's done is to let me know you needed help.''

''Not true,'' Tracy countered, wishing when she'd gotten up to get the chips she had snagged a soda from the
fridge. ''Janet arranged the meeting between me and Sergeant Phelps at the hospital. She also talked with Dr.
Kane before I did. And she found out about the chemical
gear being sent for repairs by O'Dell coinciding with the
war-readiness exercise that killed your men.'' Tracy
didn't feel disloyal to Janet. Not at all. Every word was
true.

Adam rolled out of bed and walked nude to the fridge.
Admiring his body, Tracy watched him get a soda and
then come back and crawl back into bed beside her. It
felt right, him being there. She liked it. A lot. ''Are you
reading my mind?'' She nodded toward the soda.

''Yeah.'' He slid her a wicked smile, and popped the
top on the can. ''It's scary.''

Sliding him a disgruntled look, she snitched the can
and then took a long drink. ''Janet's actions don't point
to her doing anything wrong, though. Just doing. She's
definitely more involved than we first thought.''

''True.'' Adam took the can, downed a swallow.
''We'd be wise to remember she's Intel.''

Hearing that remark from him hit Tracy with the force
of a thunderbolt. She'd surmised it. He'd confirmed it.
Once in Intel, you never get out. Janet had been planted
in Tracy's office. ''Adam, she *is* Intel. What if, after the
incident with your men, General Nestler learned the truth
about it?''

''He's Laurel's god, honey. I know you need to believe
he's not corrupt, but nothing goes on around here without
him knowing it.''

Sees all, knows all. ''Okay, that's supposedly true. But
what if he didn't know it until after it happened? What
if he only found out after your men had been killed?''

Adam frowned. ''It's possible, I guess.''

"What if Hackett, O'Dell, Moxley, and maybe Paul perpetrated the conspiracy and conducted the exercise without Nestler's knowledge?"

"And when he later found out, Nestler opposed," Adam interrupted, picking up on her line of thought. "We've discussed this possibility before. Nestler could be running interference for us via Carver, trying to help us unearth the truth. But if Nestler knew, he'd have to launch a formal investigation. That's the bottom line."

"But he couldn't, not without jeopardizing his pet project," Tracy juxtaposed. "Dr. Kane said something that's got me thinking Nestler could be a good guy in this."

"Honey, that's looking less likely all the time." On his side, facing her, Adam pecked a kiss to her shoulder to soften the blow. "But what did Dr. Kane say?"

"We need a new antidote for this sarin derivative. The one for sarin won't work."

Adam narrowed his eyes. "We wouldn't have the money to look for one unless the entire project was funded—not without announcing to the world that retro-sarin exists and we don't have an antidote."

"That's the way I see it—maybe."

Adam looked over at her; their gazes locked. "So Nestler works through Lieutenant Carver to help us get to the truth while staying out of it officially so he doesn't jeopardize the project getting funded. He avoids a formal investigation that would screw up the works."

"Carver and, I think, Janet," Tracy expounded. "She's been running interference, too. She covered for me at work with Colonel Jackson, telling him I had the flu."

"No one knows you were AWOL?"

"Only you, me, and Janet." A pang of regret and uncertainty shot through Tracy.

"And you still came back to me."

"I promised I would."

Too tender, he turned the subject. "This makes sense."

Lifting a hank of her hair, he rubbed it between his fingertips. "Hackett, O'Dell, Moxley, and Keener could be the team."

"Paul's involvement in this is still supposition, Adam. We have no concrete evidence tying him to the conspiracy."

"What about the canister? The unknown derivative of sarin?" Adam shoved up on the bed to sit beside her. The sheet slid down to his waist, exposing his chest.

"What about it?" Tracy braced a pillow behind his back. From his smile, no one had bothered with little things like his comfort. That saddened her. "Do we know Paul's producing it? That he was a willing participant in the exercise?"

"No, on participation. But Intel rumors are rampant on him producing it. We know it—"

"We *know* it, but we can't *prove* it in a court of law." Tracy took out her frustration, biting down on a chip. "Not yet. We need irrefutable proof he can't squirm out of on both fronts—production and participation."

"So let's corner Carver," Adam suggested. "Janet would be harder to coerce into telling us anything."

"Sounds like a plan." Tracy set the chips on the bedside table. "But I don't think the good lieutenant will be receptive to company at four in the morning." She rolled over, half covering Adam with her body, and slid a knee between his thighs. "Would the good Captain Burke be receptive to company?"

She'd used his title. For the first time, she'd used his title. He linked his arms around her back, fanned his fingers between her shoulders, and whispered against her mouth. "Yeah, he would."

"This is crazy, Adam." Tracy rolled her gaze to the ceiling of the car for the thousandth time. "The Officers' Club? At a First Friday gathering? Coming here is begging for disaster."

"Calm down, honey. We're not going in." Adam kept

his gaze fixed on the white lapsided building. "We're waiting for Carver to come out."

"Meanwhile, half of the officers assigned to Laurel are going in and coming out." First Friday gatherings weren't mandatory but tradition, and most people attended them. On the first Friday of each month, directly after the end of the duty day, everyone dropped by the club for a couple of hours of socializing. "Someone is going to recognize us."

"Intel Rule Twenty-Seven: hide in plain sight." He spared her a quick glance. "We're in uniform. We blend."

We *blend*? "We'll blend in prison grays, too."

He winked at her. "You'd look good in anything."

She rolled her gaze, deliberately holding it so he wouldn't miss it.

"There he is." Adam hiked his chin toward the swinging glass door.

Lieutenant Carver walked out, strutting like the brash young man he was. Seeing him for the first time unencumbered by darkness, she guessed him to be about twenty-four. He was blond, thick-muscled, just a tad shorter than Adam—about six feet—and obviously a bodybuilder. He moved fluidly down the left side of the circular-drive entrance to the club, and then headed into the parking lot.

"Let's go." Adam opened his door.

They walked over two rows of parked cars, and then toward Carver's Bronco. At the rear of it, they split up, Adam taking the driver's side of the car. Heading up the passenger's side, Tracy called out, "Lieutenant."

A smile touching his lips, he lifted his gaze across the car's hood. On recognizing her, his smile faded. "Captain Keener?"

He wasn't happy about running into her, and on seeing Adam, Carver's expression turned even more grim. He stopped and backed up a step, then another. "Oh, hell."

"Indeed." Adam took Carver's keys, then unlocked the Bronco's front door. "Get in."

Carver folded himself in, behind the wheel. Tracy slid into the passenger's seat and Adam into the backseat, behind Carver. "Start talking," Adam said.

Carver didn't utter a sound.

Tracy smiled. "That's an order, Captain."

His stern expression crumbled. "You're ordering me to disobey a direct order issued by a superior officer."

"I'm a superior officer," Tracy reminded him. "And I don't suggest you forget it."

Looking torn, Carver darted his gaze through the windshield, as if praying someone would rescue him from the hot seat. "I haven't forgotten it, ma'am. But what you're asking me to do, I can't. I have strict orders from . . . from someone of an even higher rank."

Seeing Carver's Adam's apple bob three times in his throat, Tracy knew he was weakening. "If we don't prove the truth, you could end up in Captain Burke's position, Lieutenant. You could be blamed for everything that's gone wrong since Captain Burke legally died. You'd better think about that. Our finding out the truth is your only protection."

Carver's eyes stretched wide. He blinked, then blinked again, his hand fisting around the gearshift. "Okay, you've got a point. And I have considered it, but—"

"No buts." Adam grasped Carver's shoulder and then squeezed. "Let me be blunt, Lieutenant. I've been accused of crimes I haven't committed and, because of that, I'm now a dead man. Don't screw with me on this. I've got nothing left to lose."

"I—I don't know everything," he said, his face ruddy.

Tracy interceded. Carver was willing. They didn't need muscle now, they needed finesse. "Lieutenant, is Keener Chemical producing retrosarin?"

"Yes, ma'am."

She'd known it, but hearing her suspicions confirmed

still pummeled her. "Is retrosarin the proposed product in the contract for Project Duplicity?"

He glared at her. "Yes, ma'am, it is."

"Who is Keener working with?" Adam asked, then added, "In addition to the four men who confronted Captain Keener and me with the M-16s out in Area Fourteen?"

"Colonel Hackett, sir." Carver grimaced. "He has some information on Paul Keener that Keener doesn't want made public."

"What kind of information?" Adam asked.

"I'm not sure, sir. But I know it's personal and it involves Captain Keener, sir."

"Me?" Rubbing her locket, Tracy frowned. What personal information could Hackett have on Paul that had anything whatsoever to do with her?

"Yes, ma'am. That's all I know about it, though. That's the truth."

Adam looked at Tracy. She shrugged, letting him know she was clueless about it.

Carver wiped a bead of sweat from his temple. "Hackett is ambitious—everyone knows it. He's playing politics, jockeying for that command position in the Pacific theater. Personally, I think he's angling for the assignment so that after Duplicity is a done deal, he can sell retrosarin to unfriendly factions. There's bound to be a hell of a black market, and being out in the Pacific, the colonel would have room to move without being scrutinized by Customs."

Tracy's stomach furled. "You think Hackett and Paul Keener have formed an alliance to facilitate these sales?"

"I'm damn sure of it."

Absorbing the god-awful news, Tracy stared at the dash. But it did make more of the puzzle pieces fit into place, even if it also inspired nightmares. Retrosarin would be available to every terrorist and enemy of the United States. Hundreds of thousands of people could die.

"How does Project Duplicity tie in with what happened to Captain Burke and his men?"

Carver went mum.

"Lieutenant?" Tracy prodded.

"No, ma'am, Captain." He hiked his chin and the irises of his eyes slivered into steel-blue shards. "If you want to know that, then you talk to the man who cut my orders."

"Who is?" Adam urged Carver.

He glared at Tracy. "General Nestler."

Tracy had known it. Down deep, she'd known it. But hearing him admit it still had shivers rippling up her backbone and angry tears clogging her throat. Damn it, why couldn't one—just one—of her superior officers not be corrupt? Was that asking for too much?

"The general's gone back to the office. There's a situation."

She and Adam exited Carver's Bronco and returned to the Jeep. She crawled in, still shivering, still furious, and fighting the urge to weep, now knowing firsthand how Adam had felt at being screwed over by his own.

He sat inside the Jeep. When she closed the door, he reached out and covered her hand with his. "You okay?"

"No."

"Mad as hell?"

"Yeah." She glanced over at him. "And so disappointed I can hardly stand it."

"I understand." He gave her hand a pat, then pulled out of the Officers' Club's parking lot. When he drove past the exchange and stopped at the light by the credit union, she got a sick feeling in her stomach. "We have to confront the general, don't we?"

"Yes, we do."

She squeezed her eyes shut for a long moment, again seeing her promotion, her selection, and her career sprouting wings. "That's taking a big risk, Adam."

"It is. But I think you were right and Nestler's opposed to what Hackett's done."

"I'm not so sure, anymore." She admitted the shameful truth aloud. "What if he isn't? What if Nestler is neck-deep in this and he intends to get rich selling retrosarin to enemy factions? He and Hackett could be working together. He does have a lot of pull on Hackett's next assignment. You yourself said so."

"He deserves the benefit of doubt, Tracy. We all do. And I'm going to give it to him."

"Fine. I understand why that's so important to you. But if you're wrong, he's going to kill us, Adam."

"Yes, he probably will. But I know what it's like to be condemned, and I won't do that to him. I can't."

Torn, Tracy wavered, seeing both sides of the issue. Which way was right? That she couldn't see. "So what happens if he does kill us? Who stops them then?"

"Dr. Kane." The light turned green, and Adam stepped on the gas. "He'll find the antidote and expose the truth."

Tracy squeezed her eyes shut, prayed she wasn't screwing up and she wouldn't regret this. "I suppose we have no choice. Either way, Nestler knows we're after the truth. But my instincts still say that he's working with Hackett or he would've stopped us before now."

"Not if he benefited by not stopping us, and he has. With us conducting an unofficial investigation, he's been spared from publicity and ordering an official one. That means there's no congressional block on Duplicity being funded until the investigation is complete. That antidote is vital, Tracy."

"True, but can't we try something else?" She hated risks, had sworn off taking them; she'd taken more than enough already. Slapping her hair back from her eyes, she looked at Adam. "Something less risky than a direct confrontation?"

"We have no other options, honey." His jaw clenched. "We've got to go to Nestler."

"But we could be walking right into the line of fire?"

Adam thudded the heel of his hand against the dash.

"Damn it. Don't you think I know that? Don't you think I hate the idea of putting you in this position?"

"I don't like your being put in this position any better." Tracy lifted the hand he'd pounded against the dash and kissed the heel of it, certain it was still stinging. "He won't be surprised to see us. Carver's probably called him already." Nestler would be prepared; ready and waiting for them to arrive anywhere at any time. And that thought terrified Tracy most of all.

Two blocks from Hangar Row, Adam took a sharp left. "He might not be surprised to see us, but he damn sure won't expect us to walk into Headquarters."

"No!" Tracy's heart lunged straight up into her throat. "Adam, that's crazy!"

"Maybe, but it's our best shot."

"But Headquarters is a secure building." He couldn't be serious about this. *He couldn't!* "The guards will stop us before we cross the threshold."

"They damn well better." Adam whipped into Headquarters' parking lot and stopped the car. "And when they do, then they'll know for a fact I'm alive."

Tracy loosened her grip on his hand. "Is this another of your Intel rules?"

He nodded, his eyes gleaming. "When your defense is shot to hell, attack."

She didn't like this. Not at all. It felt wrong. It felt damn foolish.

"Tracy." Adam clasped their hands. "Trust me."

Warring between doing exactly that and rebelling and running like hell, she let the battle rage in her mind. She could claim both of them certifiably insane. Who in their right mind would argue that an unreasonable defense?

When the mental dust settled, she gave Adam an earnest look. "Okay, I'll trust you. But if I end up in Leavenworth over this, I'm going to be really ticked off at you, Adam. Really ticked off—and quit smiling at me, damn it."

Still smiling, Adam opened the car door. He wasn't

antagonizing her. He couldn't help himself. She hadn't said she'd stop caring about him, only that she'd be ticked off. The woman loved him. She might be too scared or too stubborn to admit it, but she loved him. "Let's go see what the general's got to say for himself."

. Tracy stepped out of the Jeep and slammed the door shut. "Hopefully, we'll live long enough to hear his answers."

Chapter 28

Tracy walked toward the brick building, smoothing the skirt of her uniform more from nervousness than because of rumpled fabric. This was the biggest gamble of their lives—hers and Adam's—and no matter how she mentally played out the coming events, she ended up in dread. On the right side of the law or guilty of conspiracy, Nestler would not be happy to see them at Headquarters. He wouldn't be surprised, but he would be seething resentment and more angry than was safe, considering the clout of his position.

Adam opened the glass door, gave her a reassuring nod that didn't ease her trepidation one iota, and then followed her inside.

The guard at the long linear desk started to salute, but then recognition lit in his eyes and he drew his weapon. A menacing black Glock.

"We're here to see General Nestler," Adam said. "He's expecting us."

Disbelief faded to confusion and riddled the sergeant's eyes, but his expression remained passively masked. He reached over the desk, and dialed the general's office. "Captains Burke and Keener to see General Nestler."

Moments passed. Long, tense moments. Cold air streamed across Tracy's shoulders from the air-conditioning vent overhead. It seemed to burn hot, and her stomach was bent on doing more flip-flops than a landed fish. She couldn't see beyond the barrel of the Glock.

"Yes, sir." The sergeant hung up the phone, secured the door—locking others out of the building, and them in it—and then holstered his weapon. "I'll escort you."

Knowing the way to the general's office, Adam strode down the gray-carpeted hallway, sure of his steps. Tracy stiffened until her back threatened to crack, refusing to rub her locket, and stayed at Adam's side, regretting that Special Ops never shut down. Her heels clicked distinctly, announcing her every step. As they walked by office doors, people glanced up from their desks. Shocked stares rapidly replaced mild curiosity. She ignored them, certain the gossip about their arrival would spread through the whole building long before she and Adam took the elevator to the third floor.

"I thought he was dead." The secretary's whisper carried in the pin-drop silence.

"So did everyone else," a man said.

Tracy recognized him. Major Mark Mitchell, a JAG officer assigned to the general as special counsel. Scowling, he fell into step behind them.

They took the elevator up to the third floor. General Nestler's office was the second on the right, just beyond the briefing room. Tracy's stomach was lodged somewhere between her throat and her kneecaps, and it quivered as if she'd already been shot.

They passed Nestler's secretary, Beth Morinski, according to her nameplate. She sat at her desk, staring openly at them from over the tops of her owlish glasses. Her plain white coffee mug was reflected in her lenses. "Go on in," she said to the sergeant. "The general is waiting."

With a clipped nod, he rapped sharply on the door, then entered. "Sir. Captains Burke and Keener, sir." The guard stepped aside.

Tracy walked past him. Windows on two sides of the office—a total of four—all closed and sealed shut. A huge desk that gleamed and smelled of Pledge. A potted peace plant in the far corner. And two green leather chairs in front of Nestler's desk.

Nestler sat behind the desk in a high-backed burgundy one that rocked, his broad hand braced on its wooden arm, the lines in his face as hard as nails, and the look in his eyes as flexible as tempered steel. Two flags flanked his back on brass poles. Old Glory and the United States Air Force flag. Both hung perfectly still, as if they too sensed the tension in the room.

"That'll be all, Sergeant." Nestler nodded at the guard.

"Yes, sir." He turned for the door and paused. "I'll be right outside, if you need me, sir."

"That won't be necessary. Return to your post." Nestler then focused on his special counsel. "Mark, you can go on back to your office. Everything is under control here."

"But, General." Clearly surprised, he protested.

His voice remaining level, Nestler shot him a warning look. "That will be all, Major."

Resignation slid over Mark's face. "Yes, sir." He walked out and pulled the door shut.

During that conversation, Tracy remembered every word she had ever heard about Nestler. He was about fifty-five and as blond as Lieutenant Carver, but not brash or young and certainly not vulnerable. Where Carver seemed uncertain, Nestler seemed confident, controlled, and capable of anything required of him.

Tracy prayed that didn't prove to be to her and Adam's detriment.

"Please sit down," he told them.

Gunshots from the range rattled the windows. An exercise was going on. Even though she knew it wouldn't be one that ended up as Adam's had, Tracy shivered. She sat down at Adam's right in a visitor's chair.

"I expected to see you two, though I confess, I didn't think you would come here." The general's eyes gleamed. "It took guts to walk into this building."

It had. But had it been wise? That, Tracy hadn't decided.

Realizing they weren't going to say anything, Nestler's expression changed. Suddenly he looked every bit as weary as he had confident. "I guess you came for answers, not questions."

"Yes, sir." Adam said.

"Well, it's time for them." Nestler's eyes gleamed, intense and serious. "I surmise you've deduced that I arranged the fire at the brig to facilitate your escape, Captain Burke."

Captain Burke. Surely that had to be a good sign. A flicker of hope ignited in Tracy. Maybe Nestler was one of the good guys.

"Yes, sir," Adam replied. "Initially, I thought it was Colonel Hackett, but Captain Keener and I, through events such as our escape from the Lucky Pines Motor Lodge, have come to realize we have a mentor running interference. You, sir. What we don't understand is, why?"

"Hackett was on your heels," Nestler said. "A warning was necessary."

Tracy wanted answers. "Why was a warning necessary? What exactly is your role in all of this? And why did you hand-pick me to defend Adam?"

"I chose you because I knew you wouldn't stop short of the truth. No matter what, you'd keep pushing. I realize my methods have been unorthodox, Captain, but the circumstances warranted it." Nestler slumped in his chair. "As you now know, I'm fostering Project Duplicity. I told Colonel Hackett that obtaining congressional funding would be impossible without conclusive proof that retrosarin was effective. We needed a documented analysis of its potential."

Adam balanced his forearms on his outspread knees. "And Hackett agreed to obtain it."

Laurel's god nodded. "Hackett said he could get it

from Paul Keener, whom I believe you're familiar with, Captain Keener.''

"He's my ex-brother-in-law, sir. But please don't hold it against me.''

"No, Captain. Family isn't something you choose. Good or bad, you inherit it.''

Tracy set her purse down on the floor. "Keener Chemical is the sole-source selection on Duplicity, then?''

"Fortunately, yes, it is.''

"Fortunately?'' Tracy didn't follow.

"You'll understand momentarily, Captain.'' Nestler grimaced. "Hackett has tentacles everywhere—even I know that. I thought he intended to make normal requests and Keener would produce analytical data proving Duplicity's potential. I never expected Hackett would kill to get the proof—especially our own men.'' Nestler's voice turned bitter. His outrage laced it, as did his regret. "Maybe I should have realized it. Hackett's never been subtle about his ambitions. But I didn't realize it any more than I realized he would turn traitor. Now, I have to live with that.''

From Nestler's tone and the way he stared at his hands, Tracy knew he was seeing Adam's men's blood on them, and that would burden the general for the rest of his life. "But Hackett did kill, didn't he, sir?''

Again, he nodded, bowing his head. "With Gus O'Dell's help. From all I've determined, they planned and executed the readiness exercise, substituting a retro-sarin canister for a dummy.''

Adam's voice went soft. "When did you find out what they'd done?''

"After your team had been killed and you'd been arrested. And after O'Dell had told investigators you'd threatened two of Alpha team and killed them, sacrificing the other two men.''

"I didn't kill them.''

"Or threaten them,'' the general said. "I know.''

"So opposing their actions,'' Tracy cut in, "you then

recruited Lieutenant Carver and Janet Cray to assist in bringing the truth to light. You bugged Colonel Hackett's office.''

"Yes, I did. And I recruited Sergeant Phelps to feed you needed information,'' Nestler added. "Carver and Cray have been quietly working the case. The truth must be exposed and the guilty punished, but publicity of this incident could kill Project Duplicity. Timing is critical.''

"You had to prevent the project from dying.'' Tracy's revulsion sounded in her voice.

"Yes, damn it, I did. I still do.'' Nestler went on the defensive. "It's a matter of national security.''

"A matter of national security.'' Tracy grunted. "Amazing how many things are pulled in under that umbrella when it comes time to expose corrupt senior officers.''

Anger contorted Nestler's face. "Before you condemn me, think, Captain.''

"Like you thought before condemning Captain Burke?''

"That couldn't be helped. He'd already been condemned. Don't you see? Don't either of you see? The truth is so damn simple. Paul Keener has the technology. He's a greedy, money-hungry son of a bitch without ethics or morals or honor. If we don't develop retro-sarin—and an antidote to it—he'll sell it without Hackett and O'Dell, and then we'll have to try to defend against it without having the technology. That's the bottom line. The only way we can win is to develop the damn project.''

Grave, Adam rubbed at his jaw. "So to do that you sacrificed my men and me.''

"No, Captain. I didn't. Hackett and O'Dell did.'' A frown creased the skin between Nestler's brows. "But to get the project passed and funded by Congress, if I have to sacrifice you, I will. I'll have no choice.''

Tracy swiveled her gaze to Adam. His expression hadn't changed; still rock-hard and uncompromising. But she sensed his feelings. He'd known from the beginning he'd been slated for sacrifice, and his men had been slated to die.

"You're right, sir," Adam said, startling her. "You wouldn't have a choice. One life for many. That's how you would have to take it from here."

"Thank you, Captain." Nestler said that, and from all indications, he was sincere. "But I'm hopeful it won't come to that. Janet Cray and I have been working on a sequence of events and evidence to take to the OSI." He turned his gaze to Tracy. "That was a clever move, to have Dr. Kane notify nonmilitary officials along with the ones regulations require."

"Did he do it?"

"No, he didn't." Nestler admitted that deceptive maneuver easily. "I pulled him into the need-to-know loop on this and nixed his disclosure."

Adam found his voice. "So what do we do now?"

"First, we sequester Lieutenant Carver, and then we plan."

"For what?" Tracy asked, seeing the general lift the phone and issue the order on Carver.

It wasn't the general but Adam who answered her. "We sequester Carver because he broke the code of silence and talked to us. If he did it once, pushed, he'll do it again and talk to Hackett and O'Dell. Then we plan an operation. A sting that will nail Hackett, O'Dell, Moxley, and Paul Keener's traitorous asses to the wall."

"A sting operation?" The starch fizzled out of her. More covert work? "But I'm not—"

"I know." Adam cut her off. "You're a lawyer."

"A damn good one," Nestler added. "Which is why I requested you be assigned to Captain Burke's case—in spite of Hackett's recommendation, not because of it."

Tracy didn't know whether to be pleased or outraged. "Why did he recommend me?"

Adam interceded. "Carver mentioned Hackett had something personal on Paul Keener regarding Tracy."

"Nothing concrete on that," the general said. "It's supposition based solely on Hackett's usual mode of operation. But I suspect that leverage with Keener is why Hackett recommended you, Tracy."

"What do I have to do?" Adam asked.

"I think it'll be Captain Keener's expertise we need first," Nestler said.

Adam protested. "Sir, I think she's been endangered enough."

Under the desk ledge, Tracy gave Adam's hand a reassuring squeeze. "He's settled the doubt. It's okay." She turned her gaze to the general. "What exactly do you want me to do?"

For the next two hours, the three of them discussed options and played out scenarios, exploring possibilities and developing a solid plan of attack.

The intercom buzzed.

General Nestler glared at it, and punched a button. "Beth, unless it's an act of war, the President, or the Chief of Staff calling, I don't want to be disturbed."

"I know that, sir. But Janet Cray is here and she says she has to speak to you right away—about Lieutenant Carver."

"Let her in." Nestler's expression turned from concerned to grim.

Janet walked into the general's office, covered her surprise at seeing Tracy and Adam sitting there, and focused on Laurel's god. "Carver is dead."

"*What?*" The general sat straight up in his seat.

"We sequestered him in the Intel bunker. According to his guard, he committed suicide."

"He didn't." Tracy spoke before thinking. "Carver wouldn't have done that."

"I agree," Adam said, his knuckles white from curling around the chair arm.

Rapping a pen against his desk blotter, Nestler weighed their comments. "He might have done it. He was playing both sides of the fence."

Tracy and Adam locked gazes and then simultaneously looked at Janet.

She nodded. "Hackett made him an offer he couldn't refuse."

That took a moment to digest, but it didn't change Tracy's gut feeling. "I still think they killed him."

"What about Carver's guard?" Adam asked the general.

Nestler picked up the phone, issued orders to bring the guard to Headquarters for questioning, then cradled the receiver. "I think we'd better call in the OSI and counsel. Let's move this to the briefing room. It appears we have even more of a situation than I suspected."

Dread flooded Tracy. Janet signaled her to step aside. Adam must have noted it, too, because he deliberately moved away from her, giving her and Janet a chance to speak privately.

Janet dropped her voice, slowed her steps to put some distance between the general and them. "I didn't set you up or betray you, Tracy. I didn't like what I had to do, but—"

"It was your job," Tracy said. "I figure you never left Intel. Nestler planted you in my office. I understand, okay? This was important, and you did what you had to do."

Relief flooded Janet's eyes. "I tried to let you know. I put the note under your wiper blade, warning you that Adam's death and yours had been arranged. I wasn't trying to scare you to death, only to prepare you."

"I understand."

Janet blinked hard. "Don't worry about the bug you put in Hackett's office, and don't mention it. Nestler authorized a listening device. Only you and I know there were two of them."

"I won't, unless specifically asked. But I did tell Adam."

"Damn it, Tracy, I didn't want to do any of it. But you needed more information than you were getting. I had to do what I did. I tried to do the right thing. I did the best I could without burying my skinny ass and you with me. Tell me you understand that, okay? You're my best friend, and I don't want to lose you. In Intel, friends are damn hard to come by.''

''I do understand. I already said so, didn't I?'' Tracy patted her friend's shoulder and then motioned her toward the door. ''I'm not upset, okay? Once in Intel, always in Intel.'' That truth worried her. Not for Janet, but for Adam. He had received so much public exposure that he could never go back to covert operations without a new identity.

They could do that—give him a new identity. And if they did, then he would have to abandon his old one. Break all ties to it—including his ties to her. Would Adam agree to that? Would he leave her, too? He *couldn't* leave her, too!

Stop it. Just stop it. You knew the risks of getting hurt, and you took them.

''Um, Tracy, I went to the bunker.''

Her look said it all. Janet had seen the tangled sheets, Tracy's and Adam's clothes tossed together. ''Yes?''

''He's a good man.'' Janet fell into step beside her.

''Yes, he is.'' Adam was a very good man. Special. Lovable. And she did love him.

''He's even better-looking than Dr. Kane, too.''

Seeing Janet admiring Adam's backside had Tracy bristling. ''Yes, and he's mine, friend. Hands—and eyes—off. Now.''

''Got it.'' Janet muffled a little laugh. ''I can see how you fell for him. And I'm so glad to see it. Moxley's a loser, Tracy. No offense, but he's—''

''A former friend,'' she cut in. ''And a traitor.''

''That, too.'' Janet sighed, a little irked that her attempt to enlighten Tracy about Randall Moxley's character had been revealed too late. Tracy already knew the truth about him. ''So how was he?''

Adam, in bed. Janet was earthy, and thought nothing

of discussing her sexual exploits, but Tracy wasn't comfortable with that. The matter was private. Still, a little friendly torment was in order. "Better than in your wildest dreams." Truth, that.

"My wildest dreams, or yours?" Janet persisted.

"Mine are far too tame. Definitely yours."

"I knew it." Janet groaned. "The minute I saw the potato chips, I just knew it."

Tracy laughed. She couldn't help herself, then remembering the brash lieutenant, she sobered. "Janet, do you think Carver killed himself?"

"No, I don't."

"Hackett?"

"Maybe. But more likely O'Dell." Her eyes filled with disgust. "His throat was slashed, and Hackett has a thing about blood. He can't stomach it."

"He's a soldier, for God's sake."

"Not in this woman's Air Force." Janet's gaze burned. "I can't wait for his trial. Seeing him kicked out on his ass is going to be a day to celebrate."

"Seeing him stripped of his rank and his ass shipped to Leavenworth will be even sweeter." Tracy walked into the briefing room. "Wonder how big a conflict of interest Colonel Jackson would consider it for me to prosecute the case?"

Janet's eyes gleamed. "Now *that* would be justice."

Chapter 29

Tracy listened to the conversation in the briefing room, becoming more and more convinced that, while she lacked Janet's experience and that of the men sitting at the conference table, she did have something solid to offer: her belief in simplicity.

The OSI, represented by a man who looked like everyone's next-door neighbor, had been introduced only as Agent Seven. He currently held the floor. "I want a full-scale investigation."

His idea had merit, but in Tracy's opinion, it would cost them more than they would gain.

"That's a luxury we can't afford," General Nestler said. "An investigation would prevent Project Duplicity from being funded until next year—after the investigation is completed."

Mark, the general's special counsel, sided with the OSI. "The regulations are expressly clear on this matter, and they don't give us any choice but to proceed as Agent Seven suggests."

"Yes, they do." Adam adeptly refuted that statement. "If we place Project Duplicity under the 'matter of national security' umbrella, then we have the latitude to proceed."

Tracy backed Adam. "He's right, General. National security matters take precedence."

"Provided we're legally under that umbrella, I'll endorse this," Mark agreed. "We need that antidote."

General Nestler picked up the ball there, looking enormously relieved. "If we don't fund Duplicity, then Keener will have free reign with retrosarin. He'll produce and sell it outside the United States, which means we have zero jurisdiction and the U.S. is left wide open to attack from every terrorist group, malcontent, and enemy."

"But American citizens are restricted on foreign trade," Agent Seven said.

"Only if we can prove Keener's engaging in it, and that could be challenging. The damage could be done before we built our case," Tracy countered. "To be effective, we have to nix this preproduction. We have to stop Hackett, O'Dell, Moxley, and Keener. Hackett, O'Dell, and Moxley are simple. General Nestler or Agent Seven could simply have them arrested."

"Don't forget the coroner," Adam said.

"He's working with us. So is Sergeant Phelps's boss, and Sergeant Maxwell, over at the facility," General Nestler told Adam, then looked back at Tracy. "Go on, Captain."

"The problem comes in stopping Keener," Tracy said. "The military has no jurisdiction over him, or his actions. Without a contract, he's just another civilian. We can't charge him with conspiracy without hard proof, and we don't have it."

Agent Seven pointed his pen tip skyward. "We have the canister."

"Yes, we do," Tracy agreed. "But did Keener give it to Hackett, or did Hackett and/or O'Dell steal it from Keener and engage in the exercise without Keener's knowledge?"

The agent grimaced. "We don't know."

"Exactly." Tracy lifted a hand and swung her gaze from the agent to the general. "In my opinion, getting proof Keener is a willing participant in the entire conspiracy rates top priority."

Adam nodded his agreement. "Give him enough rope to hang himself."

"Provided he's guilty," Tracy said. "Hackett or O'Dell *could* have stolen the damn thing."

Adam hiked a shoulder. "In that case, why wouldn't Keener report the theft?"

"Money," Nestler said. "He'll make a fortune, contracting Duplicity. He reports it and the potential contract dies. Then he's out every dime he's expended in research funds."

"Logical," Adam said. "Or he could have elected not to report it because Hackett is blackmailing him, like Carver said. That could be the reason, Tracy."

"Yes, it could," she agreed. "But what exactly is he using as blackmail bait? Carver said it was personal and it had something to do with me. I've tried, but I can't imagine what."

Surprise flickered through General Nestler's eyes.

Janet Cray turned her gaze from the President's photograph on the wall and spoke up for the first time since entering the briefing room. "General, I know how we can do this."

Nestler stared down the long, gleaming conference table at her. "I'm listening, Janet."

"We use Captain Keener as a decoy."

"No." Adam adamantly refused. "It's too dangerous. Tracy's not even Intel-trained."

Tracy heard the genuine worry in Adam's voice and, from his look, so did General Nestler. She glanced at the others. They all had surmised Adam's worry went beyond professional limits. She should comment, at least on Janet's suggestion, but she couldn't make herself do it. Tracy owed Paul. If he was guilty, then let him be punished, but—*please, God*—not by her hand.

Janet stood up. "Tracy might not be Intel-trained, but she is Paul Keener's ex-sister-in-law, and he has asked her to marry him."

Tracy nearly groaned. Now everyone in the room except Adam was looking at her with suspicion. She laid a glare on Janet. *Thanks a lot, friend.*

Nestler frowned. "When did that happen?"

"Five years ago. After I was released from the hospital," Tracy said. "When I told Paul I was joining the Air Force and leaving New Orleans, and again after I was assigned to Adam's case and began receiving threats."

"I see." Nestler truly did. More than he wanted to, gauging by his clenched jaw.

"Sir," Tracy said, hoping to switch the focus back to the matter at hand. "I realize this relationship with Paul raises doubts about my integrity. And I'm sure that my former friendship with Randall Moxley hasn't done anything to dispel those doubts. But I give you my word, I'm dedicated to my country and to my job." She should stop there, but she had to be totally honest. "If I had a choice, I wouldn't participate in a sting operation against Paul. He was my husband's brother. My only ally at a time when I needed support badly. He's all the family I have left." She pulled back her shoulders. "But if I'm asked to participate, then I will, and I'll do everything in my power to assure its success."

"Why?" Nestler dropped his pen to the pad in front of him. "From what you just said, you'd be reluctant. Keener would sense that. He didn't get where he is by being a stupid man."

Adam reached over and clasped her hand. "She'd do it for the same reason she continued to seek the truth after I supposedly died. Because doing it is the right thing."

Tracy could have kissed him. She didn't of course, but she let him see her promise that she owed him one in her eyes.

"She will, sir." Janet added her weight to Adam's claim. "Tracy is noble to a fault."

Not sure whether to take that as a compliment or an insult, Tracy held her silence.

Nestler stared at Tracy, long and hard. She didn't flinch. She wanted to—no one could withstand such intense scrutiny without feeling discomfort—but she managed.

"I agree with Janet." Agent Seven added his opinion. "This is the way to go. Paul won't expect Tracy to act in a professional capacity. He's accustomed to seeing her as family."

"General—"

"No, Adam." Nestler raised a hand. "I understand your concern, but I agree with Janet and Agent Seven. I hate to pit one family member against another even under these circumstances, but this is our best chance for a successful mission, and I'm compelled to go with it. Tracy is a skilled and trained officer, and I trust her. In this case, in particular, trust is a rare and valuable commodity." Nestler paused and looked from person to person around the table. "Do we all agree?"

In due turn, everyone nodded.

"Tracy?"

"I agree, sir." Regret, resentment, and dread dragged at her belly. "Duty first."

"Good." Jotting some notes to himself on the pad, Nestler stopped abruptly and looked back at her. "Intel rules, Captain?"

"Military oaths, sir."

"Ah, I see." He started writing again, the tension lining his face easing slightly. "Call and arrange a dinner at your house tomorrow night. Invite Paul and Hackett."

"Both of them?" Tracy frowned. "Together?"

The general nodded. "For the record, Captain, you've just become corrupt."

Uneasy as hell, Adam listened to Tracy make the calls. Her calm caught him off-guard. It shouldn't have. Who better than he knew she had the inner strength to rise to the occasion? But it did. Because this was Paul, and she carried a lot of emotional baggage tied to him. What he'd done with Project Duplicity hurt her, made a hard task even more difficult.

Adam watched her prepare to leave the briefing room with Agent 7 and Mark for a crash-course defensive briefing. What could she learn in two hours to protect herself? Not enough. It took months of specialized training and years of practical experience to become adept at self-defense.

She could get hurt. Killed.

Every cell in his body revolted, and Adam silently cursed. He hated this plan, but there wasn't a damn thing he could do about it. The frustration of that nearly choked him.

After stepping out to confer with his secretary, General Nestler came back into the briefing room, and turned to Adam. "Captain Keener informs me she hates to cook. I'm having Beth arrange catering for the dinner."

Tracy did hate to cook. But she loved eating potato chips and drinking soda. Especially after making love. Staring at her retreating back, he saw, and even more strongly sensed, the struggle going on inside her. "She's having a hard time with this, General."

"Yes, she is." Nestler dropped his voice to a whisper. "I admire the hell out of her for going ahead with it. Despite Keener's involvement with Project Duplicity, she personally feels she owes him. In part, she feels she's betraying him. He handled her husband's funeral, you know."

"And her daughter's," Adam said, seeing Janet sipping from her mug.

She coughed, sputtering coffee. "Excuse me," Janet said between small coughs. "Did you say her *daughter's*?"

Adam nodded.

"But—but that's impossible."

"No, it isn't," Adam countered. "Tracy told me so herself."

"But Adam, it *is* impossible," Janet insisted, looking poleaxed. "Tracy's daughter isn't dead."

Chapter 30

Adam spun around to face Janet. *"What?"*

Janet cast a surreptitious glance at General Nestler, then swerved her gaze back to Adam. "Abby isn't dead."

The shock nearly bent Adam double. "But that's impossible."

"No it's not. Honest." Janet swiped a hand down the front of her black dress, smearing the sputtered coffee. "I'd never talk about this—Tracy is my friend—but my instincts are telling me something isn't right. She let Paul Keener adopt Abby, right after the baby was born."

Adam dragged a hand through his hair. "So that's what Hackett has on Keener."

General Nestler stepped into the fray. "What are you talking about, Adam?"

"Carver said Keener had something on Hackett. Something personal that involved Tracy. She had no idea what it could be, but then, having no idea about Abby, Tracy would be clueless."

"You're not making sense," the general said. "If Tracy allowed Keener to adopt her daughter, it could hardly be a secret from her. So what's Hackett got? Nothing."

"But it *is* a secret from Tracy, sir." Too agitated to sit, Adam stood and paced the length of the briefing room. "Tracy didn't allow that adoption. She doesn't know there's been an adoption."

"Adam," Janet interceded. "I'm sorry, but that just isn't true."

"You'll have to prove it to me," Adam insisted. "No offense, but Tracy would never walk out on her daughter."

"I can prove it." Janet went to the credenza at the end of the room and lifted the phone. She requested Tracy's Intel file, stat, and then sat down at the conference table with General Nestler. "It'll be here in about five minutes."

During the wait, Beth brought in more coffee. His stomach roiling, Adam could barely stand the smell. No papers in any file would ever convince him Tracy knew about Abby. "Janet, you know that locket Tracy always wears?"

"Yes." She lifted her cup and looked at him through the steam rising from it. "She lost it."

"I found it." Across the table, Adam braced a hand on the back of a chair.

"She'll be thrilled." Janet smiled. "It was a gift—her last gift from Matthew."

"That's not why Tracy wears it."

General Nestler frowned up at Adam. "Is this locket significant?"

"To Tracy, yes. She wears it because it holds her only photo of Abby." Adam swiveled his gaze to Janet. "Does that sound like a woman who would give her child up for adoption?"

Janet frowned. "All I know is I can prove she did it, Adam. I'm sorry, but truth is truth."

"Truth is truth, and Tracy giving up Abby isn't it. I'd bet my life on it." Steaming, Adam rapped the back of the chair. "Keener pulled something."

A discreet tap sounded at the door.

Janet answered it. She returned to the table with an accordion file and rummaged through it. Finally, she pulled a legal document and passed it to Adam. "Here. The adoption papers."

He couldn't make himself look at them. "You knew about the adoption because you'd read the document in Tracy's Intel file. But why didn't you ever ask her about it?"

"I'm her friend, not her priest." Janet frowned. "Tracy never talks about Abby. Never. And if you bring her up, she changes the subject."

"Why?" She'd talked to Adam about her.

Janet's voice softened. "Some hurts just go too deep."

Adam tapped the documents. "I don't care what these say, I'm telling you Tracy believes her daughter is dead." He glanced down at the shaky signature scrawled in the block.

"Well?" A frown furrowed Nestler's brow.

"It's Tracy's writing, sir. But I swear she thinks Abby is dead." He looked at the general. "If Tracy knew Abby was alive, why would she continue to mourn losing her?"

"Regret over the adoption? That's common, I'm sure."

"She didn't do it, sir," Adam insisted. "Look, I know this woman, and I'm telling you she's convinced Abby is dead."

Nestler paused, stared at Adam a long moment. "Let's say you're right."

Adam gripped the chair back hard. "I *am* right."

"Then how did Keener get her signature?"

Adam had no trouble seeing it in his mind's eye. "Tracy was injured in the car accident that killed her husband. Within hours, she gave birth—four months prematurely—and she remained hospitalized for over a month. Initially, she was heavily sedated. According to Tracy, Paul Keener arranged the funerals for Matthew *and* Abby. Tracy was too ill to attend them."

Nestler's eyes gleamed. "But she would have had to give him the authority to make those arrangements."

"Yes," Adam emphatically agreed. "And when Keener had her sign those documents, I suspect he added this one." Adam held up the adoption papers.

"Oh, God." Janet slumped back in her chair. "Her baby's alive, and she doesn't even know it!"

"But Hackett knows it, and he's blackmailing Keener with it." Nestler squeezed his eyes shut and dipped his chin to his chest. "His only brother's wife." Nestler let his gaze rove the ceiling, his mystified tone laced with disgust. "He used his niece. His only brother's widow."

Adam clenched his fists, wishing for five minutes alone with Paul Keener—and Hackett. Both of the bastards knew the truth and hid it from Tracy. Because of them, she had suffered five damn years of misery and misplaced guilt. And they'd let her. "Keener asked Tracy to marry him. Not once, but several times. How the hell could he do this and still want to marry her? How could he justify stealing her child, even to himself?"

"Money," Nestler answered. "Keener Chemical is a very successful corporation, and it has been for three generations. Yet Tracy lives only on her salary. When she became friends with Moxley and of interest to Intel, we checked her out to find out why. Matthew died before amending his will. She inherited half of his estate, excluding what was in the Keener Chemical Trust. And that was everything. Tracy essentially didn't inherit a dime."

"She told me." Adam slumped down in a chair. "They hadn't been married very long."

"Less than a year," Nestler agreed. "Looking at what we know from this perspective—that Tracy is unaware her daughter is alive—"

Adam interrupted, so furious his voice shook. "Keener didn't want to share the company fortune with Abby. So he adopted her to negate her status as Matthew's heir."

Nestler looked to Janet, who nodded. "We checked state law and, in Louisiana, you can't disinherit your children. Will or no, Matthew's assets would have gone to Abby—less fees, bonds, and separate inventory expenses. Considering the estate is worth millions, that would have been a lot of money."

"Paul stole from his brother's widow and from his

niece—all he had left of his brother.'' Adam grunted his disgust. Two minutes with the sick son of a bitch. Just two minutes. To hell with the dark alley. Maybe Keener had resented Tracy for marrying his brother, but to do this—

Adam stiffened, grabbed the chair arms. "Where is she?"

Janet answered. "Abby is in New Orleans."

"She lives with Paul Keener?" Adam asked in a disbelieving near-shout.

"No. Not with Keener, but nearby. He owns a plantation just north of New Orleans. She lives there with a housekeeper."

"I'm going to get her." Pushing against the chair arms, Adam hoisted himself out of the chair.

Nestler halted him with a hand to Adam's shoulder. "Not yet."

Adam glared at him. "The bastard stole her baby. She's mourned five years. Isn't that long enough?"

"It's five years too long." Nestler's eyes shone with compassion and pity, yet his grip on Adam's shoulder tightened. "But we have to resolve the issues here first or he'll bury them so deep we'll never get to them. There's a lot at stake, Adam, and Abby isn't in any more danger today than she was yesterday. She's Paul's legal daughter."

"Not for long," Adam vowed.

"No, not for long." Nestler looked at Janet. "Get Mark on this, Janet. I want that adoption set aside—stat. And get him to file an order to freeze Keener's assets. I think under the circumstances, any judge will agree that Abby must challenge her father's will."

"Yes, sir." Janet sprang out of the chair and to the phone. Within minutes, she was reeling off the general's orders to his special counsel.

Adam worried, "If Hackett pushes Keener too hard, he could get desperate. And if he finds out about the asset freeze, he could harm Abby."

"This will be wrapped up before he knows anything about it. Right now, she's no threat to him, son." Nestler's voice went soft. "I understand your concern, and your devotion to Tracy and her child is admirable, but don't let it get Tracy killed. She *is* a threat to Keener. That's why he wanted to marry her. Wives can't be forced to testify against their husbands. It seems reasonable to me that if she had married him, he could have brought Abby back into her life and Tracy would have held her silence to protect her child."

The truth in that had Adam scowling, and rebelling. "Any man capable of stealing his brother's child is capable of killing her."

"And any mother who learns her daughter isn't dead could kill the man who had stolen her. That could get Tracy killed. She's skilled, but with words, Adam. She's not survival- or Intel-trained, and a two-hour crash course can't possibly prepare her for something like this. Adding this kind of pressure is asking more from her than she's capable of giving."

Hard knots punched through Adam's stomach and he swallowed back a geyser of frustration. He worked at it, tamped his emotions enough to talk without ranting. "What do you recommend?"

"We let Tracy do her job without this added pressure. God knows, she'll be taxed enough. Then, after we've got the evidence we need on Keener, I suggest you take Tracy to New Orleans and introduce her to her daughter."

Adam looked to Janet. She was Tracy's friend. She cared about Tracy the woman, as well as Tracy the Air Force captain.

"He's right, Adam." Janet shrugged. "I love Tracy, okay? But she isn't cut out for covert work. She's too straightforward and honest. She doesn't love easily, but when she does, it's with her whole heart. I never quite understood why she would allow Keener to adopt Abby, but then I decided Tracy would do it if she thought it was best for her child. With her in the military, subject to all the less-advantageous perks that go with it, and with Keener being rich, I figured Tracy felt Abby, being Matthew's daughter, too, deserved the financial advantages Tracy couldn't give her. I should have known better, but I didn't. I was wrong about that, but I'm not wrong about this. If you tell Tracy what Paul has done before she confronts him on the retrosarin, she'll either kill him or get killed trying to kill him."

Valid points. Adam couldn't dispute them. He wanted to—God, how he wanted to—but he couldn't.

"One last thing," Janet said. "You're going to have a hard, hard time getting Tracy to New Orleans without first telling her the reason for going."

"Why is that?"

"Because she hasn't been back since she recuperated from the accident." Janet looked down at Adam. "She's sworn never to set foot there again, and three years ago, she refused a plum assignment because it was in New Orleans. Her commander pushed her to take the job, but she flatly refused, saying she'd put in her papers and get out of the Air Force. He backed down."

Strong feelings. Ones Adam wasn't comfortable with. Did they run so deep because of all she'd lost there, or because she was still in love with her dead husband? She'd said she had accepted his death, but this didn't sound like acceptance to Adam. And that left him at a loss. He could compete with a man for her. But he couldn't compete against a memory. Time had made her memories of Matthew perfect. What imperfect man could compete with perfect memories?

And if Adam waited to tell her about Abby, would Tracy consider that an act of honor, or one of betrayal?

The caterer delivered a gourmet dinner to die for. One Tracy had no intention of sharing with Paul Keener or Colonel Robert D. Hackett, though she did go through the motions of setting the table, chilling the wine, and arranging a bouquet of flowers as a centerpiece for the table. But if she sat down with those two and actually tried to swallow a thing, there was no doubt in her mind she would choke to death.

After pulling one last inspection to make sure everything was ready, and that the listening devices she'd planted in the centerpiece and in a potted plant near the sofa in the living room were functional, she showered and dressed in a simple black sheath and heels, did her makeup, and then paced the floor for the next thirty minutes until Hackett and Paul were due to arrive.

Hackett arrived first, wearing his uniform. He stepped into the living room boldly appraising her with his infamous interested but unconcerned Jack Nicholas look.

The sight alone made her squeamish. "Colonel. Thank you for coming."

"You made refusing impossible, Captain."

She smiled. "Yes, I suppose I did." Amazing what conclusions a man will jump to when he's wagging around a guilty conscience.

He noticed that the table had been set for three. "Are we expecting another guest?"

"Just my brother-in-law." She gave Hackett an innocent smile. "He lives in New Orleans, but on occasion he comes to Grandsen. I enjoy seeing him whenever possible." Hackett looked uncomfortable. Tracy couldn't resist the urge to watch him squirm a little. "I hope you don't mind. My husband and Paul were very close."

"Not at all." Hackett gave her the obligatory response.

By the time she seated him in the living room with a gin and tonic, Paul arrived. She had his drink ready. Scotch on the rocks.

After retrieving it from the kitchen, she walked back into the living room. The men were sitting on the sofa, urgently whispering back and forth, their expressions as tense as their hushed voices.

Tracy sat across from them in a padded chair, her nerves coiling tighter and tighter. After a few moments, she steered the conversation around to Adam Burke's case, and played the trump card she had been instructed to play. "He was set up," she said. "It was all a plan to get hard data on the performance of a chemical called retrosarin. Ever heard of it?" She looked at Hackett, doing her damnedest to stay calm. Inside, she was shaking like a leaf.

Hackett said nothing, just stared at her. She riveted her gaze to Matthew's brother. "Paul, surely you've heard of it. After all, Keener Chemical is producing the chemical. Or, it would like to produce it—provided Project Duplicity gets funded."

The men looked at each other, then thin-lipped, Hackett stared at her. "What do you want, Captain?"

"I haven't yet decided. First, I want to know why you did this, Colonel."

"I don't have to answer to you."

"Oh, but you do. You see, I have enough evidence to put you both behind bars for the rest of your lives. That might not be long, actually. Treason typically carries the death penalty."

Hackett jumped to his feet. "You stupid bitch. You have no idea what you're doing."

She sat back, casually crossed her legs at her ankles. "By all means, enlighten me."

"Terrorists have used a similar chemical against the general populace in Japan. Iraq has used it against Iran."

She lifted a finger in his direction. "That's supposition."

"In some circles, yes, but not in mine. The point is, Captain, we need retrosarin, and to get it, we needed hard data. Without that data, the project would never be funded."

Tracy folded her arms over her chest. "So you got it, by killing four of your own men."

"And saved how many?" He fisted his hand at his side. "I despise you do-gooders. Simple, small-minded pains in the ass. That's what you are. You think everything is straight and narrow, that there's only one path. Well, here's a news flash, Captain. Life is crooked. The path forks over and over again. You want to survive? Then you'd damn well better find out where the forks are before you run into them. Without this project, innocent people are going to die. You can't count how many will be saved by it, only the ones who die if you don't do it. So you tell me. Are the lives of four men dedicated to protect and serve worth countless lives?''

"So you killed them for a noble cause."

"I did what had to be done to protect the freedom we enjoy. Freedom *you* enjoy, Captain. You're damn right I did, and I'd do it again."

He believed this. That truth settled over Tracy like a smothering shroud. Saddened, appalled, wondering how someone who had done so much right had become so twisted, she looked up at him. "What about the Pacific assignment? Are you going to tell me you didn't intend to sell retrosarin to enemies of the United States?"

The blood drained from his face, and he said nothing.

Guilty as hell. Tracy swallowed hard, stared down at her hands in her lap, and then pulled together the remnants of her courage to face Paul.

"I'm not noble," he said matter-of-factly. "It was an excellent business opportunity so I took it."

She couldn't believe it. How could he and Matthew be related? "It didn't matter to you that people would die?"

"People are going to die anyway, darling. None of us are immortal. You certainly should know that."

She was looking at a stranger. This couldn't be the same man who had protected her and nurtured her back to health after the accident. The man who had mourned her loss with her, who had asked her to marry him as a selfless act to protect her.

This man wouldn't commit a selfless act.

Had he committed one back then? Or, as Adam proposed, had Paul committed an act of hatred and revenge because she had preferred Matthew to him?

"What are you going to do with this evidence of yours, Captain?"

She swung her gaze to Hackett and then stood up. "I'm going to turn it over to the OSI, along with the tapes I've made here tonight."

The men looked at each other, and Paul gave her a slow smile that chilled her blood to ice. "You mean the listening device you hid in the plant?"

An icy shiver crawled up her spine.

"Or maybe you mean the one you planted in the flowers on the table." A third man's voice sounded behind her.

She looked back. Gus O'Dell stood in the doorway, smiling.

Oh, God. She was in over her head. Guns blasted out on the range, as if agreeing with her. The floor under her feet vibrated.

Hackett slid her a feral smile. "A war-readiness exercise is under way out in Area Fourteen, Captain. Poetic justice, don't you agree?"

She glared at him. "There's no justice involved."

"Sorry to disappoint you, darling." Paul stood up. "But we suspected you wouldn't join the team. So we're going to have to remove you as an obstacle. Don't concern yourself with making threats of this evidence going public if anything happens to you, or if you don't contact Burke by a specific time. We know better, and we've taken care of everything."

The equipment had failed. She was on her own. Totally vulnerable. Adam had warned her against doing this alone, knowing Hackett and Paul were too clever, that they would spot a trap.

And they had.

O'Dell grabbed her arm and squeezed. Tracy kneed him in the groin. He doubled over.

Someone grabbed her shoulder, spun her around. Hackett. She saw his fist, aiming for her chin. The impact jarred her teeth, snapped her neck, and knocked her back across the chair onto the floor.

Hackett issued a crisp order. "O'Dell, sweep the place."

"Already have, sir. Ran a double-check, too, while she was showering. No evidence of any kind, and no more bugs. Captain Keener is on her own."

"Fine." Hackett looked surprised to hear that, but infinitely pleased. "I'd say a little training is in order, Major. See to it."

Training? What kind of—Oh, God.

They were going to kill her. To kill her, and she couldn't even put up token resistance, much less fight them. Regret washed through her and, unable to lift her arm, she mentally grasped her locket, imagined the warm metal pressing against her palm. Something brushed against the tip of her nose. She tried to open her eyes, to see what it was, but failed. Its pungent smell burned her nostrils. They stung like fire.

Chemicals. They were killing her with chemicals.

Oh, Adam, I failed. I'm sorry. I'm so sorry. Stop them, Adam. Stop them.

The spots before her eyes blinded her, and consciousness slipped away.

Chapter 31

"You *lost* her?" Adam stared at Agent Seven in total disbelief. "What do you mean, you *lost* her?"

"I mean, they've taken her from the house." Rushing past a desk in the Operations Center, Agent Seven grabbed a sheet of paper from the captain sitting at it. He scanned it, then tossed it into the shred stack at the end of the long, linear control desk. "We don't know where. Not yet."

The Ops Center never shut down; its missions ranged worldwide, and something was always going on somewhere, which evidenced itself in electronic wall maps with flashing indicators of current hotspots. Adam walked past three flashes—one of which was predictably in Iraq—while crossing the Ops Center to Agent Seven. When Adam glared down at the agent in the muted light, the dozen or so people working the current shift went quiet. "But she's wired."

"She *was* wired." Agent Seven backed up a step. "You know as well as I do that even though we both opposed it, she insisted on going in alone. They found the plants, Captain."

Adam crowded the man, and shouted, "And you didn't move in?"

"The team did move in." The agent's shoulder banged against the wall, rattling the clocks above his head that depicted time in various locations around the world. "But we were under orders to hang back. By the time the team got there, they were too late.''

Adam dragged a hand through his hair in frustration, let his head rock back onto his shoulders, and squeezed his eyes shut. He had to get past the anger and think. Where would they take Tracy? His stomach churning, his fear shoving massive amounts of adrenaline through his veins, he looked back at the agent. ''We've got to find her now. They'll kill her.''

Compassion flickered through the agent's eyes. ''Probably.''

''Captain Burke,'' a woman called out.

Adam turned toward the sound and saw Janet. Her hair was windblown, her clothes rumpled. But most significant, the fingernails on her right hand had cracked off, and clumps of mud clung to the knees of her black slacks. ''Where the hell have you been?''

General Nestler strode into the Ops Center looking like a volcano looking for a place to erupt. ''We *lost* her?''

''I'm afraid so. Yes, sir,'' Agent Seven responded, looking even more grim.

''Someone better have a damn good explanation. Failure now is *not* acceptable.''

Adam deflected Nestler's heat from Agent Seven. ''Janet, what were you going to say?''

A mixture of dread and relief clouded her eyes. She fisted her hand. ''I disobeyed orders.''

''You did *what*?'' Nestler glared at her, his expression as thunderous as his voice.

''I'm sorry, sir. I had to do it.'' She licked at her lips. ''I know Tracy. She's a great lawyer, but she's not Intel. We were expecting too much from her, putting her in a covert operation on her own. She just wasn't capable of dealing with it. It was like expecting a kid to ride a bike before she'd been taught to crawl.''

Nestler kept his temper leashed, though he had to work at it, gauging by his grinding teeth and the veins bulging in his neck. ''I realize we taxed Captain Keener, Janet.

But I wouldn't have done it unless I felt certain she could handle it. You look at her training. I look at her life. The woman knows how to suffer and endure. She understands sacrifice. And her personal ethics give her the power to perform under impossible odds. She's your friend, and you love her. I understand that, but I also understand that your feelings blind you to her true capabilities. It's not all about training. It's about will and determination. Courage, and wanting to survive. Now you tell me, in which of those areas do you find Captain Keener fails to meet standards?''

Janet's gaze slid to the gray-carpeted floor, and her shoulders slumped. ''None.''

He grunted. ''Exactly how did you break orders?''

Janet looked at Adam and smiled. ''I bugged their cars.''

Relief swam through Adam. Afraid to believe it, he quizzed her. ''Whose cars?''

''Colonel Hackett's and Paul Keener's.'' Janet's cheeks flushed. ''And Major O'Dell's.''

Understanding the broken nails and rumpled clothes, the mud and windblown hair, Adam swept Janet up and planted a kiss on her cheek. ''You're wonderful!''

Nestler's anger faded. ''We'll discuss this breach later, Janet. Right now, we need to get Captain Keener back into the nest.''

Janet nodded. ''They're at the gas-chamber simulator.''

Hearing Nestler order Agent 7 to get the MPs and a team over there *stat*, Adam hit the door to the Ops Center running, praying Tracy was still alive. She couldn't die without knowing he loved her. He couldn't lose her now. She was the only woman in his life who had ever really loved him—and she didn't even know Abby was alive.

God, please, don't make me carry not telling her on my conscience forever. Please!

* * *

Tracy awakened sprawled on the concrete floor.

Her jaw ached, her shoulder throbbed. What had happen—

Hackett had hit her.

She cranked open an eye and winced against the bright light. Shifting slightly, she bumped into a tire and tried looking again. A red fender. The car she and Adam had taken out to Area Fourteen to retrieve the canister. He'd put it inside the chemical-simulator chamber to decontaminate it. With it inside, the chamber was crowded.

Oh, God. They've brought me to the gas-chamber simulator—to kill me.

She looked down at her feet, wishing for her Pooh slippers. She desperately needed an attitude now. Instead, she saw black heels, her black sheath, hiked up on her thighs.

"She's awake."

Randall? She shot a glance at the window in the chamber door. Though it was closed and locked, his voice carried inside. Odd, that. But it did, and it was him. And past his shoulder, she saw the red light flashing on the control panel's desk. She rolled onto her side, setting off an explosion inside her head. They'd drugged her, but clearly not with retrosarin. Thankful for that, she grabbed the wheel well under the front fender of the car and pulled herself to a sitting position for a better look through the window. Inside the hangar, she saw them all: Randall, Hackett, O'Dell, and Paul Keener. And Randall, of all people, was armed with a pistol.

"It's gone too far," Hackett said. "We have no choice, Gus, we have to kill her."

Paul nodded his agreement. "The sooner the better. They'll be looking for her."

O'Dell shifted his weight from foot to foot. "We kill her, and the OSI will be all over us. They know too much. I say we cut our losses and run. We can be out of the States within the hour."

Hackett blew up, losing even the façade of control.

"We have to have this project, Gus. Quit fighting it, and push the goddamn button."

Tracy looked up the walls to the ceiling, saw the metal pipes leading to the silver jets that would spray lethal chemicals into the chamber. Claustrophobia set in, and she broke into a sweat.

At the simulator control panel, O'Dell firmly crossed his arms. "I'm not doing it, sir."

"Spare me from idealistic incompetents!" Paul lifted, then dropped, the heel of his hand.

The button lit up.

Pressure hissed from the jets.

Tracy gasped. She was going to die. *To die!*

"No!" she screamed out. "No!" She clawed at the wall, at the door, beating against the safety glass she would never break. Gasping, she held her breath, desperately scanning for something, anything, that could get her out of the chamber alive.

Her gaze came to a dead stop on the red panic button. When she had first seen O'Dell in the chamber, he'd been shaming a lieutenant for pushing it.

You've got the tools. Trust your gut, and use them.

She could push the button. But unless one of them pushed the green button outside the chamber, she'd contaminate half of the base.

And she'd still be dead.

Just like Adam's men. Just like Reuger's men.

She had to choose. She could take them all with her, but the airborne chemical would contaminate innocents, too. Or she could die, and trust Adam to demand justice.

She had to do the right thing. She did have the tools. Faith, honor, devotion to duty, an oath to protect and serve. She didn't want to die. *God, but she didn't want to die.* She wanted to live. But she couldn't kill innocents. Even if a miracle occurred and she survived, in killing innocents and breaking her oath, she would already be dead.

Reconciling herself, regretting that she'd never told

Adam she loved him, she stopped fighting and sat on the hood of the car.

The car! Had Adam left the chemical gear in the car?

She slid down, rushed to the window, and looked into the backseat.

It was empty.

But Randall was screaming. "What the hell is she doing at the car?"

Trying not to breathe, her lungs burning, begging for air, she cupped her locket in her hand. She was hearing them not through the door, but through the jets. How could that be?

"Why did she stop fighting it?" Randall sounded stunned.

"Maybe it's not working." Hackett looked into the chamber.

It took everything she had in her, but Tracy smiled at the bastard. She couldn't get out of here alive, but she could make them think she was going to. She needed a key to the car. Adam would leave one with it. He prepared. He always prepared. Where would he put it?

She checked under the floormat. Too obvious. The visor, glove box, and under the hood.

"What the hell is she doing?" Randall asked.

Paul glared at her through the window. "Don't worry. The woman is mechanically inept. She can't hot-wire the damn thing."

Light-headed, she dragged her fingertips along the underside of the bumper. She had to do everything possible to give Adam and the team time to find the men here. Her hand bumped into a small metal case. A magnetic metal case.

Pulling it away from the bumper, she slid open its little top. A key. Feeling an enormous sense of satisfaction, she raised it so the men gawking at her through the window could see it, then got into the car and cranked the engine, seeing little reason to worry about carbon monoxide poisoning.

"It's not working. She should be dead," Hackett insisted. "O'Dell, check out those controls before the crazy bitch drives out of there and sends us all straight to hell."

"Something's not right," O'Dell said, sounding frantic. "The oxygen-level reading inside the chamber is normal."

"How the hell can that be?" Hackett ran over to the controls and looked for himself.

Tracy revved the engine, not believing it, not daring to breathe.

Yet Adam had been here. He'd disposed of the biohazard gear they had contaminated.

I showered at Environmental and made a few simulator adjustments.

He had told her that. He had! But surely he hadn't rigged the chamber. That would have been a monumental undertaking, taken more time than he'd been gone from the bunker.

But he could have rigged the control to give a false reading.

Paul stood, arms crossed, an assured smirk twisting his mouth. "She won't drive out, Hackett. Her conscience won't let her. She knows she'll kill half the people on base. And that, my idealistic sister-in-law would never deliberately do."

Tracy raced the engine. Foot on the brake, she yanked the gearshift into Drive.

"The hell she won't," Hackett shouted. "O'Dell, turn the goddamn simulator off and get her out of there—now."

Tracy warred with herself. Should she warn O'Dell to clear the air first?

He spared her the decision; the green light lit up. Sweet air swarmed through the chamber and Tracy cracked open the window, felt it breeze over her skin.

She glanced at the clock imbedded in the dash. Though it seemed that hours had passed, in truth, it had been just over a minute. She got out of the car.

The chamber door opened. She stumbled out, bumping into Randall, who dropped his gun. She dove for it. Caught in a tangle of flailing arms and legs, she felt the trigger, and pulled it.

A shot sounded.

The men backed away, and Tracy rolled to her feet, took aim on them.

They raised their hands. Hackett looked sour. Randall, stunned. O'Dell, resigned. And Paul, amused.

"Tracy, don't do this," Paul said. "You're only prolonging the inevitable. You can't win."

She hated him. With conviction. "You're a disgrace, Paul Keener. I'm so grateful Matthew isn't here to see this. I'd rather he be dead than to see what you've become."

Paul narrowed his eyes. "You always were difficult."

"Difficult?" Rage poured through her, set her hand to shaking. From the corner of her eye, she noted the chamber door. "Get in there. All of you."

"Stay where you are," Paul said, cocksure, confident. "She won't do it."

No one moved.

She fired the gun, shot Paul in the foot. "Move your asses. Now."

The men shuffled into the chamber, Tracy locked them inside, and then walked to the control panel.

"Jesus Christ, she's going to gas us!" Randall screeched.

Her chest heaving, Tracy set the gun down on the simulator control panel, then held her hand above the red button and stared down at it. One push. Just one push, and she could rid the world of all of them.

"Keener," Hackett called to her. "You kill us and you lose everything."

She looked through the window at him. "Yes, sir, I do. But the world gains." Could she do it? Should she? She didn't want to kill anyone, but if ever anyone deserved to die, it was this sorry-ass group of men. "We all know I'm too young and idealistic. Maybe it would be worth everything to spare the rest of the world from all of you."

"Tracy, *please*!" Randall shouted.

"Darling," Paul added. "I'm all the family you have."

"Yes, and you were going to kill me, you bastard."

"If only you had married me, then none of this would have had to happen."

"Shut up." Hackett glared at Paul. "She'll know soon enough what a greedy bastard you are. Don't antagonize her."

Bent over the panel, her hand flat on the metal casing beside the button, she looked up through her lashes at Paul. *Marry him? Marry him?* The urge to push the button ripped through her like a lightning bolt rips through a stormy sky, setting her whole body to shaking. They deserved to die. All of them deserved to die. She should push the damn thing. It'd be right. It'd be justice.

Would it be right or just? Do you want to be just like them? Do you?

She stiffened against her conscience, trying to ignore it, but she couldn't shut out the truth. If she pushed the button and killed them, then she would be stooping to their level. She'd be guilty of all she hated. She'd be making a mockery of her life's work, her ethics. Sweat trickled down her temples. But so many would be better off without them. Her fingers inched up, hovered over the button. *So many . . .*

A vision flashed through her mind. A vision of herself at eighty, facing the mirror.

"No. No, you're not taking this away from me, too. No!" She dropped her fisted hand—and punched the framing beside the button.

The men screamed.

And that scream proved she had done the right thing in letting them live. She'd devoted herself to the system, to the law. Now she had to prove her faith in it by trusting that system to work. By letting them be judged.

The hangar door swung open, and a flurry of activity at its mouth snagged Tracy's attention. MPs armed to the teeth, Agent Seven, General Nestler, and Janet rushed in.

And Adam.

Oh, God, Adam! Tracy ran to him.

Adam opened his arms, suffered the impact of her ramming into his chest, then wrapped his arms around her and held her tight. He buried his face at her neck, cupped her head with his hand. She was alive. *She was alive!*

And babbling.

He let her ramble, unable and unwilling to let her go, scanning the hangar over her shoulder and spotting the men locked inside the simulator chamber. How in hell had she managed to get them inside it?

Seeing the gun on the simulator control panel, Adam understood. How she'd gotten the weapon from them would come out soon enough; she was already rushing through events, filling in the blanks. Tracy might not be trained, but she'd performed as if she had been schooled by the best. "You disarmed Randall?"

She nodded, her fingers curled at Adam's waist, digging into his sides. "They locked me in there, Adam, and turned on the simulator. I tried not to breathe and they decontaminated before letting me out because they thought I was going to drive the car through the wall."

"Ah, you found the key."

She nodded. "I knew you'd have one stashed somewhere." Her expression turned serious. "Do you think I'll live?"

"I'm sure of it."

"How can you be sure?"

He gave her his most devastating, heart-melting smile. "Trust me."

She smiled, and pressed a kiss to his neck, squeezed him tightly. "When I thought I was going to die, my whole life flashed before me. I regretted, Adam. I didn't want to die with more regret, but I almost did."

Agent Seven had Hackett, O'Dell, Paul Keener, and

Randall Moxley handcuffed and lined up outside the chamber, reading them their rights. Adam considered grabbing the gun and killing them for what they'd done to Tracy and for what they'd tried to do to the world, but he held Tracy instead. She'd endured it, and she'd chosen to let them live. Adam had to respect her decision.

He looked down into her tear-streaked eyes, knowing he should tell her she hadn't almost died. He'd disconnected the gas. The only thing flowing into the chamber was air under pressure. And he would tell her. Just as soon as she answered a question for him. "What did you regret, honey?"

"Failing you."

His heart felt squeezed. He bent low, pressed a kiss to the corner of her eye. "You didn't. You couldn't."

General Nestler cleared his throat.

Tracy turned, but Adam kept his arm draped over her shoulder, kept her close to his side. Coming so close to losing her, he couldn't let go—not yet. Not until not losing her had time to sink into him and feel real.

"Go ahead and take Tracy home. We'll mop up here." The general slid Adam a knowing look, as if he understood that need to hold. "In fact, take a week of leave. Both of you. By the time you get back, I'll have everything straightened out."

"Thank you, sir." Adam smiled.

"Congratulations on the success of your most recent covert mission, Captain Burke. And thank you for your cooperation and assistance in helping him effect his cover, Captain Keener." Laurel's god's eyes twinkled and he rubbed at his temple. "You realize, of course, Project Duplicity will be funded."

"It's vital to national security," Adam said. Keener's lab had produced it. It wouldn't take long before others had the ability. Funding the project was the only way to ensure an antidote, to protect civilians and the military from attacks. "Only God knows what Keener's done with it already."

"We'll be finding that out, I assure you," Nestler said. "The JAG has already obtained the judge's approval on those, er, other matters, Adam. Keener Chemical has been locked down."

Tracy found her voice. "Dr. Kane has a sample, sir. You might want to send someone from Environmental to retrieve it."

The general's eyes gleamed. "Retained for safe-keeping, eh?"

"Yes, sir," she met his gaze easily. "I didn't know whether or not to trust you. I'm sorry, but that's the truth, sir."

He smiled. "Are you sure you haven't been Intel-trained, Captain?"

She smiled back. "Only trial by fire, sir."

"Captain Burke." General Nestler looked at Adam. When you return from leave, we're going to to have to discuss your future. You realize your exposure during this mission has halted your days in covert operations."

"Yes, sir." Only a tiny hint of regret tinged Adam's voice.

"I suggest you consider management in Intel. Less travel." A knowing gleam lit in his eye. "Easier on the family. Of course, we could give you a new identity. Think about it and we'll discuss it after your leave."

Adam nodded. "I'll consider all options, sir." He hoped to come out of this with a family. But whether or not that family would agree to become his, he'd have to wait and see.

Janet joined them. "I considered standing by and keeping my mouth shut about something, then figured, what the hell, I'm in trouble already for breaking orders."

"Under the circumstances, we'll forget that," Nestler told her. "But don't let it happen again, Janet."

"No, sir." She cocked her head to look up at him. "General, Captain Keener's promotion board meets in a couple of weeks. What do you expect the odds are of her making major?"

He tried not to smile, but the hint of one curved his lip. "I'll do what I can."

"Janet, stop." Tracy glared at her friend, mortified. No one talked that way to a general officer, and Janet damn well knew it. What had happened to all her worrying about burying her skinny ass in rubble?

"Why? If you want to know, you ask, right?" Janet shrugged, then looked back at the general. "That promise does extend to her Career Status selection, too, doesn't it?"

Nestler's eyes twinkled. "I'll report Captain Keener's service to all interested parties, along with my recommendations. Her OER will carry my endorsement, but the decisions are, of course, up to the selection boards."

Janet beamed at him. "That's great, sir."

Tracy had to swallow a gasp. He would do all he could with both of them, and in his position, he could do a lot. "Thank you, sir."

"My pleasure." The general nodded. "Dismissed, Captains."

Adam gave Tracy's shoulder a squeeze, then led her to the hangar door. They stepped out into the sultry night air and started walking across the asphalt toward the brown Jeep.

Tracy looped an arm around his waist. "A week off." She let out a sexy moan. "What are we going to do with it?"

"Take a vacation together." Adam smiled down at her. "You're going to love it, Tracy. That's a promise."

"I'm sure I will." She leaned her head against his arm. "But we start out tomorrow."

"Honey, I think you'll really want to—"

"No, Adam. Tomorrow." She stopped and looked up at him, splayed her hands on his chest. "Tonight, now, I need to be close to you."

Adam debated, but he'd been in her current position too many times. She didn't just want to be close, she needed it. Needed to feel safe, to make the transition from life-threatening circumstance and situation to normal life. She'd looked death in the face, and survived. Now, she needed affirmation of life, to feel loved. "Okay, tomorrow."

She gave him a crooked grin. "Let's go home and make love."

He pretended a lightness he didn't feel. "Have you got chips and soda?"

"You bet."

"Then how can I refuse?"

"You can't." She pinched his ribs and got into the Jeep. When he got in on the other side and closed the door, she added, "Not that you want to. You need to love me as much as I need to love you."

"That, counselor," he confessed, pulling her into his arms, "is a fact."

They didn't make it to Tracy's room before making love. Honestly, they had to work at it to make it from the garage into the kitchen. Stretching from her seat on the kitchen table to watch Adam get a soda out of the fridge, then a bag of chips from the pantry, Tracy thought she just might love that eagerness.

Unwinding and downloading, they talked about events, then went into Tracy's bedroom, showered, and made love again. This time, slow love, without the urgent need for affirmation of life interfering, and Tracy loved it, too.

Snuggling against Adam's side, her head at his shoulder, her hand on his chest, she sighed her contentment.

"Ready for your chips?"

"In a minute." She rolled her head back on her neck, brushing his chin with the tip of her nose. "I really need to stop the junk food addiction, and the caffeine."

"What you need is a substitute." Adam gazed down at her, the look in his eyes still as warm as when he'd been making love with her.

She wrinkled her nose. "Like carrot sticks or celery?"

"Or me."

"Mmm, sounds appealing. Show me what you have in mind."

"I have every intention of doing that," he said. "But it could take a good, long while."

A lifetime maybe? She pushed back a little to better see his face in the lamplight. "Then you'd better tell me about your job first."

"We need to have a serious talk about your priorities, woman."

"I'm serious." She touched his chin. "Nestler offered you a new ID so you can stay in the field. Are you going to do it?"

"No."

"Why not?" Back to pulling teeth again, she hiked the sheet up over her shoulder.

Adam pulled it around them, and snuggled down beside her. "I'd have to cut all ties. I don't want to do that. Do you want me to do that?"

"No, I don't." She shouldn't push it. She was courting disaster. "What ties specifically don't you want to cut?" Bloody hell. She'd pushed it anyway.

"I'd have to leave you forever, and I'd rather not." Adam let her see his feelings in his eyes. "I'd rather be tied to you forever."

Her heart was stuck somewhere in her throat. "Is that a proposal, Burke?"

"Yeah, counselor, I guess it is."

Afraid to breathe, she tilted her head to look up at him. "Do you love me?"

He hesitated, dropped his gaze to her locket. He caught the disc between his forefinger and thumb. "There's a part of me that really admires you for still loving Matthew. And there's a part of me that envies the hell out of him. In all my life, no one has ever loved me that much." Regret filled his eyes. "But he's gone now, Tracy, and I'm here."

"Do you love me, Adam?" she asked again.

"Yeah." He swallowed hard. "Yeah, I guess I do."

"Then I guess I accept your proposal." She kissed him long and deep, rekindling the fire between them. And when they'd satiated it, she again nestled to him, content and happy for the first time in five years. "I love you, too, Adam."

He sighed contentedly against her mouth. "I know, counselor."

"Arrogant becomes you." She nipped at his neck. "So where are we going on vacation?"

Adam sucked in a deep breath, then took the plunge. "To New Orleans."

Stroking fingertip paths on his chest, Tracy stopped dead in her tracks. "I don't go to New Orleans, Adam. Not even for you."

He kissed the stiffness right out of her. "You'll want to go. Trust me."

Trust him. Sooner or later his trust tests would stop. And she wouldn't have to prove herself. As wounded as he'd been, that could take a while. But the wait would be worth it. Still, this was New Orleans.

Dear God, New Orleans!

Don't be stupid. You can't go back there.

Shut up. For him, I can. I will.

Finally! Thank God . . .

"All right," she said, taking a leap of faith. Opening her eyes, she clasped his sides and looked up into his face. "I'll have a hard time being there. All the memories, you know? But I'll go. Because you asked me to do it."

"Will you do one more thing I ask you to do?"

This was important; she sensed the tension in him. "If I can."

"You can." He cupped her face in his big hands. "Marry me right away, Tracy. I promise, you won't regret it."

She gave him a watery smile. "Absolutely."

*   *   *

Tracy stared at the split between I-10 and I-12. Adam continued on straight ahead, on I-12. "You missed the turn," she told him. "New Orleans is that way."

"I know. But we're going this way."

She snitched the soda can tucked between his legs. "Exactly where are we going?"

He gave her a sly smile. "You said you trusted me, counselor."

She took a drink from the can, then put it back between his legs. "I trust you enough to marry you." And seeing a garbage can at the roadside, she knew how to prove it, once and for all. "Adam, stop. There, by that garbage can."

"Why?"

"Just do it, okay?" She winced. "Without taking out those people's mailbox."

He pulled up to the can, and braked to a stop.

Tracy reached into the back seat and unzipped a small case, then pulled out her Pooh slippers. "My dad used to say 'When the world's kicking your ass, hon, kick back. Just make sure you're wearing steel-toe shoes.' " She smiled softly. "I never could quite make myself go for those steel toes."

"So you settled for soft, cushy Pooh heads the size of baseballs."

"Yeah." A little melancholy, she grunted. "I can still kick ass, but I have to kick with compassion."

"Nobly, eh?"

She nodded. "Otherwise, I'm just another steel-toe thug."

Adam's eyes glittered. "They're safe, like Intel masks."

Again she nodded. Giving the slippers a farewell look and a silent thank-you for helping her through some really tough times, she let down the glass and dropped them through the window into the garbage can.

"Tracy? What are you doing?"

She turned back to Adam. "I don't need them anymore. I have the tools. You told me to trust my gut. Well, my gut is telling me to trust you, Adam. And I do, with all my heart. We love each other. I don't need an attitude or a mask. With you, I can just be myself.''

He cupped her chin in his big hand, his smile so tender it brought tears to her eyes. ''Thank you, honey.'' He kissed her lips.

When they parted, she wrinkled her nose at him. ''I'd better warn you. I have a penchant for lace and silk.''

''I think I can live with it.''

''Good.'' She smiled. ''So, does this mean I can know where we're going?''

''No.''

When he didn't expound, she frowned at him. The man wasn't going to tell her a thing. ''Whatever,'' she said, curling up on the seat beside him. Adjusting her seat belt, she rested her head against his shoulder.

Adam loved her pouting as much as he loved everything else about her. Her lashes fluttered, then touched her cheeks, and she dozed off. A flicker of uncertainty stole through him. She'd be thrilled to get Abby back, and angry as hell at him for not telling her sooner.

He passed an eighteen-wheeler, then steered back over into the right lane. She might as well get over it. She was stuck with him. And he'd make sure she never regretted it.

Following the directions Janet had given him, he exited I-12, then drove east, out into the country. Ten minutes later, he pulled the car to a stop outside a huge white plantation home, nestled in a grove of oaks.

A flash of movement at the right of the house caught his eye. A child sat on a swing. She was muddy and leaves clung in her blond hair. It was a mess. A wild tangle. Just like her mother's.

He looked down at the sleeping woman who had done the impossible and captured his heart. He hadn't dared to want a family before, afraid he'd end up with one like his. Family could cut your heart right out of your chest.

Could be used against you on the job. It was a soft spot, vulnerable to attack. Family could hurt you, hate you, and make you feel there was nothing in you worth loving.

Tracy had a family. She had him and Abby. And soon, she'd know it. They'd make a good life together. He'd had so little practice at loving, at being a good husband, and none at being a father. He could hurt them both, learning how to love them.

But, oh, he wanted this woman. Risks, pain, dangers— all of it. He wanted both of them. Her and Abby. The child would always hold a special place in his heart. She'd been robbed of five years of love. Knowing how those loveless years felt, he understood how desperately she needed love. And as sorry as Adam might be at giving it to her while learning how, he'd do his damnedest to make sure she always felt loved down to the tips of her toes.

Because even though family could encumber and cause pain, the people in it could also love. And he wanted their love. He craved it, needed it. He needed them.

"Tracy." He touched her shoulder. "We're here."

She awakened, stretching and grunting, and seeing nothing but the plantation home, she gave him a puzzled frown. "Where exactly are we?"

"Look." He pointed through the window at Abby.

Tracy turned her gaze, and saw a little tomboy. About six, the child stood on a swing, hanging by ropes from an oak limb. In the stillness, she could hear the child's laughter. And from this distance, the little girl favored Matthew. Her heart felt a little tug, but she couldn't seem to look away from the child. "Why are we here, Adam?" Tracy made herself look at him.

His eyes were glossy, shining overly bright, and his voice went husky thick. "We're here to get your daughter."

Shock streaked through Tracy. Fury chased at its heels. "That's not funny. Why are you being cruel? You know Abby is dead."

"She's not, honey." Adam clasped Tracy's cold hand, bent her rigid fingers in his. "Paul stole her from you. When you were in the hospital and you signed the papers for Paul to handle the funerals, you didn't sign papers for Abby's funeral. You signed papers for Paul to adopt her."

"I would *never* do that!"

"No, you wouldn't. Not if you'd known. You were medicated, injured, mourning. He deceived you, honey."

"No." She shook her head, stiffened, staring at the child. "He's a bastard, but he wouldn't do that to me. He wouldn't do it to Matthew."

"Paul did it, Tracy."

"Why?" She cried out with all the anguish in her heart. "Why would he steal my baby?"

"Abby would have inherited Matthew's half of Keener Chemical. That's why Paul asked you to marry him, so he'd retain control. But you refused. So he adopted Abby to keep the family fortune."

Tracy didn't want to believe it. Didn't want to believe Paul capable of this. But the evidence was there on the swing, laughing, right before her eyes.

Emotionally devastated, she stared longingly at the child. Five years. The first five years of Abby's life, and Paul had stolen them from her and from her child.

The hunger in her eyes brought tears to Adam's own. He blinked hard and fast. He'd refused to protect her, and she'd cried for him. Then he'd protected her, but shielded his heart. She'd shattered the shield, and he'd cared about her, and then he'd come to love her. And now he did what he hadn't done since he was eight years old and his mother had told him he'd been a mistake and she hated him. He cried.

"She's alive, honey," Adam said softly, pressing his lips to her hand. "She's alive and we'll have the rest of our lives together. Mark Mitchell, the general's special counsel, has gotten the adoption set aside and the judge has frozen all Keener assets. Mark's also contacted the

Keener Chemical board of directors. They've ousted Paul from the chair and their number two man is filling in until they receive orders from the court. Mark checked him out, Tracy. This interim chair is a good man. Keener's looking at life in Leavenworth for conspiracy, attempted murder, and murdering my men, aside from the charges regarding Abby. Mark says you and Abby will end up with all of the Keener Chemical assets—at least the run of the trusts, which holds the bulk of the assets, and everything that would have belonged to Matthew.''

Jolted by his words, Tracy swiveled her gaze to him. She would have the rest of her life with Abby. She couldn't seem to catch her breath, to take it all in. ''You've known about this for some time.''

''Not long. I would have told you sooner, but you didn't need the added pressure.''

''You didn't want me to kill Paul Keener.''

''That, too,'' Adam confessed. ''Or for you to be killed, trying to kill Paul.''

''I can't tell you what this means to me.'' She squeezed his hand. All those years of regret and would-have-beens. *Now Abby would be walking, talking, getting her first tooth. Now, she'd be learning her colors, her numbers, drawing pictures for the fridge. Now, she'd be taking swimming lessons, baking cookies, getting on the bus for her first day at school . . .* Years of what she would have been doing, and Tracy would have been doing with her. Years of hearing Abby ask, ''Mom, how big am I now?'' And Tracy marking the frame of the kitchen wall with a pencil, then measuring with the tape to show how much she'd grown. Years of memories of the big things, and the millions of little ones that Abby had experienced without her. All because of Paul. Oh, God, all because of Paul. ''I've missed so much.''

Adam gently squeezed her hand. ''She's alive and in your life, Tracy. You'll do new things. Look ahead, not behind. The past can't be changed. You've got a whole future.''

"Yes. Abby's alive. Alive and in my life." She gasped, and looked up at him, tears streaming down her face. "Oh, Adam. It's . . . a miracle. Just the greatest miracle."

"For both of us." Worry shadowed his eyes. "I know I won't be the best father, but I promise you, I'll try."

Father. Abby. That's why Adam had solicited Tracy's promise to marry him right away. He didn't want to be separated from her or Abby. He wanted to live by example. Her heart swelled. "You will be the very best kind of father because you know what it's like to need one. You have the tools, Adam. A loving heart. A protective spirit. The desire to make a child and a woman feel cherished." Joy bubbled inside her. Poor Adam never before had had a family, but he wanted one. And they'd build one together. A strong, full one.

He gave her that special smile. "You really think so?"

"I know it." She cocked her head. "But if you need a written contract, I know a good lawyer."

He laughed. "No, I trust you, counselor."

She opened the door, and stepped out into the sun. Nestler would correct the misconceptions about Adam, Command would know the truth. The guilty would be charged, tried, and convicted—Tracy would see to that. Their professional lives would go on, and their personal ones, too—together, with Abby.

"She's seen us." Adam clasped hands with Tracy.

She squeezed his hand hard and gulped. "How am I going to tell her this?"

"The words will come," Adam promised. "You're good with words."

He had so much faith in her. She hoped a little would rub off, and she'd feel it herself.

The child ran to them, coming to a stop about three feet away. Squinting up against the sun, she studied Tracy's face, her hair. "He told me you would come. But I didn't believe him."

Tracy dropped down to her knees, bent in the grass. "Who, darling?"

"Uncle Paul. He called this morning and said my mom wasn't dead. That she was coming to get me today. But I thought he was telling me a story again. He tells lots of stories."

Tears clogged Tracy's throat. "This one is true, darling. I am your mom, and I've come to take you home with me."

Delight shimmered in the child's eyes, and she flew into Tracy's arms. Tracy hugged Abby long and hard, and didn't fight against the tears sliding down her cheeks.

"Is he my daddy?" Abby whispered against Tracy's chest. "Uncle Paul said he was dead, too, but you weren't."

Adam smiled at her. "No, honey. Your daddy died in a car wreck. But I'm going to marry your mother, and I'd like to be a dad to you." He touched her cheek. "Is your heart big enough to love both your real dad and me?"

"Maybe." She slid him a measuring look just like Tracy's. "Do you tell stories?"

"He tells the truth," Tracy said, her heart full. "Only the truth."

"Oh." Abby swiveled her gaze from Tracy back to Adam. "Then I guess it's probably big enough. We'll have to see." She cocked her head. "Do you give hugs?"

His heart slammed into his ribs, stuck in his throat. He'd never hugged a kid in his life, or been hugged as a kid. But he remembered how much he'd needed to be hugged. "Yeah. Yeah, I give hugs."

Abby swung an arm around Adam's neck, pulling him into the circle she shared with her mother. Adam let his eyes drift closed, gently rubbed Abby's narrow back. After all these years of being alone, he now had a family. His own family. *His.*

Tracy couldn't bring herself to let go of either of them. It was too new. Tears glistening in her eyes, she locked gazes with Adam. "I love you both very much."

She accepted Adam's kiss, and then Abby's, dreaming of a new beginning with her daughter and the man she loved. And in her mind, she saw the familiar mirror and, in it, the eighty-year-old woman she would become . . . and she smiled, free of guilt, free of regret.

Free of duplicity.

*Don't miss Vicki Hinze's
next novel of gripping
romantic suspense*

ACTS OF HONOR

**Coming from St. Martin's
Paperbacks in January 2000**

It's a world where nothing is as it seems, where danger and passion are one and the same, where all the rules have been rewritten—and everything is painted in...

SHADES OF GRAY

A novel of romantic suspense by Vicki Hinze, acclaimed author of *Duplicity*

"You want intrigue, danger and romance? Ms. Hinze proves she can supply them!"

—*Romantic Times*

"A wonderful combination of romance, family drama and out-and-out thriller. Her characters are wonderful and vivid, the plot engrossing, and the setting is utterly fascinating. A terrific read."

—Anne Stuart, bestselling author of *Moonrise*